W9-ADI-416

Advanced

Mythology

by

Jody

Lynn

Nye

Meisha Merlin Publishing, Inc
Atlanta, GA

This is a work of fiction. All the characters and events portrayed in this book are fictitious. Any resemblance to real people or events is purely coincidental.

Advanced Mythology Copyright © 2001 by Jody Lynn Nye

All rights reserved by the publisher. This book may not be reproduced, in whole or in part, without the written permission of the publisher, except for the purpose of reviews.

ADVANCED MYTHOLOGY

An MM Publishing Book
Published by Meisha Merlin Publishing, Inc.
PO Box 7
Decatur, GA 30031

Editing & interior layout by Stephen Pagel
Copyediting & proofreading by Josh Mitchell
Cover art by Don Maitz
Cover design by Neil Seltzer

ISBN: Hard cover 1-892065-46-0
        Soft cover 1-892065-47-9

http//www.MeishaMerlin.com

First MM Publishing edition: September 2001

Printed in the United States of America
 0 9 8 7 6 5 4 3 2 1

This book is dedicated to the real Diane
and
to the memory of my precious Lila.

Advanced

Mythology

by

Jody

Lynn

Nye

Prologue

The russet wooden casks were laid on sturdy cradles to sleep undisturbed in the cellar until their liquid contents should mature sweetly into drinkable dreams. Marm trod softly along the dirt floor between the rows, listening to one here, turning one there, mentally taking note of which of his distillings were close to being ready to consume. Though he was not considered especially sure-footed for one of his Folk, his steps wouldn't have been audible by most animals, nor by any of the Big Folk, with their puny rounded ears and their big, threshing feet.

Marm, like most of his family, stood about breast high to a Big person. If it hadn't been for the beard on his broad, fair face he would have looked like a child not quite into his teen years. His skin was smooth and unlined. His thick hair, cut just above the collar of his shirt, glinted dark gold in the cool circles of light issuing from the lanterns hung along the walls.

A faint rasping sound attracted his attention. He lifted his head, listening with all his might. His elegant ears, nearly five inches high, swept up in a slanting arc from behind his cheekbones to tapered points at the top. Marm turned slowly, trying to detect from which direction the noise had come, and decided he must have heard a truck bumping along the road that ran along the front of the 20-acre property known as Hollow Tree Farm.

Did his Big neighbors only know that in the midst of this drowsy farm country in the heart of rural Illinois lay a veritable village of people they considered to be mythological—impossible, even—they might have been lost in wonder. But he *liked* them to think he and his existed only in fairy tales. It was far safer for him and his loved ones that the Folk should never be discovered. Even those Big Folk who had come to be trusted in the village begged them to be careful not to reveal themselves. The Folk knew what to do about that. They'd laid charms around the property that kept out those who didn't belong and fooled prying eyes into thinking there was no one special here at all.

Marm was happy to keep himself to himself. Let others go off adventuring and dare the gaze of strangers' eyes. He loved the quiet life with his family, his work, and his beloved brewing.

He glanced speculatively at one of the kegs. Each one had been brought laboriously from their old place to this new place, one at a time, driven slowly and secretly from their last home. Each had been carried down the stairs with Marm beside it all the way, and installed on wooden support brackets that had been a joy to make, of whole wood that they could afford at last, so they wouldn't tip, or rock or leak. The sweet essence within had been brewed with their own fruits and herbs, better than anything the Big Folk had at hand. In fact, his liquor was considered very good by the standards of his own Folk. Marm was proud of his skill. When special occasions arose it was always his brews that people hoped for to toast the celebration. His eye came to rest on the barrel he knew had been fermenting the longest. Like the others, that one's contents had had over two years to settle. It might well be worth tasting. He reached for the wooden cup that was hooked to his belt.

A shadow flitted past his head in the dimness. Marm waved a hand to ward it away from his face. A bat? Perhaps he'd better get one of the others who was wise in the way of wild creatures down here to check. It'd be wrong to keep wild animals trapped, even by accident. He knew how he'd feel about being locked in a cage.

The wine barrels were much larger than the casks. The newest of these held a special place in his heart and that of all the Folk. This wine had been pressed from grapes grown on vines tended by their own hands on land that they could at last call their own. Such a thing hadn't been true, Marm stopped to think, for over a hundred years. He and his had lived a secret, timid existence, running from one place to another. The last home they'd had, in the bowels of Gillington Library at the heart of the Midwestern University campus, had lasted over five decades, but it hadn't been theirs, not really. Hollow Tree Farm *was*. It belonged to them. They even had a legal deed showing ownership. After so many years, the Folk could stop wandering and worrying. They were putting down roots, magical as well as physical, delving deep into the earth, spreading out, feeling themselves safe and secure and set. Wine, which couldn't be hurried and couldn't be agitated, and didn't like to be moved, was a good symbol of their new rootedness. Marm laid hands on the nearest barrel, sensing the bubbling within and laying a blessing on it at the same time. When the time came to drink this vintage, he wanted it to seem as though they were quaffing pure joy. Yes, Marm thought with satisfaction, stamping on the hard dirt floor, feeling the charm of protection that enveloped the farm under the soles of his feet. Yes, a body did best when he could call a place home.

He liked being down in the cellar, where it was cool and peaceful. Not that he didn't care for his extended family, but when tempers frayed there were fewer places than before to flee to. And lately, there'd been more arguments than usual. Everyone seemed to be picking a fight with everyone else. Well, it was a busy time, what with orders to fill, and no energetic Keith Doyle to run hither and yon at their whim.

He lifted the lids of each of the tuns. The heady aroma of yeast and grape must tickled his nose. Marm wrinkled that feature as he checked the level of liquid against the wall of the barrel. Every vintner knew of the natural evaporation of a quantity of fermenting liquid. His Folk called it the Wee Ones' tipple. The Big Folk called it the 'angels' portion,' supped by divine beings, perhaps in exchange for blessing the wine. The angels in these parts certainly were thirsty. The level was lower at this stage than any other wine he'd ever made. Perhaps the cellar was too dry. That was bad. It could lead to the barrels shrinking or cracking. Sinking a trifle of magic into the floor, he strengthened the charm protecting the room, sealing it against the outside, and adding a provision to preserve more of the natural humidity of a cool, stone-walled cellar, though not enough to allow mildew or harmful molds, so that it wasn't sinking into the wood.

The shadow whisked past him again. Marm ducked back, feeling it almost touch his skin. Definitely something here, something that ought not to be. It made him cross that someone had been falling down on his or her duties to make certain the living spaces within the old farmhouse were fit to live in. He'd have to go and find out who should be responsible, and have a few words. Bats, indeed!

A suspicion roused itself in his normally placid mind. What if it wasn't the Wee Ones taking sips from the barrels? What if it was one of the others, sneaking draughts of the maturing liquor? How dare they interfere with his business?

Marm stomped up the stairs, not troubling to blow out the lanterns hanging on the walls.

The fire-snake coiled in a corner of the cellar underneath one of the wooden brackets, waiting until the noisy-footed being had gone away. It had not been easy to get into this place, and that was wrong! The snake was not accustomed to having its path blocked. Throughout all time its kind had gone where it wished. The walls of this structure had never presented an impediment before. Now a power lay around them, sealing the building as tightly as an egg. The snake tasted the air with its tongue. The power was foreign to this area. The snake didn't like the flavor. It *had* liked the liquid in the barrels, and did not appreciate being disturbed from its drinking by the being who had just departed.

Spreading scaled-feather wings, the snake slipped into the air and flitted toward the smaller kegs. Choosing the one that smelled best, it prepared to pass through the wood as it had before. A film of water met it, solid, not liquid, yet it was not cold. The snake withdrew, shaking its head, hating the sensation. It nosed the lid of the keg up instead, and drank its fill.

Noises above reminded it that this was a hostile place. Time for the snake to leave. It made for a shadowy corner. Its nose banged into the wall. The snake backwinged, then rushed at the corner again. The solid masonry repelled it backwards several feet. It could not escape! It had not been easy to find a hole to come into this place, and now it found its exit barricaded as well. The large being had closed off the hole in the barrier it had made. Angrily the snake rushed at the walls, banging them with its nose. Its unblinking eyes saw no break in the barrier.

The traditional underground roads had never been blocked since time began. The snake felt ill-will towards the newcomers. Their arrogance must not be left unpunished.

It slithered into one of the barrels and took a long drink. Too much of the sweet liquid gave it a headache, stirred its already aroused temper. The intruders into this land should not benefit by their deeds. The snake left a curse on what was left of the bubbling liquid. Whoever drank from these barrels now would suffer misfortune.

The snake was still unsatisfied. That was not enough of a punishment. It swarmed through the unprotected inner wall of the cellar, into the drain pipes, and slithered toward the upper reaches of the house, tasting and probing as it went. It would make these newcomers sorry they had ever interfered with the course of nature.

Chapter 1

The ancient midnight-blue Mustang pulled cautiously onto the Midwestern University campus and crept along a side street in front of the dormitory buildings. A slender young man with red hair, sitting in the passenger seat, looked around nervously. There seemed to be no one at all at the wheel.

"Okay, Enoch," Keith Doyle said, keeping an eye out. "Can you see the open space ahead on the right? Let's try parallel parking. Pull up to the car ahead of it..."

The small black-haired male in the driver's seat glared up at him. His hands clutched the wheel tightly. "I know the rules for parking in parallel. I would do better without narration."

"Okay, okay," Keith said, holding his hands up in an "I surrender" pose. "I just thought I could help."

"I have used up the last of my nerves in the trip all the way here from the farm," Enoch said. "Let me make the attempt on my own. You can correct me if I have made a mistake." Keith shrugged and sat back. Enoch might look like a scrawny twelve-year-old boy, but he was a grown man in his late forties, a talented woodworker, a puissant scholar, and possessed the temper of a wolverine.

Enoch let his foot off the brake and, peering forward through the gap over the dashboard and below the top edge of the wheel, eased the Mustang gently up beside the large red van parked in front of the empty length of curb. Suddenly, the doors on both sides of the van popped open. Enoch slammed on the brake.

A middle-aged man in shorts climbed out of the driver's seat. He gave Keith a friendly but harried glance. The man did a double-take. Keith, knowing that he saw the driver's seat behind him as empty, gave him a friendly grin. Shaking his head, the man walked around to help the teenaged girl now at the rear of the vehicle to flip open the back hatch.

"This'll take a moment," Keith said, without glancing around. "Unless they're planning to unload everything on the grass. Nope, just a couple of suitcases at a time. Good. Okay, they're gone."

"Hmph," Enoch snorted, throwing the car in reverse. The old car skimmed by the red van and angled into the space. The huge steering wheel rolled through the black haired elf's hands as the car came to a rest, perfectly centered between the van and the car behind. Keith applauded as Enoch slammed the gearshift to P for Park and turned off the ignition.

"Nice job. In no time at all we'll have you going over the roads in an eighteen-wheeler." He turned toward the back seat. "Don't you think that was a nice job parking, Holl?"

"Hmm?" Another small figure, this one resembling a twelve-year-old boy with blond hair under a baseball cap between his tall pointed ears, round pink cheeks and chin, turned from staring out the window. He blinked blue eyes at the two in the front.

"You're in another world today," Keith said. "I thought daydreaming and looking blank was my job."

"Things on my mind, Keith Doyle," Holl said. A line creased the skin between his brows on a normally cheerful face. He was Keith's best friend among the Little Folk. In fact, if Keith was thinking about it, his best friend anywhere. He hated to see Holl preoccupied. The blond elf had been unusually silent since they'd left the Folk's farm. No amount of teasing or prodding from Keith had so far persuaded Holl to open up. Not really unusual, since the Folk tended to be more private than Keith was, but the worried expression he wore whenever Keith asked him a question made the worry contagious. Keith wondered if he should push the matter, and decided to wait until they were back at the farm.

"Should we wait here?" Enoch asked hoarsely, glancing at the steady flow of students and parents burdened down with luggage.

"Why don't you come with me?" Keith asked. "I have to get my class assignments. It'll only take a little while. You'll can go...incognito."

The two elves looked at each other.

"I don't like it," Enoch said. "It's a matter of pride. I rarely covered my ears when I went about Midwestern before we moved."

"How often did you go out in broad daylight?" Keith asked.

Holl shrugged.

"Few notice, but it's the one who does that will make trouble for us," he admitted. "All right."

Keith could never help but be impressed by the illusion they crafted. It was hard to believe that they weren't really changing, but only appearing to change. The tall, elegant points of their ears seemed to melt before his eyes, shrinking to rounded lobes. Because he was so used to seeing them in their normal configuration, these human-sized ears looked much too small. But at least they wouldn't attract notice. That was the last thing he wanted to have happen.

Solicitously, he shepherded his two friends toward the School of Business. He hoped there was no one around with advanced perception who could see that his companions weren't the youngsters they seemed to be, but mythical beings who were twice as old as he was. In the back of his mind he always worried that someone would come along one day and snatch the Folk up from under his nose and he'd never see them again. They were very important to him. They represented more than friendship, more than a business arrangement. The Folk were the fulfillment of a dream that he'd had ever since his parents had started to read him fairy tales. They were magic. In spite of his hopes and boundless determination, he could not have predicted until the day that it happened that he would ever meet someone who no ordinary person really believed existed. Keith was aware of the privilege he enjoyed, interacting with them whenever he wanted to. He'd caused them some problems, but he'd helped them, too. The fact of which he was most proud was that he had helped them to found a viable business that allowed them to be financially independent. They might look like everybody's idea of leprechauns, but the part about the pot of gold was a myth. That they liked him made him so happy he felt like breaking into a dance right there in the middle of campus.

Instead he filled the silence. Enoch was never a talker and Holl was buried in his own thoughts.

"I'd love to be able to finish off my classes in a year, maybe a year and a half, so I can get out there and get a good job," he said, as the two elves stalked cautiously around a pack of chattering undergraduates. The few who glanced around turned back immediately, uninterested in a pair of children. "The counselor told me there would be no problem getting into the right classes. The course load for an MBA isn't *that* heavy. I can be out again soliciting orders for you in between assignments."

"Since you bring up the subject of assignments," Enoch interrupted him with a sharp look, "the Master was not best pleased that you sent him your last essay at one minute to midnight last week."

"Hey!" Keith protested, hands in the air. "*Technically* it was still Thursday."

"*Technically* doesn't please him. Everyone had gone to bed except for the few reading messages from overseas. Imagine their surprise when the wee flag on the mailbox icon went up, and it was from you. Keva thought it was an emergency and went to roust him from sleep."

"Uh-oh," Keith said, guiltily. "I'm sorry. I've been really busy. And c'mon, I graduated! I thought I was done with essays and research papers, at least for the summer. Imagine my surprise back in June when I discovered you'd gotten an e-mail account, and the first message I get from you is an assignment for five pages on the change in art in the New World between pre- and post-Columbian periods."

"From my father," Enoch said, "not from me. He is the teacher, and since you have not said otherwise, you are still his student."

"True. Thanks a lot. In spite of working my summer job— which was full time, by the way—and going to see every relative in my family I have been turning my essays in to the Master faithfully by the due date. I've been kind of short of time."

"Too short to visit us for many weeks now," Enoch said, with a significant nod towards Holl, who was walking along in a trance a couple of paces behind them. "Some have missed you greatly."

Keith nodded apologetically. "I've missed all of you, too. Wish I could have gotten down here more often. Well, I'll be back here full time next week. You haven't had any trouble getting orders out without me?"

"You know we need to learn to cope without your presence constantly underfoot, you precocious infant," Holl said, catching the last statement and hurrying to walk alongside them. "All's well. The delivery service gives us no trouble. They take the cartons from the box on the porch, sign the book, and away! The next we know a check from the vendor appears."

"And a bill from the delivery service," Enoch said, his dark brows drawn down over his nose. "And *they* cannot visit our customers and learn if they are happy or not."

"Well, I can help with that when I get back down here," Keith said. "Starting next week."

The J.F. Compton School of Business of Midwestern University was living up to its name. The doors of the building were opening and closing in a neverending rhythm as students came and went with piles of books and papers fluttering in the August sunshine.

Enoch and his brother-in-law sat down on a low brick wall that surrounded a concrete terrace before the door while the Big student disappeared into the building. Enoch consulted a mental map. Unless things had changed over the last couple of years, Keith needed to go to the auditorium on the lower level, just above the ancient steam tunnels that the Folk were accustomed to using as hidden paths around the campus. He ought to be gone for at least half an hour. He glanced at Holl, and found himself meeting worried blue eyes.

"Don't you say a word to him," Enoch said. "This is still *your* worry, and yours alone."

"I was not going to," Holl said, peevishly. "It's unjust. I still feel that Keith Doyle's input would be valuable. I don't intend to place the burden on his back. I am content to bear that. What's wrong with counsel?"

"The Conservatives hold that we're becoming too dependent upon this gentle fool, so much so that we're losing the ability to cope on our own."

"He's not a fool," Holl corrected him. Enoch nodded.

"No, to be fair, he's not. But the Master has spoken. You'll not bring it up. This is a worry we will solve among ourselves."

Holl sighed. "I won't say a word." Restlessly, he got up from his perch and wandered out onto the broad lawn behind the wall.

When Keith Doyle returned, bearing a sheaf of papers, Enoch was sitting on the wall alone.

"Where's Holl?" the Big student asked, plopping down beside him.

Enoch pointed out onto the green that lay between the business school and the new library beyond. The small figure sat slumped in shadow against a huge sycamore tree, his hands busy with some small object or objects. Keith guessed that Holl was whittling. He was a real artist, capable of creating the most life-like shapes out of solid wood, bone or whatever he could cut with the titanium-bladed knife he carried. Keith got up to see what he was doing, but Enoch put a hand on his arm to hold him back.

"He just wants a few moments on his own. This place holds many kindly memories for us. It will give him peace."

Keith watched the distant figure dash something away in frustration. "Enoch, is something going on? Holl's not acting like himself. He's been silent as a clam all day. Nothing wrong with Asrai, is there?" Keith adored Holl's baby daughter.

Enoch grunted. The black haired elf could be remarkably taciturn when he chose. "The weight of office," he finally said.

"Oh," said Keith, thinking that he understood. Holl was the heir apparent to the leadership of the Little Folk, and was constantly undergoing 'tests' set him by the senior members of the village.

Enoch knew what was really troubling his sister's lifemate, but had no right to bring it up to the Big student, for all he'd proved his worth and his quality time and again to the Folk.

There were some roads one had to go down alone.

"Do you think he wants to talk about it?"

"No," Enoch said shortly.

Keith shrugged. "Okay. We'll give him some mental space." He sat back and squinted up at the sun. "It's a nice day, anyhow. I don't mind the wait."

"No time is ever wasted," Enoch said. "You can work on your assignment for me while we await him."

"Now?" the Big student asked, surprised. He glanced around at the hundreds of strangers standing, sitting or sprawling on the terrace. "Here?"

"You can practice magic and subtlety at the same time," Enoch said. "Try something small."

Keith glanced around, then gathered up a handful of crisp, narrow leaves from underneath the nearby bushes. He cupped them in his hands, and closed his eyes to concentrate. Enoch could feel a trickle of the charm he was using. Something to do with cohesion.

He was always a bit surprised that any Big Person could feel, let alone use the power of nature. His folk had long ago consigned the Big ones to the phylum of a lower life form, but for better or worse Keith Doyle was different. Books of legend were plentiful about the exploits of human enchanters in the past. Though Enoch assumed most of the legends weren't true, he should not have been surprised to find one magician in a generation, especially one who claimed close family ties to a land where the Folk had lived for a thousand years or more.

"Ta-daa," Keith said, opening his hands. A pigeon with feathers of shiny brown and gold hopped off his palm and fluttered to the terrace, where it began at once to peck at the ground.

"That is not very real looking," Enoch complained. "The eyes are dull, and it is too thin."

"C'mon, transformation is hard," Keith said.

"And ye've only had all summer to think about it."

Keith shrugged. Thinking hard about how real pigeons looked, he tossed the remaining leaves one at a time to the ground. The bird hopped over and picked them up. With each bite the simulacrum seemed to take on substance, getting rounder, plumper and glossier. It looked up at Keith and cooed.

"No more leaves, birdie," he said, showing it his empty hands. It ambled away, rolling from side to side on its round legs, and joined the real pigeons milling about on the sunny side of the terrace. "That could be a shock to any ornithologists hanging around. I'd better undo it before we go."

"So ye might. That was better," Enoch said, grudgingly. "What else can you do?"

Keith glanced toward Holl. The dejected posture and faraway, forlorn expression his friend wore worried him. He started to get up again. Enoch cleared his throat.

"And where do you think you're going?"

"I want to talk to Holl. He's really worried about something."

A solid dose of Keith Doyle's solicitousness might break down Holl's resolve. Enoch stood up directly in Keith's line of view. "Leave him be. You have work to do. You're not the equal of us yet."

"Enoch, that'll take me years, if ever. All I want to do is talk to him."

"You'll not distract me away from your task with your worry and your fussing. It won't be many minutes before he's back with us. Let me see what parts of your lessons you've retained since I saw you last."

"You're just like your father," Keith grumbled goodnaturedly.

"Thank you," Enoch said. "Well, then?"

Keith pulled a piece of string from his pocket. He stretched it out between his hands and whipped it around in a circle until it seemed to form an solid oval. Concentrating hard, he aimed a mental pencil at the space inside. Slowly, an image began to form. He'd done this kind of thing dozens of times on his own. It was more difficult with a critical eye peering over his shoulder. He could see in his mind just exactly the image he wanted to create: a portrait of his two friends. Transfering it outside his head took care. He was just getting the general shape of their faces and the color of their hair into place when a hand reached into his field of vision and snatched away the string. The image vanished.

"Hey!"

"You ought to be able to do it without a physical component, nor a stage to set it on," Enoch said. "What you're doing is stuff for children."

"Dola uses a piece of cloth for *her* illusions."

"Dola *is* a child, but far more learned in her art than you are. Once she lets go of the crutch there'll be no limits to her ability. Try again. In mid-air. No fancy passes. Keep your hands down. Mind only."

"C'mon, Enoch, I can't."

"Can't or won't? Lazybones."

"Them's fightin' words, pardner," Keith grinned. "Okay. I like a challenge. Here we go." He threw his legs over the wall so he was in shadow, facing the open common, and hunched his back with his shoulders forward.

"What's wrong with you?"

"I'm sort of wrapping myself around my work so no one can see it," Keith explained.

"That won't help," Enoch said. "There are those sensitive to the feel of the world around them who would know what you are doing if you were locked in a lead room."

Keith glanced around. "I know. I just hope none of them are hanging around the business school. And if anyone asks, I've got an excuse ready: holograms."

"Well, no more excuses from you to me. Make your image."

Letting the muscles in his back relax, Keith picked a point in the middle distance. It was harder than he had anticipated to create an image in the air without a physical point to focus on. He'd never tried it before. He found it easier to draw upon memory than to keep looking at Enoch or Holl. Thin face, round face. Black hair, blond hair. Dark eyes, light eyes. Features...?

A fly buzzed into the space, sailing through the insubstantial noses. Keith waved a hand at it, erasing part of his image as he did so. "Oops. I turned over my Etch-a-Sketch." Having gotten the hang of placement, he was able to restore the sketchy portraits in only half the time it had taken him before. He filled in details, like the lines beside Enoch's mouth, the arched brows, and the rounded lobes of his ears that looked as though they ought to be detached but weren't. He sat up, easing the tight muscles in his back.

"Not bad, huh?" he asked.

Enoch eyed the image critically. "Passable," he said. "You could have done better."

"I think it's pretty good. Hey, Holl," Keith jumped off the wall, scooped up the image, and started walking, towing it along with him as though it was a balloon. "Is this really so awful?"

Enoch was so stunned he paused for a moment before running after him. What Keith Doyle was doing at that moment out of pure instinct was much more impressive than he could know. He hurried to catch up.

Not that Enoch was concerned that Holl would deliberately break his word not to talk, but he knew the Big student was very persuasive. He might be able to worm information out of them before they knew what they had said.

"Hey, Holl, take a look. Is this really so bad?"

"Don't ask me," Holl said, glancing up briefly from the carving he was doing. It was an incredibly lifelike rendering of a primrose. He had learned a lot over the last many months from Tiron, a newly arrived Little Person from Ireland. "Enoch's teaching you. I'll not second-guess him."

"Holl, what's wrong?" Keith asked, dropping to the ground beside him. Holl looked up at Keith, then glanced at Enoch. His eyes dropped back to his work.

"Nothing at all."

"Why don't I believe you?" Keith asked, encouragingly.

Enoch couldn't deter Keith Doyle forever. The lad was a force of nature. Best to present a diversion.

"Keith Doyle," he began, clearing his throat, "I meant to ask you...."

Surprised by the tentative tone, Keith looked up at him. Enoch was so self-sufficient. He let his illusion fade away.

"What's wrong?" he asked.

"I myself have a concern that you might know something about."

"Sure. What is it?"

To Enoch's relief, they were interrupted by a high pitched thread of music like the first line of a jig. Keith's face went blank for a moment as the music repeated. Grinning sheepishly, he fished in his back pocket and came up with a small, flat wireless phone with a case the shimmering blue-green of a dragonfly's carapace.

"Sorry," he said. "My graduation present from my grandmother." He poked the RECEIVE button. "Hello?"

"Keith?" asked a woman's voice. "Your mom gave me this number. This is Dorothy Carver. Remember me?"

"Hey, how are you?" Keith asked. "How are things at PDQ?"

"That's just what I wanted to talk about," Dorothy said. "They've made me a creative director."

"That's great!"

Dorothy paused, then chuckled. "There's days when it's great. And then there's days when I wish you'd gotten this job instead of me."

"You were the best choice," Keith said firmly. "Things can't be that bad, can they?"

"No, they're not. They're good. In fact, that is why I am calling you. Perkins Delaney Queen is wooing... a company. I can't say more than that yet. It's a big deal. They've got a new product, and a big budget. PDQ wants them, of course, but the customer is going to want something offbeat. A new approach. That's why I'm calling. I need a goofball like you in there pitching ideas, helping out the usual suspects. Can you drop in here Monday morning and meet the client?"

"Monday?" Keith said, frowning. "Sure. I don't have to be down here again until Wednesday."

"Where are you?"

"Midwestern University. I start my Master's degree program next week."

"Oh."

"Why?" Keith asked, concerned by her flat tone of voice.

"Because if the client likes your suggestions he's going to want you on the creative team," Dorothy said. Keith felt his heart start to pound with excitement. "I can't promise you anything. That's our war cry, you remember. No one can promise anything, but this could bring you to the attention of the big wheels here. Who knows what that could mean?"

"Wow." The wheels in Keith's head were beginning to spin, figuring out the possible changes in logistics. He was already on his feet and pacing up and back on the grass. "That'd be great. I would love to have a regular job in advertising."

"Regular, hah," Dorothy said, with mock scorn. "Nothing around here's regular. Of course, if you screw up, my behind's in the blender, too, you know."

"I won't let you down," Keith promised her, hitting the END button. "Yahoo!" he cried.

Everyone in the park turned to look at him. Keith just grinned back.

"What's the excitement?" Holl asked. Keith explained.

"This could be my big chance," he said, pacing faster and faster, unable to keep still. "There was no room for me last year, and otherwise I'd have to wait until after I graduate to apply. Think about it! If I come up with something for the client that they would never have thought of, I could get hired as a freelance contractor, or even an entry-level position. Paul, the intern advisor from last year, told me I was good at ideation."

"An artificial term," Enoch said, looking as though the taste was sour in his mouth.

"So is every brand name in the world," Keith said. He flipped the little phone end over end into the air and caught it high over his head. "Wow. That'd solve a *lot* of problems. I could sure use the money."

"What for?" Enoch said. "But for your tuition, your expenses are small."

"Well," Keith said, embarrassed, "Diane's starting to talk about what happens when the two of us graduate. She's hinting that it's about time I make some kind of commitment. And I want to!"

"And what's holding you back?"

"I want the moment to be perfect," Keith said, and his eyes grew dreamy, taking on the green of the trees around them. "I want to have an engagement ring in my pocket—in a velvet box. A red velvet box. No, blue. She likes blue. And soft music playing, with the moon overhead."

"So now yer ordering the moon around?" Enoch said, with affectionate irony. "So this fantasy of yours takes place outside."

"Maybe," Keith said. "It'll depend on the weather. And then I'll say something poetic—I'm still working on that part. I don't want it to be hokey, but it has to express how I feel about her. And then I'll ask her to marry me. And after she says yes, there'll be fireworks, and maybe champagne."

"It sounds like a well-thought-out moment," Holl said. "But in the course of a year, you can earn enough for a nice ring on commissions alone."

"But there's more," Keith said. "By the time I propose I want to have enough money in the bank for a down payment on a decent house. I don't want us to have to live in an apartment. My family's always lived in houses. I like having a yard. Someday I hope we'll have kids, so I want to live in a nice area with a park nearby." He grinned. "All right, so it probably won't happen that way. It's just a dream."

"It's a good dream," Holl said. "We'll help in any way we can."

"Thanks," Keith said. "I appreciate it. The best thing you can do is not to tell Diane a thing. I want to surprise her."

"I promise you, Keith Doyle, you have a gift for the unexpected. It doesn't need our help."

Keith whistled at the sky. "I hope something comes out of this meeting Monday. Even a freelance contract would go a long way toward the cottage with the white picket fence."

"And roses climbing around the door? But what about school?" Holl asked. "You've only just finished registering for your classes."

"Midwestern has weekend and evening programs for MBAs," Keith said blithely. "There's even a distance-learning section. Uh-oh. I wonder if I can get into it at this late date. I'll have to see my student advisor." He grabbed his new schedule and looked at his watch. "Too late today. I'd better get home and make sure my good suit is pressed. PDQ's into 'business casual,' but I can't show up for a meeting in khakis."

"Hold!" Holl said, planting himself in front of Keith, bringing him to a reluctant stop. "You're not going anywhere yet. You haven't got the job. This appointment is only an opportunity, and an uncertain one at that."

"But it's the kind of thing I've always hoped for," Keith said.

"And it is not until Monday. You have not seen Diane yet, have you?"

"No," Keith said, smacking himself in the forehead as he pulled his mind back from potential futures. "She said she wouldn't be home from work until four o'clock. Hey, it's nearly four now! Come on. I'll drop you off at the farm and come back into town."

"Don't bother," Holl said. "She's there."

"Where? At the farm?"

"Take us back, Keith Doyle," Enoch said, a trace of mischief in his dark eyes. "They'll have had time enough now."

"For what?" Keith asked.

"You'll see."

Chapter 2

From the two-lane asphalt road, it looked as though a car could drive straight across to the old, white farmhouse all but hidden behind the overgrown hedges and stands of mature trees. Within a few feet of passing the white-painted, wooden split-rail fence, however, the crushed-stone driveway began to dip down a steep hill. At the bottom of the first slope, the drive crossed a ford that in the wet season ran with eight inches of water, and up another hill to a gravel parking pad beside the house.

As he negotiated the slope, Keith became aware of a painful sensation in his head that made him grit his teeth. It grew so fierce he couldn't concentrate on the trickle of water ahead. He braked the car gently to a stop.

"You've got the electric fence turned up too high," he said.

"Apologies," Enoch said. The blackhaired elf stretched out his hands and seemed to tear apart invisible curtains. Immediately, the discomfort plaguing Keith died away so suddenly he felt as if a constricting shell had fallen off his body, leaving him limp against the seat. He worked his jaw.

"I know I haven't been here in a while, but I don't think I was ever this sensitive to the repulsion."

"We've had a few too many unwelcome visitors lately," Holl said ruefully. "Salesmen, inspectors, poll-takers, nosy travelers—more than ever before—so we've made the place somewhat less inviting."

"Less inviting!" Keith whistled. "And the delivery driver and postal carrier come in through this? They must have nerves of steel."

"We've given the driver immunity, but the postal carrier still dislikes coming in here. She leaves our mail in the box on the road. We'll attune the spell to welcome you once we are inside."

Keith felt the protective barrier almost clang closed behind him as he eased the Mustang up the hill and in beside
Diane's small, white Saturn. He frowned at the other two cars.

"Who else is here?" he asked.

"You'll see soon enough," Enoch grunted. "Come along.
I've had enough of riding in this steel box. I will have metal
burn for a week."

"That's fine talk for someone who works on a drill press,"
Keith said, following him in the kitchen door.

A dozen of the Little Folk stood around the custom-height
counters chopping vegetables, tearing salad leaves, or rolling
out pie crusts. Keith looked around at them fondly, admiring
just the look of them, their *there*-ness. An expression that his
grandfather used to use came to mind as appropriate to the
scene: it did his heart good.

"Hi, everybody!" he called.

"Keith Doyle!" Most of the Folk left their tasks to greet
him. Tay, his ice-white hair and beard startling on a face that
looked ten years old, came over, wiping his floury hands onto
the breast of his apron. His small fingers grasped Keith's with
a surprisingly powerful grip.

"Well, well, we've not seen you in a while."

"No," Keith said, with regret. "I've been really busy. Mmm,
something smells delicious!" He went over to the examine the
pots bubbling on the low stove, and took a taste from a big
saucepan with the wooden spoon propped up inside it.

"There, now, stop that," scolded a little silver-haired female, who hustled over to rap him on the knuckles. Keva was
one of the finest bakers in the world and Holl's elder sister.
Keith didn't know her exact age, but she was over a hundred
years older than her brother. "One of these days, you're going
to have a sup of boiling laundry."

"That'd be okay. Fiber's good for you," he said, irrepressibly.

"Welcome," said Maura, Holl's wife, coming up to squeeze
his hand. Her chestnut-haired beauty had matured with marriage and motherhood into a warmth like a fine patina. "Asrai
has been asking when her Big uncle would come to call. She is
talking more now than ever."

"Can't wait to see her," Keith said. He calculated in his head. Asrai must be a little over two years old already. He couldn't keep up with time.

"Keith Doyle!" Dola abandoned the strawberries she had been hulling and came running up to spring into his arms for a hug. The little elf girl, now nearly thirteen years old, had always been a pet of his. Another one who was breaking out of childhood, but slowly, in the way of her kind. She had always worn her long blond hair loose, but now it was braided in a complicated bun at the back of her head, probably to keep it out of the fruit salad she was making.

"Hi, Dola. You're looking beautiful." Keith swung her in a circle and set her down gently. "Where are Marcy and Diane? In there?"

He heard a noise in the main room beyond and started toward it. Dola trotted alongside him and tucked her hand into his.

The very next blink, Keith's eyes sealed shut. He tried to pry the lids open with a thumb and forefinger, but they wouldn't budge. It was as if they were made of single pieces of flesh. "Hey, no fair!"

"Come along," Dola said, guiding him forward. Keith put out his free hand, feeling for the wall. "You will spoil the surprise."

"What surprise?" Keith demanded. "What's going on?"

Though his sight was blocked, his other senses were in perfect working order. Around him many voices that he knew were speaking in whispers and giggling. He could feel bodies passing close enough to him to set his invisible whiskers on alert. And, best of all, he could smell lots of luscious food including, to his delight, some of Keva's bread.

The rush of light when his lids finally parted was as shocking as a skyrocket. Packed into the bright room around him was the entire population of Little Folk with a sprinkling of Big Folk faces Keith knew as well. The long, thin face with the stringy black hair belonged to Pat Morgan. The light-skinned African-American wearing a cashmere sweater-vest was Dunn Jackson, a fellow former student in the Elf Master's special extended educational courses under Gillington Library. The ancient woman with eyes as blue as cornflowers was Ludmilla Hempert, and supporting her, the tall, taciturn man with mahogany-dark skin and eyes was Lee Eisley.

"Surprise!" From the midst of the crowd, a lovely girl with a blue-green eyes in a heart-shaped face, wriggled her way out of the crowd to give Keith a kiss. He returned it with enthusiasm.

"What is this?" he asked.

"It's a party," Diane Londen said, her blue-green eyes gleaming with mischief. Diane led Keith forward into the center of the room, and everyone clustered about, patting him on the back or shaking his hand.

"I can see that, but what for?"

"We didn't know whether you would figure it out or no," Maura's emerald-green eyes were bright with glee. "A celebration of your graduation."

"And ours," said Marcy Collier. A shy beauty with black hair and very white skin, Marcy had fallen in love with Enoch. Since the end of the last school year, she'd been living at the farm full time. The shy girl had become a reserved but much more confident woman. Keith was pleased. She needed stable roots to blossom, and she'd gotten them. "But mostly for you."

"But I graduated months ago," Keith protested.

"But not from my class," the Elf Master said.

A stocky, older male with red hair and beard and gold-rimmed glasses balanced on his nose, the master emerged from the midst of the throng. The others parted respectfully to make way for him. He rocked back on is heels to reguard Keith.

"Until your lahst assignment I did not accept that you had demonstrated the requisite knowledge to earn the degree of Bachelor of Arts neither according to the charter of your unifersity, or to me. I am now satisfied. And, now, about your definition of vhen a paper is due…" His eyebrows lifted meaningfully. Keith opened his mouth to protest.

"Later, later," the Master's wife, Orchadia, said, laughing. She put a brimming wooden cup into her husband's hand. "A toast."

"Yes, a toast to the good ones who haf vorked so hard," said old Ludmilla Hempert, the retired University cleaning woman who had been the first Big Person the elves had learned to trust. Moving slowly but still with an upright spine, she came over to kiss Keith on the cheek. Her flower-blue eyes twinkled. "I am glat to see you here again with my little ones."

"Thanks, folks," Keith said, deeply moved. "I'm really delighted."

"Speechless?" asked Pat, Keith's former roommate.

"Never." Keith grinned. "I'll think of something to say after I've eaten. It seems like weeks since I've had a square meal. And nothing as good as this."

"We wait for you to begin," the Elf Master said, cordially. He gestured toward the long table under the window, which had been laid out as a buffet. Sliced meats and cheeses covered one huge platter beside a basket of rolls. Salads galore followed, most of them made with fresh fruits and vegetables from the community garden. Keith took Diane's arm and escorted her to the end of the line.

"Congratulations," said Tiron, swinging into line with Catra, the Little Folks' Archivist on his arm. "Didn't know any Big People who had the wit or the endurance to measure up to our standards, and here's four of you. Will wonders never cease?"

"Thanks, I think," Keith said. "How's things going?"

"Oh, well, well," Tiron said, patting Catra's arm possessively. She gave Keith a sly grin. He thought he understood the byplay.

Tiron was the newest member of the community, imported personally, though unwittingly, from Ireland by Keith in a suitcase that had formerly been filled with the student's clothes. He was a carver of enormous skill and matching ego. He had also acquired a reputation as a ladies' man. Keith wondered what had happened to Catra's longtime boyfriend Ronard. There he was, in the crowd near the kitchen door. His blazing gray eyes were fixed on the back of Catra's tightly-coiffed chestnut head and Tiron's curly dark one. Keith suspected that Catra was getting tired of waiting for Ronard to jump the broomstick with her—all right, so the Folk didn't use broomsticks in their wedding ceremony—but Ronard wasn't getting the message. The newcomer was good looking, very talented, and not at all ashamed to toot his own horn. He was a good prospect, or a good lever to pry a reluctant suitor off the fence. Ronard wasn't the only person who looked disgruntled. Catra's younger sister Candlepat, the village flirt, was pointedly not looking at Tiron as she swept through with a platterful of cookies and pastries. Keith thought for one moment of asking what was going on, but decided he didn't want to bring up weddings. Not with Diane in earshot.

"Leave that be! You should never have brought that up in the first place."

At the sound of angry voices Keith glanced over toward another serving table set against the wall across the room. It held a selection of beverages in barrels, bottles and punch bowls. Marm, the Folks' brewer, seemed to be having a furious argument with Tay, Dola's father. Marm appeared to have won the battle. He snatched a wooden mug from the other male's hands and brought it to Keith.

"It ought to be my honor to offer you the produce of our cellar," Marm said, shamefacedly, knowing that everyone had been watching them. "Imagine, I don't know where the young ones lose their manners." Tay flushed, staining his ice-fair skin the color of the wine. "The first pressings from our own vineyard, come to maturity. You're responsible for this vintage, in a way."

"And I didn't have to stomp a single grape," Keith said, solemnly, raising the cup to his lips. "Delicious. Wow! It packs a little kick, too." Marm looked smugly pleased.

"The cup's my contribution," said Tiron. "It's a gift for you from us all. It will last forever, and nothing you put in it will sour or poison you."

Keith examined the wooden mug. His name was etched around the base. The handle was a simple carving of a unicorn, so perfect it looked as if it had just that moment reared up to look into the interior. "Thanks, Tiron. It's beautiful."

"And if you tip it up too often, all we'll see is the backside of a horse," Marm guffawed. "And there's one on the cup, too."

"I have something for you, too," said Catra. She offered Keith a sheet of marbled paper. It looked like a letter, written both in English and the elves' language. Little of it was comprehensible except for Keith's name inscribed in large characters in the center of the page, but he recognized the format.

"Hey, a diploma. So I'm officially an *Artis Baccalaureatis* of the Select Learning Academy for Leprechauns and Others under the Master, otherwise known as SLALOM?"

The others laughed. The Elf Master pursed his lips. "It is gut that you yourself cannot go farther downhill in your studies."

"Yeah, but I can dodge like anything," Keith said.

In spite of his worries, Holl grinned.

"You've started something again, widdy. Now they'll all be calling it that."

"I won't get one of those just yet," Dunn said, "but you know what it's like." Sheepishly, he pulled a sheaf of papers rolled into a cylinder from his back pocket and handed it to the Elf Master, who raised his eyebrows as he scanned the first page. "Trying to make a buck makes it hard to get to my homework, but I'm trying. As long as I'm working for my brother I can't get down here again for at least a year."

"Hey, I understand. I know I'm lucky to be able to go on for an advanced degree." Keith examined the document, wishing he could read it. Although it was set out in a graceful calligraphy that would make the sheepskin printers die with envy, the sheet was plain. "Beautiful. But shouldn't you doll this up a little bit? You know, a seal and a ribbon, or a portrait, or something?"

"The document fulfills its function," the Master informed him, austerely. "You should not need a literal reminder uf your accomplishment, but as Lee Eisley told me some years ago, it is uf psychological benefit. It says vhat it needs to say. No more is needed." Lee met Keith's eyes and shrugged.

"Well, you could make it fancier. Just for fun." The Master raised his eyebrows, but Keith rattled on, caught up in the idea. "I could design you a seal like the one the University has, maybe even a school logo. Hey, that reminds me…"

"Enough!" the Master said. Reluctantly, Keith let the idea drop. For the time being.

"Let us eat," Orchadia said. "The cooks will be sadly disappointed in us if everything spoils."

Chapter 3

"What are your plans for the fall?" Maura asked, guiding the Big Folk to the end of the buffet table. She took their wine cups while they filled plates.

"Full schedule," Keith said. He spied a bowl of huge strawberries like fat, speckled rubies and helped himself to a hearty scoopful, taking in the tangy scent with appreciative sniffs. The fruit and vegetables the elves grew not only looked more perfect than anything he ever saw in a store, they tasted like Aristotle's absolute of ideal flora. "Just got my classes sewn up."

"My schedule's mixed up," Diane said. "I've only got six required courses left, but the history section I want won't be offered until January. The food service wants me to stay on, so I'm spreading out my classes three and three. That means," she said, with a sly look at Keith, "I'll have some free time."

"Mmm," said Keith, leaning over to offer her a strawberry and a kiss. "I'll take all of it."

"I'm glad the party hasn't been until now," Diane continued. "I've hardly been around since the end of last term. I went home for a while, then I was in Chicago for a while visiting Keith, then I went with my roommates to New York for a weekend. Then, my summer job has been keeping me very busy."

"I know," Keith said, putting the free hand, the one not carrying a plate of sandwiches and fruit, around her waist. "I've hardly seen you myself."

"Well, that'll change," she said. "I'm working after class this year in the general nutrition department, but apart from that I'm all yours."

"Mmm. That's all I need to make this year perfect." Keith leaned in for another kiss, then drew back with a mischievious look in his eyes. "Perhaps you can help solve a mystery that's always puzzled me," he said, working his brows up and down like Groucho Marx. "How can they take perfectly good ingredients and turn them into school food?"

"I hope I never find out," Diane said, laughing. She filched a sandwich from his plate. "I'd much sooner learn how you folks make such incredible bread."

"If you inqvire of Keva," the Elf Master said, his eyes glinting behind his gold-rimmed glasses, "I know she vill be both pleased and flattered."

"So, are you still living in that phone booth we moved you into back in June?" Pat asked Diane.

"Sure am."

"Why?"

"Because I can afford it on my salary and financial assistance," Diane said firmly. "I don't have to have a roommate. I grew up with four sisters and one bathroom. This is my last chance to have a bath all my own." She shot a pointed look at Keith. He pretended to look innocent. Holl knew he was thinking of the house in the suburbs with two baths he was hoping to buy. The other Folk smiled. They were looking forward to one wedding, and anticipating another one. They would celebrate for Keith Doyle with the greatest of joy; for all he'd done for them, it was the least they could do in return.

"And you, Keith Doyle, will you really be living in that small box on the edge of town?" Marm asked, glowering at them for slowing down the buffet line.

"It's got everything I need," Keith said, moving ahead and picking up cherry tomatoes and carrot sticks. "Bedroom, kitchenette—all right, just a stove, a sink and a refrigerator at one end of the bedroom—and a bathroom. More than enough."

"It is a suitcase, Keith Doyle, smaller than your old dormitory room," Enoch pointed out.

"Well, a suitcase is all I plan to use it for: keeping clothes in. And sleeping," Keith said. "I'll be spending all of my waking time in class, studying, or with Diane or my other friends, or here."

"Would you not have been happier sharing larger quarters?" Marm asked. "Diane is living in a small place. You are living in a small place. Would it not make sense...?" The Elf Master moved a hand and Marm abruptly stopped talking. Keith guessed that he had sealed Marm's back teeth together momentarily to keep from embarrassing Diane, but it was too late. She was blushing.

"Sure I would," Keith said, deliberately misunderstanding the question to take attention away from her, "but breaking in a roommate takes time."

"Besides," said Pat, with a theatrical sigh, "who else would put up with him?"

Keith flipped a hand toward Pat. "See? And it's just simpler not to have to explain about you and the ears." He gestured in the direction of his own. "Listen, it's my own space, however small. You notice it's on the side of town nearest here. It is a lot better than spending another term in my old room at home. Even though my younger brother is finally out of there. He's starting college, too."

"Not here?" Enoch asked, alarmed. "Two Doyles in one place?"

Keith grinned. "Nope. I love Jeff and we get along better these days, but this town ain't a-big enough for the two of us. He got a full scholarship to architecture school in Seattle. In fact, he got a pile of scholarships, some from the weirdest places. He attracts good fortune, especially the financial kind." Keith gave a mock sigh. "Nobody wants to support a budding wizard, but they're all over fairy godparents."

"You do enough good on your own," Holl assured him, joining the line behind Enoch and Marcy. "But are you certain you won't be lonely?"

"I won't have the time," Keith said, briskly, glossing over his private doubts. "But I will miss living with Pat."

"That makes one of us." Patrick Morgan grinned at him over Holl's head. "I put up with you for four years," he said. "That should have earned me a medal, not just a diploma."

"No, Pat's my problem now," Dunn said, slapping the taller man on the back. "Making a stab at the legit-i-mate theater

doesn't pay worth spit, but I can hold on for now. I'm programming for my brother's company. He got some venture capital recently. That means I'm paying the bulk of the rent right
now, until the money runs out. Then we'll both be washing
dishes somewhere to cover the rent of our opulent three-bed-
room riverside apartment. But, whatever. I'm doing my part to
support the arts."

Pat fanned himself with a fluttering napkin. "I have always relied," he said, in a breathy Southern accent, "upon
the kindness of strangers."

"Yeah, right," Dunn said, turning back to the food. "You
folks wouldn't be interested in investing in a budding software giant, would you?"

"Not in this market," Holl said, with a rueful smile. "You
can imagine the expressions on the faces of the Conservatives if we propose investing the money earned from their
painstaking labors on the whims of the Internet marketplace. There is still considerable disagreement about the
computer."

"I can hardly believe you have one, even though I know
I've sent lots of messages to it," Keith said, around a mouthful of sandwich. Diane had recovered her composure, and
was eating chicken salad. "Too Progressive even for you?"

"Not you, too," Holl groaned. "It is a good machine, and
a worthy investment."

"Would you like to see it?" Dola asked.

"Sure."

She grabbed his hand. "Come along, then!"

"Not now, child!" Orchadia scolded. "Let the youth eat
his dinner."

"It's okay, Orchadia," Keith said, letting himself be dragged
into the kitchen, to a handsomely made cabinet on wheels.
Holl and Enoch followed along, with Diane and Marcy behind
them. Importantly, Dola pushed aside her relatives working at
the kitchen table, and opened the doors.

"It is the very most recent con-fig-ur-a-tion," she said carefully, showing off the features. "I like the scanner. It is as though
the computer has an eye. It copies images nearly as well as we

can. The printer is very fussy, though. Catra has had to speak to it many times to produce what she wants."

"Very nice," Keith said, as Dola turned on the unit. The screen came to life in an instant. Keith put his plate down and came closer for a look. He read the drive properties enviously, noting the speed and capacity. "Much nicer than the setup my folks gave me as a graduation present. Where's this cable go?" He traced the striped ribbon coming out of an opening in the side of the case down to the floor and under the kitchen table. A couple of the elves had to get out of the way for him to see the tall white box it led to. "A server? Your own server?"

"Yes, and in the way all of the time," Keva snapped. "I'll break an ankle on it one day, and all will rue it, you mark my words."

"No, it's not in the way, grandmother," Dola said. "You never put your foot under this table."

"Do not show disrespect to your elders, girl!"

"Why?" Keith asked.

"Why here?" Holl asked.

"Yes, and there's no good reason for it," Keva said, sailing away in high dudgeon.

Holl grinned after his indignant sister. "It does no good to point out to her that this is where the telephone line enters the house, making it the most logical location, and the most out of the way of daily tasks. Keva keeps threatening to throw a cup of flour into the workings. I'm afraid one day she will."

"No," Keith said, waving his hands. "Why a server at all?"

"So as not to have to interact with Big Folk and your service providers," Holl said patiently. "They want details, and once you are in their clutches, they gather more. We don't want anyone tracing our comings and goings, nor especially our contact with the others. And the monthly cost—the Archivist researched it most thoroughly and determined it was worthwhile to buy our own. The domain names are registered to you, by the way."

"Thanks for telling me," Keith said, with a good natured grumble. "The way you're going, I'm going to wake up one day the potentate of a small country—all on paper."

Dola turned off the computer and rolled the cabinet back against the wall with the help of her great-uncles.

"Beautiful carving on those doors," Diane said.

"I…" Tiron began, and the others turned to look straight at him, "couldn't have done it better meself." Holl turned back, abashed to think the newest member of the household might be in the mood to stir up trouble. He was ashamed for lacking trust.

"That *is* a handsome cabinet," Keith said. "A new design?"

"This is one-of-a-kind," Enoch said. "I built it especially for the computer and its attendant pieces. It is like the rolling wardrobes we saw in a catalog fair Marcy brought home one day."

"Nice! Are you thinking of moving into the furniture business?"

"Not furniture. The market is too crowded at the low end and too chancy at the high," Enoch said flatly. "We cannot afford quality wood for speculation. I'll not make another. Unless," and his grudging look belied the generous words, "ye'd like one for your own."

Keith was touched. "That's really nice of you, Enoch, but I don't think I could get it up the stairs to the room I'm renting. I really like it, though. Look at that satin finish. Is it real rosewood, or just a varnish?"

"There's no just-a-varnish about it," Enoch said. "I took a piece of oak and enhanced the grain a bit to smooth it out. It is much stronger than rosewood. Which it needs to be, in this household, with all the racketing about it gets."

"The computer is popular in the evenings especially," Maura said. "That is when we receive the Internet mail."

"Hmph!" Keva said, pushing them aside to attend to a cooking task at the opposite end of the room.

Enoch snorted, watching her strut away. "And the Conservatives are there for every word. Don't let them tell you they aren't, and if they didn't see the use of it beyond what we Progressives espouse, they'd have put it out the door already. All gather around in the evening to read the messages from our folk left behind in Ireland. The Niall has a computer of his own, and a fine one by the sound of it. And even the old ones see the Internet as a solution to not having every new book and periodical to hand because they are no longer living in a library. They read more journals and scholarly digests now that they do not have to slip volumes away one at a time. They have greater access to material from all over the world. It's not often the box is not in use."

Keith grinned. "That's one way to worm the computer into their hearts. Give 'em more than they can handle, and they won't remember what they did without it. At least you don't get a brain ache from too much education."

"That's never your problem, Keith Doyle," Holl said, but it was a half-hearted sally.

He shouldn't have said anything. Keith glanced at him, curiosity writ large across his thin face. Marcy leaped into the breach.

"Come and see *my* graduation present," she said.

"What is it?"

"It's down in the barn," Marcy said. She took his and Diane's arms and firmly turned them toward the door, ignoring their questions. Enoch led the way.

"Careful, I'll spill my potato salad!" Diane exclaimed, laughing.

Marcy pointed out the new kitchen garden, where the cooks had planted dozens of exotic species of herbs and spices in sunlit plots like squares of emerald. She reached out to bruise a sprig of lavender. To Holl's nose, its scent was strong enough to perfume the air for yards around, but the Big Folk only seemed to be able to perceive it when they were right on top of it. Diane plucked the top of a stalk and put it in Keith's breast pocket. Marcy showed them the basils, thymes and mints, naming them all with help from Enoch. Holl trailed along in their wake, keeping well back to avoid uncomfortable questions. He was grateful to Marcy and Enoch for keeping Keith distracted. His Big friend was kind-hearted, and already knew that something was troubling him. But he had given his word not to speak about it, and he wouldn't.

The other Big visitors had little sensitivity to magic, but he was suprised Keith hadn't sensed the problem going on in the house yet. The argument between Tay and Marm over the wine was just another symptom of the bad feeling that seemed to pervade the entire house—no, the farm—with a psychic miasma like the smell of mildew. Everyone was on edge, and had been for weeks. Tensions that normally bubbled under the surface broke through, worrying everyone. Accidents were more prevalent than could just be put down to chance. Intrusions from the outside were becoming more frequent, as county inspectors for this and poll-takers for that had appeared on their doorstep, or, more troublingly, inside the borders of the land around the house. Small wonder that tempers were flaring: the Folk had been scared into remaining inside the house, when they were just becoming used to having an outside it was safe to go.

More than one person had wondered aloud, once the thrill of owning their own home had worn off, whether they had done the right thing and wound up in the right place. Half the Conservatives had declared the house unlucky. To Holl's horror, several were campaigning to be put on a ship or jet airplane, no matter what, and sent back to the Folk who still lived in Ireland. If their fears were forcing them out into the world, away from the safe haven they had created here, things were bad indeed. He wished he could consult with Keith, but he'd been forbidden. Even the Master had suggested Holl relied too heavily on Keith's assistance.

The Master was right, of course. Keith had been invaluable so many times that it was easy to take him for granted. Now that they were out in the world again after half a century, they ought to learn to be self-sufficient in *all* their needs. That included working out social pressures that came with their new liberty.

Perhaps, Holl thought sadly, following the others around the barn, they were not ready to live unprotected. Perhaps the transition ought to have been gradual, though Holl had no idea how that could have been accomplished, with or without Keith Doyle. They'd had to be so very quiet, both physically and magically, while living in the basement of Gillington Library. Now voices were freed and magic was loosed—and people did not like it when they couldn't feel the protective walls around them. Holl noticed that a few of the Folk no longer went outside except to race between house and barn as though enemies lurked all around them, just out of sight. Not that Holl hadn't felt the sensation himself, though he put it down to uncertainty rather than scrutiny.

All the same he wished he could talk it out with a sympathetic and technically disinterested ear. Keith ought to have insights that would be valuable to Holl. If nothing else, it would be good to talk to someone who didn't live in the middle of the problem. Every time the doorbell rang, everyone jumped halfway out of their skins. Every time a truck drove by on the bumpy country road, everyone braced themselves to scurry to a hiding place. It was at the Conservatives' urging that the repulsion spell around the property had been strengthened to a point that pained those that must pass through it. Gradually they were turning what was to be a home in touch with nature into a secured camp. They couldn't go on like that, but Holl didn't know what to do to turn it back.

Chapter 4

Beyond the old barn, now given over entirely to the production of wooden goods, the Folk had built a pole barn to contain their farm equipment. A gravel drive that intersected with the original driveway led out around the front of the house to serve it.

Keith glanced over his shoulder at Holl, trailing behind them, as he crunched down the slope toward the oversized door.

"What's with Holl?" Keith asked Marcy in an undertone he hoped wouldn't carry over their footsteps.

"Why do you ask?"

Keith made a face. "I always get suspicious when people answer a question with a question. There's something eating everybody. The farm is not as...happy-go-lucky as it ought to be."

"Really, there's nothing specific," Marcy said, nervously.

"Uh-huh," Keith said, with a dubious expression. "Well, it doesn't seem okay." She looked so alarmed that Enoch cleared his throat with a pointed 'hem!' Keith relented. "Never mind. I'll get to the bottom of things, once I'm down here again for the year. What's this present?"

"Take a look," Marcy said. With a flourish, she threw open the pedestrian door beside the large one and flipped a switch.

"They bought you a *car*?" Diane exclaimed, as the overhead lights flicked on. Looking like it was there by mistake beside the muddy animal trailer, the tractor and the rusty, vintage harvester was a dark green Chevrolet Suburban. "Holy cow. Look at the size of the thing. I like the color."

"I know it's not really a car," Marcy said, with a laugh. "It's a truck. And it's really almost more a present to *them,* since I run all the errands they can't. It's got heavy shocks for carrying wood, high-traction tires and a trailer hitch. And it gets awful mileage. I don't mind. It handles well. It doesn't feel industrial. They've done things to the suspension and the seat to make it comfortable, and it's not noisy at all. It's nicer to ride in than my parents' fancy car."

"Nice," Keith said, flipping up the hood to examine the engine with the avid interest of an amateur mechanic. "I've seen these going for thirty, forty thousand dollars." He stopped, and looked at the others suspiciously. "Where'd you get the money?"

"Fair and square, Keith Doyle," Enoch said, sourly.

"eBay," Marcy explained. "The computer's only been here for a couple of months, but you know how fast the Folk learn. Once they saw how many different things people were selling, Tiron carved a bust of Candlepat out of beechwood, and we put it up on the web for sale. It sold for nine hundred dollars."

"Wow!"

"It could have gone for more, but we didn't want to attract too much attention," Marcy said. "But we bought a digital camera with the proceeds. They made more things, all of them one of a kind carvings, good ones, photographed them and uploaded the images. Those auctions are fierce. You ought to see how fast the price goes up."

"I'll bet," Keith said, doing calculations in his head. "What about merchandise for the gift shops?"

"Oh, the bread-and-butter pieces are still being done. Not everyone is good enough to create high-end art, but we…" she paused, blushing.

Enoch took her hand and squeezed it. "Ye can say 'we.' You're considered one of us now." He glared at Keith, daring him to contradict the statement. Keith held up his hands.

"Hey, I've already stopped seeing the difference in height."

Enoch gave a curt nod. Marcy made a little face and continued, her confidence restored. "*We* are thinking of making the higher-class art a business."

"Well, I hope they don't stop doing the bread-and-butter," Keith said. "I need the commissions." He started to say more, but realized Diane was in the room, and clapped his mouth shut. A surprise wasn't a surprise if the surprisee heard about it in advance.

"You'd do better on the commissions from fine art," Enoch pointed out. "It would be worth your while to visit galleries as our representative."

"Why not?" Keith said, thinking of moonlight and blue velvet boxes. "I'll need a nicer suit."

"Have you not seen the television reports from art galleries? They wear nothing but plain black. That shouldn't be expensive."

"Now there you're wrong," Diane said positively, getting into the spirit of things. She'd made no secret of the fact she wanted to see Keith start dressing a little more fashionably. "*Armani* black will set you back several hundred dollars just for a *shirt.*"

"Armani black is an expensive color, then," Enoch said.

"You have no idea. But if Keith wants to look the part, he'll have to get some."

"I'll look like a lighted match," Keith said, wryly, tugging at his red hair. "But anything for a sale."

"So, you two," Diane said, as they locked up the barn and headed up the hill toward the house, "when's the wedding?"

Marcy's face fell. She came to a halt and clutched Keith's arm. "Could we wait to go back inside for a moment?"

"Is there a problem?" Keith asked.

"Oh, not with them," Marcy said, gesturing at the lighted windows above. "I just don't want any of the others to hear. Not this. You're the only ones who might understand. It's my parents."

"Should I go away?" Holl asked.

"Should I?" Diane asked. Marcy caught at the other girl's hand.

"Oh, no. If you could help…"

Marcy looked so desperate, Diane dropped the jealousy that had been brewing inside her, and her mother-hen aspect, as Keith called it, manifested itself. She squeezed Marcy's hand comfortingly. "Whatever I can do. What we both can do. Right?"

"Right," Keith said at once. "Dr. Ruth and Dr. Spock at your service. Only Enoch's got the ears. What's up with your folks?"

"Well…they don't really like the fact that I'm living down here with Enoch. They've been after me to introduce them to him, but I'm still nervous about it. I'm trying to find a good way to bring up the subject so they won't reject us immediately. I tried to tell them the truth before…"

"But they weren't exactly receptive to having an elf as a son-in-law," Keith finished.

"No. The subject is especially a sore spot with my mother. Mom already hates the idea that he's a…woodworker."

"She ought to feel lucky," Keith said at once. "Anyway, Enoch's not just a woodworker, he's an artist. Look at that cabinet he made."

"She'd be happier if my fiance was a doctor or a lawyer."

Keith scoffed. "Anybody can marry a doctor or a lawyer."

"But the biggest question," Marcy said, dropping her voice to a near whisper, "is how I bring up…his height."

Keith and Diane nodded. No one was fooling themselves by pretending that it wouldn't matter how different Enoch was from Big Folks. The ears and the magic apart, he was the size of a preadolescent boy, with a face to match. It would take particularly special parents to get past that right away, especially if they hadn't met Enoch under circumstances where they could get to know his personality before they judged him on his appearance. Which they couldn't, since their daughter had already said she was going to marry him. Keith wondered how his own folks would have taken it if his girlfriend was one of the Little Folk. Marcy looked upset when he grinned.

"I'm not smiling at you," he assured her. "I was thinking what it would have been like if our situations had been reversed."

"How would you get your parents to come around?" she asked, quickly.

"Oh, well, it's not really an equivalent situation," Keith said, giving her a sheepish smile. "I can't remember a day in my life when I wasn't talking about legendary beings. In fact, my parents were probably *expecting* me to come home and tell them I'd married a fairy woman. I hope they weren't too disappointed when I started dating Diane. Oof!" he said as Diane punched him in the arm. "It's just as well, though. It'd be a heck of a commute from Fairyland to Chicago."

"What can we do to help?" Diane asked, putting a hand over Keith's mouth.

Marcy held up her hands helplessly. "What should I do? How can I convince them I'm not kidding? He's a good man. I really want them to like him. I…I can't push them."

"I," Keith said, holding up a declamatory finger, "am an expert in the art of push. I offer my services as a go-between. Your folks used to like me. I'll be happy to go convince them that neither Enoch's occupation or species, if you want to call it that, are detrimental to your future happiness, but the fact that they won't give you their blessing would."

"In two-dollar words or less," Diane added.

Marcy smiled with relief. "That's exactly what we need." He'd never stepped over the line with her, and had always given his support to what she really wanted. "You're a true friend. It won't be easy. My dad's even more set against it than my mother."

"The difficult we do right away," Keith said, loftily. "The impossible just takes a little longer. Is this what you wanted to ask me about this afternoon?" Keith asked Enoch.

The black-haired elf nodded. "I didn't think you were listening, the way you hare off after every newest idea to come your way. Fair Marcy is grieved over the way her parents resist her intentions."

"They think she's still a child, huh?" Keith asked, sympathetically.

"That's the long and the short of it," Enoch said glumly. And, catching the gleam in Keith's eye, added, "none of your attempts at wit, eh? They're as sorry as your spellcasting."

Keith caught at his chest in mock protest. "I was doing fine! That pigeon was a work of art!"

"Aye, well, it's good my father isn't instructing you in that. You'd not have graduated yet."

When they returned to the farmhouse, Pat was doing a spirited impression of the director of his latest play.

"No, no, no, no, no!" Pat shouted, pointing at Keith. "You were much more red-headed when you came in before. Do it *again*, and give me *intensity*."

"So, vhat do you think?" the Master asked. Over the teacher's head, Marcy gave Keith a frantic look not to mention what they had been talking about.

"It's a great present," Keith said, giving her a calming nod. "You'll have to let me know how it works out for you. Pretty soon I'm going to have to think about replacing my old car. For the time being, though, it'll have to last me."

"What if something comes out of this Chicago call?" Enoch asked.

"What Chicago call?" Diane wanted to know.

Keith explained the conversation he had had with Dorothy.

"Oh, no," Diane said, unhappily. "So you're going to be up in Chicago now? When did this happen. We were going to have so much time together this year."

"It's only a potential opportunity," Maura said, placatingly, "not an actual one."

"It's just one meeting," Keith added. "I get a chance to show off. Maybe I can cadge a lunch out of Dorothy, and I'll be back before Wednesday morning. Don't worry! The whole thing will probably go nowhere. I'm just glad they're still thinking of me at PDQ. That means there might still be a door open for me after graduation."

"I hope it will work out for you, Keith Doyle," Holl said. "Harnessing that hyperactive imagination of yours to work for a living would be good for you." But Keith could tell Diane didn't like the idea.

"And since you will be back among us do you intend to continue in your instruction under my tutleage?" the Elf Master wanted to know.

Keith was delighted. "Can I? That'd be great. But I thought you said I had graduated."

"And you haf. From the first lefel of unifersity education. There are many to go, and many subjects you might study. Hmm? Vould you like to continue?"

"Yes, I would," Keith said at once. "You bet."

"Gut. Perhaps you vould like to explore the history of the field in vhich you are so interested, eh? Eight to ten pages. In light uf your travel plans, three veeks until it is due."

Keith's face fell. "Homework again already?"

Marcy came over to break it up between her father-in-law elect and her friend. "Let him enjoy what he's earned, please, sir."

"Uf course, my dear," the Master said, the suspicion of a smile lifting the corners of his mustache. "I am too eager to teach, it seems."

"It sounds as though you've filled every moment of the coming year, Keith Doyle," Orchadia said. "Do you never dream of a time of peace and quiet?"

"No time for it," Keith said. "There's still so much I want to do. For instance, I'd still like to get all the supernatural beings in the world together for a big party—that is, all the ones who can get to it." He looked hopefully at the Folk.

"If I ever see any, I'll tell them you're looking for them," Holl said sourly. He and Keith had an ongoing argument about whether the Folk could claim a supernatural origin. Holl felt they were perfectly natural beings; humans were the ones who had lost touch with nature.

"No, it'd be great," Keith exclaimed, waving his arms with enthusiasm. "The air sprites already showed me they've seen all kinds of creatures. If they come, it would be the most amazing party ever. It'd be a chance for everybody to get to know one another, maybe work out differences, settle ancient feuds. I mean, look at all the legends for which there's still no really good explanation. People still think you're legendary…"

"And with good luck they always will," Enoch said, alarmed.

"…Yeah, but think of all the other beings like you who fall just under the radar. You would have a lot in common with them. Maybe you could work out strategies for dealing with us

Big Folk. And maybe they'd figure out that there are some of us who would treat them with respect. Pixies, titans, medusae, mermaids…"

"You have to find these first," Holl said, his eyebrow raised skeptically.

"I will," Keith said, full of confidence. "Somehow."

"Some of these of vhich you speak could not attend because of geography and physiology," the Master reminded him. "And vhat uf the vuns who are bigger than your kind? Chiants, und others."

"Well, then the party will have to be held outside," Keith said, not missing a beat. "I don't know what sort of things they eat, but I know from all the books they like good liquor and beer. I can bring in some kegs."

Marm cleared his throat. "Well, my brewing is known far and wide as the best around. I'd be most pleased to offer beer for the party, if I can come to it."

Keith grasped his friend's shoulder. "It wouldn't be a party without you," he said. "That would be great. Your beer is the best I've ever had."

"How much will you need, and when will you need it?" Marm asked. "A good brew takes longer than overnight."

"I don't know yet. Lots, I hope. I haven't had much luck in making contact with other kinds so far. I try when I have time. The air sprites have been giving me these tantalizing glimpses of beings racing over the landscape, but I haven't caught up with any of them yet. By the way, the sprites send sunrises to Tay and Holl."

Tay grinned. "Since I'm unlikely ever to clamber into a balloon again I'll probably never see them, but I am glad they remember me kindly. Give them greetings from me."

"You bet."

"And if you succeed in making contact with every being that can walk, crawl, swim or fly, where do you propose to put them all?" Holl asked. "Your parents' home, in the midst of the Chicago suburbs? That'd be a subtle get-together, with giants towering over the trees, and salamanders burning holes through the fences."

"Well, I was sort of hoping to have the party *here*," Keith admitted. The group fell silent. A few of the older elves looked shocked. Keith bit his tongue. *Uh-oh, too soon*, he thought. He saw his glowing plans die away to ash. But not all the faces were unhappy.

"That is not an unreasonable request," the Elf Master said, after a moment's pause.

"Really?" Keith asked, relieved. "I thought I'd have to do a lot more persuading. It would be okay with you?"

"Yes, uf course. Don't be so surprised. You haf done much for us. It is a small thing to ask. Ve vould appreciate a chance to show our gratitude. And ve vould enjoy such a gathering."

"Thanks, sir," Keith said. "Wow. Yeah! I'd better start making a list of what I'll need."

"I can get you cold cuts at cost from Food Services," Diane said. "Their produce doesn't hold a candle to yours, though," she told the Folk.

"With time enough we can persuade the fields to produce what you need," Siobhan, Dola's mother, said.

The others gathered, clamoring to add their own offerings. "The best cheese you've ever tasted, boyo." "You'll need a mort of bread and rolls, will you not?" "Candy! What about sweets?"

"You guys are great," Keith said, overwhelmed by their generosity. "This is going to be one terrific party."

"We'd be only too happy to help," Maura said. "When would you want to hold it?"

Keith did some mental calculations. "Well, this is August. Say sometime next spring. It'll give me a chance to fill out the guest list. I've got to figure some way to get the word out."

"Take care you don't attract anything unwelcome," Holl warned, "such as more of your own kind. I don't think they would enter into the celebration with the spirit you hope for."

"I'll make sure that no Big People even figure out what I'm doing," Keith assured him.

Chapter 5

The gold pendulum swung wildly back and forth over the map of the central United States. Gradually, it slowed and began to describe a smaller oval. The tall, gaunt woman holding the end of the little pointer's chain shifted her wrist until the oval spiraled in to an ever-diminishing circle over one spot on the face of the central United States.

"There, isn't it as I have told you?" the woman said, with a triumphant look. Her dark eyes seemed to have a red fire within them as they focused on the man in the upholstered armchair with his legs propped on the foot of the bed. "It chooses this place."

"Bah," Everette Beach said, rolling his pale eyes up to the stark white paint of the hotel ceiling. He had short, light-brown hair shot with gray. The thin nostrils in his spare face made it look as if he was always recoiling from smelling something bad. "There are six hundred square miles in this area. I expect you to pinpoint exactly where you think this 'psychic realm' is located. I want an address, not a general area. We need to find that energy cell."

"It does not cry out 'I am here,'" Maria Katale said surlily. She sat with her back very straight in the pseudo Louis XIV chair. "It beckons. It hints. You did not tell me that United States is so *big*. The power broadcasts its influence over a larger area."

The stocky, dark-haired man beside her cleared his throat. "In our country, the area she shows you would be much smaller. At least she gives you where to seek."

"I can't help it if your education didn't include geography lessons," Beach said. "I had the impression that your original target was farther south than Chicago. Now your circle stretches all the way from Milwaukee to Springfield. I'm not impressed.

I don't want to go back and tell them you brought us here so you could do some shopping."

"It is not me; it is the spirit guides," Maria said. "If first they say it is south and now they say it is north, what of that? The spirits do not anchor themselves in the physical world. They give me the impression, the clue. We must seek on our own. I will tell you if we meet the true magic. It is here."

Beach, disgusted, flung himself to his feet and glared down at Maria. Stefan stood up between them, his five-foot-eight frame an inadequate bulwark against their employer's six-foot-two. "She knows, Mr. Beach. She was much respected in the...old regime. She is genuine. Just because you do not like her answers does not mean she is of no use to you."

Beach threw up his hands. "I want answers, not impressions, Stefan. I'm not saying I believe in all this mumbo-jumbo. If it exists, I want to lay my hands on a source of genuine magic. *If* it exists. I'm still not saying I believe you. I could have gotten better results tossing a dart at a board."

"You must not doubt Maria," Stefan said firmly. "Our...former...government respects her highly."

"If she's so good why don't *you* have...our target...already in your possession? Why would you need to work with me?"

"Money," Stefan said. "Maria is exact, but she finds by circling around her prey, like a cat. It takes time, and we could not afford the search on our own. So we are willing to share the fruit of our efforts. We have the same goal, eh?"

"I doubt it," Beach said. An expatriate Australian who had served in numerous U.N. peacekeeping missions, Beach had had a chance to see the vast difference between the haves and have nots in the world. More problems could be attributed to the curse of capitalism than would ever make the headlines of any newspaper—after all, they were owned by organs of the rich. He had quit, taking his connections with him, and set out with a new goal in mind: to rid the world of pernicious Western influence. Money. There was too damned much money in this country, none of it flowing into the right pockets, the pockets of the people. Capitalism enriched the very few out of the labor of the millions. The world was overbalanced in favor of the big guys. Everette was proud to be part of the effort to right that balance.

He had no trouble enlisting numerous like-minded, highly trained people to his cause. The main problem they had was the very one they were battling. In order to overthrow the moneyed powers, one had to *have* money. It'd be a nice irony once he succeeded, but a pain in the down-unders while he was working to achieve his goal. To get his stake money he hired himself and his force out for industrial espionage to the new superpowers, the megacorporations, under the *nom de guerre* Dotcommunist. It told everyone what his eventual goals were. He liked the idea of weapons that didn't rely upon billions in research and development. Stefan had come to him from the former government of an Eastern European power, a former satellite of the former U.S.S.R. His deposed masters had been on the edge, they said, of finding the source of supernatural power. Beach was intrigued. If his sources were right about what they were chasing, they'd have counterintelligence 'equipment' that no technological power in the world could equal— or detect.

It wasn't that the West didn't know that such things might exist. In response to a Russian effort in the 1950s, the US and other western nations had started chasing psychics and magic, but the effort had never gone anywhere, probably because the scientists working on the research been debunked, ignored or laughed out of whatever chamber they'd had to go into for funding. On the other side of the Iron Curtain, the east had never stopped looking, testing, probing, building on the scant evidence that had made them believe in supernatural powers in the first place. And then the Soviet Union broke up.

The evidence the satellite states had that made them believe in magic was put away into vaults. Everette had seen some of it when he was stationed in the Eastern Bloc: a wealth of documents in an unfamiliar alphabet, written on parchment, leather and primitive paper in inks that laboratory tests showed was made from nut juice, soot, ochre and other pigments. In spite of the materials' ephemeral nature, the inks had not faded and the papers resisted even the slightest crumble. That alone had excited scientists and scholars. They couldn't pinpoint precisely when the documents had been made. They defied traditional carbon-dating, but the provenance, the chain of ownership, went back at least to the 15th century, if not before.

But there was more. They had artifacts. They sounded simple: wooden knives that cut as well as steel, a box that kept food, even milk, fresh at room temperature indefinitely, and several other things. In Everette's estimation, what they were looking at here was forgotten technology, like the architectural skills that had built the Pyramids, moved the trilithons of Stonehenge, not magic, but it was still amazing compared with modern electronics and inexplicable in the face of its great age. He was intrigued. He had never told anyone back home about what he had seen. Only when he left the Foreign Service, citing personal difficulties, did he go back and try to find the things and the people who knew about them he'd seen. The Eastern European governments needed money. Without Soviet money they'd been left behind by the rest of the world and were desperate to catch up. They weren't willing to sell Beach their goods, but they allowed him access to them. His intention was to build up a spy ring, but only if he could get to the source of these things, if it still existed. The Europeans assured him that it must. They showed him more documents, written on modern paper. That told him that the creators of these goods must be somewhere around.

There was more. He'd read contemporary accounts of people who claimed to have eavesdropped on voices heard in hollow hills and under tree roots. Most statements of that kind would be dismissed by skeptics as the ramblings of the insane or the attention-hungry, but they were remarkably consistent in kind. A few contained transliterations of what they had heard. Beach had put a couple of his linguists on the job. His first thought was that the subjects had overheard isolated spy installations, but they couldn't find a correlation with any language they knew, nor did the spoken transliteration appear to coincide meaningfully with the written documents.

Stefan had also produced Maria and her psychic gifts. Dowsing with a pendulum was her specialty, alongside occasional clairvoyance. She'd done a reading for Beach that impressed him enough to commit resources, at least for now. They had never convinced the skeptical Everette that they weren't chasing rainbows, but that wasn't his problem. If it was enough to get him to his goal, that was all that mattered.

One might say he was a spy, but he was a sincere spy. Human nature being what it was, he assumed that everyone else was committed to the cause partly out of naked self-interest. He was taking a fee from Stefan's bosses for a share in the results, true, but it was a tiny fraction of what he could earn doing corporate espionage for any of the enormous international corporations that were large enough to be considered countries in their own right without worrying about such artificial boundaries as borders. They did battle without armies, in the media, in the boardrooms and on the stock exchanges, destroying lives and depleting resources with the stroke of a pen or a computer key. He especially hated advertising. It was the devil. It told lies about inferior products to sell them to the hordes of feeble-minded, hypocritical people who cared about nothing further than instant gratification, the satisfaction of the moment. Bleat, bleat, bleat about human rights, until you asked captalists to pay more for a pair of designer sneakers because the underage, foreign child worker that made them only earned fourteen cents an hour, then they shut up quickly, not liking to be held accountable for their choices. Why with all its resources the United States, for example, didn't have colonies in space at that very moment was that they couldn't focus on the future because the pretty baubles of the present were too enticing to ignore, and their weak-spined government didn't want to risk getting tossed out of office to pursue the issue.

Everette pushed his idealism back. He was there to get whatever it was they were chasing, or destroy it so it couldn't be used by the powers that be. The West didn't need any more advantages than it already had.

But Beach wasn't relying solely upon the powers of one unreliable psychic. He had a team of other operatives in this

country. Some had been here for years, like his chief communications operative, just waiting to be activated. Ming Na-seh
hailed from Sydney. She was now a naturalized citizen and a
highly placed executive within one of the telephone companies. Others, such as most of his enforcers, had to rely upon
tourist visas. Lying about seeking employment while within
the borders of the United States, Beach chided them in his
mind. Tch tch. Beach hoped that he could accomplish his mission before their visas ran out. He didn't want to have to activate another shift.

In the meantime, Ming was proving invaluable. She had
provided the latest piece of evidence that brought Beach to
the United States.

Most of the newspaper-reading public had by now heard
about a computer program being run by the Central Intelligence Agency called Carnivore. It scanned millions of e-mail
messages and other electronic communications every day. It
was supposed to be used only to inform the C.I.A. about drug-
runners and other criminals, but self-interest being what it was,
Beach doubted that they stopped there. With a combination
of favors and cash, he'd staked a couple of young hackers to
create a better program than theirs, which he nicknamed 'Omnivore.' Capable of world-wide infiltration of the Internet, it
scanned graphic and multiple language transmissions as well,
and it excerpted the surrounding text of any reference it found.

It turned out to be money well spent. Omnivore had detected e-mail messages containing that alphabet rocketing back
and forth across the Atlantic. The gateway servers turned out
to be of no help. They were supposed to provide the source
location of messages, but his people were unable to discover
the senders. They pinned down a part of Europe as the most
likely point of origin. It was far easier to try and trace the
American side of the correspondence.

They had been lucky. The coding on the e-mail showed
that both sides were using a smaller server gateway instead
of one of the huge services. Ming had turned Omnivore to
search for the name across all e-mails being sent. The closest
she had come so far to pinpointing its location was some-

where in central Illinois. But here was Maria saying that the source wasn't in the center of the state at all. Beach was frustrated.

"Are you certain you aren't sensing any magic?" he asked Maria again.

The woman deployed her pendulum once more, swinging it out on its chain over the section of map. It reacted as though it had a mind of its own, though. Instead of describing a circle or oval, it leaped and hopped erratically. Maria captured it in her other palm, hiding it from the keen eyes of the two men. "There is nothing."

"Try again."

"I cannot," she insisted. "The powers have stopped speaking to me. I must try again later."

Beach regarded her with exasperation. "We're not here just to chase some linguist's wet dream of a lost language. We're here for the goods, if there are any."

"We will find it," Stefan assured him. "When Maria finds it, she will know. She will be positive."

"Good! Then we will take our...advantage home with us."

"Be careful," Stefan cautioned him. "You don't want the U.S. State Department knowing what you are doing."

"Why?" asked Beach, humourously. "It is not illegal for us to be in this country. We are tourists. It says so on our visas. Besides, they think you are Bulgarian."

"Perhaps we can go shopping," Stefan said. "Since Maria must rest, I would like to look for things for my wife. She has given me a list of many things she has seen on the Internet. It would be good to bring her at least one of them."

Bourgeoise. Beach rolled his eyes.

Chapter 6

Keith was almost buzzing with nerves by the time he followed Dorothy into the boardroom. He was excited to be back at Perkins Delaney Queen. The suite of offices hadn't changed much since Keith's last day as a student intern several months before, except perhaps to replace the modern art sculpture made of tiny pieces of brass and steel in the glass-walled foyer with another equally weird abstract construction of colored aluminum cut into elongated zig-zags. Keith thought of the graceful, curved lines of the Little Folk's carvings and thought how well they could do in the mass market. Perhaps later he could drop in on a few galleries and feel them out. He had a few photographs in a portfolio of some of Enoch's and Tiron's latest creations. The works would sell themselves; all he would have to do is hold up the pictures and take orders. At the moment, though, Keith felt his mind sliding into 'ideation' mode, ready to pop creative notions out one after the other. He hoped he could come up with something that would stick. Dorothy was counting on him.

Dorothy Carver, her chic suit-dress of coral-red picking up warm highlights in her medium-dark complexion, introduced Keith to the men and women around the table. She defered to the plump man at the head of the table. His very black hair was touseled, and his small mouth was framed by a neatly trimmed Van Dyck beard. "Bill Mann, president of Gadfly Technology Corporation. Jennifer Schick, vice-president in charge of sales," was the slender, brown-haired woman with intense, blue eyes beside him. The tall man with the domelike head fringed with the remnants of bronze hair was "Theo Lehmann, head of engineering. Mr. Mann, you've met W. Jason Allen, our president," she nodded toward the elegant. bearded, strawberry-blond man wearing an Ungaro suit and a collarless shirt at the other end of the table, "and Peggy Gilmore, our executive creative director; Doug Constance, creative director; Rollin Chisholm, art director and Janine Martinez, copywriter. Keith Doyle, one of our...freelance copywriters. And you know Paul Meier, who will be the group director for your account."

Keith grinned at Paul, a medium-sized man with black-brown hair and sallow-tan skin who had been Keith's supervisor during his semester there. Doug Constance, about Paul's age, had thick blond hair and a pale gray silk Italian jacket, both elegant and expensive-looking. By contrast, Peggy, a slim woman with light-brown hair, Rollin, a burly but muscular dark-skinned African-American, and Janine, tall and heavyset, were casually dressed. Everyone shook hands. Keith sat down in the empty seat beside Dorothy, perching on the edge of the chair, ready for whatever was to come. She gave him a warm smile, looking poised and ready. In the several months since the two of them had worked together she had grown in confidence. Out of a soft leather briefcase she took a sketch pad and a pencil, and Keith remembered that her artistic ability was one of the skills that had qualified her for the internship. She doodled when she was nervous. She didn't touch pen to paper; instead she waited patiently for everyone to settle down.

"Gadfly?" Paul asked.

"All the good names were taken," Ms. Schick said, with a wry grin. Everyone chuckled. That was a good sign, if the client was willing to break the ice so soon. One of Paul's current crop of interns from the boardroom up the hall took orders for coffee. Keith, who liked his very sweet, was glad to see no one watched him while he poured four packets of sugar into the cup.

Bill Mann nodded politely as his coffee was set down before him, but he kept his arms folded while Ms. Schick dealt out sheets of paper to everyone.

"Just a reminder that we can't proceed until we have non-disclosure agreements from everyone," Mann said. After a glance, most of the others pushed the sheets away or tucked them into their notepads, but a couple of the PDQ executives joined Keith in filling out the form. Keith read through the paragraphs above the lines asking for his name, address and date of birth. The language of the document alarmed him with its threats of penalties, fines, legal fees and so on if he broke any of the clauses therein contained. He looked up. Paul caught his panicky gaze and nodded slightly, understanding his concerns without having to ask.

"Standard boilerplate," Paul said, very casually. "I see the same thing every day." Gratefully, Keith scrawled his name and pushed the paper toward Ms. Schick.

Mann reached over to take the paper off the table, leaving the wide expanse of shining black marble open. Once the papers were collected and put away, Dorothy stood up and faced the clients with the same anxious expression she might have if she was about to dive off the high board into an unfamiliar pool. More than just her job was at stake. A big campaign for a big client could mean millions of dollars for PDQ. Failure might mean half the staff in the room could be looking for work within days. Keith found he was holding his breath, and let it out silently, not wanting to be the one to attract attention. Dorothy smiled at the visitors.

"We want to thank Gadfly for giving us this opportunity to offer our services. We understand that your company's primary focus is personal technology. That's an exciting field. We have the experience you're looking for to promote your product, and we have the numbers to prove it. We know that if you hire us we will give you the best possible exposure, and bring in the maximum number of customers in the demographics. PDQ can present advertisements in any medium, and we welcome customer involvement. You tell us what you want, and we'll do it."

Mann and the others nodded. Keith knew from Dorothy's hasty briefing that PDQ was only one of a dozen or more agencies that were being given an audience, and almost certainly not the first to present that day. The primary approach had been made to Gadfly by the upper management of PDQ. The real test that determined whether they got the account would come later.

"So…" Allen said, when the silence went on too long, "what *is* the product?"

"One thing at a time," Bill Mann said, his resonant voice slow and unhurried. "You know the old saying about how you only get one chance to make a first impression. We want your first impression of our baby."

Mann gestured with one large hand to Lehmann, who lifted a box to the tabletop. "In there is the prototype of the GF Mark One. It doesn't have a name yet. Name it. Give us one we really like, *the* one, and the account's yours. Believe me, we've heard from a dozen agencies already. You can't believe how many wrong ideas we've heard already."

Peggy smirked, tossing her long hair. "Yes, we can."

"Well, Gadfly was founded by people who like to work by the seat of their pants. So, we want to know if you're like us. That's why your creative people are here. We don't want a big-time production until we're sure we can work with you. I promise you, we've thought of as many dumb names on our own as anybody can. We don't like one of them. We want to see how you think."

The PDQ staff shifted uneasily. Keith, who was already quivering with nerves, had to sit on his hands to keep from springing up.

"Usually," Dorothy said carefully, "you give us the details of what you want, and we bring it to you later, for your approval."

"Nope. Not this time. We want more. No, we want *now*. That's how we work. It's a test. We make up our minds very quickly. Inspiration's usually the best indicator of how people think. I speak for the rest of the guys—guys being a unisex term in our office," he said, reaching out to touch the table before Dorothy and Peggy, "so what I like here today goes. Got it?"

"Whatever you say," Dorothy said, looking at her fellow employees. The customer was always right.

The PDQ staff nodded warily. Keith didn't want to say out loud that brainstorming and quick inspiration were pretty much how he had been taught to work on ad campaigns, but the staff wasn't used to doing it in front of the client. Though they were all seasoned professionals in their field, such a challenge put them under a kind of pressure they weren't accustomed to handling. They accepted Gadfly's terms, then waited as the cardboard box was passed from Theo Lehmann to Jennifer Schick.

Keith leaned forward in anticipation. He saw some of the other, more experienced execs sitting back, seemingly cool and disinterested, but it was a pose. Were they frightened of making a bad impression, or did they really not care any more after so many years in the business? Keith hoped he'd never become that jaded.

No such ennui plagued the people from Gadfly. They were up about their product, almost bouncing in their seats with excitement. They could hardly wait as Ms. Schick opened the box.

"All right, ladies and gentlemen," Bill Mann intoned proudly, "Gadfly presents the GF Mark One, the next great step in personal electronic technology. This is the One-Dee version. We'll probably be in in One-Eff by the time we go to market, but it will look just like this. Jen?"

'This' was a small blue-gray box, about six inches long by two and a half wide by an inch high. Jen Schick turned it in her hands. One flat side of the unit was mostly made up of screen. The other had a small keypad, earpiece and mouthpiece. "As you can see, it's a personal digital assistant. And a cell telephone. But it has dozens of other uses. You see the modular design. It's amazingly versatile. It can do just about anything you want it to."

Everyone watched her hands intently as she flipped the small device in her hands. Keith studied it with fascination. It wasn't really a box, but a stack of very thin panels held together by tiny hinges. The other copywriters were murmuring to one another and making notes. Dorothy drew furiously on her sketchpad.

Ms. Schick turned on the unit. The screen came to life on a crisp, colorful graphic rotating over a black background. Keith was impressed by the sharpness and resolution. So were the others. The technician grinned at their coos and hums of admiration.

"High-res monitor," Lehmann said. "We got tired of screens where you couldn't see the small details."

"User interface is multiply configured," Ms. Schick continued. "With the stylus," which popped out of the side of the unit, "you can use it as a normal palmtop. The screen is touch-sensitive, so you can pull down the menus, or doodle on it, write in the character box or touch the character keyboard that pops up. But what sets this little guy apart from the others—among many other innovations—is the keyboard." Jen Schick held onto the screen and flipped the rear portion down and away from the rest of it, pressed a minute catch, and opened out two of the panels, which turned into four, snapped out flat. "This one is big enough for even a touch-typist with big hands to use. We recessed the keys slightly so you get a slight 'reward' action when you press each solenoid. There are several PDA units out there with keyboard peripherals, but they aren't integral to the unit. Closed up, some of them are bigger than their PDAs."

Theo Lehmann spread out his hands side by side. "You can use your thumbs across the breadth of the keyboard, but you don't have to. The majority of the workforce does not need to be retrained for this platform."

An approving hum rose from the PDQ executives. Even Dorothy was nodding to herself. Keith couldn't take his eyes off it. He thought it was wonderful.

"Memory?" asked Rollin Chisholm, his voice husky.

"Forty gigs running on a 128 Mhz FlagChip IC, in the original configuration," said the engineer. "The next generation will have more. It runs real Windows or Linux or any other system you want to install—with its own mini CD-ROM, you don't need a docking station. It's an extraordinary device. It deserves extraordinary treatment."

"We agree," Dorothy said. "It's amazing."

Keith watched the engineer fold and refold into different configurations. Ms. Schick flipped the keyboard shut but left the unit folded out into two panels so the telephone keypad was beneath the screen. She set it down on the desk, where it stood by itself.

"This little ring here," Jen Schick went on, twisting a stubby cylinder that was mounted along one end of a long edge on the upright portion, "is a camera eye. The GF Mark One will take over 600 pictures on a memory stick or ten times that on a writable mini-CD. It can record an hour of video or more, depending on how much resolution you want. The drive is back here. You can see that we've reduced the drive size so that it doesn't add bulk. The drive is Theo's baby. We're ready to license out the patent to seven other companies, but we want to get our own unit to market first." Lehmann tilted his head with a modest expression.

"Incredible," murmured Allen. "The disk drive is thinner than a checkbook."

"The camera lens will swivel in any direction. You can use it as a digital video camera and record on a disk or stick, or send streaming video over either your wireless phone line or the Internet. Of course it's fully Internet compatible. One of the things we thought the camera feature would be good for is teleconferencing. You just point the lens back at yourself while looking at the person you're talking to on the screen. Of course there's a wireless headset so you can set the unit down or have it on your lap. It makes the Mark One's uses almost infinitely expandable. It'll share data through the usual modem configuration, but there's an infrared eye right here," she pointed to a minute square of dark plastic at the rear of the screen section. "You can make your own videos and send them out on the web in no time. It could revolutionize newsgathering. It's got clipart and moving clips you can use to customize your video. The character generator works off the word processing system. But look at this." With the stylus she scribbled out a command, and the image on the little square screen changed to show a pair of spaceships zooming through the black void shooting red laser bolts at one another. "It updates high-res video instantly."

"That's beautiful," Keith said. "Is it real?"

"You mean, is it a working prototype? It is. Here. Look. I'm running computer adventure game. The processor is very fast, but it consumes very little energy."

Several of them leaned forward. Doug had his hands stretched out as though he'd like to get them on the little unit, but they let the marketing director continue to demonstrate the device.

"You can watch movies on it—the power-saver feature can run the hard drive flat out for more than twenty hours, and it can record from over-the-air signals. You can download books from the net. It'll hold a library's worth, including illustrations. It can store MP3 files, or play music recorded on mini-CD. It's practically a whole personal entertainment system. Everything but the dance floor," Jen Schick added.

"Do you want us to use that?" Janine Martinez asked, pausing from making notes. She put the end of her pen in her mouth, raised her eyebrows quizzically. The crew from Gadfly looked at each other, exchanging silent questions.

"Maybe," Mann said, cheerfully. "Give us a name first, and we'll go for the whole download."

They seemed outwardly to be happy-go-lucky, casual people, but underneath they were watching and wary, steel-lined, not going to take anything they didn't like. They hadn't gotten to be a multi-million-dollar venture without being determined.

"So," Mann asked, "what do you think?"

"I am in love," said Doug Constance. "It's so small, but it's got everything. It's amazing."

"Other handhelds have these features," Schick admitted, "but no one unit has them all incorporated into one. We do."

Keith just stared raptly, watching them turn the little screen around to face the keyboard, flip up so the digital camera eye is pointing at one of them, the little screen out to the side to use as a viewfinder, back again to use as a palm-top surface.

"What about wireless Internet?"

"At present the Internet function is disabled, but it's ready to go as a telephone and wireless browser," Mann said. "I'm not letting it connect because I just don't want anyone lurking on the web to scope out the configurations prematurely. This is a big deal for us."

"Of course," Dorothy said. "We're all enormously impressed."

"Touch the Internet icon, then write in any URL," Lehmann said, pointing over Keith's shoulder, as he took the device around the table, demonstrating it for each PDQ staffer in turn. "You'll be able to web surf in full color with practically no lags. The important things about it are the long battery life and the thinness of the components. They'll bend but not break."

Fold, flip, turn. Keith saw his own eyes stare back at him from the little screen. They were wide with excitement. This was the most exciting techno-toy he had ever seen. He had to have one for his own.

"Factotum?" suggested Jason Allen.

"Oh, come on," Doug Constance said. "Half the people out there will have no idea what that means."

"Packhorse? Mule? Suitcase?" suggested Rollin Chisholm. "I'm throwing out ideas here—Office Entertainment System?"

"Nope," said Mann, tersely.

"Smartpack?" Janine Martinez offered.

"No way."

"Palm Pro?"

"Too close to the competitors," Paul Meier said. "Fingertip?"

"Uh...nah."

"Encyclo-PDA?"

"Y'know, every single agency in Chicago has come up with that one."

"Really?" said Peggy Gilmore, narrowing her eyes. "I thought that one was pretty clever."

"We really ought to try New York, too," Lehmann said to Mann. Dorothy stiffened. Paul leaned over and put a hand over hers.

Lehmann noticed the gesture and seemed genuinely abashed. "Sorry. We think out loud too much. Corporate culture." He pointed a finger at his head pistol style, and pulled the imaginary trigger. "You know, no people skills."

"This thing doesn't need a campaign behind it," Paul said, admiringly. "The thing writes its own ad copy. Just write down everything it can do."

"Use the list as wallpaper, said Doug, excitedly. "Transparent, over a photo, maybe the user's hand and a train window in the background. It'd make a good and sticky ad—one that keeps your eyes on it for a long time."

"Yes," Dorothy said, sketching the unit in Lehmann's hands and filling in scribbles around it to indicate words. "Good."

"HE for Home Entertainment?" suggested Chisholm. "HE's the one you want to take everywhere with you? Turn HE on, and HE'll turn you on?

"No," Paul said. "Male customers will think it sounds like they're taking a guy on a date."

"Okay, SHE? Single Home Entertainment? Women are less sensitive about hanging with other women."

"PE?" added Parks. "Personal Entertainment?"

"No," Mann said. "PE sounds like gym class. It's still going to be the Gadfly Mark One no matter what handle you hang on it."

The Gadfly guys seemed nonplussed by the babble going on around them. They couldn't be impressed, having heard initial pitches from a dozen companies. They listened as the staff threw out idea after idea, saying 'no,' or simply shaking their heads.

"Everyone will want one of these," Constance said. "Can you think of one single person in the world who won't want one? This will galvanize the industry. Gadfly could sell a million of these in the first week."

"But it needs the right approach," Paul Meier said.

"The right name," said Mann.

Keith sat watching Ms. Schick manipulate the Gadfly unit while the others argued over his head. He wasn't the only copywriter that Dorothy had brought in, but she trusted him. She wanted him to succeed for her. He was grateful for the chance. He didn't want to let her down.

He couldn't take his eyes off the device. The flat hinges allowed the PDA to be turned inside out and upside down, revealing more and more uses. An infinity of utility. He didn't even notice Dorothy's desperate eye, so intent was he on the device. It bent every which way, like someone folding a piece of paper.

"Origami," he said, dreamily.

"How about the Pocket Secretary?" Chisholm proposed.

"Too much like an infomercial," said Lehmann.

"The Office Box?" Constance offered.

"What?" Mann asked. "What did you say?

The blond executive started. "The Office Box? I know it needs work."

"No, him, the bug-eyed one," he said, pointing at Keith. "What did you say, son?"

Keith grinned, embarrassed. "I said 'origami.' The Japanese art form. That's what it reminds me of. They can take a piece of paper and fold it into anything you want. It just made me think of it, the way you can twist that around into so many different shapes. It can be about anything you want it to. Can't it?"

The executives smiled slowly at one another.

"Dude," said the president of Gadfly Technology, "you're the man."

Chapter 7

"...And they said right there and then that PDQ had the account," Keith said. He sat perched on the arm of an old couch at one side of the barn workshop next to Holl's worktable. He just couldn't stop talking. The whole world had changed so much in a single day. "Mr. Mann kept repeating it over and over: 'Origami.' It just came out, but he really liked it. Ms. Schick called their office and cancelled all the other appointments. They want me to start full time on the project, effective yesterday. We're all supposed to start thinking of how to make the campaign work. Dorothy was really happy."

"And you, too, I should imagine," Holl said, continuing to plane a board glass smooth. He ran his finger along the surface, and attacked an invisible rough patch with a cloth coated with jeweler's rouge. A splinter of the wood grain lifted and snagged the cloth. "Pah." With the most delicate touch, he sent a tendril of power into the wood, causing the grain to adhere together more strongly. He gently eased the splinter back into place. The board was a mite too well-seasoned for fine carving. Tiron had warned him that the storage area in the barn was too dry, but Holl had disagreed. He'd checked it himself not a week before. It had been all right then. At least, he thought it had been. If this piece was a representative sample the room *was* too dry. From then forward he'd better check more closely. The Folk couldn't afford to lose all their quality hardwoods, not with winter order season nearly upon them. "It helps to speed along your dreams, doesn't it?"

"It sure does," Keith said, slinging himself backwards into the depth of the couch. All around them, the Little Folk were working on wooden boxes, lanterns, jewelry and ornamental pieces, raising their heads to listen occasionally to Keith. "You're going to be amazed—PDQ is offering me $200 a *day* as a freelancer."

"Very generous."

"Oh, yeah," Keith said happily, watching Holl's hands. "You can't believe how amazing this Mark One is. It has every single thing you can think of. It's set up for interactive games on the wireless web. It could be used as a smart card. Pay your bills. Buy movie tickets. Invest in stocks. All from a handheld computer that I could put in my pocket. It's got a mini-DVD. That's going to be the hard sell. Since people are already investing in full-sized DVDs they probably wouldn't want to buy all their movies in the miniature format, but for the road warrior, you know, the traveling executive..."

"Ugh!" Dola exclaimed, throwing up her hands. She sprang up from the couch. "I have heard all this nonstop all the way from Chicago. At least spare the repetition until I have gone again."

"Sorry, sweetheart," Keith said, tweaking a lock of her hair. "I know I bent your ear about it, but I'm in gadget-lust. I want one of these things, Holl. I don't care what it costs." He dropped into a reverie, seeing one of the shapely units in his own hands. "It's a full personal computer that receives television, radio and shortwave signals along with digital/analog telephone. And a pager. You can websurf for hours and listen to, say, the BBC World Service at the same time. It's designed so well that the transmission signals don't interfere with one another. The TV doesn't get lines across it from the shortwave radio band. It can handle wireless fax. It's got DVD, infrared, serial and parallel connectors and a USB port. It's set up for GPS, walkie-talkie, still *and* motion picture camera, voice recorder, video games with stub or touchpad joystick; it's got e-book capability, and it can carry up to 20 amenity cards—like grocery store and department store passes—in a password-accessible database. Practically every electronic gadget there is, in miniature. They're working on scanning capability, too. I think," Keith said, dreamily, "I'll call her Doris."

Dola looked at Keith, met Holl's eyes and shook her head.

"Haven't you already got pride of ownership already?" Holl asked. "You've given it a name."

"Origami is the brand name," Keith corrected him. "If I owned something this wonderful, it would deserve a personal name. Even the power source is new. It can last practically forever between charges. I wonder if I can make up a slogan to relate to that?"

"And if this is such a marvel that a man can't resist owning one the moment he sees it, why doesn't everyone know about it?"

"Well, because it's not on the market yet. The campaign won't get under way for a couple of months. Nobody knows about it. That's why we had to sign nondisclosure…oh." Keith felt his cheeks burn. "I suppose I shouldn't even be telling you." For the first time he seemed aware that he was surrounded by dozens of people, all listening intently with hearing far better than his. Tay, nearby, tipped him a sly wink. "You won't tell anyone, will you? I'll get into incredible trouble. You ought to read the form they made me sign."

Holl chuckled. "You can rely upon our discretion. But this must chafe at your open-hearted soul, not being able to talk. You can hardly restrain yourself now."

"Yeah," Keith said. "I have to learn to keep my mouth shut. I must have babbled at Dola for more than three hours solid. Sorry, honey."

"Well, it was better than the terrible music on the radio," Dola said, graciously.

"Dola will have to go back in a couple of weeks or a month to film commercials," Keith told Holl and Tay. "They only needed her for a day this time to photograph her with the new season's shoes for the Fairy Footwear catalog. They'll do anything to keep her. She's a natural in front of the camera." Dola preened.

"I am glad you're enjoying your job, daughter," Tay said. "I don't see it lasting forever."

"Nor do I," Dola said, with a maturity beyond her years. "Big Folk have no attention span at all. Even while I speak to them they are thinking of a dozen other things. They will find another face to sell their product. In the meantime I like seeing the city."

"It gives you a good connection to the outside world," Holl said. "I prefer gentle interaction to the fearful avoidance we've become accustomed to practicing."

"Take care, uncle," Tay said, with a wry smile. "You preach an ultra-Progressive lifestyle, and it will enrage the elders."

Holl shook his head. "No matter what I say it will enrage them. They do not like Dola going among the Big Ones. They're afraid one day she will not come back." Keith felt ice in his belly as Holl said that. It had happened before, and turned the whole village upside down.

"Well, I'll take Dola up and back whenever I'm around," Keith said. "I'll make sure she's all right."

"We appreciate that. Even the Conservatives acknowledge that you can be trusted—a main objection is with Dola allowing herself to be photographed in the first place."

"You don't know about advertisers," Keith said, cheerfully. "They have no idea that she's the real thing. They assume she's a kid who likes to play dress-up. Everything in their world is artificial."

"Are you certain you can exist within that culture?" Holl asked. "You are the one who insists that things be real."

"I'll be fine," Keith assured him. "I can always find a job in a different field if it goes sour, but for now I like advertising. It's fun."

"And what about school? The Master will expect you to attend classes and produce your homework on schedule no matter where you are—and no more last-minute transmissions, either. But what about your regular program?"

"I already called my advisor. I've got an appointment in the morning to talk about changing my program to Saturdays from full time," Keith said. He took a sheaf of much-folded papers out of his pocket and flipped through them until he found what he wanted. "You see? This'd be much neater if I could keep all my lists on a PDA," he said. "I could have it search my lists for keywords."

Dola groaned and threw up her hands.

"...Here it is," Keith said, finding the right note. "Ten thirty. I've checked the schedule, and I've got it all planned out. It may be a struggle to fit me into the classes, but they should understand about job offers that can't wait. It might take me five years to earn my degree instead of two, but I can't let an opportunity like this get away. It's the fast escalator to a job with PDQ. Dorothy thinks my chances are great even if the client changes its mind. It'll mean a lot of commuting, and a lot of work, but it'll be worth it. I think it will be fun."

Dola, becoming bored with adult talk, stood up from the couch.

"Thank you, Keith Doyle, for taking care of me and driving me up and back and taking me to the shopping center." She gave him a sly smile, a conspiracy between friends. She pitched her voice louder. "I am sure everyone will like their presents." At the word 'presents,' heads began to perk up all over the workroom. She dragged her duffel bag from where she had dropped it near the door to the center of the room. Her father watched over her shoulder as she zipped it open.

"What have you done, daughter?" Tay asked, indulgently, as the girl ostentatiously removed package after package from the suitcase. "Bought out the whole of the fabric store?"

"Fabrics?" asked Candlepat, abandoning the music box she was assembling. Even dour Catra left the bookkeeping on her desk to gather around the little girl, who handed out bundles right and left. The recipients cooed and exclaimed over the parcels, holding up the lengths of colorful cloth against themselves, bursting out with ideas about clothing and fashions. In the middle of the rainbow, Dola sat happily dealing out presents.

"Boy," Keith said. "I could learn a lot about advertising from her. She's a natural. Look at her grab their attention with one word."

"Like advertisers, she plays upon their self-interest. She brought them presents."

"What a memory she has, too," Keith said. "She dragged me all over the place picking things out. She went out of there with a pack on her back with something for everyone, just like Santa Claus."

"Ah, well, they're her wages," Holl said. "She knows some of it must go for the support of us all, but the rest is hers to enjoy as she wishes. And she enjoys sharing. She hasn't a single selfish cell within her."

"I have notions and buttons. I did not forget the elastic this time, Aunt Maura," Dola said, with authority, handing over a flat package. "It is white. I hope that is what you wanted."

"Perfect, my darling," Maura said, hefting Asrai to her other hip. Quick as lightning, the two-year-old reached past her mother's hand for the paper-wrapped packet and unwrapped it. She looked at the stringy tape and tried to pull it off the card. It snapped back into shape. Asrai regarded it with a puzzled expression so funny Keith laughed. "Thank you so much. Is that the flannel for Asrai's sleepers?"

"Yes," Dola said. "Do you like it?"

"I think so. I can't quite see it." Maura twisted, trying to maneuver a very active baby on her hip and unwrap a package at the same time. Marcy came to the rescue.

"I'll take her, Maura," the darkhaired girl said, kneeling down. The baby leaped into her arms, cooing. She loved Marcy. All the children did. Asrai snuggled close to the much bigger human, chattering out a running commentary on the present-giving.

"Not long before Asrai's running everywhere," Holl said, watching with parental pride. "And she talks like a magpie, though I can't understand nineteen out of every twenty words."

"Maybe she's speaking magpie," Keith said. Marcy's great with her. Holl saw her cradle the little one with an expression of hungry yearning.

"Aye, it wouldn't surprise me about my little sprite... I wonder how long she and Enoch will wait to have their own babes." The Big student beside him nodded, knowing Holl wasn't talking about Asrai.

Holl was sorry for Enoch, even as he rejoiced that his enigmatic brother-in-law had found the lifemate of his heart. The

Big Ones did not live as long as his kind. Still, as Shakespeare put it so well, t'was better to have loved and lost.... Marcy was a good addition to the village, whatever protests her family and the Conservatives might put forward. She fit in well with the personalities, some of whom were strident and difficult enough that even their relatives found them trying. She was biddable but not easily pushed when she chose to stand her ground, took instruction, had a scholarly mind and a sense of humor, though very gentle, and liked a good discussion. It was sad that her family wasn't taking her romance seriously. He couldn't have borne that himself, though that was just the opposite of his own life, where everything he did was taken too seriously indeed. But he'd always been taken a mite too seriously, perhaps. A more pompous soul would have taken advantage of that. Holl grinned. He'd been pompous enough with Keith Doyle, but the boy did invite it, acting as foolishly as a colt.

"I don't think it'll be too long," Keith said, watching Marcy dandle the child, who was so small in proportion to her. "But I know her: not until they get married. I haven't had a chance to talk to her folks yet, but I'll have plenty of opportunities now that I'll be up there most of the week. I'll be in at PDQ full time, for now. I've arranged to move into the Crash Site with Pat and Dunn. Poor Pat thought he'd gotten rid of me, but at least I can take on part of the rent and lift the burden off Dunn and his venture capital."

"That's a very heavy schedule," Maura said sympathetically. She came over to show Holl the fabric for baby clothes. "Are you sure you can do it?"

"Oh, yeah," Keith said, blithely. "I've got it all worked out. Dunn's working on this voice-recognition software that ignores exterior noise. I'm testing it for him in my car—you know what kind of a rumble my engine makes. So far it's terrific. I can do my homework while I drive. If I install it in your computer or Diane's I can print out at either end of my trip. It's perfect. No down time. Chicago on weekdays, college on weekends. See, everything's under control."

"And where will you live on these weekends?" Maura asked. "You are giving up your rooms here to pay for your share of the apartment."

Holl had to laugh at the stricken look on Keith's face. "You can stay here, widdy. We'll find a bed for those long shanks of yours."

"Thanks," Keith said, wiping imaginary sweat off his face. "I thought for a moment I was going to have to ask Diane for the use of her couch. She's not going to be happy with the situation anyhow."

"I applaud you, Keith Doyle, but the lovely Diane is not going to like the change."

Keith smacked himself in the forehead. "I forgot to call her." He took the blue-green cell telephone out of his pocket.

"No, use our phone," Holl insisted. "A local call will surely be less costly than your per-minute charge. The Internet banner ads are full of details about them. It is a costly indulgence that in this case is unnecessary."

"Thanks," Keith said, hoisting himself to his feet. He brushed an accumulation of sawdust off his front and backside. "You have got to see Doris, Holl. It's amazing."

"I'll take your word for it," Holl said. "In the meantime, keep it to yourself."

But Keith found that difficult to do. Nearly everyone in the workroom had been eavesdropping, their sensitive hearing picking up every word over the sound of power tools, and it instantly became the subject of intense gossip. When Keith went into the house to use the telephone, they were waiting for him. At the head of a contingent of Conservative elves, Keva marched up to confront Keith, hands firmly clamped to her hips.

"What's this nonsense you've been filling my granddaughter's ears with?" she shrilled. "All this machinery, this technology—it's unnecessary!"

"But it's fun, Keva," Keith said. "Sure you can live without it, but it's like anything else: it's meant to make life easier."

"I don't need my life made easier!"

"Well, you know Big Folks," Keith said, sitting down on the floor so he was at eye-level to her. "We're lazy. We like labor-saving devices. It all started with carpet-sweepers, you know. They were mechanical, not electronic. And typewriters with moveable type..."

Keva interrupted him with an impatient wave. "This thing you want, this Doris, doesn't sweep floors. What's it really for?"

"Well," Keith said, "it helps organize the little things in your life. If you want to make lists or take notes, you can do that. If you want to take pictures, it takes pictures. It can carry games you can play anywhere. Or video. Or if you have time when you're traveling it can teach you how to play the piano. The piano emulation software is going to be included as an extra." As the expressions around him grew more uncomprehending, Keith took off on a full flight of enthusiasm. "This device is capable of full streaming video, audio, interactive gaming, shared gaming through infrared or radio-wave connection, or fully online, either modem or wireless web. It has a huge memory, a fast processor, and shielded interfaces. You can even get an earpiece so you can listen to music or talk on the phone while the unit is open on your lap. Uh..."

He realized he had made a mistake. The more technical his babble became, the more sour the faces of Keva and those other Conservatives in the kitchen grew. In fact, he had made another mistake in sitting down. Now he was crowded by angry Little Folk, all complaining at the top of their voices. He had no room to get up without stepping on someone's feet.

"Must ye amuse yourself to death?" demanded Curran, white-haired clan chief of Holl's family, going chin to chin with Keith. "That's the trouble with ye Big Folk. Ye won't enjoy real life, when it's right underneath yer nose."

"Do ye need so many toys?" Shelogh asked. She was Catra's and Candlepat's mother. "A camera, if ye have no talent to draw yourself, a book and a pad of paper give you all the same pleasure, with no batteries. "

"But everything's all in the same toy," Keith pointed out. "With it you don't need the rest, including pen and paper— even books. It'll hold several in memory. Saves lots of weight.

You'd like that." He appealed to the Master, who appeared behind the other Folk. "You can go to a lot of sites and download all kinds of books. Lots of them are free."

"Even so, this device is unlikely to haf afailable books for download ve vould find uf interest."

"True," Keith admitted. "So Newton's memoirs are unlikely to be digitized. For now. But if you had a PDA, your *notes* would be in one place."

"Until you ran out of batteries," Tiron pointed out dryly.

"I've got a secret weapon," Keith said, with a sly tap at the side of his nose. "Enoch taught me how to recharge them. But look, you're already surrounded by technology. It's here. You use it every day."

"Too much surrounded!" exclaimed Aylmer. "Telephones! Automobiles! Helicopters!"

"Central heating," the Master pointed out, in a calm voice. "Vashing machines. Power tools. Vhy should ve not make use of that vhich is already here and available? That vhich ve do not vant is easily rejected. Ve should take advahntage of reliable power that doesn't exhaust the user to maintain."

"We're forgetting our past," Keva argued. "The Old Ones would ne'er fall into such ease."

"Och, that's not so," Tiron said, with a dismissive wave, "and it would be as well to know that the Old Ones are interested in the new ways as well as the traditional ones. The Niall would like this Pee-Dee-Ay as much as Keith Doyle, so he would. Why, they had their computer months before we did."

"Hmmph!" Keva snorted. "And now just because we all have the evil boxes doesn't mean it's was a good thing for us to do."

Tiron looked as though he wanted to laugh, but kept it in, for which Holl was grateful.

"And do you not like hearing the voices of those you thought were lost to you forever? I know my kin do. They'd not have let me go unless they could be certain of my well-being. This is so much less expensive than long distance telephone calls." He looked around at the crowd of Conservatives, matching them sneer for sneer. "Well?"

"It's all Keith Doyle's fault anyhow," Curran began, trying to stir up his fellows again. He might have succeeded if Holl had not marched in at that moment and cut Keith out of the crowd.

"Shoo. He needs the telephone. You don't want your voices heard, do you?"

Most of the Conservatives fled in alarm. Tiron sauntered out, slapping Holl and Keith on the backs as he went. *Cock of the walk*, Holl thought, *but I'm grateful for his support.*

The Elf Master was the last to leave, his blue eyes watchful behind his gold glasses, and his mouth pursed in amusement.

At last Keith was able to get to his feet.

"Boy, now I know how you feel in the middle of a crowd of Big Folks," he said, brushing off the seat of his pants. "It's a real disadvantage."

"I apologize for that," Holl said, making sure the last of them was gone. "They're all looking for a scapegoat to shout at, and you fed one of their pet complaints to bursting."

"Still bent about the server under the table?" Keith asked.

"Oh, yes," Holl sighed. "Though they consider it a concession to avoiding further interference in our business. Any mention of it sets them off."

"Sounds like the symptom of something else," Keith said wisely. "Any problems I ought to know about?"

"Big Folk sniffing around," Holl said shortly. "They almost spotted some of us early today, and not the young-looking ones who are easy to explain away. It was sheer carelessness. And we discovered that there were holes in the barrier spell that protects the edge of our property. If it is not there our presence all but cries out that we are here. We must guard ourselves a little more closely. It's a burden, but one we're used to carrying."

"I wish I could swap problems with you," Keith said, lifting the telephone receiver.

"Oh, no, you don't, my friend," Holl said, under his breath. "No, you don't."

Chapter 8

"I'm sorry," Keith said. He'd said it again and again over the last hour. He had a deep well of apologies to draw from. It looked as though he was going to need the whole aquifer. Diane had sat through about half the recitation of his revised plans, then burst into furious tears, scolding him for thoughtlessness, unreliability and not thinking of anyone but himself. Keith weathered the storm, trying to figure out how to make the situation better. He couldn't. It was his choice and his fault. He pleaded for her to understand.

"It's a great opportunity for me," he said, trying to catch her eye as she stormed past him, pacing from wall to wall in the small apartment. "I could wait another year, maybe two, for a break like this, and then there might not be any room for me. I just jumped for it when it happened. I'm sorry. I should have called to run it by you."

"I was looking forward to spending a lot of time with you this year," Diane said, her eyes still red. "It was nice being able to *count* on having you here for your master's program during my senior year. I missed you a lot during your semester up in Chicago. This is our last year together before… before it all gets real."

"I know. I've missed you, too." Keith felt helpless in the face of her unhappiness. He caught for her hand. "Look, I helped Dorothy get the account. That's all I was supposed to do for her. She and the rest of her team can take it from there. I am the weakest part of the chain. My inexperience could even sink them. They don't need me to keep it going. If you don't want me to go to Chicago, I'll turn them down. Dorothy will find someone else who knows what he's doing."

Diane turned away and looked out the small window. She was silent a long while. Keith wished he *had* thought to call her before accepting the position in the first place. It had seemed so obvious at the time, but now he wasn't so sure. He couldn't be in two places at once, and she *had* been counting on him. They didn't get much time together when he was down here full time, what with their school and work schedules. He hoped he hadn't destroyed the trust the two of them had been building for three years. He loved her so very much.

"No," she said at last, turning around. "You're right. I can't be so selfish. It's a good opportunity. This is what you like doing. I hope it works out for you. I want you to have what you want. It's for both of us, right?"

"Of course," Keith said, relieved. "It won't be so bad. I'll still be down here every weekend. It's a five-day-a-week job. Unless they're cranking on something, everyone goes home about 4:30."

Diane's blue-green eyes crinkled, seeing the funny side even though she was still sore. "Including junior copywriters? Including hyperactive ones who see a future for themselves at the company?"

Keith grinned. "Including those. By five every Friday I'll be on my way down here to throw myself at your feet." He dropped to his knees before her and threw his arms open wide.

"Oh, get up," Diane said, in mock exasperation. "I just wasn't ready to deal with you being gone again."

Keith sprang to his feet and put his arms around her. He was glad when she nestled close and put her head on his shoulder. He stroked the silk of her hair, thankful to be forgiven. "Hey, it might not last. It depends on how long the project lasts, and what they want me to do. I could be out the door again tomorrow. Then I'll be back here full time."

"No, I don't want that," Diane said, firmly, lifting her head to meet his eyes. "It'll be okay. I'm all right. But you'd better call me every day. I just get lonely."

"You'll never know I'm gone," Keith promised her. "The phone company will declare a dividend based on my bills. It could bankrupt the state. Whole markets might collapse!"

Diane laughed and shook her head. "It's hard to stay mad at you, you idiot."

"My one saving grace," Keith said. "Uh, I know it's a lot to ask, but could you, well, keep an eye on the farm for me? I hate to leave everyone in the lurch, but maybe you can look after each other."

Diane shook her head. "You've got to stop trying to be all things to all people," she said, wistfully. "Once in a while it would be nice if you were just all things to one person."

"I know," Keith said, ruefully. "I'm not very good at delegating."

Diane grabbed him by the lapels and looked deeply into his eyes.

"Learn," she said.

"So you've invited the Big One to live here each and every weekend?" Curran demanded, standing up. "How could you be so foolish, with the troubles we're havin'? Bill collectors? Hikers invading aur land? And what about that man fro' the Preservation Council? He's a persistent one!"

Holl stood at the center of a village conclave. Upon hearing the news his clan chief had called for a full meeting with all attending. The Conservatives, mostly older Folk, were massed on one side of the large living room. The Progressives filled the other. Holl stood in the middle, cramped and hot between Catra, the Archivist, taking notes, and the Master, seeming at ease in his deep chair. He would have been more comfortable if they had agreed to hold the meeting outside, as was their new-made summer custom, but the elders insisted they didn't want even the possibility of being overheard. Early in the summer the Folk had had plans to build on an extension to the house to use as a regular meeting hall. No one had brought it up recently.

"I don't regret the impulse at all," Holl said, and the Progressives sitting behind him murmured their agreement. Only the Elf Master seemed neutral on the issue. "It's a small favor. We have plenty of room in the workshop. It's not used at night, and it's warm and insulated. Why shouldn't he have the use of a bed? He'll be spending little time here except to sleep. Between travel, classes and his ladylove, he's got a full schedule. It would have drawn his attention if I had not made the offer."

"But he must be here at least some of the time awake," Aylmer pointed out, "since he is continuing his studies under our Master's tutelage. We should haf been asked. It is a community, after all."

"And I vill claim his attention," the Master assured him. "But there is a point that must be considered. Ve cannot belief that Keith Doyle vill be blindfolded and deaf during his stay. He vill know that something troubles us."

"It's a curse," Shelogh announced, her voice thin with stress. "There is a curse upon this place, and we should stay no longer. We discovered one homestead. Why not find another?"

"It is not so easy as that," Tay said. "We were lucky, and we had the services of Keith Doyle to help us search."

"It is not a curse," Enoch said. "What do you call a curse that only works its evil when there's a break in the charm around the house?"

"What do you think causes the holes to appear?" Dierdre, Shelogh's clan leader, asked.

"Logic would suggest," said Catra, "that something's either coming in or going out. But which?"

"Logic vould suggest," the Elf Master said, gently, "that perhaps something came in, then vent out, and so on."

"You are amazingly cool about this," Catra said, giving him an odd look.

The village headman turned his gaze fully upon her. "But consider: if it is a curse it vould be vorking all uf the time. If it is a being that meant us serious harm, ve vould know that, too."

"We don't know what it wants," Shelogh said, throwing up her hands.

"We don't know if it's an *it!*" Candlepat said. "It could be a curse upon the land where this house was built. It's more than possible that a Big Person living here would have no conception of it; they're so insensitive. They might only have had the feeling something was wrong."

"Vhy else vould the owner haf sold so cheap?" Aylmer added.

Everyone stopped talking for a moment to consider that idea. Holl waited warily for someone to break the silence. It didn't take long. They all burst out talking at once.

"We should never have come to live where Big Folk have been. It's wrong!"

"A curse could be working all the time. We may not notice," Marm said.

"No, I disagree. It's awfully directed for something that's a general curse upon the house," said Tiron. Tay nodded.

"Maybe we should have been looking at one person."

"Aren't we going to a lot of trouble to imagine what we cannot touch, see or sense?" Maura asked.

"It reqvires more infestigation," said Bracey.

"Has no one noticed that it all seems to happen whenever someone goes down into the cellar?" Tay asked, trying to get everyone's attention. "One person in particular?"

"And which one person are you pointin' a finger at?" Curran demanded. "We all go down the cellar."

"Well, we've all gotten sick from Marm's wine," Tay began. "That vintage he served at the graduation party..." The round-faced male sprang at him and stuck his chin at the white-haired youngster.

"You take that back, you stick-insect! You chose the keg. It could be you that took some not ready to drink and made us all ill."

"D'you think I can't read the signs?" Tay insisted, standing his ground, though his face was as white as his beard. "—No, I can read ones that are well-drawn...Perhaps you've ceased to care if yours are legible."

"You pup! I am the most careful person who lives here! Not like you, pushing your nose in where it doesn't belong!"

Tay cocked back his fist and drove it into Marm's eye. The brewer staggered back a pace, but was quick to respond, grabbing the younger male by the back of the neck. Tay batted at his hands, trying to free himself. His teeth were bared like a beast's. By now everyone in the room was on their feet. *Heaven's help, this is not like us*, Holl thought, alarmed. He pushed in between them, shoving them apart.

"Stop!" he cried. But the two didn't listen. They ignored him, circling one another warily. Marm was not a practiced fighter. Holl easily ducked under a punch he swung, grabbed him around the body and shoved him toward his wife and family. Tay lunged, but Holl was there, holding him around the waist. He stopped, tossing his head like a frightened horse.

"Don't you dare brawl like Big Folk," Holl scolded them. "They can go so far away from each other that they'll never meet again, but we must stay close. All the world's against us. We only have each other. Choose your words with care. An accusation now that is found later to be without a basis..." Holl let his voice trail off. Tay took the point, but Marm was too angry to let it drop right away.

"He's accused me of poison. I will not rest with that ringing in my ears."

"Well, Tay?" Holl asked.

Tay let his gaze drop to his shoes. "I take it back." He raised his face, his eyes ablaze. "But I still say there's a curse, whether it be on him or not."

"Well, I say there's not," Holl said. "We'll go look and see if there's something else in the cellar. Who is with me?"

Enoch stood up. His father turned a mild look of reproof upon him, and he sat down.

"Vhy should more than one go to look?" the Master asked. "It is not a large place. You cannot profe a negative."

"All right, then," Holl said, mentally squaring his shoulders. "I will see if there's evidence of a positive."

He strode out of the room. The others watched him go in silence.

"Why?" Enoch demanded, as soon as Holl was gone.

The Elf Master sighed. "It is a test, my son."

"Bah," Enoch said. "Some community." He stalked out after Holl.

He found Holl crouching near the back wall where pipes entered the house from the well, examining something. The fair-haired male glanced up as Enoch came in. Enoch thought he saw hope and relief flash across his brother-in-law's face that somebody had come to keep him company, but the expression was gone as soon as it registered. He was grateful, for the thousandth time, that Holl was to be the next Headman of the village, and not him. Imagine, having to keep one's temper all of the time.

"Any negatives or positives?" he asked.

"You cannot call it good news," Holl said, rocking back on his heels, "but yes. When Marm threw a fuss the other day about the protective spells being broken I came down here with the others. I felt the seal myself. Something has been trying to pierce the spell since then. See for yourself."

Enoch came closer and extended his hands, sensing, almost listening with his fingertips. The power that should have surrounded the foundation like a seamless garment was nearly holed through, almost as though fire had been applied, melting out an irregular circle. Together, they strengthened the protection, smoothing out the roughness.

"But did it come from within or without?" he asked. "Are we constantly trapping something in here that wishes to be elsewhere, or do we have an intruder? And what does *it* want?"

Holl stood up. "For once I agree with Candlepat. Is it an it? We might merely have stumbled upon a force of some kind. This *feels* old. Timeless."

"Hmph. Because we don't know the source of it. It is only unfamiliar. Don't mistake strange for ancient."

Holl studied the wall. He didn't say aloud that he wished Keith Doyle was there with him, but he did. He missed that cheerful courage that Keith had displayed on their visit to Europe, his open willingness to try anything, blundering forth good-naturedly into everything, trusting that every situation would come out all right, and carrying on like a hero when it did not. The expression on Enoch's face told him he knew what Holl was thinking. Holl, ashamed to be caught, put Keith out of his mind at once and concentrated on what was before him. "The old house itself could be registering a protest, now that there are 80 of us living here instead of two elderly Big Folk."

Enoch shook his head. "Those of us with good stone-sense went over the foundation a dozen times since we've moved in here. The old ones insisted. They thought the house might come down around us. It hasn't, and it won't. The house is not to blame."

"The only feeling I get from this is a troubling one, of uneasiness," Holl said, trying to put into words what he felt. "And anger. I feel that something is very angry."

"Could it be another creature?" Enoch asked, raising his eyebrows.

"How would we know?" Holl replied. "We've spent all our years trying to avoid other beings. I'm not certain we'd recognize the evidence if it was here."

"Could it be the Earth herself? We've always tried to live in harmony with nature, but I was so small when we last lived on our own I don't know what it should feel like."

"I couldn't know," Holl said. "I was born in Gillington Library. I've never lived elsewhere. But I will say there's nothing in the shape of the burn that correspond with the shape of the Earth's energies here." Holl touched the wall once more. He felt nothing but the coolness of fieldstone and concrete and the hum of the spell. "We'll just have to wait until the next incursion, and hope we can catch whatever it is while it's happening."

Enoch looked toward the stairs and let out a snort. "They'll not like 'wait and see' as an answer."

Holl chuckled. "I am sure they'll accept it, if I ask for volunteers for the vigil first."

Enoch nodded, following his brother-in-law out of the cellar. And there was another good reason they'd named Holl as heir apparent: he had an agile mind.

Chapter 9

"If Mr. Collier has a moment to see me," Keith offered the middle-aged African-American woman a winning smile as she picked up the receiver of the complicated-looking telephone system. "I've got to get back to my office before eleven. I've got a meeting I can't miss."

"I'm asking his personal assistant right now, sir. If you'll just wait for a little while?" She spoke into her headset microphone in a low voice for a moment, then pushed another button on the keyboard. She nodded at Keith. "Burghart, Collier and Associates; good morning, may I help you?"

Keith stepped back, brushed down the front of his russety-tan suit jacket and straightened his tie. He started paced back and forth among the burgundy tweed chairs. He'd been thinking about this moment all yesterday evening while driving back to Chicago, and all morning while he was getting dressed.

How best could he get Marcy's point across without being too pushy? He felt that he ought to approach the moment as if he were an advertiser trying to win a customer. How would Enoch play as a product? *Try Enoch brand Son-in-law*, Keith thought, playfully. *Compact, effective, last for centuries, g....* No, he'd better stay *far* away from phrases like 'guaranteed satisfaction.' But this was serious. He promised himself he'd play the matter completely straight, for Marcy. She was trusting her whole future happiness to him. That was a sobering notion.

"Keith Doyle?" a man's voice asked, startling him out of his thoughts. Alan Collier came toward him with his hand out. Though the rest of her features had come from her mother, Marcy had inherited her wide, dark-blue eyes, straight black hair and white-white skin from her father. Mr. Collier stood slightly taller than Keith, and his wiry frame and athletic grip suggested he worked out regularly at something like handball or tennis. "Hey, guy, it's been a couple of years!"

"Hi, sir," Keith said, returning the handclasp firmly. "Yeah, I think it's been since sophomore year."

"Good to see you. C'mon back. Coffee?" He led Keith through the door into an elegant suite of rooms. "Becky was saying just the other day she wondered what had become of you."

"Same as Marcy. Finished my bachelor's degree. I'm in grad school now."

"Cool," Mr. Collier said, gesturing Keith to a chair. "So, what can I do for you?"

Keith glanced around, trying to figure out just where to begin.

It was a handsome office, suitable for a partner of the firm. There were signs of money around the room, but very little wood. Almost all chrome, leather and black melamine. Keith found it cold. He felt like blurting out that his prospective son-in-law could go a long way toward improving his office furniture, but that would impede Marcy's chances of happiness, not improve them.

"Have you seen Marcy lately?" Mr. Collier asked.

"Well, yes," Keith said. "Just the other day. In fact, she's why I'm here."

Mr. Collier raised his eyebrows, looking hopeful.

"You know she's living down on Hollow Tree Farm," Keith began. "She's really happy there."

"We haven't seen a lot of her in the last couple of months," Mr. Collier said, reproachfully. "Her mother and I were wondering why."

"Well, she's been a little shy about facing you," Keith said.

"Oh, not us! We're her parents. We love her."

"I know," Keith replied. "You see, she's been seeing this guy. Well, he's a good guy, but he's not what you'd call the usual kind of person. She wants you to meet him, but she's not sure how…she wants to make sure you like each other." Keith cleared his throat. Better start over. "I don't know whether she's mentioned it a lot, but she's really interested in getting married. Soon. What she wants more than anything else is to get your blessing, yours and Mrs. Collier's. It's really important to her."

Alan Collier eyed him askance. "She's not... pregnant, is she?"

"No! I mean, I don't think so. I think they're waiting. She's really serious. I mean, Marcy and Enoch."

"Are you sure you're not here on your own behalf, Keith?" Mr. Collier asked, with a 'between-us-guys' kidding expression. "Marcy used to talk about you a lot."

"No, sir. Not for myself. I'm committed. I mean, I've got a girlfriend. *Very* serious."

"I think there's still a spark of something there," Mr. Collier pressed. "You wouldn't be here if you weren't still fond of my daughter."

"I did have a crush on her," Keith admitted, "but I don't any more."

"You were stuck on her for a long time during your sophomore year. Long enough for it to turn into real romance?" Mr. Collier asked.

"No, sir," Keith insisted, puzzled as to the direction the conversation was going. It was as though Mr. Collier wasn't hearing what he was saying. "We both grew out of it. We have someone else. Each. Marcy's more like one of my sisters. I've got three. It's Enoch she's interested in." This wasn't going well. The more he talked, the more Mr. Collier looked convinced Keith was thinking the opposite of what he was saying. Keith was just making it worse by trying. He'd better get out of there before the man got the idea he really was there to make a bid for Marcy's hand. "I'm sorry, sir. I'd better go."

"Come anytime," Mr. Collier said, genially, standing up. "You're just like one of the family."

He can't face it, Keith realized, hurrying down the street in hopes of catching a bus. *Now I know what Marcy's been up against. It's like I'm just knocking on the door. He's not letting me in. I'll have to try again.*

Keith looked at his watch. He'd better get moving. It was a long way back to PDQ.

"I want this to be big, really big," Doug Constance said, leaning forward conspiratorially. Keith and the others, Dorothy,

Paul, Janine and Rollin sat poised around the conference table in the largest boardroom at PDQ. Pinned to the felt boards around the room were photos and schematics of the Origami in dozens of different configurations. Inspiration, Keith thought. "We have a chance to change people's perceptions about communication and productivity. One-unit offices are the the wave of the future. One-unit computer systems keep all your data in one place, one very portable place. One-unit entertainment systems will give you an endless range of options for movies, games, music—and they're all the same unit. We save space. We save resources. Brainstorm on it. Not you, J. Pierpont Finch," he said, as Keith sat up with his mouth open. "Let's hear some other ideas before you blow us away."

Keith let his mouth close. This was the second major strategy meeting on the Origami. Now that they had conditionally won the account, it was up to them to prepare what Dorothy called 'the dog-and-pony show.' The president of the company had gone back to his corner office, leaving the rank-and-file to hash out the details of the account.

"What are we selling here?" Janine asked. "The convenience? Every PDA is convenient."

"This is more than a PDA," Paul said. "It's a handheld computer."

"That takes too long to say." Doug waved a hand. "Do enough people know the difference? I know *I* don't."

"Let's assume the person on the street will find out. Let's just tell them what it is," Janine said.

"I think we ought to concentrate on the battery life," Rollin said. He and Janine were a team, having worked together for the last couple of years. Keith envied them their chemistry, their easy give and take. "That's miraculous, twenty hours. My laptop poops out in three."

"Yeah, but my cell phone lasts for more than three days," Paul said.

"With this you don't sell a battery," Janine argued sharply. "It's a machine. What it *is*. How long it lasts is gravy, not a selling point."

"Oh, yes it is," Rollin said, with an exasperated look at his partner. "What good is it if it's out of gas?"

"How about the combined features?" Keith offered. "Being able to record music off the air and dub it into videos...?"

"Is anyone but technogeeks going to like that?" Doug asked.

"Man, these days *everyone* is a technogeek," Rollin said. "Start a conversation in a bus terminal, and homeless people start coming up to you with their cell phones."

"Is it universality or exclusivity we're trying to promote?" Dorothy asked.

Rollin grimaced. "You know most people will end up using it to play solitaire."

Paul laughed. "A truth, but an ugly truth. Do we make use of it?"

"How about an ad with the cards all jumping out to become features of the machine?" Janine asked.

"I think that would get really confused, visually," Dorothy said.

"Don't make it look like gambling," Rollin said. "Bad connotation."

"All right, folks, this is what we've got from the big boys," Doug said, holding up a sheaf of documents. "We're going to take this a step at a time. Two television commercials, one for now, one for the holidays, to run in 10-second, 30-second and 60-second blocks. A billboard. Full-page ad for the glossies. Newspaper ad, to run in full-page in the tabloids and half-page in the full-sheets. They've got a company up the street working on the design for the box, but we're providing the wrap.

Doug started leafing through the briefs. "Janine and Rollin, you did some really good work on the Daiyenu Play System. You can do that. This is for the big time, remember. Gadfly can still decide they don't want us for media ads, even after we spend a million dollars for them." The team nodded. He turned over the next sheet of paper in the stack. "Billboard. Outdoor displays, worldwide..." He looked at Keith, then put it on the bottom of the stack, shaking his head.

"We'll take that," Janine said at once, holding out her hand. "I've got some great ideas."

"Uhh…" Doug said, "maybe we'll work on this one closer to the end of the rotation. You work on the TV ads first. We'll need the lead time for post-production."

Keith was getting more nervous by the moment. So far, Doug hadn't offered him an assignment. He could understand the executive's reluctance to trust thousands of dollars and the account to the hands of an inexperienced parttimer. He knew Doug considered his outburst on the product name a fluke.

Keith smiled absently at the intern who brought around everyone's order from the coffee shop. He peeled off the lid and glanced into the murky pool. The cappucino was too dark to have been made with a single espresso. Keith hated bitter coffee. He took a handful of sugar packets out of the box on the table, shook them down, and tore all the corners off at once, keeping his eyes on Doug, willing him to hand over a brief. He stirred the sugar into the coffee, took a big swig, and nearly spat it out across the table. The intern had already sugared it for him. Not wanting to make a fuss, Keith drank the syrupy brew.

The jitters came on gradually but with the force of a slowly charging rhino. Before he knew it he was getting dirty looks from the others for tapping his pencil on the table. He put the pencil away, but then he didn't know what to do with his hands. He found himself playing with a rolled-up napkin, shredding it into strands and twisting them around. Dorothy gave him an odd glance. He looked down between his hands, and discovered it was turning into a miniature cable-knit sweater. It had the mark of glamour on it, meaning he'd been using magic without thinking about it. Enoch would have given him an 'A' in miniature magical macrame and told him not to do it in public.

"I used to be dynamite at construction-paper snowflakes," he said, tossing the scrap of paper aside. He put hands under his thighs and sat on them.

"And we've got a full-page ad here for the executive journals: financials, airline magazines, Newsweek, WSJ. Something classy and understated..." The pent-up energy just exploded in Keith. He had to move or self-destruct.

"I'll take that one," he said, springing to his feet. "I've got an idea." Everyone looked at him. He sat down.

"Okay, Keith," Doug said, surprised, handing over the paper. "All right. Let's come in later and talk about it some more. There's a dozen other briefs pending. We need to get the vital ones out of the way now."

"I'll take Keith for a while," Dorothy said, grabbing him by the shoulder. "Should we meet back here about four? We ought to be able to hash out some initial ideas before quitting time."

The others nodded, leaning together to look over their data sheets. Dorothy held onto Keith's arm and marched him out of the room. He smiled over his shoulder at the others. His hands were shaking. He took a couple of deep breaths before Dorothy swung in front of him and shook a finger under his nose.

"What was with you in there?" Dorothy asked on the way out. "You were more hyper than ever."

"Double caffeine and eight sugars," Keith said. "Next time I'll taste it first, I swear."

"God, I bet your mama had to keep you on a leash as a kid."

"Nope," Keith grinned. "We had a fenced-in yard."

"Well, come on before Doug comes out here and takes that back."

Keith followed Dorothy into her small office. She closed the door behind them and waved him to a chair by the window. The high-ceilinged room had a non-insulated brick wall suggesting that the building had originally been a factory or a warehouse. The rest of the office was furniture-mart modern, complete to the melamine storage units, all of which were stuffed and overstuffed with sample books, binders and sourcebooks. Jammed along the wall were a desk and a drawing table. Under the window was a small table piled high with papers and books. Framed on the wall along the top molding were copies of news-

paper and magazine advertisements. Keith guessed by the style
that they were her work.

"We'll have to find you a cubicle," Dorothy said, standing
with her hands on her hips, looking around. "It's an office, but
it's too small to swing a cat. I don't usually have a perma-
nently assigned creative partner like Rollin and Janine, so
they're not wasting any extra space on me. I can find you a
desk, or you can take that little table by the window."

"I'm happy to be anywhere," Keith assured her. "The table's
fine."

"Uh-huh," Dorothy said, with a summing-up look, as she
swept sample books off its surface and put them in a heap next
to her desk. "We'll see how you feel later on when we're bumping elbows. We'll see how *I* feel. I may want to throw you to the
wolves or stick you in the fire-escape stairwell." She sat down
and waved him to the other chair. "So what's your great idea?"

Keith held out the creative brief. "This is for the airline
magazines, right?"

"And Newsweek, and fifty other glossies."

"Yeah, but we can do something dynamic with the Origami
for travelers. How about just a really simple headline: 'Ready
to take off when you are.' We could make it look like it's about
to take flight."

Dorothy's eyebrows went up and she reached for her drawing pad. "I like it. Yeah. You know, I looked up a book on
origami after the first meeting. It's around here somewhere."
She and Keith bent down to sort through the books on the
floor. "Yeah. Here it is. There's one classic design that's supposed to be lucky." She paged through until she came to a
pinched figure with bent points coming off it at several angles.
"It's the crane, the symbol of long life. The legend is that if
you fold a thousand cranes your wish will come true."

Keith's eyes danced. "That's great. It pulls in a feeling of
magic. That would be good."

"If we don't say the word 'magic'," Dorothy said, shaking
her head warningly. "You would not *believe* what things are
taboo. You can have people with tattoos selling brokerage accounts, but the second you bring in the pixie dust, you're toast."

"Too bad," Keith said, waggling his eyebrows. "Magic is my middle name. Well, one of them. I like the idea of the crane, though." He scooted his chair closer as Dorothy started sketching. "Can you make the Origami look like the origami? The keyboard looks like a pair of wings, but the head and neck would be too wide."

"I think I can do it," Dorothy said, slowly, concentrating as she worked. "Oh, yes, look at that. If we change the perspective, tilt it a little and give it a back light, they'll see the outline as much as the screen part. Yes, I like that. Here, what do you think?"

"That's terrific. You really can draw! You said a thousand cranes," he added speculatively, after a moment. "What about having one in the middle, and 999 others fading off into the distance?"

"No, little boy. If you really want to draw the eye, you don't want more than three main elements in your design. Any more than that, you lose focus."

"Well, there's only one product," Keith reasoned. "They'd be all the same element."

"Yes, but you want the name and the company as well. You don't want those surrounded by clutter. But make it clear by emphasis and placement what you want them to look at first. That would be the unit itself."

"Make sure the screen shows," Keith said, scooting his chair over so he could see better.

"I know, I know. Don't bother the lady while she's working."

"Wow, that's great," he exclaimed, as she changed the whole perspective with a few pencilled lines. "Yeah, it just jumps out at you, doesn't it. That's just right."

Dorothy glanced at him. "That's what I think, too. No argument?"

"None at all," Keith assured her. "It's terrific. It works just like you said it would."

"It all started from your headline," Dorothy acknowledged. "This is screwy. We're just too compatible." She raised her chin defiantly. "This is just 'cause I knew you from before."

"Maybe," Keith said, carefully, not wanting to read too much into the moment, "maybe we just think alike."

"Wouldn't that be weird," Dorothy said, dropping back in her chair and looking Keith square in the eye, "if it turned out that we were thrown together over a year ago because we were meant to work together? I mean, we had some mojo going back then, when we were coming up with fake ads for Paul, but this is just falling together, bang-bang-bang."

"Is that why you called me?"

"No," Dorothy said, going back to the sketch. "I told you, Gadfly came across so weird at the first meeting with the top bananas that I wanted someone with a different perspective sitting in on the creative pitch. You always came up with the strangest things, at the drop of a hat. I thought they were going to ask for the usual dog-and-pony show, like a lot of the big accounts do. I had no idea that their idea of an audition was to name the product. I struck lucky there, too. They could just have easily taken a walk over to a different house. Every agency in Chicago was ready to pitch them. Tech companies are big, big money. I remembered that you had a creative mind, and you were easy to work with. Seems I was right." She shot a quick glance at him. "It's too much to hope that I was sensing the copywriter I'm going to be paired with for my whole creative life. You know, there's some legendary teams out there. But that would be too scary."

"I don't know why," Keith said. "I believe in magic, so seeing the future's not that far out of range."

"Now, don't you go talking like that and scaring the customer," Dorothy scolded him, rapping him on the wrist with the pencil.

"It'll just be between you and me," Keith assured her. He leaned closer to see what she was doing. "I think the image ought to be higher up on the page."

"I was just moving it!" Dorothy exclaimed. "Hmm...I think...just slightly above center line. Yes."

"That's it!" Keith said, excitedly. "Sorry, I know the art's your department, but where it is right now, your eye has to go to it." He piled junk on the layout page around her drawing. "See? It's still the first thing you see."

"I know, little boy, I know. Let Mama work, okay?"

Dorothy lettered out Keith's headline on a 4x6 card and held it at different angles to the image of the 'crane.' "I like this spot best," she said, setting it on the page at a 45° angle above and to the right of the picture of the Origami. "This way, the dynamic line of the image draws your eye diagonally up to the headline. Since people read from left to right, they'll look at the picture first, the headline second. And...we'll put the rest of the copy into a block in the lower right section of the ad. If we leave the left side of the ad clear except for the picture, it'll be stronger than having copy run straight across. It says we think it can speak for itself."

"It can talk," Keith said, grinning. "It can do anything. I can't wait until it's for sale. I hope I can afford it."

"And the elements form a triangle. Hmm, company name and logo at the bottom in bolder print, maybe two or three points larger. That's visually interesting. I like it."

"Me, too," Keith agreed. "I'd better work out some copy, then."

"We can slot in dummy copy for now," Dorothy said. "Let me get the keyliner to run up a rough for the others to look at. Hot stuff, Keith."

"The same to you," he said, sketching a bow to her. "You know, we really do work together pretty well."

Dorothy eyed him up and down with a half-smile as she picked up the ad sketch. "We do, at that."

When she returned from the production department, Keith was sitting at the table staring out the window and tapping his pencil against his teeth.

"It'll be done soon," Dorothy said. "I caught Cary with a free moment. What're you thinking?"

Keith swung around, the pencil still at his lips. "That poster is still up for grabs," he said, thoughtfully.

"What poster?"

"The one that's going to be used for billboards and bus wraps. I want to do that one, too."

Dorothy shook her head. "I think Doug's going to give it to Rollin and Janine."

Keith sat up eagerly. "No, I think we can do it better. I want to do it. Badly. How do I get Doug to let us have it instead of the others?... It is *us*, isn't it?"

Dorothy gave a big, mock sigh. "It's us. For better or worse. You get an ad that'll have prominent exposure by doing a good job on this one."

"Do you think he'll go for it based on 'Ready to take off...'?"

"The way things are done these days, you have to have a rough of the billboard for them to look at." She saw that his eyes were dancing. "You have an idea already."

"Yes," Keith said, barely able to stay in his chair.

"What is it?"

Keith leaned in close. "Doug all but designed it himself. Remember what he said? A photo of hands operating the Origami, with an overlay of words, all the functions the Origami has. It'd be so simple, and I think, totally effective."

"You'd have to have a killer headline."

"I do," Keith said, jumping up and spreading his hands across the sky. "'One of everything.'"

Dorothy stared at him, a slow grin starting on her face. "It's got a bundle of meanings besides the obvious, and it'll make people read the overlay. Yes, that's so simple they'd jump for it. And Doug will like it because he's already thought of it."

Keith smiled wide enough to swallow his ears. "That would *never* have occurred to me."

"See? You belong in advertising," Dorothy said, picking up her sketch pad. "You lie like a master."

But Janine and Rollin had decided to make a pitch for the high-profile poster, too. The keyliners were kept busy that afternoon, as both teams hurried to have a rough layout ready to present. At four o'clock, both teams appeared in Doug's office, clamoring for the assignment. As Dorothy predicted, Doug was already inclined toward the design he had suggested so offhandedly.

"I like yours, too," Doug assured Janine and Rollin. "It's kicky. I like the headline, 'Fold it your way.' Don't get me wrong. I'm sure we'll be able to use it later. But this one is good. I'm surprised." He nodded to Keith, who acknowledged it without speaking. He had wanted to show Doug that the idea had come from his own suggestion, but Dorothy told him not to bring that up unless asked. The others would already know it. "And," Dorothy had said privately to Keith, with a grin, "they'll be kicking themselves they didn't pick up on it first."

"It'll be expensive to do," Rollin argued. "It'll need a fresh overlay for every language. We'd have to get translations of the features for each country the ad goes to."

"We'll have to have that anyhow, for the box layout," Doug said. "We'll already have all the descriptive copy in hand. The owner's manual is in eight languages including Russian, Chinese Mandarin and Japanese."

He turned to Keith and Dorothy. "So, what's going in here?" he asked, pointing to the image of the Origami screen, still blank.

"We're still working on that," Dorothy said. Keith had pleaded with her not to put anything in that Doug would demand in the final. He had an idea, and wanted nothing to interfere with it. "We have to figure out what won't detract from the overlay."

"Yeah," Doug said, stroking his chin. "All right, kids. Put some thought to that. Show me on Monday or Tuesday. In the meantime, good work."

"Slick," Rollin muttered to Keith as they left the room. "You trying to do us out of a job?"

"There's enough assignments for everyone," Keith said sincerely. He didn't want to create ill-will among the full-time employees.

"Back to work, Doyle," Dorothy said, pointing toward her office. "I've got to e-mail the rough to the client. They might kill the whole thing anyhow," she added, with a meaningful look toward Rollin and Janine. "You never know."

Grudgingly, the other team withdrew. Keith didn't wait. He strode back to Dorothy's office and closed the door. He needed privacy for a telephone call he wanted to make.

Chapter 10

"It's perfect," Keith said, spreading the sheet out on the kitchen table for all the Little Folk to look at. He'd made the drive from his apartment to the farm in record time that Friday evening, the old Mustang practically flying down the long Illinois highway on pure excitement. It had been a glorious summer evening, full of birds calling as they soared over the lush, green cornfields, but all Keith could see in his mind was the layout for the advertisement. "The empty screen is just sitting there. It has to have something on it. Why not put the invitation to the party out all around the world for free, courtesy of Gadfly and the Origami? 'Come one, come all, to the Mythical Beings Grand Reunion!' This will be on billboards, walls, posters, even on the sides of buses, in every country that buys electronics. Everyone will see it."

"Everyone who lives in a city, you mean," Maura corrected him, joggling Asrai on her hip as she helped put away the dinner dishes. "Why would you think that most beings like ourselves will be within range of seeing this advertisement?"

"There'd be at least one poster near places like Midwestern. That's where I found you folks, isn't it? And the folks who see it can pass along the news to others."

"That is, assuming they know any others," Holl said. "We don't."

"What if there are no others?" Maura asked.

"Sure there are," Keith exclaimed. "You know the air sprites. They've told me they have seen lots of beings not strictly human or animal. And there's that grouchy guy I ran into in Scotland. Who knows? There could be *hundreds* of races and thousands of beings out there who are just dying to come to a great party. The trouble is, getting the word out is very tricky. I didn't want it so obvious that we'd get fairy-hunters or

UFOlogists showing up. It's just supposed to be a nice party like a family reunion. A big family, with maybe a few more, uh, unusual talents than most."

"Many of the creatures of legend are no more family to us than you are," Catra said. As Archivist she stayed as neutral in village disputes as she could, but on this issue Keith knew she was more of a Conservative.

"I dinna like it," Curran said, his white eyebrows low over his bright blue eyes. "And so we'll be invaded next spring by a crowd o' strange beings, comin' and goin' as they please, who'll know where we are forever after? I still dinna care much for the trampings in and out of Big Folk...er, present company is excepted, o'course."

"Thanks, Curran. But it'll be fun. You'll see," Keith promised. He observed the elders exchange sour glances. Evidently their faction was still not completely on board about the party. He hoped they would still let it go forward. The Master had given his approval, but he could still withdraw it if there was enough of a popular outcry. He'd have to sound Holl out on the subject later. It'd be impossible to pull the invitation back once it had gone out around the world. He didn't have to hammer that home; they knew it. He would know by the time he went home if he was going to be able to do it or not. Mentally, he crossed his fingers and looked hopeful.

Catra looked over the advertisement. "The text would have to be brief. There's little room there."

"It's going to be a poster," Keith replied. "The available area will be at least a foot across, and much bigger on billboards. Naturally we want to avoid any recognizable words. Is that a problem?"

Holl tilted his head, reading the text that Keith had written out. "Like any other migratory people, we've picked up words from the lands we've traveled through. A few of German, many English and Irish, a scattering of other tongues."

"Well, could it be done without using any adopted words?" Keith asked. "Go back to the base language without confusing anybody?"

Holl shrugged. "I don't know if anybody but our folk would be able read it, new words or no."

"Yeah, but it's my best shot," Keith pleaded. "If I use sign language or symbols somebody might figure it out. I thought that if you used your own alphabet, we'd minimize the possibility of unwanted guests. And, if no one at PDQ can read it, they won't be tempted to cut any of it out. Besides, it'll look pretty."

"That it would," Maura smiled. Keith's eyes grew dreamy.

"Just think," he said. "By next month, it'll be on buses in France, on billboards across the US, on hoardings in Germany and the UK, in magazines in Japan…maybe even on the Internet!"

Eyebrows went up all over the room.

"You may get more than you can handle, Keith Doyle," Maura warned him.

"Better too many people at the party than too few," he said cheerfully.

"Perhaps seven lines of print, then?" Catra asked, already interested.

"You'll do it?" Keith asked, delighted.

"I see no reason, unless the Master objects."

"Not at this time," the red-haired schoolmaster said, his blue eyes glinting with amusement behind his glasses. "A most creatif solution to a difficult problem. I congratulate you, Meester Doyle."

"Thanks, sir," Keith said, reddening with pleasure. "It was just such an opportunity I couldn't let it pass. I had to grab for the assignment."

The teacher nodded. "Uf course. And how goes the progress on your other assignment?"

Keith blanched. "I, well, uh…"

Catra cleared her throat and shook the paper at the two men. "I can have this for you before you go Sunday night."

"That would be terrific," Keith said, grateful for the rescue. "I told them I wanted to play with it a little. Dorothy will let me get away with this. So long as I'm discreet, that is."

"Too late," Catra said, chuckling. "You're a living billboard yourself, but a benevolent one."

"Thanks, I think."

She departed, already muttering phrases to herself under her breath. The Elf Master turned to Keith.

"And now, Meester Doyle, about your essay?"

Keith smiled winningly. "Could I turn it in at class on Sunday?"

The Master peered at him over his gold glasses. Was that a twinkle Keith could see in his eyes? "Very vell. I hope you are as confincing in your paper as you haf been this efening."

"Would you like some coffee or tea?" Maura asked, setting Asrai in Keith's lap.

"Coffee would be great," he said, gratefully. "I'm half asleep after the drive. By the way, dinner was terrific. I didn't know how hungry I was. Hiya, pumpkin," he added, tickling Asrai under the ear.

The toddler giggled. "I'm not pumpkin."

"You're not? Then why do you have a green stem?" He touched her on the top of the head. Asrai wriggled off his lap and ran to look in a mirror.

"You will make a fine father one day," Maura said, watching her daughter with great fondness.

"Yeah," Keith replied, a trifle wistfully. "I hope so."

"How goes the progress on making your dream come true?" Holl asked, carrying a tray of mugs to the table. He set down Keith's personal mug before him. Maura filled it with coffee.

"Well, you know, the salary sounded like a huge amount of money when I started, but I've got so many expenses. To give Dunn a break I'm picking up half the rent on the Crash Site right now."

"Such an unfortunate name," the Elf Master said, stirring milk into his tea. Asrai discovered she did not have a pumpkin stalk growing out of her head, and ran back to jump into her grandfather's lap. Keith grinned at the resemblance between them, especially the owlish gaze. Asrai's hair was a softer auburn, not the Master's carroty red, but her eyes were the same color and shape, and she had that firm family chin. A good thing Holl was a diplomat at heart. "But I do understand the reference."

"It's only appropriate half the time. It *looks* like three guys live there, but Dunn's programming hardly ever crashes. He is the most cautious guy in the world."

"He has always maintained good scholarly habits, mit the exception of timeliness. His latest assignment is qvite late."

"You wouldn't believe how much he's got going," Keith explained, quick to defend his friend and roommate. "His brother is trying to raise venture capital for Uhuru Enterprises. It's an excruciating process that takes months, if not years. I've offered to help him set up his presentations, but they're not ready to show off yet. There's a lot involved. And I thought advertising was complicated." Maura poured more coffee for Keith, and tapped the side of his cup with her finger. He smiled at her and took a hearty sip. "Thanks. This is really good."

"How is this vocal-recognition program different from what's for sale already?" Holl asked.

"Well, you can organize different parts of your dictation by using voice commands," Keith said. "It works really well. I've been using it to divide my notes into personal, business, school and your class," he addressed the Master, then decided he'd better not dwell on that subject for long.

Holl, watching his expression, laughed. The Master wasn't going to tease him any longer. Keith had apologized, and that was all the teacher ever asked, that and getting the assignments in as soon as possible. Keith was allowed a great deal of leeway for his generosity and willingness to let them make a fool of him. He never cared if he was the butt of their jokes, so long as he was allowed to be there among them. He would always be bigger and slower than they were, and he accepted the differences without rancor or resentment. He had remarkable grace of character. The Folk could have done far worse, Holl reflected, than trusting this one Big Person, out of the millions and billions. He could have revealed them to the world, but he kept their secret almost dearer than his own life.

"And do you still enjoy the job, now that you must answer to PDQ as an employer, rather than as an educational experience?" Holl asked.

"More than ever," Keith said, happily. "I'd like to keep going on the creative side, but sometimes I think I would like to get out there and find them clients. PDQ is a good firm. They treat their customers with respect, and they have a lot of fun making up the accounts. I mean, it's a bloodthirsty business, but I like a challenge. Say, when are you going to let me do a campaign for you?"

Curran and the other elders looked alarmed. "A campaign?"

"To vhat end?" the Master inquired.

"Well, to advertise Hollow Tree's products," Keith explained. "We could really increase orders with the right kind of ad. If I pay for studio time, I can use the agency's equipment and get a really professional look. Christmas is coming. How about a flyer mailed out to retail stores with new offerings for this year? The right look could even get you into the department store chains."

"No, thank you," Holl said, firmly. "We are doing well enough with the accounts we have. Too much expansion would stretch us past our capacity. If our needs exceed our income, we will work out a different way to earn money."

"Like the high-class art," Keith said, nodding. "Well, how about a website? I know you bought Hollow Tree Industries dot-com. I checked. It's in the registry with my name on it."

Holl cleared his throat. "Our action was mostly to secure it to prevent another from taking it and ruining our reputation. We are proud of the quality of our work. We wouldn't want anyone wandering about on the Internet pretending to be us."

"So why not use it?" Keith asked, reasonably. "You've already got an account with the shipping companies. You could set up a mail-order fulfillment service pretty easily."

The Folk looked at one another.

"Now, that may be of interest," said Holl. "We could sell our wares at a further remove from the customer. We will one day saturate this market. In fact, the day is not long in coming. Very well, we will talk about it."

"Not now, if it's okay with you," Keith said, fighting back a yawn. "Wow. I didn't realize how keyed up I was. Where can I sleep?"

"We've set up a bed for you in the workshop," Maura said. "I'll show you. If you wouldn't mind watching Asrai, father?"

The Elf Master, arm around his granddaughter, waved them out of the room. "Go. Sleep vell, Meester Doyle."

Maura returned in a few moments, shutting the kitchen door quietly behind her.

"Abed already," she said. "He took a moment to telephone to Diane, but he couldn't do much more before he dropped off. I hated to do that to him."

"He needed rest," the Master said. "A simple charm of restfulness does him no harm. And ve haf not yet handled the situvation at hand so as to escape explanation. There are things he has no need to face. They are our business."

"Keva in a pet is one of them," Holl agreed. A disaster had struck at the heart of his formidable sister's pride. Keva's bread had fallen. Every loaf of the day's baking had come out of the oven flat. Candlepat, with commendable tact for one who was usually focused upon herself, had tried to make things better by bringing in recipes for serving focaccia. Others gave their best efforts, too, but nothing had salved the old female's feelings. She had never, *never* had a batch of bread fail in all her long life. The shame of it had driven her to their clan's room, where she had spent the rest of the day, refusing dinner and any attempt to lure her out. Anyone who had approached her had returned looking half-chewed from the scolding. Keith was a favorite of hers, but even he'd be unlikely to escape a tongue-lashing.

"Surely she'll be herself in a day or two," Curran said, lowering his wiry white eyebrows. "The lass's had her dignity wrung out. All have been under a strain that'd strangle a dragon, so it would. Whate'er wee beastie is muckin' about around here bids fair to tear us apart."

"We don't know there's anything here, Curran," Holl said, wearily. He'd hoped the old one wouldn't bring up the subject again. "It could just be a run of bad luck. A trend can feed on itself when all are under a strain, as you say."

The eyebrows climbed high on Curran's forehead. "Bad luck, you say? And wasn't it just you who told me yersel' that the bad luck comes in bursts? Nor have these auld eyes missed that they come coincidently alongside breaks in our barrier charm. That smacks of intelligence, do you not say so?"

"I would," Holl said, "but I can't prove it. It only seems intelligent because of the coincidences. It is possible that there's a mindless force underneath this place, or that we've brought something into the house that's causing the problem. I hardly know where to start."

"Research it," the Elf Master suggested. "Vhere experience fails, see vhat other observers have written in the past. Vhat you say is true: there are many possibilities. Explore them. You may type a message this efening to the Old Vuns to ask for their advice vhen ve activate the computer later on. I recall that there are many records of interest that may be of assistance."

Holl glanced at the clock. Still a few hours to go before the new tradition of gathering before the computer screen as though around a cosy hearth, to share messages with their distant relations. He doubted they had much to say about troublesome spirits in the New World, but it would do him good to ask. Suddenly, his sensitive hearing picked up the sound of feet stomping up the cellar stairs. He identified Marm's pace before he burst into the room. The plump brewer's face was dark red with fury.

"There you all are!" he snapped. "I want justice! Some fool's been meddling with the mead meant for New Year! A quarter of the barrel gone so far!"

"No one would take half-fermented mead," Holl said.

"I marked the barrel," Marm announced. "Two fingers lower in the wood, the level is, than the last time I complained to you. That's quarts gone, much more than the Wee Ones' share. It'd be the young ones again, causing their mischief. Why wouldn't they want a sugary drink? We've got to pay for soda. The bees' bounty is free, but it comes only once a year."

"There's more honey," Curran said, with a dismissive wave. "The hives are fair drippin' with it. Start a new batch."

"I can't rob the hives now," Marm explained. "They're filling up for their wintering over. I'll not treat the bees so badly!"

"Well, ye should ha' kept a closer eye on yer barrels, then, if we canna do without."

"Do you accuse me of neglect?" Marm demanded, his usual placid manner gone.

"Friends, please," the Master said. Maura picked up Asrai and withdrew with her to a corner, out of the way. The little girl was wide-eyed with alarm.

"I'll not have everyone in your clan attacking me. What if I demanded that each family brew for itself?"

"And bake for itsel', too?" Curran asked. "Ye'll do without bread if I've aye to say about it!"

"Oh, we will, eh? It'd be better than the flat cakes we had for breakfast!"

Holl winced, hoping that Keva couldn't hear the insult. "Let's calm down," he said. "You'll wake the house."

"Calm down?" both Curran and Marm bellowed, rounding on Holl.

A tremendous crash interrupted them. They knew at once it came from the cellar.

"My mead!" Marm shouted, running for the stairs. Holl came right behind him. Others, alarmed by the noise, spilled out of the bedrooms, the sitting room, the garden, and piled down the stairs to see what was the trouble.

As soon as Holl reached the bottom of the stairs he smelled it. Not the sweet, yeasty aroma of liquor, but concentrated sweetness. His heart sinking, he yanked open the door to the canning room. Sure enough, the floor was littered with shattered crocks and jars. Their contents glistened with jewel colors in the fitful light from the lanterns carried by the other Folk just behind him.

"Marm!" Shelogh shrieked. "What have you done!"

"I have touched nothing," Marm snapped, rounding on the older female.

Rose and Olanda pushed past the crowd into the room. Olanda looked as though she wanted to cry. Rose, more stoic, pressed her lips together, but her face was pale.

"All of the raspberry preserves," the younger female groaned. "Half the apricot and half the apple butter from last summer. And the pickles! The crocks are split!"

"It is terrible," Rose said. "Ve can ill afford to do mitout for the vinter."

"What in the world were you doing bumbling around down there?" Bracey asked Marm.

"He's *always* down here," Tay said.

"Enough!" the Master annouced. "Marm vas upstairs mit us vhen the noise came."

"Maybe the shelf supports came loose," Enoch suggested. He and Marcy stood on the stairs looking down over everyone else's shoulders.

Vardin, a red haired male about his own age, looked up at him, his eyes narrowed. "Don't you impugn my work. I secured those braces with good bolts and a charm beside. Maybe there were too many jars on them."

"Never," Rose said, emphatically.

"What'll we do?" Olanda asked, as the others helped her to her feet and began sweeping up glass and goo. "This would have fed us through the winter." The Folk grunted agreement, looking at the ruin of a summer's work.

"It's not as bad as that," Holl said, trying to soothe them. "We can *buy* more preserves. With the cash from the fancy goods we sell, we can have all the preserves and honey we wish."

Almost as one, the crowd turned on him. "*Bought* jams?" Curran sputtered. "Oh, so you want to turn into one of the Big Ones, do ye? Eatin' that filthy muck. Ye...Progressive, you!"

Holl flinched. "I only meant that it isn't the tragedy it was once. We won't starve. We're no longer entirely reliant upon what we make and what we can put by."

"You have to admit to our prosperity," Enoch said.

Curran shook his fist at the Master's son. "Ye can say that becayse ye're well out o' reach, young pup. Well, if it's not *this* clumsy lout, then who is responsible?"

"It is not me!" Marm insisted. "I've been telling you that someone has been down there. No one's paid me any attention."

"No one's been down there that shouldn't be! It's a curse!"

"Nothing's down there," Enoch said wearily. "Feel it. The charm's not broken, not even tried. How could anything get in to harm us?"

"We must have let it! Who is meddling with the protections?"

Everyone began shouting. The Master raised his hands for silence. They ignored him.

"Hush," he said, having to raise his voice until it could be heard above the din. "Vriends... *please...QVIET!* May I remind you that Keith Doyle is asleep in the barn. Howefer inferior his hearing may be to ours, he cannot fail to hear you if you all yell."

Every mouth snapped shut.

"If you vill all go back about your business, ve vill try to determine the reason the pantry shelfs haf collapsed. Now, who vill clean up?"

Several of the Folk came forward to assist Olanda and Rose in mopping up the fragrant mass of goo.

The Master gave Holl a quick glance. "As I haf said, Keith Doyle is asleep in the barn."

"I don't need it spelled out for me," Holl said, a little testily. "I have promised. I will say nothing about it."

"I know. But now you must find out what *it* is. Observation is the best means to enlightenment. By the vay," the Master said, as he climbed the stairs after the others, "it is true. The others must learn to lif mit the inconveniences of their own prosperity." His eyes glinted. He left Holl to supervise the mopping up.

The Folk all worked in silence. Everyone had his or her thoughts about what was occuring, and no one had the energy to start an argument. Once the broken crockery had been disposed of, and the old flagstone floor scrubbed to primeval newness, the others went up the stairs, blowing out most of the lanterns as they went, leaving Holl on his own in the cellar with a single light drawing a pool of gold around his feet.

Holl propped himself up against the wall and stared at the ceiling. He had no idea what he was waiting for, but it had seemed the right thing to stay. Above, he heard the hum and urgent static of the computer connecting to the Internet, meaning that the others were gathering together for the nightly reading of messages. He felt lonely sitting by himself. Maura had gone out to their small cottage to put Asrai to bed. He wished she or Enoch would come back and keep him company. Or Tay or Marm. They were good friends of his, and of each other, when they weren't under such extraordinary strain. Most of all, he wished Keith was sitting with him. The Big student had a gift for accepting that which he could not understand.

Holl's keen ears picked up his elder sister's high voice reading aloud from the screen. Not that anyone needed to be read to, but it had come to be a tradition. A sympathetic note from Aine, one of the Old Ones, regarding a letter that Shelogh had sent about Big Folk snooping around outside the farm.

"'Well, and if they're attracted to something, you must get rid of it at once,'" Keva announced. "'Big Folk are like ants. When one finds a tasty spill, it attracts others, like bad luck begetting bad luck.' And there you are," she said. "She thinks it's bad luck afflicting us."

"Ah," some of the listeners, mostly Conservatives, intoned in agreement.

Holl fell into a kind of trance, his only active sense his hearing. He wished he could be up there with his friends and neighbors, voicing his own opinion. He could hear them, but they might as well have been on the moon as at the top of the stairs. An uncomfortable feeling of unbelonging dogged him, making him seem an alien imprisoned within hearing, but not sight, of his own kind. The isolation reminded him of the latest Joseph Campbell book he'd been reading, about vision quests and the search for a protective totem. The Folk could certainly use one. Aine was right. Sooner or later one of those meddling Big Folk was going to wander onto the land and into the house, and their secret would be out for once and all.

He heard a light *plunk!* and lowered his gaze to focus on the barrels. Was Marm right, that one of the youths had been meddling with them? Holl hooked one of the small lanterns off the wall and went to inspect them. The lids of the barrels fit snugly but were easy to lift off. Holl opened the first cask at the end of a row and took a deep sniff. The rich, appealingly heady scent of fermenting liquor rose up to meet him. That might tempt a young one to try it, but one sip of immature beer was usually enough to dissuade one from seeking a second. True to his word, the brewer had marked each cask on the inside. One or two did show a succession of dropping levels.

The fifth one he opened smelled sweeter than the others. This must be the mead. As Marm had said, over a quarter of the barrel was empty. Poor fellow. He never hurt a soul. All he sought to accomplish in life was making the best beer in the world—which he bid fair to do—and someone had gone fiddling with it. Holl thought he'd better see how many more of the casks had been tampered with, then he could go up and have a word with the Master.

He pried open the next barrel of mead.

A force knocked him flying. Holl banged into the wall and lay staring, half-stunned, as a gout of red and yellow flame erupted from the barrel and caromed off the ceiling like a billiard ball. It rebounded off the floor and bounced around the room, zooming so close to his ear he could hear it sizzle. Before he could scramble to his feet, it smacked into the far wall and seeped into it like a drop of water soaking into a dry sponge. Holl ran to investigate. The wall was hot, but there wasn't a mark upon it. This was nothing he'd ever seen before, especially not from a barrel of beer.

"Look out!" he cried, dashing up the stairs. "There's a fireball on the loose!"

"Vhat is this?" the Master asked, rising from his seat beside Catra, who sat at the computer keyboard. The others rose from their places around the computer screen.

"I think I've seen what broke the jars," Holl explained. "Some kind of stray emanation. It was hot. It went into the cellar wall."

"What was it?" Enoch asked.

Holl shook his head, trying to get a clear picture in his mind. "I don't know. Some force."

"In the walls?" asked Aylmer. "Vhere did it go?"

As he said that, the computer screen went dark. Dola and Borget hurried over to see what was wrong.

"The electricity is gone," the boy said, looking up with concern. He grabbed a lantern and crawled underneath the table. "The wire is intact, but there is no power."

Holl saw a ring of orange hiss along the cable. He jumped forward, grabbing the children by any part he could reach, and yanked them free just before the ball of flame poured out of the server.

The Master recovered his wits sooner than the others. He clapped his hands over the sides of the white box. Fire flew out from it, zipping away along the many wires. Bracey threw his arms around the monitor and CPU as his brother Aylmer flung himself across the keyboard to protect it. The flames doubled back upon themselves like a snake in a tunnel. Finding that they could not go back the way they'd come, they boiled up into the air, collecting into a roiling, crackling, red-yellow mass.

Several of the Folk who were talented with controlling fire converged on it, hands outstretched. It bounded up toward the ceiling, ricocheted, and flew towards the fuse box. Borget was nearest. Determination steeled his young face. He put himself in between the box and the ball of fire.

"Oh, no, you don't," Holl cried, concentrating on the charm for snuffing out flame. Just before the fireball reached the boy, Holl flung himself in front of it. It struck him full in the chest. Holl staggered backwards, gasping, heat scorching the front of his torso and the cold of the steel fuse box burning his back. The floor slapped him in the backside. He'd slid down the wall without ever feeling his legs collapse.

"Uncle!" Borget cried, crawling to his side.

"Help him!" Rose cried, running over.

Holl waved her away, getting to his feet on his own. "I'm all right," he said.

"I'll get Maura," Marcy said, starting toward the door.

"No!" Holl pleaded. "There's no need to disturb her. I am fine. Is the computer all right?"

Borget scrambled to his feet. He and Dola went over to the cabinet and searched the cables and components inch by inch.

Rose gestured for someone to bring her a lamp. "Let me see," she insisted, holding Holl by the shoulder. She bent to inspect the front of his shirt. "It feels a trifle crisp, but not burned. You did vell vith the dampening charm."

"I didn't use it," Holl said. "It didn't burn me."

"What *was* it?" Curran demanded.

"I thought I saw eyes in the midst of the flame," Olanda insisted.

"It acted with intelligence," Enoch said.

"I perceived only a potential instinct for survival," his father disagreed. "I vould be pressed to insist upon intelligence." The two of them faced one another, looking profoundly alike in spite of the differences in hair color and age.

Dola piped up. "Where did it go?"

"Not into this boy," Rose said, standing up and slapping Holl on the shoulder. "It just disappeared."

"It's in the house," Candlepat said, shivering as she looked around the ceiling.

"We must root it out and prefent anything like it from happening again," Aylmer said. "Ve vill increase the protections around the house. This proofs ve haf not adequate safeguards."

"This could be kickback from the spell we already have around this place," Holl said. "Keith Doyle remarked upon it himself. We are pouring so much energy into this area that it is almost certain to rebound upon us. I think we may have created our own monster."

But no one listened to him. They were already arguing about the best way to reinforce the charm of protection. Enoch glanced at him over the crowd and shook his head. Holl gave up trying to get their attention. His chest hurt. It felt as though someone had struck him with a battering ram. Maura had a draught that would help him sleep. He pushed open the kitchen door.

"Got it!" Borget crowed, triumphantly. Behind Holl, the computer sang to life. He stepped out into the night.

Chapter 11

"I'll go out and get breakfast," Keith insisted, for the fourth or fifth time. "Thanks for asking me, but I can find something. Really." The kitchen was full of cooks, yet nothing was getting cooked, except tempers. He tried to catch Keva's eye, but she wasn't looking at him or anyone else. Holl, head propped up on his palm, sat beside him, looking as though he hadn't slept much. Keith's cheerful queries about how everyone had slept had been met with uneasy glances or glares.

"Stay," Maura said, laying a hand on his arm. She was the only one who didn't seem to be involved in whatever was eating everybody else, but he could see worry in her eyes, and did not want to add to it. He wondered if it was about him. Even Dola didn't meet his eyes, concentrating on playing with baby Asrai. Maybe Holl had caught flak for letting Keith stay. Despite the expense he'd better find a place of his own. "It's all right."

"No, really," Keith said. "I've got to get to class by nine. Thanks." He started to rise from the bench at the long table. Several of the Folk hurried over to pull him back down to his seat.

"Wait," Dennet said, his kindly eyes pleading. "It will be ready soon."

Keith waited, but his invisible whiskers were twitching with curiosity.

A tapping came at the back door. Everybody turned to look. Diane leaned in, smiling.

"Morning, everyone!" she said. Keith sprang to greet her. "Hi," he said. "This is a surprise."

She smiled impishly. "I've come to drive you to class."

"That's great of you, but my car's okay."

"No, I want to," Diane insisted. "You've done all this driving. Besides," she added, lowering her head so her blue-green eyes glinted like jewels through her long eyelashes, "I want to have you at my mercy."

Keith grinned. "Yes, ma'am." He went for his backpack, which he'd stowed under the table next to the server.

"What about your breakfast?" asked Laniora, a fellow student in the Master's class. "The eggs are nearly done."

"Well..." Keith began, torn between hunger and escaping from the tension in the house. "Diane's here, and everything."

"I wasn't trying to invite myself for a meal," Diane said, with hope that turned into dismay as she watched them bustle around her. She was surprised that the Folk didn't at once invite her to sit down. She looked at Keith with alarm.

The telephone rang, making everyone jump. Dennet seized it.

"Who is calling?" he asked. "No, we do not wish to cable service. I have told you many times: the installer has never come, because we don't want him. No, you may not send a representative to see!" Dennet cradled the phone with a bang, then looked surprised at the force of his action. "I apologize," he told the Big students. "They have been relentless."

"Do you want me to go to the office and tell them to lay off?" Keith asked. "I think I've seen it right near campus."

"Thank you, no," Dennet said, though his face was pale. "It is just one of many unwanted calls. Whether our number is unlisted or no, they always seem to find us. It is disturbing."

"Welcome to modern technology," Diane said, with a snort.

"And do you not care for the tools of convenience?" Laniora asked, challenging her. If there was someone you could call a militant Progressive, Keith thought, she was one. Diane was taken aback.

"No, I mean, there's...I get all sorts of calls I don't want, too. Everyone does."

"We are not everybody," Keva said. "I'd rip the cord fro' the wall if that'd stop the interruptions." Pointedly, she looked at Keith and Diane.

"Well, I'm really sorry to intrude," Diane said, stung. "I've got to be at work by nine." She tossed her hair back defiantly, glared at Keith. "Are you coming?" She strode out, head held high, not looking back.

"Uh, yeah, I'd better not be late. Um, thanks for break-fast," Keith said, hurrying to pick up his backpack. He ran out the door behind Diane.

"I've never been so embarrassed," Diane said, leaning over the wheel of her car as she zoomed down the hill and up out onto the road. "What's with them?"

"I don't know," Keith said, trying not to stomp on an imagi-nary brake on his side of the car as they skimmed around cor-ners, narrowly missing farm equipment, mailboxes and squir-rels that hesitated on the narrow pavement for one breathless, heartstopping second before hightailing it into the nearest tree. "They've been like this since I got up, snapping at each other, forgetting things. They're not usually like this. They didn't mean to make you feel unwelcome. You know that."

"I can't help it," she said. Keith leaned over to put his arm around her. She froze. Quickly, he pulled back. Diane turned to him, her eyes blazing. "I've never felt comfortable with them. Every time I go over there, I feel like I am being checked out by a zillion relatives, and they're all looking out for *you*. Just you."

"That's not true," Keith said, very gently. "They love you, too. They care about you. You know that."

"No. They're your thing, not mine. I don't know why you have to spend so much time with them when you could be with me. I miss you so much!"

Keith thought desperately, trying to come up with a joke to defuse the moment. "I'm not used to being fought over. Hey, slow down and let me enjoy it for a second."

For answer, she stepped hard on the accelerator, until the little white car skimmed over the top of a hill. It launched into space for a moment, coming down hard on a patch of gravel.

"You haven't talked to me. I hardly know what you're do-ing all week," Diane said. "Do you think I would tell anyone if you didn't want me to?"

"I had to sign a confidentiality agreement," Keith said. "I had no choice."

"But you told *them*, didn't you?"

"That was different," Keith said.

"Different *how*?"

"Pull over. Come on, please? You're scaring me." Pretending terror, he clenched his teeth and bugged out his eyes. He leaned over and clutched the dashboard with both hands. He held on until Diane screeched to a halt at a stop sign. She pulled over onto the gravel shoulder, her hands clenched, her face contorted between tears and laughter.

"I'm sorry," she said. "I don't know what got into me. I do love them, but I love you more."

Keith scooted over, oblivious of the jab in the ribs he got from the emergency brake handle, and put his arms around her. "It's okay," he said, as they sat just leaning on one another. Diane let out a sigh, and her body relaxed. "They're having a bad day, and it's catching."

"It's whatever I had to drive through to get onto their property, too," Diane said, gesturing toward her ears with a vague hand. "It's not like it was in the library. It feels as though I'm coming into an armed camp. I feel better now, but I don't think it was me. Something back there made me want to run screaming."

"You're right," Keith agreed. "It's bad. No one is telling me what's up."

"And the famous Doyle Snoop System isn't working?"

Keith waggled his eyebrows at her. "It will, my dear. I'm just giving them a chance to twist themselves into a rope of their own making."

"*That* didn't make any sense."

"I know," Keith said, shifting back into his seat and letting out a mighty yawn. "I'm not really awake yet. I slept like a log. It'll take me another century or two until I can stretch out my roots."

"*You* need coffee," Diane said, definitely, and put the car into drive.

They stopped for a bite of breakfast before Diane dropped him off in front of Midwestern's business school. Keith took his coffee in with him, prepared to dump the cup if he had to, but several of the other fifty or sixty students in the airy lecture hall were clutching their own caffeine wake-ups. They needed it. The teacher in Business Management, Professor Larsen, a lanky, fast-moving man with cavernous eyebrow ridges above round blue eyes, spoke rapidly and seldom repeated himself. Because of his schedule change Keith had missed the first Saturday class. It took him a while to catch onto Larsen's style. Once he did, he found the class stimulating but exhausting.

Graduate classes were offered in a format more oriented toward peers than students. The lectures were long, but Larsen gave the class a chance to respond to the topics he covered. When the discussion flagged, the professor tossed out a challenge to the group, demanding they learn to think about each business problem from several angles. Suggestions and arguments flew too fast for manual note-taking. Keith vowed to bring a tape recorder the following week.

A brief lunch break was followed by the second three-hour course, Franchise Organization, taught by an Asian woman, Dr. Li. Slim, compact and dark-haired, she was Larsen's physical opposite, but his match in lecture delivery. By the time Diane came for Keith at 4:00, his fingers were numb.

"Now, you see," he told her, as they drove off campus. "If I had Doris, I could have typed all my notes, or recorded the teachers to transcribe later. And hey! If I used Dunn's software, the notes could transcribe themselves!" Keith threw his arms behind his head. "Yeah. That'd be great."

"Terrific," Diane said. "And if you could get the computer to organize your notes into thesis form there'd be no need for you to go to class yourself."

"Hmmmm…" Keith intoned, speculatively. "I wonder if the guys at Gadfly are open to suggestions… could I get a bonus for putting them together with Dunn?"

"All right," Diane announced. "I don't want to hear about Doris all day long. I'm beginning to think she's my rival."

Keith sat up at once. "Never! Don't you know you're my one true love?"

"Well," Diane said, "start acting like it."

Keith bowed as low as he could, considering the shoulder harness of the seat belt. "Your wish is my command."

She smiled, her skin glowing golden in the autumn sunlight. "That's what I like to hear."

They spent the rest of the day just driving around the central Illinois countryside, chatting and catching up on the news of the week, enjoying one another's company, and simply being together. Keith concentrated on going along at a leisurely pace, trying not to let the thoughts of homework, advertising, the unfinished essay for the Master or the Little Folks' worries interfere. It was a warm and lovely afternoon, the prelude to a happy weekend.

Sunday afternoon, they arrived back at the farm in time for the Elf Master's class. Keith realized Diane had been right: there was a palpable sense of ill-feeling in the air. And, he realized with dismay, they'd come into the middle of another argument.

"...If the young ones hadn't filled up the postcard for a free T-shirt—which is big enough to cover a mattress besides—we wouldn't be overrun now with unwanted offers," Ligan complained. He was the oldest of the Master's clan, a frail-looking male with a few pumpkin-colored streaks left in his thinning white hair and beard. "Givin' out the telephone number, as if they'd no one to consider but themselves!"

"We never wrote down the telephone number," Borget insisted. The small boy stood his ground in the face of the Conservatives.

"They've other ways of obtaining that information," Catra added. "Don't blame the child."

"Whose side are ye on?" Ligan demanded, rounding on the Archivist.

Keith grabbed Diane's arm and began to back out of the kitchen. Calla, Holl's mother, caught sight of them and waved them in. She gave them an apologetic smile. The Folk in the kitchen looked around at her gesture. They seemed surprised to see the two Big students behind them. They'd been so intent on their discussion that they hadn't heard them approach. That was *not* normal, Keith thought. His invisible whiskers were on full red alert.

He held up a disk. "I've got my essay," he said. "Can I use your printer?" Abashed at being caught fighting, most of the Folk cleared the kitchen.

"Of course you may," Catra said, grateful for an excuse to break up the discussion. She sprang to open up the cabinet and turn on the computer. Dola took the disk out of Keith's fingers and inserted it into the drive.

"You must have lunch with us before class begins," Calla said, hospitably. "The weather is so fine we're picnicking outside. You ought to have a decent meal under your belt before you go running back to Chicago." She took their arms and led them out of the house and around onto the grassy slope in between the house and the old barn.

Once he was outside, Keith wondered if he'd ever want to go inside again. The difference in atmosphere between the house and the yard was palpable. Everybody outside was smiling and relaxed. It was the house, he thought. He'd have to pull Holl aside for a private conversation. The Maven was on the far edge of the slope, turning sausages on a grill over a fire that belched clouds of smoke. If not then, Keith amended, perhaps later.

Different, too, was the elves' mood. They seemed far more relaxed and cheerful. Everyone crowded around him and Diane, greeting them and asking questions.

"Apologies, dear Diane, for the morning," Dennet said, drawing her toward a comfortable corner near the side of the house. "You caught us out of sorts earlier. A personal matter that should never have affected you. Never do we want you to feel you do not belong among us."

"Well, thanks," Diane said, mollified, with eyebrows raised toward Keith.

"There, you see?" Keith said.

A few of the volunteer cooks brought them food, and someone ran inside for an armload of pitchers. Keith found himself on the lawn with a cold drink and an audience as he described their Saturday afternoon out.

"I stopped by to see a few of the old clients," he said, answering Marm, who was thoughtfully carving the top knob of a beechwood cookie jar in between bites of his lunch. Keith got up off his back pocket and fished out a few crumpled papers, which he handed over. "Three of them gave me orders. You've got most of them using the fax or the Internet to send in orders, but they like seeing an actual person once in a while. Face-time is important. I'd be happy to stop by once in a while during the weekends. That is, when I have time," he added, meeting Diane's eyes.

"He's a born salesman," Diane said, half-teasing and half-proud. "He started talking about the empty spaces on the shelf and how good your items would look in those spaces. Before you knew it, they were throwing money at him."

"Just to make him quiet down and go away, no doubt," Enoch said, darkly. He sat at Marcy's feet at the foot of the porch steps.

"Probably," Keith agreed cheerfully.

Marm read over the papers, chewing. "Two of these are substantial," he said.

"Holiday orders," Enoch said, knowingly. "It's beginning already."

Tiron came to peer over Marm's shoulder and pulled down the edge of the first page with the tip of a forefinger. "Ah, these'll be easy to fill. Ye'll be able to deliver them next week, my word on it."

"Perhaps," said Candlepat, "but I wanted to work upon museum pieces and special orders."

"That would be good, too," Marm said, amiably.

"Well, we can't do both," Tiron insisted. Candlepat and Enoch immediately rounded upon him with their objections. Keith groaned. They were fighting again, but it sounded like the normal rivalry to him, not the uncomfortable acrimony of before. Marcy caught his eye and beckoned him over to where she was sitting. He and Diane tiptoed over.

"Anything on my problem?" Marcy asked, in a whisper.

Keith shook his head. "I dropped in on your father. I honestly don't think he heard me. He kept dodging the subject."

Marcy sighed. "That's the way he's been with me." Enoch took her hand firmly in his and squeezed it. She squeezed back.

"I'll go back," Keith promised. "Maybe I can take him to lunch where I can keep him away from other distractions, and really get his attention. I'll find some pretext. What do you think?"

"He likes you. He might think you...you're..." Marcy waved her hands helplessly.

"I'll make sure he knows what I'm there for," Keith said, "I mean, who. And why. I'm not Cyrano de Bergerac. I think it's a great idea for you to get married, and I understand completely that you want your family to go along with it. But look at it from your folks' point of view for a moment. I think they're kind of confused why you're not bringing them together. Your dad has probably got the idea that Enoch is a monster or something."

"Why would he think that?"

Keith looked from one woeful face to the other, struck by a blindingly bright flash of the obvious. "Because they've never seen him?"

Marcy's eyes dropped. "You're right. They haven't. My mother's been hinting like crazy. But I'm afraid if we go up there they'll reject us. I...won't be able to handle it. I'd be so hurt."

"Pictures don't have any feelings," Keith said, temptingly. "We could photograph Enoch. I'll take the photos up and sell your dad on him."

Marcy's dark blue eyes widened like saucers. "That's perfect."

"That's exactly the right thing," Diane said, eagerly. "If he brings pictures, your dad will see he has nothing to worry about."

"Right! It'll be just like a campaign," Keith said. "Present him in the best light, and they'll fall in love with him on sight. Hey, that rhymes! I could make a poster."

"None of your nonsense!" Enoch snapped. "I'm not a...a pair of shoes."

"Nope," Keith said. "More like a work of art." Enoch snorted.

"I think it's good idea," Marcy said, dropping down from her step until she was sitting beside him, her eyes pleading. "It means so much to me. I want them to like you. And I want them here for the wedding."

"Oh, all right, lass," Enoch said, relenting and putting an arm around her shoulders. "It's a hard adjustment to make, when we've been so careful not to let ourselves be photographed."

"I won't let the pictures out of my hands until they get to your folks," Keith promised solemnly. "Now, where do you want to take these pictures?" He glanced around the field. "The trouble with doing it outside is that there's no scale, and that's half of what we want to sell your folks on. I think we ought to take them at your workbench. We're not hiding your profession, we're bragging about it."

"If you say so," Enoch said. "Oh, but that's another thing that's been going wrong. The expensive digital camera has ceased to function. The Conservatives are taking it as another sign that technology is our downfall."

"Really?" Keith asked. "Where is it?"

Enoch led them into the workshop and pointed him toward a table in the middle of the room where odds and ends accumulated. He brushed off a light dusting of sawdust and took the camera out of its case.

"Yow!" Keith exclaimed, as it fell back to the table with a clatter. "It zapped me!"

"Oh, no," said Marcy. "Is it broken? Everyone's been so careful."

Keith looked it over carefully. "Oops, look at that: the battery hatch is jammed. That might be the cause of both problems." He flipped it open, tipped out the battery, blew dust off it, returned it to its place, then pushed the switch. With a musical hum, the camera warmed up. "How about that? No charge for the emergency repair."

Enoch glowered. "They'll be saying it's because you're one of the Big Folk that it works for you."

"C'mon," Keith said, "you don't believe that. Okay, sit down and work on something. Smile. Look natural."

But Enoch couldn't. Nervously, he took up a half-finished box and one of the yet-to-be-attached sides. Setting one of the sides at the proper angle, he concentrated on the charm that would join the pieces of wood as though they were cemented together. Keith, behind the camera, found himself scuttling around trying to capture Enoch's face with the lens.

"Smile!" Keith called. Enoch tried, but the smile faded and his brow furrowed as he got interested in what he was doing. "I'm not getting any good pictures. C'mon, Enoch, you're only supposed to *pretend* you're working."

The blackhaired elf frowned up into the lens. "This is unnatural," he said. "Pretend? Smile? You try it."

"No problem for me," Keith said, peering at him through the viewfinder. "I've had cameras shoved in my face from before I could hold my head up. Look, just sit still and smile. Hold something in your hand, if you want."

"I don't want to do this," Enoch said, starting to get up. But Marcy looked so sad that he sat down again. "Ah, well." He picked up the box and a chisel, holding them awkwardly in his hands, almost as though he had them by mistake. The chisel slipped out of his hand and clanked to the floor. Enoch bent to retrieve it just as the flash went off.

"Damn!" Keith exclaimed. He poked at the buttons on the back of the camera to erase the last five photos. "These aren't turning out very well. That last one was a blur."

"It'll be okay," Diane said. "Just sit tight a little longer, and we'll get a good one." But Enoch wasn't paying attention to her. He was looking over her shoulder. She turned around, and tugged on Keith's sleeve. He glanced up.

While they'd been trying to take pictures, the others had crept into the room to watch. Keith was embarrassed for Enoch's sake. What had begun as a simple task was turning into a spectacle.

"Hey," Keith called. "Look at the birdie!" Enoch dragged his attention woefully to him. Concentrating as hard as he could, he made an absurd little yellow bird appear on his shoulder and let it void, dripping white down his shirt front. Enoch grunted.

"Not bad," he said, pointing a finger at Keith. "Fine speed of enchantment and an even appearance, but can ye do nothing without that touch of foolishness?"

"You were just supposed to look at *me*," Keith said, sternly, "not criticize my bird."

The others tittered. Enoch rose from the bench.

"I've had enough," he said. Marcy rushed to him and laid her hand on his arm.

"Please," she said. "For me. Just one more time."

"I don't know what to do!" Enoch said, resentfully, sitting down again. "Look *natural*, this big fool says. How do you do that?"

Tay, in the midst of the crowd, caught Keith's eye and nodded toward the door. Keith nodded back. The white-haired elf slipped out for a moment. He came back in a few seconds, with Dola in tow.

"Let me help," the girl said, bustling importantly through the crowd. "I know what to do, uncle. I have done many photo shoots now." Marcy made way for her. She plumped down beside Enoch. "Pretend he's got to see all your front teeth." She opened her lips in an exaggerated smile. "Do you see? So, when I relax slightly, the camera sees a friendly look that it likes."

When she did it, it looked very pretty. When Enoch followed her example, he looked like a fox caught at bay. Keith took several shots, then brought the camera over to show him the results.

"How grim you look, uncle," Dola said, frankly. Enoch looked up at Keith, who nodded solemn agreement.

"Oh, aye?" Enoch asked, surprised, as he scrolled through the pictures, seeing one grimace after another. "I had no idea...do I look like that often?" he appealed to Marcy, as he handed the camera back to Keith. She bit her lip.

"Not very," she said at last, in a small voice. Enoch let out a sharp burst of laughter. He put his arm around her, pulling her cheek to cheek with him. "Lass, you're a poor liar."

Keith backed up and started snapping pictures again. Marcy dropped her head, looking sheepish. Enoch looked at her with a fond smile. She looked up into his eyes. They'd forgotten all about the crowd.

A few moments later, Keith interrupted them. "These'll do the trick," he said, waving the camera in the air. "Let's print 'em out!"

They took the camera inside and fed the memory stick to the computer's docking unit. The entire collection popped into sight on the screen. Keith sat down on the low stool in front of the keyboard and went through them, checking off the ones he wanted to use.

"See?" he said. "You actually look handsome in these."

"Well, thank you for a useless compliment," Enoch said sourly, watching over his shoulder. "No, I take that back. I appreciate the help. These are fine. You did well."

Keith examined the files critically. A few of the shots he'd taken at the beginning were good enough to use. The ones with Marcy were really sweet. You could tell how much those two were in love.

"Your folks won't be able to resist these," Keith assured her. She leaned down and kissed him on the forehead.

"Thank you, Keith. You're an angel."

Keith printed four images on each page. As they rolled out of the printer, one of the Folk cut them apart and set them in a neat stack. Enoch popped out the memory stick and put it back in the camera.

"You can save these on the hard drive," Keith said. "You have lots of spare memory."

Enoch shook his head. "We're doing that no longer. Not after what you've told us about the hungry program. We regret now that we were so free in sending images up and back to Ireland. We've removed all the others. Better not to keep them where they can be stolen all unawares."

"That's a good idea," Keith said, thinking of the man who was chasing him. His heart raced for a moment, wondering if anything that had been left on his hard drive during the robbery could have identified the Little Folk or led an outsider to their front door.

All the elves turned to look toward the front door. Within a few moments, the Big Folk could hear what they had heard: a car pulling in on the gravel drive.

"The others are here," the Elf Master said. "It is time for class."

After Keith had seen Diane off, he threw his bag and briefcase into the front seat of the Mustang and prepared to climb in after them. Catra emerged from the house, fingers ink-stained, followed by Holl and the Master.

"Keith Doyle, wait!" Catra offered him a sheet of paper.

"I have done my best to be brief but cordial," she said. "It contains a concise description of you and your home, so they know where and to whom to respond, and the way to come here for the party. I sent it to the Niall to check for continuity. In all our years apart, we've never hosted a gathering, so I was not certain of the proper words to use." She seemed anxious for approval.

"I'm sure it's fine," Keith said, surveying the graceful calligraphy with pleasure. "This is gorgeous, Catra. You're sure, now?" he said, looking into their eyes.

He didn't mean whether Catra was certain of the wording. If the Folk were giving him the text, it meant they'd decided that he could have his party. This was irrevocable. He knew it, and they knew it.

"We're sure," Holl said, his eyes gleaming with mischief. "If for no other reason than as a reward for getting Enoch to smile for five entire minutes on end. It'll be a memory we'll treasure forever."

Keith laughed. "Thanks. I'll accept under any circumstances." He studied the page. "Hmm. There's no way I can use a keyboard to input this into the ad. I'll have to scan it."

"I could have done that," Catra said, frowning.

"Oh! Well, if you can set it out in a square for me, so I don't have to cut and paste it, that'd be great."

"No trouble at all." She disappeared back into the house. He heard the printer warming up. In a few moments she returned and handed him a printout and a disk. "The paper is cleanly white, so it ought to do well for your purposes. If it will not do, the disk contains a jpeg."

"Thanks for this," Keith said, stowing the paper in his notebook for safety. "I'm really grateful for this, and for everything. Want anything from Chicago?"

"Not this time," the Master said. "Come and go vith our blessinks."

"Such as they are," Holl said under his breath, watching Keith's ancient car drive away. "The quality's really not worth handing on."

Chapter 12

Keith followed Paul Meier toward the boardroom.

"It's so different not being with the other interns," Keith said, glancing back over his shoulder at the door at the far end of the corridor. The current crop of students, two women and two men, watched them go with looks of open envy.

"Yeah, you're one of the big boys now," Paul said, giving Keith an avuncular slap on the back. "You can come and hang out with us in there anytime. You've got the kind of energy they're cranking. I'm too old to relate. Or so they say."

"Is that a real client, or something you thought up to keep them busy? A rock group called Skim?"

"Oh, they're real, all right," Paul said. "Nice bunch of guys. One really astonishing guitarist who maybe could grow up to be Eric Clapton, with an act of God. Good lyrics like Sting or the Moody Blues. Even tunes I can recognize, and I admit to owning Cole Porter albums."

"You're not *that* old," Keith said.

"No," Paul sighed, "but I miss melody. We had a group come to us, called themselves Pap Smear. What did they think, we were going to get out there and plaster the world with posters of gynecological exams? I told them to change their name and come back when they could play their own instruments. Bands have always had weird names, back to the beginning, but do they have to be obscene?"

"Some of them are pretty good in spite of their names," Keith said.

"Yeah, but admit it: kids are embarrassed to ask for albums by them. You know why they started putting condoms behind the counter in drugstores? People were shoplifting them because they were too embarrassed to ask. I bet the same thing happens in music stores. You're forcing little girls to go in and shop for the latest thing from Hole."

"Paul's on a rant again," said Dorothy, coming up between them and putting an arm through each of theirs.

"Damn straight," Paul said, allowing himself to be towed into the boardroom.

"Yeah, but it's our job," said Doug Constance, tagging along behind. He liked to get Paul going.

"All right," Paul said, trying to break loose to face Doug, but Dorothy held on. "Never mind the kids. What about their poor grandparents, who grew up in more polite times? I'm buying music for my nephew, who one minute ago was chanting along with Barney, and the next thing you know he's giving me a birthday list that has names like Rage Against the Machine and Popped Zits, for all I know. I can just imagine my mother having to go into the record store."

"And we're right in there writing ad copy so the kids will buy them, right?"

"Yeah," Paul sighed, sinking into his chair. "Right. I'm piling wood on the pyre around my own feet."

"You died in a good cause, man," said Rollin, who was waiting in the boardroom, propped up against the wall. "Our bottom line salutes you."

Suddenly inspired, Keith plastered an imaginary headline on the air with one hand. "'Skim: All of the music, none of the fat.'"

"Yeah." Paul chuckled. "Not bad. You want in on the brainstorming session?"

"Yeah!" Keith said. "If the group comes in to meet the staff, can I come and meet them?"

"Sure, kid."

Jennifer Schick, Gadfly's marketing director, arrived at that moment, followed by Teresa carrying a box from the coffee shop on the corner. She pushed a cup in front of Keith. He looked up at her in surprise. She gave him a shamefaced little smile. It was meant to be a peace offering from the team. He tasted it, then beamed at her. Sweet, but not enough to send him to the moon. She must have been watching him during the earlier sessions. He raised an eyebrow at the size of the cup. 'Short' meant short meetings. 'Medium' meant business as usual. A 'lofty' brew meant a long meeting had been scheduled.

"It's okay: it's half-caf," Janine told him. Keith pantomimed wiping sweat off his forehead.

"All right," Dorothy said, tapping a sheaf of papers on the table to square it. "We've got a lot of work to get done. Welcome, Jen. I think you're going to like what we've got for you. First, let's look at the storyboards for the commercials. Janine and Rollin have worked on the first one together. I think it'll give just the right play with a touch of whimsy. It makes use of as many features as we could work in. And for music..."

With a dramatic flourish, Dorothy reached for the T-shaped control in the center of the table. The lights dimmed, the screen at the front of the room descended, and the agency's million-dollar multimedia system took over.

To the tune of the 60's hit, "Bend Me, Shape Me," the Origami did a little boogie across the screen, twisting into several configurations. Behind it, wrapping around it and flowing like draped silk caressing it were game graphics, stock ticker numbers, obvious pager messages, GPS instructions, as a mellifluous man's voice said, "Play a game. Write a memo. Keep in touch. Chart your course. Be productive. Have fun." The camera zoomed in on the screen to show a close-up of a young man's face, obviously the user taking movies of himself, followed by a quick glimpse of what looked like regular TV programming. The unit folded itself up, and stuck itself into the pocket of the young man's polo shirt. "Origami. The new perpetual motion machine from Gadfly."

"Nice work, Rollin and Janine," Jennifer said, applauding. "Fun."

"A lot of people have been getting the 60's and 70's angle," Dorothy said, encouragingly. "We couldn't resist it. Kids will like it because it's bouncy, and people who grew up at that time will associate it with their youth. Excuse the jerkiness of the images. That was just a computer-animated mockup, not the way the commercial will look when it's finished. That'll be up to the production house, but I promise you we keep a close eye on their work."

"I understand. Sure. Can we get the rights to the song?"

Doug Constance cleared his throat. "Yes. We've priced it out."

"Excellent!"

"This'll play on CNN as well as WB," Rollin said. "Even the stuffy shows like Meet the Press are trying to shed the gray-suit image. Also, they *are* the Boomers who grew up with the song."

"Terrific. Politicians try so hard to look net-savvy these days." Jennifer grinned. "Kind of sad, really, but that keeps 'em buying our product. Nice work."

"The demographics for CNNfn, Wall Street Week and Headline News are at the bottom," Paul pointed out helpfully. "There's a print ad for *Wall Street Journal* and *The New York Times* that ties in."

One by one, Dorothy demonstrated PDQ's work in progress for the marketing director. The box and inserts were displayed and approved. Jennifer went over each graphic and advertisement with care. She made notes to herself with a stylus on the screen of an Origami unit that fit into a pocket of her purse. Keith watched her with envy rising in his heart. He *had* to have one.

Quarter-page ads, full-page ads, catalog inserts for Sharper Image, Brookstone's, Amazon.com and the major department stores were examined and passed or sent back for changes. Jennifer laughed over the choice of eight proposed logos.

"I can't call this decision," she said. "Theo would go on strike if I made this choice unilaterally. Can we come in next week for it?"

"Sure," Dorothy said. "Since you want to start your big push for Christmas buying, the big launch will be the day after Halloween. We've got time."

It couldn't have been the caffeine that kept Keith twitching until Dorothy got to the bottom of the stack of layouts, to the ad with his hidden invitation. He desperately wanted Gadfly to like his work. He really believed in the product. Paul had always said it helped if you could fake it, but his admiration of Gadfly's little computer was completely genuine. If only he could have one. He wanted an Origami for his very own with a visceral yearning that knotted his stomach muscles, but more importantly for now, he wanted to get his party invitation sent out around the world. The ad had undergone dozens of changes over the past couple of weeks, as every department in the agency had had its say, but the basic idea remained intact, and so had the text on the screen. Jennifer Schick could sink his hopes with a single word.

Let it pass, he pleaded mentally. *Let her like it!*

"Here's the final layout of the poster advertisement." Dorothy handed around an oversized sheet to each person at the table. "None of this leaves this room, of course. I get it all back when we're finished."

Jennifer nodded. "So far we've managed to keep the project under wraps, but I don't know how long we can do it. Rumors are starting to fly that we've got something new. Buzz on the 'Net is that we're coming out with a compact PDA, but they're missing the big news items. No one knows about the extended-life power supply or the Firewire compatibility. And no one's guessed that the keyboard and CD player are all part of the same unit."

"Well, the second these go out it'll be big news all over the world," Dorothy said. "I've got a press release on my hard drive ready to go to the PR people just before the ad hits. We'll be targeting techno-news on CNN, the web and all the other media services. They'll want interviews."

"We're ready for 'em," Ms. Schick, sitting back with a satisfied smirk. She held up her copy of the poster and gave it the same careful scrutiny as she'd given all of the other pieces. Keith was relieved to see that the wording in the mockup of the Origami remained unchanged. He checked his crib sheet from Holl, every letter in place, and smiled at Dorothy.

"Good headline," said Jennifer Schick, nodding approvingly. "'One of Everything.' I like it. Several meanings all in one slogan. Everyone all over the office has been quoting it. We might like that on tote bags for the Consumer Electronics Show."

"Attaboy, Keith," Paul said, slapping him on the shoulder. "Jennifer, we can get you a price from fulfillment companies, unless you have one you are already using."

"Bring 'em on," she said. "We've got lots of money for giveaways. Let everybody carry our ad around." Paul made a note on his pad.

"The campaign will go out on trial in nine cities," Dorothy said, reading from a list, "including four in Europe: London, Berlin, Amsterdam and Paris. We're not ready to go head-to-head in Helsinki yet against the Nokia monopoly—maybe in a couple of weeks if the first trials go well. We're prepared to tweak as needed. Bus wraps, billboards, hoardings, ads in trains. No one's going to open a newspaper without seeing an Origami. And for those who don't read newspapers, we're preparing a blitz on the Internet. We've got banners going out over the lead week's top ten websites and all the major search engines' home pages. Our page is ready to launch. All it takes is your approval to push the button."

"Looks hot," Schick said, nodding over it. "I'm just curious, by the way: what's this stuff on the screen?"

Paul leaned over to glance where she was pointing. "Dummy copy. We use it to indicate language. Nothing special."

"Does it mean anything? Are we insulting people in Armenian? Is it 'screw you' in Moldavian?"

"Uh," Keith said, shifting to sit up straighter, "no. It's, er, a poem in another language. An ancient language. I thought it looked good. Everyone's always using that Latin cutout stuff. I wanted this to be different. Let the customers know it can communicate in any language."

"We could use Japanese," Janine said.

"That won't fly in every country," Paul said, shaking his head. "What about China? That's a big market and getting bigger. They prefer English."

"And the French prefer French," argued Janine. "And the Germans prefer German."

"We've already got to pay for translations for the overlay," Doug said. "What's the difference?"

"The difference," Dorothy said, patiently, "is that the text is included in a graphic, not by itself. Changing the screen means changing the image entirely to get the shadows and glare spots on the plastic screen set right. They have to appear to lie on top of the text, not under it. This is okay. It won't distract anyone from looking at the image, and it won't stir up national prejudices because even if they can translate it; it's something from an ancient culture. God forbid someone might get it and think we're intellectuals."

"Good compromise?" Paul asked, glancing around the table.

"Okay with me," Doug said.

"I like it," Schick said, holding the text this way and that as if it would help her understand it. "It's a poem, you say?"

"Yeah," Keith said. "A welcoming poem. Blank verse."

"Cool."

"Good?" Dorothy asked, looking at the other two copy-writers.

"Sure," Rollin said. He was still smarting a little about losing the poster to Keith. Not wanting to rub in his success because he needed the good will of the permanent staff, Keith offered Rollin a friendly, sympathetic look. Janine elbowed Rollin heartily in the ribs until he gave Keith a grudging smile. Crisis averted. Keith was very pleased: he'd gotten what he wanted, three times over.

"Good," Dorothy said. "Everybody better hand me back the sheets. Except you, Jennifer," she added. "You can take yours back with you."

Alarmed, Jennifer held up her hands. "No, thank you. I'd forget my head if it wasn't glued on. I don't want to carry anything I can lose. Too much is riding on keeping this all under wraps. E-mail everything to Bill. He'll give you final approval. I'll tell him it's got mine."

"Anything else?" Paul asked, putting both hands on the table?

"Uh," Keith said, uneasily, "what's the price of the...the Origami going to be, when it comes out?"

"About $1,500 to $1,800," Jen Schick said.

"Ouch!" Rollin said, falling back against his chair with his hands clasped over his heart.

"I know it's a shocker," she offered, apologetically, "but it's a complete palmtop computer full of new technology. We're hoping the price will drop rapidly in the first two years, but we've got to make back our R&D. Sorry."

"Oh," Keith said, in a small voice. So much for Doris becoming his soon. It cost just about the same as an engagement ring, and that took priority in his life. Maybe he could start a second savings plan to buy an Origami. There was a trickle left from his wages and the money he was putting by for his party.

Jen Schick noticed the long faces all around the table. "Hang in there for the Mark Two. It won't have a keyboard, so it ought to be a lot cheaper."

Keith shook his head. His heart belonged to Doris. No other pocket computer would do.

Chapter 13

Stefan looked up at the office building on La Salle Street, and scratched his head. "This place? It does not look like a wizard's stronghold."

"What are you expecting?" Beach said testily. "A castle with glowing turrets? This is modern America. If Ming says that a transmission containing the lingo was sent from here, that's all it is. We don't know if it originated from here, or if it's a waystation between two points that haven't been detected."

"How do we find that out?"

"We talk to someone," Beach said. "We ask questions."

He'd been keeping a close eye on the Perkins Delaney Queen agency all day. God, American security was lax. They had locks on the doors, but they let you in on any pretext whatsoever. The receptionist had admitted Beach into the PDQ building at 8:00 A.M. because he claimed he had a delivery for one of the names on the personnel list provided for his convenience in the lobby. She'd paid little attention to him thereafter. If he'd been serious about destroying their business the bomb squad would have been picking up pieces, and no one would have connected it to the man in the natty gray suit who'd only stopped in for a moment and strolled casually out afterwards. Nothing about the suite of offices suggested that anything remotely mysterious was going on inside, but Beach knew better.

"Two weeks ago," Stefan exclaimed. "What we want may have gone away from here by now. The program should work faster than that."

"You fool, Omnivore has to sort through billions of messages every day," Beach snapped. "The miracle is that we got word this fast. It's only dredged up the image. It'll take time to resurrect the whole of the message it was inserted into."

Stefan frowned. "Then how did we find the location so quickly?"

Beach grinned like a death's head. "Because Perkins Delaney Queen most obligingly put their address in the lower corner of the page."

He had the sheet containing the sample of mysterious typography folded up in his inside breast pocket. It had been inserted into the midst of a graphic, presumably being sent from one business to another—but Beach wasn't that naïve. Both addresses had to be covers for something else of a higher level. Ming had been very excited about the find. A healthy dollop of text, in a combination, the linguists had assured Beach, were in the same language, but this particular combination of words had not been seen before. They had no record of similar phrasing, not even in the precious documents locked up in the stronghold in Eastern Europe. Therefore, it was new. And it was in the midst of an advertising layout, where nearly everyone would overlook it, except the person or persons it was meant for. Therefore, someone at the agency knew this lingo. Follow the lingo, he thought, and you find the source.

Someone in there knew what it meant. The place looked so very innocent. He could only guess what secret government machinations were going on inside. The Americans, with their vast resources, didn't need the further advantage of magic. *He* wanted it. It rightfully belonged to the disenfranchised of the world. He needed an inside contact. Beach was prepared to go to any lengths: threats, bribery, blackmail. All he needed was one vulnerable employee.

He'd counted almost a hundred men and women entering the building in the morning. Most of them did not leave the building at lunchtime. A privileged-looking few in executive-level clothing left in clusters or taxis in the early afternoon. Several food-delivery services entered, carrying white cardboard boxes or bags to feed the rest. But one boy, a slim young man with red hair, had emerged onto the pavement, walked to the nearest east-west street and hopped a bus going east. Leaving instructions for his enforcers to keep watch on the agency,

Beach hailed a taxi to follow him. Stefan and one of the men took the cab that pulled up behind.

When the bus reached the lakefront, the lad swung out, hiked into the big park and found himself a seat by the fountain. Excellent. The sound of the water would cover their…negotiations. Beach gave him a chance to get settled. He stood admiring beds of gold and bronze asters planted throughout the huge lakefront park, pretending that he was an ordinary tourist. Though his expression was bland, inside he was tense with anticipation. He waited a while longer, then approached.

Keith sat on the bench and stared out at the faint gray-blue line of Lake Michigan. The bright sun glinted off the sails of the boats nipping in and out of the breakwater past the end of Navy Pier. Keith began to wonder if he'd made a mistake coming to Grant Park to study. There were too many distractions in a nice day like this. His eye followed sailboats out through the breakwater. Birds circled above his head, calling for a handout. People milled around Buckingham Fountain, enjoying the nice weather, wondering how long it would be until fall kicked in. With a mixture of pleasure and guilt Keith closed his textbook on his finger to take in the scene. He should have taken Paul Meier up on his offer of a meeting room at PDQ. How could you think about administration issues when lake gulls were crying, and children were clamoring at their parents to let them wade in the fountain? Keith grinned, remembering countless times when his father had had to haul him and his four siblings out of the water. That was before the city had freshened up the statuary and relined the pools under the dancing water. Buckingham looked amazing now. Chicago had an inferiority complex next to the rest of the world, but in Keith's opinion it had nothing to worry about. It was a serious city, deserving of its rating as one of the great places. Okay; so it wasn't as old as London, or as busy as New York, but it had an identity with charm and style.

"I'm writing copy again," he said, with a deprecating grin at his own flights of fancy. He opened the textbook, but his mind refused to settle down. The place was so alive. It would be a great spot to practice magic. He'd been working on making a little flame appear, real fire. Such a display would be small potatoes to the elves, but he was proud of it. How would it be, he thought, if he created a tossing, dancing fire right here on the palm of his hand, that would emulate the spray of the fountain? Holl would probably tell him not to be so frivolous. Maybe. The blond elf was capable of his own fanciful acts.

Keith was dismayed that Holl had backed out on his promise to come up to Chicago for a visit. The two of them had promised Maura a few days of doing touristy things, like seeing the Art Institute and the museums, and maybe going to a play one evening. She was shy about coming out among Big people, but with Keith and Holl both looking after her she ought to be fine. Dola could reassure her, but the older ones never listened to the younger ones, even when they were right. Some things were the same no matter how tall a person was. Keith had also been counting on the privacy to ask about what had been eating Holl since before the school year began. The young elf had avoided any and all private chats while he was down at the farm on weekends. Keith hoped it wasn't something *he'd* done.

He'd have to turn on the charm. Christmas shopping wasn't all that far away. Holl liked to indulge Maura. She rarely asked for anything, and she took such pleasure in small favors. She'd talked longingly about seeing the sights. How could Holl say no? The holly and ornaments would be up the day after Halloween. Keith brightened. That was the day the Origami ads would debut, and Keith could show off what he'd been doing. Except for asking for their help on the poster, he'd kept the rest of his work secret.

If they did come he'd have to move home to his parents' for a couple of days. Space in the Crash Site was already at a premium, what with three active men occupying a small apartment with one bath. There'd be no privacy for Maura. Keith's folks had offered their hospitality. They liked the Little Ones. Keith was surprised how well his parents took in their stride the presence of mythological beings occasionally occupying their guest room. Of course, they'd been raised on *The Lord of the Rings*. Maybe he should be surprised that it took an *extra* generation to discover the Little Folk.

Better buckle down to the wonders of Entrepreneurship. There was a test on Saturday.

The bench creaked when Beach sat down. The boy wriggled to a more comfortable position as the boards under his bottom shifted. Amazing that, after what he considered an unforgivable miss by Maria, good old technology managed to pin down a source of the lingo almost under their noses. She must have been wrong all along about the downstate location. Omnivore was a godsend. If the boy had any connection to his goal, he would discover it.

"Nice day," he said. The boy glanced up, surprised, and gave him a pleasant grin, stranger to stranger. He had clear, hazel eyes that picked up the color of the trees. Guileless. A perfect target.

"Yeah. Beautiful weather." The boy went back to his book.

"What's the name of this fountain?" Beach asked.

"Buckingham," the redheaded boy said, making brief eye contact, still friendly. "Named after some politician, I think." His eyes dropped back to the page again.

Beach waited for a moment.

"Good view."

Eyes up. "Yeah." Down.

"What do you know about this?" Beach took the graphic image from his pocket and shoved it across the bench toward the youth.

Up. Glance at the paper. Down. Pause.

The boy's eyes came up again, this time meeting Beach's gaze squarely, mouth agape, his narrow, freckled face pale with alarm.

"What can you tell me about this?" Beach pressed, leaning closer to the young man. "What?"

"Nothing!" he sputtered, springing to his feet. He snatched up his papers and books in his arms. Beach stood up, but by then the young man was sprinting across the pavilion.

Stefan appeared from his place of concealment and folded his arms, nodded significantly toward the disappearing youth. Beach shook his head. No, there was no reason to detain the young man. The fact that he fled from Beach when confronted with the words meant he had seen them before. It was not a mistake. PDQ knew something about the lingo. The agency must be the front for a deep-cover operation. *Good camouflage*, Beach thought. He'd have to remember that some time when he needed to establish an organization that no one would question. Now, to find out more about PDQ, and just how much they were concealing.

How could that man have a copy of the Origami ad? Keith thought, his heart pounding as he raced back toward PDQ. The top secret file, for which he'd signed a confidentiality agreement, promised solemnly he wouldn't reveal to a single human being, a complete stranger shoves into his face right there in the middle of the park. And not only that, one of the very same ads *he'd* worked on. How could the man have gotten hold of it?

"How could this happen?" Dorothy asked, glaring at Keith, who told his story in between gasps for air. She had dragged him and Paul Meier into her office and locked the door. "Those Origami ads are highly confidential material! It had to go out of here in someone's pocket." Her eyes blazed.

"Not me, I swear," Keith said, holding his hands up in surrender.

"Then, *who?*" Dorothy demanded.

"Now, now," Paul said, taking hold of her shoulders. "It's not Keith's fault. It's a good thing that he brought it to us. We might never have found out until it made the papers in the morning. What did the guy want, Keith? Did you recognize him?"

"No," Keith said. "I've never seen him before, anywhere. He had a husky voice, and some kind of accent. All he said was 'What can you tell me about this?' I babbled out something like 'I don't know,' and got away from him as soon as I could. I *didn't* say anything about the project."

"Good for you. All right." Paul sighed and leaned against the door. "We're going to have to tell Jason. He's got to decide what to tell the client."

"The leak could be on the Gadfly end, too," Dorothy said. "They had to approve the layout. It was transmitted to their home office."

Keith shook his head. "It couldn't be. This was the new ad, with the dummy copy in place and the new headline."

"It's not likely to be Gadfly anyhow," Paul said reasonably, though his face was grim. "Why would they shoot themselves in the foot? It's only a couple of weeks until this ad premieres."

"Then that means it's us," Dorothy said, woefully. "We've got a leak or a mole. This is bad. I...I don't know what to tell Jason. This is my first big account!"

"I'll take care of it," Paul promised.

He left, closing the door of Dorothy's office behind him. Dorothy flopped down in her chair and stared at the wall in front of her. Keith had recovered his breath.

"What can I do?" he asked. Dorothy seemed to recall he was there. She sat up, reasserting her professionalism, but Keith could tell how shaken she was.

"Work on catalog copy for the Origami," she said. "We still need blurbs for the Sharper Image and the e-shopping outlets. And nothing leaves this room, you understand me?" she asked, putting a finger under Keith's nose. Then, she turned her back on him, her head drooping. Keith reached out, setting a reassuring hand on her arm, but she shook him off. After a moment, she settled down and began to work on the piles of paper overflowing her desk. Nothing he could say or do could console her. This could be the ruin of months of work.

Keith was disconsolate, too. He sat at his little table, doodling on his legal pad, trying to drag his mind away from the encounter in the park. He kept wondering if he could have done anything differently. It was unfair to blame him for the leak—he would *not* have broken confidentiality. Then he remembered: he had shown the advertisement, the very same advertisement, to the elves. But they'd never let anyone else see it. Why would they? But the fact that he *had* let someone else see the top-secret ad made it hard for him to deny that it was possible he was to blame. He moped through the hours remaining, unable to concentrate. By the time the day came to a merciful end, he hadn't produced any useful ideas, but he'd nearly worn himself out feeling guilty.

Word of the leak hadn't spread through the company yet. On his way out, people said goodnight to him in exactly the same friendly way they'd said good morning. Keith made for the elevators, eager to get home so he could do some serious thinking in private.

"Look, you're wanted, man," Cary, the keyliner, gave Keith a poke in the ribs. Following his glance, Keith spotted Paul Meier standing in the doorway of his office. The executive beckoned him over and pulled him just inside, out of earshot of passersby.

"How bad is it?" Keith asked.

"I won't lie," Paul said, frankly. "The brass is upset. We've got a meeting with them in the morning. Go home and try to think of anything you can about the man you saw. If you see him again, call me right away." He gave Keith a small slip of paper. "Here's my cell phone number and my home number. I know it's not your fault, but I'm not the one you have to convince."

"Paul, I swear…"

"Forget it. Go home." Paul slapped him on the back. "We'll defend your honor in the morning."

"Yo?" Dunn called from the main bedroom when Keith opened the door of the Crash Site. "Who's there?"

"Me," Keith called back. The apartment door opened into a small area wider than a corridor yet narrower than a foyer. The building was old, so the most generous dimension of any room was its height. The apartment had graciously high ceilings framed with mahogany-stained molding and white plastered walls. Their simplicity appealed to Keith not only for their elegance but as being less difficult to keep clean, a real consideration with three twenty-something men in residence.

The apartment was a sprawl of rooms, most of which had come to be used for other purposes than those for which they'd been built. To the left of the foyer were the small living and dining rooms, the latter of which overlooked the street. Beyond it lay the kitchen and a small room that used to be a scullery or maid's quarters. Pat, who needed to practice his lines at all hours, lived there. To the right was the one and only bathroom, tiled and possessed of an enormous claw-foot tub an elephant could swim in, and thick-walled white-enameled sink and toilet that looked as though they had been made by Fisher-Price for a life-size dollhouse. Beyond the bathroom, Dunn's and Keith's rooms were back to back. Keith's, the smallest habitable bedroom, had originally been a nursery, which had become a walk-in closet. Dunn had set it up for use as a home office, until Keith had pleaded for shelter. Now all the computer equipment was crowded into the master bedroom, but the prior arrangement meant Keith had a jacks for the house telephone and modem lines already installed when he moved in. His furniture, bed, desk and dresser, left him with almost no room to walk, so unless he was working on his computer or sleeping, he spent little time in the bedroom. It wasn't a perfect situation, but it was better than most alternatives, and the three men knew each other well enough to avoid stepping on one another's toes.

Dunn emerged from his room, strutting like a symphony conductor. "Just so you know, I am The Man. I have debugged ten and a half million lines of code, and it is beautiful."

"Congratulations," Keith said. He hooked the strap of his briefcase over the back of a chair, shifted a pile of unfolded laundry and threw himself on the couch. "That is a heck of a lot of hard work."

Dunn looked at him with eyebrows raised high on his forehead. "That's not the level of enthusiasm I'm looking for, but I'll take it. Sit down and have some cold Chinese takeout and tell me what's bugging *you*."

Keith told him the story of the man who approached him with the confidential ad layout, without going into details about the product. "I don't know where he got the ad from.

It's impossible that anyone could have seen it. Nobody out-side the agency or the client has. It'd be all over the Net if word had gotten out." The full force of that thought hit him, and he paled. "Or it could be. Oh, my God."

"Does PDQ send any of their ads by e-mail?" Dunn asked.

"Well, yeah. All the time. It saves them a lot of time and messenger fees. But they use a very sophisticated encryption program. It's suppposed to be foolproof. It cost them thou-sands."

"Money can't promise smarts." Dunn's smooth forehead wrinkled into three horizontal bars. "Encryption's only any good if your hacker's smarter than the other guy's hacker. Sounds like maybe someone's running a capture program on your agency's line. Have you ever heard of Carnivore? It's a program that the CIA uses for scanning people's e-mail and the Internet. *Supposedly* they're looking for specific keywords. Supposedly it's meant to help stop crime. And supposedly they're getting approval from the Department of Justice be-fore they go any further and read the mail. *Supposedly*. Prob-ably some hacker already has something bigger out there, bigger and meaner, that can read anything, even heavily-en-crypted files. Tell your boss. He'll want to know their se-cured system isn't."

"I'll tell them," Keith said. "But if they didn't want to leak it to the public, what did the guy want?"

"Who knows?" Dunn asked. "Is Gadfly hostile-takeover material?"

"It *shouldn't* be. I don't really know what their financing is like."

"Maybe this guy is just poised to swoop down on the com-pany when it goes public," Dunn said. "Ask me how I know. We've had all kinds of feelers from people who want to talk to us when we're successful, not all of them nice."

"I have no idea," Keith said. "All we're doing is helping them with their publicity. PDQ has never had a problem like this before, not one where so much money was at stake."

"The world is changing, my man. Maybe they should ask Uhuru Enterprises to write them a new program. Hint, hint."

"Thanks," Keith said, turning toward his own room. "I hope they don't just shoot the messenger. Are you online?" he asked, glancing back.

Dunn picked up a white carton of almond chicken. He gestured at Keith with a pair of chopsticks. "All yours."

It was a relief to shut the door between himself and the rest of the world. Keith hit the computer's ON button. He threw his briefcase into a corner and flopped on the bed as the screen hummed to life. The icons scattered themselves over the picture of Diane that he used as his wallpaper. He hoped he had a message from her or Holl. He felt like writing to someone about what had happened to him, and then realized he didn't even want to think about it.

The small mail icon in the bottom of his browser screen showed a dozen messages. Half were junk mail, as usual, but one was from Diane. He brightened. It looked like a nice long letter. He could really use a good love letter to take his mind off his miserable day. Underneath it was a short message from Hollow Tree. Keith reached for the mouse. If he read that one first and got it out of the way, he'd have all evening to enjoy Diane's note and compose a reply.

Just as he clicked on it, the lights flickered. Keith looked up, hoping the power wouldn't go out. The landlord claimed the building had been rewired within the last two years, but the electric company had brownouts and blackouts all the time. He glanced back at his screen. It had frozen up. The cheerful home page of his Internet Service Provider didn't respond no matter how frantically he moved the mouse.

Keith swore and rebooted the machine. The roommates had surge protectors and battery backups on every computer in the house. Power outages should not affect them. When his opening screen finally appeared, he dragged the cursor over to where the e-mail icon ought to be. It wasn't there.

That was unusual but not unheard of. Keith checked the "recycling bin," but it was empty. Oh, well, the icon was only a shortcut. He opened the program menu and chose the mail program. Frustrated, he waited for it to come up. Keith felt as if he was waiting forever for the modem to engage. Finally, he decided it wasn't going to. He smacked the desk with both hands. Diane's message was stuck in limbo and he wanted it out! He tried closing and opening the program, clicking all the on-screen buttons, but nothing helped.

He went out to find Dunn.

The programmer shook his head. "Sounds like the program got corrupted. You say you had a brownout?" he asked, standing up from his computer. His array of equipment wouldn't have shamed NASA, with multiple screens and every gadget known to technology-loving mankind.

"Just for a moment," Keith said. He trailed after Dunn, who marched purposefully in and took over Keith's basic computer setup. His long hands flew over the keyboard like a concert pianist's.

Dunn let out a short exclamation as the screen went blank, then the opening logos came up.

"You've got gremlins. The program's toast. We'll have to reinstall your e-mail. Where's the disk?"

Keith started flipping through the CD-ROMs in his storage case, then stopped. He ran his hands through his hair, leaving it standing on end. "At my mom's," he said.

"That's okay. I've got the basic browser. We can get you online to download it all over. That's not all bad: you can get the latest version. I don't need the modem for a while."

"How long will that take?" Keith asked.

"Oh, an hour or so."

Keith had a horrible thought and leaned over his roommate's shoulder. "What about my mail?"

Dunn shook his head. "Did you have it backed up?"

Keith groaned. "No. But there was a letter from Diane in there!"

"Sorry. It's gone." Dunn was genuinely sympathetic.

"Oh, well," Keith tried to put the best face on it. "She prefers a real phone call anyway."

"That's the spirit," Dunn said. He used his own disk to get Keith on line to the download site, then went back to his own work.

Keith flopped back on his bed, watching the progress monitor on the screen while he dialed the phone. He didn't think his rotten mood was one he ought to share, but the moment Diane answered, he felt the tensions of the day melting into a warm pool of contentment.

"Hi, sweetheart," he said. He caught a glimpse of the sappy smile he was wearing in the mirror over his dresser. He stuck his tongue out at his reflection. So he was in love. So what if it made him look goofy? It was the best thing in his life.

Chapter 14

The next morning Keith found himself on one side of the long conference table with the top staff of PDQ on the other. Jason Allen and his executives from both the creative and client sides of the agency interrogated him like a prisoner under the lights, asking him to repeat details of his encounter with the man in the park over and over again. He had wanted to get the attention of the brass, but not like this! The group was split regarding how much culpability he bore for the meeting.

Some of them who remembered him for accepting the industry award on their behalf for the Judge Yeast account were inclined to think he was innocent. Most of the others were clear that they thought he had something to do with the man choosing him out of all the people who worked for the agency. Keith felt as though he'd walked into another argument between the Progressives and the Conservatives, with the Conservatives demanding bombastic punishments for an alleged error. But this was no minor error. The loss of the Gadfly account—Doris!—meant hundreds of thousands of dollars, something the vice president of accounts kept bringing up with agonizing monotony. Paul and Doug sat flanking Keith, for which he was grateful. The error, if it was one, could have an impact on their careers, too. Dorothy, on Paul's other side, held herself as erect as a queen. She was as much on trial here as Keith was.

Keith kept trying to defend himself. "Look, all I was doing was studying…"

The vice president of accounts interrupted him. "What were you doing out there anyhow?"

"The weather was good, and I just wanted to get away…"

"What if you were needed during that time?" one of the women from the client side demanded.

"Ellen," Paul said, stepping in as he had several times during the last hour and a half. "Keith's entitled to a lunch hour. He has a cell phone. Dorothy and I both have the number. That's not the issue."

"And who else had that number?" the executive asked, glaring at him.

"Lots of people." Keith shook his head. "Look, check my phone records. No one called me…"

"They could have arranged ahead of time," said an angry man from Media. "Just like they arranged to get a copy of a confidential document!"

"That had nothing to do with me!" Keith exclaimed.

Paul patted the air with his hands, trying to bring the volume down. "Keith is not our problem. Whoever actually let the ad out is our problem. Keith brought this to us as soon as he could."

"We're going to have to tell the client," W. Jason Allen said, leveling a grim gaze at them all. He reserved a special glare for Keith. "You, do not talk to anyone outside this office, do you understand me?"

"That's ridiculous," Paul said.

"He hasn't done anything wrong, Jason," Dorothy said, jumping in to shield her protégé. Keith shot her a grateful glance, but she wasn't looking at him.

By the time the meeting came to an end, the group was still split. Like the juries in the television lawyer shows, they seemed to avoid or meet his eyes depending on whether they thought he was guilty. Keith followed Dorothy, keeping quiet until they were in her office. The brass filed past the door, looking in curiously, as though, Keith thought, they were hoping to catch him handing over agency secrets to some guy in a trench coat and fedora.

"Thanks for defending me," he said.

Dorothy's jaw was set. "Don't thank me now. If I get canned because I brought you in, I'll gitcha."

Keith bowed his head. "If I'm guilty I'll let the boom fall, but I didn't do anything!"

Dorothy looked over her shoulder. "Go on, get out of here for a while. They don't want to see you while they think about what they're going to say to the client. If I'm scared, they're feeling it double. Triple. Go on."

She didn't sit down until Keith picked up his briefcase and jacket and left the room.

When the door slammed behind him Keith felt as though it might as well be for the very last time. He felt as alone as if he were the last man alive. He looked up and down LaSalle Street. Where should he go? Everybody on the sidewalk was walking quickly and purposefully. They all had places to go, people to see. Nobody wanted him where he was supposed to see, and he wasn't supposed to talk to anyone. At that moment, that was what he wanted more than anything else on Earth. He fingered the small cell phone in his pocket. *Off limits*, he thought, sadly. He started walking north, trying to stifle his gloomy mood, but it hung on. He would loved to have called Diane or Holl or his parents, or anyone, but the executives would be probably fire him if he dared approach any human being or reasonable facsimile thereof.

An idea struck him. He stopped in his tracks, grinning with relief. He *did* have somebody that he could talk to, maybe, and not at all human, or even close. Scanning the skies, he picked up the pace.

"One for lunch?" the hostess at the 95th Floor restaurant asked.

"Um, yeah," Keith said, and turned on all the charm he possessed. "Is there one right next to the window? I'll wait if I have to."

The woman consulted a plastic-coated floor plan daubed with grease pencil. "No problem. I've got a very nice table. Please come with me."

Keith rubbernecked as he followed her. It had been a while since he'd been to the top of the John Hancock Building. He couldn't have asked for better weather. A few fluffy clouds floated around to the west, but over the lake the sky was clear, bright blue. He settled in at the table with its vertigo-inducing view, and thought hard about being visible. He hoped that they could hear him.

The waiter had already delivered his Coca-Cola by the time they arrived.

Sun behind clouds, the air sprites sent as a message to his mind. Keith studied the filmy white beings dancing on the air just outside the window. Each was no larger than a cat. Their slender, winged bodies were nearly translucent, tapering away to wisps where feet might have been on a ground-bound creature. He tried to figure out which was the one he had met first, but decided that what details set them apart to one another just escaped his powers of observation. The large eyes in their otherwise featureless faces regarded him with sympathy.

"Yeah, I feel a little gloomy," Keith admitted. "Things have been rough at work."

A picture of a box with his picture on the lid opening appeared in his mind. "Reveal what I'm talking about, huh?" He tried to organize his thoughts like a slide show, giving them a series of pictures of his job at PDQ: playing with the prototype of the Origami, working with a laughing Dorothy, leaning over a layout of the "One of Everything" ad, the faces of the people he was working with, especially Paul, then the strange, narrow-faced man and the ad copy in his hand. That last image was burned into Keith's memory as if with a branding iron. He'd never forget the shock of the moment, and wondered if there was any way he could have handled it better. The sprites hung on air currents outside the window, dancing like kites. He never knew just how much they could understand, but they sent back parts of the images, including a large image of the vice president's angry face to show they knew one of the things that was troubling him.

"You're right. That is what's bothering me. I know I'm not responsible for the leak. Everything was going so well, too," Keith said. "If they pull the ad, I don't know what I'll do. I was so happy I managed to get the invitation incorporated into it. If they let it pass it will go all around the world! Every creature that can read it will know they're invited. I just hope that I don't miss anyone. Holl, you remember him?"

Holl's face appeared in his mind, blond hair flying, cheeks and ear-tips red with excitement and cold, brow furrowed with worry. Keith recognized the image from their balloon ascent, more than a year before. "Right. He sends his greetings. I wrote up what I wanted to say and his people translated it for me. It looks kind of pretty. Maybe English looks like that to people who read a different alphabet, but I doubt it. As long as people see it. That's the important thing."

The sprites sent pictures of billboards, murals from the sides of buildings and a streamer pulled through the air by a skywriter. Keith grinned. "You guys want my job? You'd probably tick off fewer people than I'm doing."

Sun behind clouds, the sprites said, very positively.

"You don't think so, huh?" Keith paused and glanced around to make sure no one was watching him, "Any news on other magical beings?"

The small white creatures began to dance excitedly on the air, describing figure-eights and Immelmann turns. In his mind, Keith saw a two-legged shadow stride across a twilit landscape. At first he wondered why they were sending him pictures of a human being, until the figure passed a water-tower. In proportion, it seemed no higher than a beach umbrella.

"Cool," Keith breathed, just as the waitress plumped his plate down in front of him. The woman, about his own age, gave him a very puzzled look. Behind her, the sprites fled. "Um, I mean, thanks. I'm really hungry."

She gave him another odd glance, disgorged a ketchup bottle from her apron pocket, and stalked away. The sprites returned at once. Keith attacked his sandwich and fries with gusto.

"'Scuse me while I eat," he whispered, behind the cover of his glass of soda. "I never thought I'd be hungry again. A giant? You saw a giant around *here?*"

He almost got dizzy as the perspective of the image in his head zoomed out and out, until he was looking down at the Earth from miles up. The sprites commanded the air all the way up to the top of the atmosphere, possibly higher. The view in his mind's eye tilted to the right. He saw a broad stripe, a highway. It centered itself in his vision, then scrolled up as his point of view traveled south then east at speed. It took him a while to recognize landmarks. Then, he reconstructed the whole map in his memory.

"Near *Madison*?" he squawked, then shrank down in his chair as the waitress came up.

"Everything all right here?" she asked, with the sort of expression that suggested *she* didn't think so.

Keith gave her an apologetic grin. "Yup. Thanks." Wow, he thought. A giant in Wisconsin. Maybe Paul Bunyan was down from Minnesota visiting the Dells…nah.

Outside the window, the sprites danced in the sky. Shaking his head in wonder, Keith ate his lunch. Nothing cheers you up like knowing you aren't the only person on the planet Earth, he thought.

He paid the tut-tutting server and prepared to leave. Over her head, birdlike eyes offered him a kindly farewell.

"Thanks," Keith thought at them, hoping they understood. "Keep me posted if you see anyone else. Nice to see you."

The image of a setting sun appeared in his mind. Keith enjoyed it most of the way toward the elevator, when a hand reached out and caught his wrist. *The spy!* he thought, alarmed.

Worse than that, it was Mr. Allen from the agency. It was a shock to see the face he'd just been thinking about appear right in front of him.

"Hey, Keith," the executive said. He was seated at a table for four with three other men, all in expensive designer suits that must have cost thousands each. Keith felt underdressed in his off-the-rack best. "This is Keith Doyle. We've just brought him on as a copywriter."

"Hello, sir," Keith said, nervously. "Um, gentlemen." He pointed back toward his table. "I was just…"

Allen gave a humorous glance to his companions, then addressed Keith.

"I saw you talking to the birds out there. Lake gulls?"

"Something like that," Keith said. They must have watched his animated conversation with the sprites. They must think he was crazy. He felt his cheeks burn. "I just talk to them when I have something on my mind. I hope that's okay. They're not human, after all."

"Oh, sure," Allen said, with a genial nod. He leaned back and crossed his long legs. Gadfly must not have been too upset about the revelation of the ad leak. "And do they ever talk back?"

Keith paused for a moment, wondering what the man would do if he told him the truth.

"Oh, yeah," he said, trying not to grin all over his face. "All the time."

On the way out of the Hancock Center, he passed a woman with long black hair and armfuls of shopping bags staring up the side of the building with a fascinated, wondering expression on her face. She must be a tourist, Keith thought. He followed her rapt gaze, taking in the crossed girders and high tower just visible on the roof. It was a pretty impressive sight, all right.

Mr. Collier leaned out into the waiting room. His face brightened when he saw Keith.

"I thought it was you. Come on back. I was going to get a Coke. Want one?"

"Thanks," Keith said. He followed the man to his office and waited patiently for him to finish the motions of hospitality.

"So, what can I do for you?"

Keith brought the photos out. He'd arranged the stack carefully. The best one of Enoch, the one with the least dour expression, was on top. He slid it across to Mr. Collier. "I thought you might like to see the man your daughter wants to marry. This is Enoch."

Mr. Collier took the picture, and leaned back in his chair, relaxed. "Hey, he was a cute kid. Marcy's been so cagey about bringing him up here I was afraid he was deformed or something. When was this taken, when he was about ten?"

"No." Keith glanced at the fancy leatherbound desk calendar. "About two weeks ago. I've been kind of busy or I would have brought them in sooner."

The chair lurched forward and Mr. Collier sat up. "You're kidding, aren't you? My daughter's dating *a child*? This is…disgusting."

"He's not a child, sir. I swear. He's one of the Little Folk. An elf. I know Marcy told you. You should have believed her, sir. She's telling the truth."

No time for the easy build-up. Keith fished through the collection and found the good picture of the pair side by side and cheek to cheek. It was a tender moment, full of warmth, trust and, yes, passion. Snapping the shutter had been such an invasion of privacy at that moment he'd almost been ashamed to do it, but it was a good shot. Without saying anything, he passed the picture across the desk. Mr. Collier saw his daughter, noticed her expression, and started to push it away. To give him credit, he stopped at the last moment, to study Enoch's face. It was not a child's face in that instance, but mature and very loving. Marcy's father's brows went down, then way up. Keith knew he'd spotted the ears. You couldn't miss them. His hands began to shake. The shock must have hit him hard.

When Mr. Collier spoke again, his voice was hesitant.

"How old *is* he?"

"About fifty," Keith said. "But don't worry about the age gap. That's considered a medium-young adult in their culture. And they've really got a lot of interests in common."

"He's... a good... man?"

"He's great," Keith said, firmly. "He's a very good friend of mine. I hang out with them all the time when I'm down there. Enoch's brother-in-law, Holl, is my best friend. He and his wife are as close to me as any Big People in this world. Closer than most."

"This Holl is one of them? And his wife, too?"

"Yep." Keith had to give Mr. Collier credit: he was trying to grasp the ungraspable. He just started talking, trying to give the man a chance to absorb it. "I've been trying to figure out a way to tell you about them, so you wouldn't get excited and judge Enoch by the fact he only comes up to the middle of your chest. That's never made the slightest difference to me, or Marcy, or any of the other students— the lucky ones," he amended, "who've gotten to know him and his people. They're intelligent, kind, generous, and very patient, which is good in my case. They've helped me in a thousand ways. Enoch's father tutors a special class of just a few Big Folk at a time. College level. Better than college. He's a terrific teacher. I sure wouldn't have done as well without them, and they've been my friends. I think maybe Marcy's the only one of us ever to fall in love with one... I mean, the only one I know of who intends to marry and settle down with one of them. On this side of the water, that is. There's a lot of relatives in Ireland. They've been keeping in touch by e-mail. The Internet's terrific, but there's never a good substitute for face-to-face contact. That's just my opinion. I'm planning a big party to have all the Little Folk in the world come to get acquainted. You could come, too, if you wanted." Mr. Collier continued to thumb through the pictures, stopping longer and longer on each one. He turned up a slightly dazed face to Keith.

"Do you mean my daughter is the *only*... human being down there?"

"Well, she does kind of stick out in family portraits," Keith admitted, "but she fits into the society really well. Better than me, in some ways. They all like her. She's accepted. She's not alone, sir, and they never stop her from associating with other people. She just doesn't want to, very often. Well, you know her. She's kind of shy. They're good at bringing out her best. She's gotten a lot more assertive since she started dating Enoch." His chatter was giving Mr. Collier a chance to recover his wits. When he spoke again, he was an ordinary parent.

"I don't like the idea of her living in a commune."

Keith almost smiled. "It's not a commune, it's a village. Everyone respects everyone else's privacy. They've got 20 acres, and I wouldn't be surprised if they weren't trying to buy some more of the surrounding land. Holl and Maura live in a cottage outside the main farm house. I'm pretty sure that's what Enoch has in mind for Marcy after they get married. Right now Marcy has a room of her own."

"Really?" Mr. Collier focused on Keith's face, his eyes boring intently into Keith's own.

"Oh, sure. They want her to feel welcome. I owe her a lot, Mr. Collier. She introduced me to them. I want her to be happy.

I know you do, too. I just wanted you to see that the truth isn't
so scary."

Alan Collier nodded slowly several times. He squared the photos in a neat stack, but he didn't give them back to Keith. He put
them on his side of the desk. Standing up, he extended a hand.

"You've given me a lot to think about, Keith. Thanks for
coming by."

Keith retreated, not wanting to undo all his good work by
overdoing. "Thank you, sir."

As soon as he could get to his home computer, he brought up
the e-mail program. He wanted to send the good news to Marcy
before her father called her. He typed out as much of their
conversation as he could remember, finishing up with a triumphant note of his own. "Your dad didn't quick-shuffle me out
like he did the last time. I think I got through," he said. "Tell
Enoch the photos made all the difference."

Keith punched SEND, and waited for the modem to connect. It worked, praise to Dunn. Keith read the news on his
browser's home page, scanned a few online computer-ware
sites, partly out of personal interest and partly out of fear of
seeing news about the Origami leaked, then clicked over to
the e-mail portion. There was a message from Diane dated the
evening before, after the two of them had gotten off the phone,
a long one, judging by the amount of memory on display. He
skipped it to save for last. The other messages were mostly
spam, but he had a couple of real letters. His brother Jeff wrote
from Seattle to say that he was doing well in his classes, and
he'd met a really terrific girl majoring in computer design. He
wanted to impress her with some of the image magic that he'd
seen Keith using. That sounded like he was moving too fast
for his elder brother, who felt exactly like his father when he
wrote back with some strong advice to hold off before he blew
the big secret. Too many people in the world freaked out when
faced with the real thing. Magic was one of those things you
saved for when you were sure the relationship was stable, like
maybe his silver wedding anniversary. He hoped Jeff wouldn't
think he was nagging.

A message from Holl turned out not to be a letter but instead contained a forwarded message from the chief of all the Little Folk in Ireland.

"The Niall felt there were corrections that ought to be made to the text of your invitation," Holl's accompanying note said. "Catra's translation was essentially accurate, but there ought to be a few more words of courtesy used."

Keith groaned. He should have foreseen that something like that could happen. He scrambled to hit the reply button.

"I can't change it," he typed. "If you give me their address I'll send him an apology. The graphic's finished and the keyline has gone to the client for approval. I don't want to draw attention to the text by making a big deal about it. If I try, they may pull it altogether."

He worried as he sent the message that if he refused to alter the wording, the elves might withdraw their permission to use the farm for his party. What would he do? Unless he did pull it back in the next few days, it would go out all over the world, and there he'd be, having promised a gala celebration, but with nowhere to hold it.

The message from Diane was full of love, with a little scolding toward the end that he hadn't been keeping up properly with the promise of a letter every day. Maybe he should just call her again. Keith glanced at the clock. She wouldn't be back from work for hours yet. He had a while. He could use the time to browse the net for data he needed for the paper on franchising he had to turn in to Professor Larsen. Keith wrote Diane a long letter, telling her all his news and promising a phone call the next day between her classes and work, and hit SEND.

The screen froze. Not believing his eyes, Keith grabbed the sides of the monitor. The program had crashed. Not again!

"Dunn!"

The warbling of Everette's cell telephone barely aroused anyone's attention in the crowded observation deck. He flipped it open and put it to his ear. "Beach."

"Are you near your computer?" The excitement in Ming's voice came across clearly even over the tinny earpiece.

"No." In fact, he was on a version of a snark-hunt. A couple of hours before, Maria and Stefan had pounded on his door, demanding that he come with them at once to the John Hancock building. A vision had led her, Maria had insisted. She had seen magical wonders, flying around the crown of this oh-so-astonishing building. Surely the place was blessed! Running around, trying to see what it was, what had called the spirits to guide her here. The place was soaked with deep emanations, recent ones. It was a shame Beach couldn't see, but they were there for those who could perceive them. Surely they couldn't be far from the goal of their journey!

"Tourists," he explained to passersby who regarded the two excited foreigners with a mixture of amusement, pity and scorn. "They don't even have electricity where they come from." He returned to the phone. "What do you have for me?"

"Another transmission!" His operative's voice was triumphant. "It came through the same server some time last night. Heading for a different destination than the last, not as detailed. Only a text of the language, with no other material surrounding it. But there was a change in the typography. An *alteration*." Ming savored the word. "We have a fluent speaker with access to a computer not far from where you are."

"Fantastic," Beach breathed, watching the antics of his pair of operatives as they ran from window to window. Maria seemed to be trying to get closer to something only she could see or feel. She was so convincing he wondered at his own doubts about her talent. "It came from the agency?"

"No way to tell until Omnivore dredges up the surrounding data," Ming said, ruefully. "We still haven't got anything on the original message yet. It could be days. Weeks."

"I don't want to spend weeks at it," Beach snapped. "Boris and Natasha here will drive me mad by then." He snapped the phone shut on Ming's chuckle. He needed more data. Omnivore was amazing, brilliant, but it moved too slowly. Nothing to be done about it, he'd have to get into the place and look for himself. He looked around for Maria and Stefan. They were plastered against one of the floor-to-ceiling windows, gabbling to one another. "Come on, children!" he called. The scenery shifted alarmingly as he walked. Good God, but this building gave you vertigo. "If you're very good and come with daddy now, he'll buy you a nice ice cream before you go back to the asylum!"

"But, Beach!" Maria complained. "We are in the presence of emanations!"

He took her arm and turned her toward the elevator. "If anyone was storing magical artifacts up here, *someone*, probably the janitor, would have noticed it by now. *We* are busy exploring other options. Come along."

Chapter 15

Bracey jabbed Holl hard in the ribs. "I told you someone was bumbling around out here."

The two elves lay on their bellies in a hollow just a few feet from the edge of the road. The men who busied themselves around the open hatch of their truck were so near that Holl could have reached out and tugged their pants legs. He read the logo on the vehicle's white-painted side.

"It's just the telephone repair men," he whispered.

"And why, in the name of Mother Nature, would they be right here, miles from anywhere, unless they were spying upon us?" Bracey asked.

"I suspect because we have the only telephone for miles," Holl said. "Keep your voice down. They may not be able to hear everything we say, but it would only take a word."

"But why now?"

Holl sighed, burying his face in his forearms momentarily. "I would have expected them sooner. The telephone has not worked correctly since that fireball bounded around the kitchen. Someone farther along the same wire must have complained. There, you see?" he asked, as one of the men, wearing rubber gloves and pants and a helmet with a little light above his brows, clambered up the nearest telephone pole. The two elves watched as he poked at the wires and transformers.

"The circuit breaker's shot," said the shortest man. He seemed to be in charge. "Someone go ring the bell and see if anyone's home."

Holl began to back out of his hiding place, more silently than a mouse. "We'd best find Marcy and ask her to answer the door."

"We cannot let them come through to the door," Bracey whispered indignantly. "They are intruding."

Holl glared at him. "They're doing their job. Do you want to draw the attention it would bring for them to be stopped at an invisible wall? Let us hurry. We want this line fixed as much as they do. And we'd best put a protecting on these men."

"On Big Folk? Whatever for?"

"Because if one of them gets hurt it will start questions being asked," Holl said impatiently. "And our homeowner's insurance is not large enough to handle multiple claims. *I* will do it. Go find Marcy."

Grumbling under his breath, Bracey withdrew, leaving Holl to make his charm. He hoped that whatever had jumped out of the mead barrel at him the other night would leave the visitors alone, for an accident like that would bring not only claims adjusters and lawyers, but curiosity-seekers.

"…So I said, it's great if you want us to come up with a killer ad campaign for them, but until they get a better phone service system I'm not the one you want to write copy for them," said a young man in a royal blue dress shirt with a white collar to an older woman in lime-green pants and a baggy white cotton sweater. "I spent half an hour on hold trying to get one lousy part for a home entertainment system cabinet. They've got like one woman answering calls for the whole country." The young man put a pretend phone to his ear. "'Thank you for calling Starter Furniture Boutique. Our coffee breaks are very important to us, so please sit there listening to our Muzak until we get back from Sumatra.'"

His companion laughed. "What if you did one of those 'good cop, bad cop' campaigns, where that's how Brand X treats their customers?"

"That'd be great, until someone called Starter Furniture and figured out where we got the idea…"

The two of them walked down the stairs of the PDQ building and turned right, passing near enough to the darkened doorway where Beach and his minions stood hidden that he could have touched them. O'Dell, one of his operatives, swung a detector in an arc.

"Still two body-heat traces on the third floor," O'Dell said.

"We can avoid two," Beach said. "Go on."

His men slipped past him, Stefan keeping a lookout while Miller undid the lock. Cat burglary was an art. No longer was it necessary to rappel down a wall wearing black spandex and a balaclava. Modern burglars made a civil approach through the front door, disabled the alarm system, then gave the security cameras something to look at besides themselves while they went about their business. Beach reminded them sharply that they were to leave everything as they found it.

"Cleaner, if possible," he said. "We don't want them having an idea that we were there. All we want is information."

Vasques and Wyszinski were a team he had hired there in Chicago. They drove VW's as a compliment to their last initials, an affectation that Beach found irritating, but they were good at searching. They had been private detectives who had had their licenses yanked for impropriety, but the state board couldn't remove their knowledge. They went right to the files on the second floor, handing off folders to Beach and the other three to read over, looking for signs of the calligraphic characters of the mystery language or any reference thereto.

A click made them all raise their heads. It sounded to Beach like a footstep on a concrete floor. Could the infrared detector have missed a janitor in the cellar? Unlikely. O'Dell was thorough. But the men held as still as statues until they were sure the noise wouldn't be repeated.

About half an hour into their illicit visit they heard the elevator. O'Dell held out his instrument and nodded. Both heat traces from the floor above were departing. They had the place to themselves. That was good, because the job was likely to take all night. The office was awash in paper. Apparently the place really did function as an advertising agency. Whatever was going on *sub rosa* was deeply buried.

It wasn't until they accessed the mail room computer at three o'clock in the morning that Beach began to see signs of his quarry. He almost smiled over Vasques's shoulder at the screen. PDQ was so careful about the security coding of what it sent out over the web, it never thought to protect the computer from which such transmissions originated.

On the user log they found four files of approximately the right size dating from the day Ming insisted the first graphic had been sent. The second one they opened, addressed to "Gadfly Electronics" turned out to be the right one. There, on the screen, was the lingo, exactly like the copy he carried around in his pocket. The attached note was telling someone called Jen to look it over and give PDQ their approval as soon as possible. Beach made a note of Gadfly's e-mail address for further investigation. Who were they, and what were they using the magical language for?

"Who routed this to the mail room?" Beach asked. He was so excited he was gripping Vasques's shoulder with iron fingers. The man paid no attention, rapt on the screen, his face glowing in the reflected light of the screen. He typed in commands, brushing aside firewall programs and password prompts like cobwebs.

"Dorothy Carver," Vasques said, pointing at the name. A few more commands brought up a screen from Personnel. "Creative director."

Beach nodded to the other men. They scattered, looking for the name. In a moment, Wyszinski reappeared, cocking his head toward the rear of the floor. The window of Carver's small office faced another building where people were still working late on an autumn night. Beach lowered the blinds and hoped that no one across the way would think it odd to see lights in Carver's room. Together the five of them turned over every sheet of paper, every computer file in the office, until they found a copy of the graphic. Carver's initials were in a small box in the lower left hand corner.

"What's this?" he asked, puzzled. The device on the page showed a blank screen. "The lingo didn't come from Carver. It was added later. Keep looking until you find one with writing in this section."

Miller was the one who found the prize. On a cluttered desk in a different department he came across the finished page. Another set of initials joined Carver's: KD.

Back to Vasques and the Personnel files. KD had three matches in PDQ's roster: Kirby Deane, an executive vice president; Kenneth Drabble, media services; and Keith Doyle, copywriter-trainee. From evidence unearthed during a search of his corner office Deane turned out to be on vacation in Tahiti and had been for three weeks. He couldn't be the source. Kenneth Drabble was deceased. That left Keith Doyle, age 22. Beach frowned. How could Doyle, a trainee, be the source of a sample of a language that no one spoke, that was associated with magical artifacts and powers? Perhaps he was the government agent they were looking for.

"Where's his employment record?" Beach demanded. On his commandeered computer Vasques clicked through the files until he came to a screen headed with the name "Keith Doyle." Beach leaned in, unable to believe his eyes. The photo in the record was of the redheaded boy he had approached in the park. *He* was the key to all this? Beach was filled with respect. The youth had seemed naturally flustered when he was confronted with the graphic. He had *lied* to Beach. Tricky. They'd have to be certain not to underestimate him again. "I want a copy of that, and make sure there's an address on it. We need to pay a visit."

Keith spotted the revolving blue lights on the street as he got off the bus. Funny place for a traffic stop, he thought, hiking down the block. But the police car wasn't there to write a ticket. Men and women in uniforms were coming and going from one of the apartment buildings. As soon as he realized that the building was his own he broke into a run.

The stern-faced black police officer at the door wouldn't let him in.

"But I live here," Keith protested.

"Then why doesn't your driver's license show this address?" the officer asked.

"It's temporary," Keith explained, starting to pull files and letters out of his briefcase. "I don't know how long I'll be working in the city…"

He heard Dunn's voice say, "Wait a minute. Doyle, is that you?"

His roommate appeared around the corner. He looked half worried to death, his mild face creased around the mouth and forehead. Pat Morgan was behind him, looking more bedraggled than usual.

"What happened?"

"We had a break-in," Dunn said, wearily. "I just went out to get some lunch. When I came back, the place had been tossed. I couldn't have been out of here more than forty minutes."

"What did they take?" Keith asked, alarmed. "Your program?"

Dunn's face was grim. "They blew my monitor, but your computer is all over the place."

"Oh, shit!" Keith hurried toward his bedroom. He was prevented from entering by a female cop, while a male technician, on gloved hands and knees, searched the carpet with a powerful flashlight. The tech rose, dusted his hands together, and sighed.

"Nothing," he said. "A very professional job. No footprints or fingerprints. I think Mr. Jackson must have interrupted them when he returned from outside, so they didn't have time to steal it after they took it apart. Was there anything on your computer that would be of interest to thieves, Mr. Doyle?"

Keith panicked for a moment, worrying whether anyone had opened his e-mail program and read the messages to and from the elves. Then he remembered that the program had been wiped. Nobody would get any information from it. "Nothing," he said, with relief. "Just the usual. Games. Word processing." His eyes widened in alarm. "My essay!" He sat down heavily on the bed. The Master was going to kill him if it was gone. There went four late nights in a row doing research on the Internet.

The tech grinned. "Nothing serious, then. Good."

Pat was helping the other officers as they went over the place trying to figure out if anything was missing. Whoever had come in had pulled every book off the bookshelf, tossed clothing out of drawers and pushed over all the furniture. Keith wondered how many thieves there had been to trash the place so thoroughly.

"Can we take this now?" asked the detective who was help-ing Dunn. He pointed at Keith's monitor. "Will it be compat-ible with your CPU?"

"I'll make it work," Dunn said, determinedly. "Nothing had better be wrong with my drive. I'm writing software for my brother's company. They're depending on me."

"Would it be easy to copy?"

"No way. People are in and out of here all the time. My machine is password-protected and encrypted. It works better than the alarm on this place."

"Now, Mr. Jackson," the detective said. "We got here about the same time you did."

Keith trailed after them as they took the monitor into Dunn's room, hooked it up and booted the machine into life. Screen after screen demanded passwords, which Dunn typed in with uneasy looks at the police and his roommates.

"It's okay," Dunn said, his shoulders slumping. The ten-sion in the room eased. He pointed to the latest entry on a usage history monitor in the bottom right corner of the screen. "They started it up but they couldn't get through the chastity belt. We'd better check the other guys' hard drives."

Keith's computer had been started, too. His usage history had been wiped, though neither he nor Dunn could say whether that was due to the problems he had been having with his e-mail or not. Pat's computer, much more basic than either of the others, had been started, too.

"No way to tell if anything had been copied," the detec-tive said, making a note. "Maybe you two should start using passwords from now on."

"Yessir," Keith said, automatically, but his mind was else-where.

In a while the police and their analysts departed, closing the door behind them. Pat and Dunn waited until the crowd of footsteps went down the stairs and out onto the street. Then they both descended on Keith.

"All right," Pat said, "which one of the little guys did you piss off?"

Keith raised his hands. "None of them! Honest to God. Everyone thinks I'm the newfangled cat's meow. But..."

"But, what?" Dunn demanded.

Keith hesitated. He wasn't completely certain, not with the way Holl had been acting, refusing to talk about what was troubling him. Maybe...no. After all this time they'd certainly be more direct with him. They'd been friends a long time. "Could this be from the guy who followed me that day?" he wondered. "That Carnivore program that made a copy of my ad?"

"Nope," Dunn said automatically. "It's supposed to pass unseen through protections, and if it's messing with you, it'll be messing with every computer attached to the modem line in this apartment, and it's not. Besides, if they can rip your hard drive over the phone, why come in here and redecorate for us?"

"I don't know," Keith said, worriedly. "I don't know."

Beach's people assembled in a safehouse far away from the handsome hotel room he used as his headquarters, to go over their booty.

They had watched the apartment building for several days, getting to know the ins and outs of the inhabitants of apartment 3D. The lanky white man with long, black hair was an actor. His hours were the farthest off an ordinary workday, but he tended to come and go at approximately the same time every day except Mondays. Their target, the redhead of average height, left in the early morning, then came back around suppertime or later. Beach's greatest concern was the light-skinned black man, who spent most of his time at home. He only seemed to go out late at night. VW had followed him to what they called a "Nerd Bar." Otherwise, he seemed to live on carryout food, which he went out for in the late afternoon. An interval like that was their best chance.

They had lain in wait until midafternoon, when the actor had left, carrying a duffel bag and a bottle of water. A couple of hours later, the black man emerged, heading for the main street where all the takeaway restaurants were. As soon as he was out of sight, Beach and his men went in.

"Make it look like a robbery," Beach ordered. Wyszinski started taking photographs, and Vasques started looking for computers. Though there was one setup in each bedroom, all evidence pointed to the fact that the highest-tech array belonged to the black man, not the target. It seemed Dunn Jackson was a programmer.

"Scan his drive anyhow," Beach said, grinning. "Just in case he's working on something I can use later." Vasques echoed his grin, putting a read-write CD into the drive.

Like little children throwing snow over their heads, Stefan and the others were throwing the three men's possessions in the air, going for the greatest amount of mayhem. Beach enjoyed the spectacle for a moment, until Vasques came to tap him on the shoulder.

As Beach had hoped, Doyle's hard drive not only had that seven-line example of the lingo on it, but the alteration of the test that had so excited Ming.

"This proves he's got something to do with it," he said, slapping Vasques on the shoulder. "Where'd it come from?"

Vasques shook his head. "No way to tell. He could just be a mule, bringing the text in to PDQ."

"But for who?" Beach asked. "We need to learn more about his connections."

The e-mail program was no help. It contained a single love-letter from a girl named Diane.

"Hot stuff," Beach said, with a lecherous glint in his eyes, "but no use to us." He straightened up, raised his leg and kicked in the monitor. The screen burst, showering glass everywhere. Vasques leaped up, swearing. "Take it apart. We'll analyze the hard drive back at the safe house." The private detective nodded and started pulling wires out of the rear of the plastic box.

Stefan came running on crepe-soled tiptoe. "The man is coming back!"

"We're through here," Beach said. "Never mind. Leave the computer." They departed through down the fire-escape stairs just as they heard Jackson's key fumbling in the lock.

The break-in had borne precious little fruit. Beach needed to look elsewhere for answers. The advertisement had been commissioned for Gadfly Electronics. It was time to investigate them, and any other lead that came his way.

Perhaps, he sighed, dusting himself off in the alley, *even from Maria.*

Chapter 16

"The first fifteen are complaints," Catra said, presenting Holl with printouts of the e-mails that had arrived since phone service was restored. "From our customers, saying that they have been trying to get in touch with us. Only those who write to the postbox are not upset. Both Marcy and Keith have picked up the mail for us several times since the...disruption."

Holl shook his head. "I'm almost inclined to side with the Conservatives, for once. If we had not become so dependent upon the new technology, we would not be out of touch with those who are relying upon us."

The Archivist glanced around the busy workroom with an impish expression. "Do not say that too loudly. They'd gloat if they heard you."

"There's more they could gloat about if they wished," Holl said, glumly, but he kept his voice below the level of ambient noise. "Keith Doyle has mentioned that he has had many disruptions in his e-mail, too, and always after he has opened a message from us."

"So has the Niall," Catra replied, thoughtfully. "So it can send mischief coursing up wires if it chooses. It does begin to look as though we are dealing with a type of intelligence, doesn't it?"

Holl nodded. "Thank you for not saying 'I told you so.'" But she'd be the only one who wouldn't be celebrating the petty victory of being right. The smug expression on Aylmer's face, as the older elf stood varnishing boxes at the next table, told Holl he'd overheard the conversation. The Conservatives were vindicated. Well, knowing that fact wasn't going to help clear it out of the house. "It doesn't matter. We must be rid of it. If our disturbance is an aware being, perhaps I can try and communicate with it."

His keen ears caught whispers as he strode out of the workshop. Everyone knew where he was going, but no one volunteered to go with him. Catra had given him a look of pity.

Her remark was an interesting one. This presence could and did affect transmissions leading out of the house, but it was still there, working its malign will on them all. That suggested that it couldn't or didn't want to leave. In Humanities studies, the Master had made them watch cinema westerns. The hero was always having to confront the intruder and inform him his presence was unwelcome. "This town ain't a-big enough for the two of us," the hero would say. But the villain never wanted to leave without a fight. Westerns reflected battles over territory. Well, the Folk had made this farm their home. It was too small for them and an unsocialized spirit that made everyone cranky, destroyed their winter stores and spoiled their e-mail.

Steeling himself, he marched down the cellar stairs.

The room was cool and dim after the warm autumn day. It took Holl's eyes a moment to adjust. Nothing looked out of the ordinary. He felt along the walls, seeing if the spell protecting the wall had been interfered with. All was intact. That meant the intruder was still within the house somewhere. Could it be back in the liquor barrels? Warily, he sidled toward them. One after another, he flipped their lids up and let them drop back into place. No fireball. Nothing but the liquor and Marm's watermarks. Lower again, Holl noted with dismay. One lid toppled off its barrel and clattered to the stone floor.

"Hey, down there!" Dennet's voice came from above.

"It's me, father," Holl called out. "I'm…"

Dennet cut in, not unkindly. "I know, I know. Be careful, then." Word had come up the hill as quickly as he had. Holl smiled.

His father was proud of Holl's status as Headman-in-Waiting, but he disapproved of what he called abuse in the name of proving his son's worthiness. After all, the Master was unlikely to step down from his post for many years to come. If now was any moment to judge by, Holl didn't feel ready, and might never feel ready. Some candidate he was, jumping at shadows.

He sat down on the floor and let his mind reach out, trying to sense the stranger.

His sensitivity expanded outward, listening. He'd used the same questing to reach out to his people while he had been abroad a few years before. Without trouble he felt the presence of his parents and sister, pottering about in the kitchen above. A bit farther than that were dozens of people he knew. He could pick them out one by one: Dola, Borget, Celebes, the Master, Olanda, Tiron, Candlepat, and the rest that he had left behind in the barn. Farther yet, Marcy and Enoch, stealing a moment alone on the slope of the hill. It wasn't easy to be in love in a crowd. The older Folk, charitably, smiled and let them be. The less kindly passed remarks about making a spectacle of oneself in public. Holl, who was just as much in love with his lifemate as he was the day he'd discovered the depth of his feeling, let his enigmatic brother-in-law and his chosen have as much peace as they desired.

He was so distracted by his thoughts that he was not prepared for the jolt of pain. Holl jumped, realizing he'd let his mind-touch go all the way to the protective spell about the perimeter of the property. Heavens above, no wonder the Big Folk were complaining of headaches. But he'd missed his quarry. It was no longer within the confines of the house. How?

He brought his consciousness inward, going more carefully now. Enoch became aware of the scrutiny as it passed over him and felt irritated. Holl sent a mental apology to him, hoping the sense of it would get through, though he was less adept at sending than receiving. Very few among them could transmit a specific message or feeling. It was why, Holl's mother would always say, their ears were several times the size of their mouths. It was a better thing to listen to the sounds of the world than to make more.

How constricted the homestead seemed. Every blade of grass was irked by the one rubbing against it. Nests seemed too small for the birds. Blacksnakes in the kitchen garden hissed though there was nothing holding them at bay—but wait! Something *was* there with them, something…alive? Could that be their intruder? Holl prepared a charm of containment, hoping to stop it in place long enough that he could run up the stairs to examine it.

It became aware of him at the same moment, and flitted. Holl felt the astonishment of the snakes, normally imperturbable and short-sighted, as their tormentor departed. The moment passed, and the strong impression was gone. Holl was disappointed. He'd missed his chance. The enigma was gone.

No, it wasn't. It reasserted its presence, not far out of the vegetable garden. In fact, it seemed to grow larger and larger, filling his inner vision.

Holl opened his eyes in alarm. It had felt his spell. It must be coming towards him! Then he felt the presence stop short.

He sprang to reinforce the protections around the cellar. They were intact. After that last attack, the Folk had sealed all the conduit, the pipes, the cables and wires running in and out of the house. Nothing should be able to go through them at all. Half of the village were certain they'd shut the intruder out, and half were afraid they'd locked it in the house with them. It looked as though the former were right.

A click and a gurgle from the far side of the room made him jump. Then, the sound of running water overhead reminded him that those were the noises the electric pump made. Holl laughed sheepishly. He was letting familiar things play games with his mind.

He was glad they'd managed to shut it out, even if they didn't know how they'd done it. He'd better go warn the others that it was still on the grounds. Perhaps he could persuade the village to open the shield spell around the property's perimeter and release it to the rest of nature. He started for the stairs.

Through his thin-soled shoes he could feel a rumbling in the ground. Earthquake, in this part of the North American tectonic plate? Surely not!

And then, from the drainpipe in the center of the floor, a fountain of gold-red fire poured upward. Holl threw his arms up to protect his eyes.

The long thin stream gathered in the air, coiling in around itself like a rattlesnake. Holl dropped to a crouch. Adhesion, his favorite means of holding something in place, wouldn't work. The snake-being, for a being it was, wasn't touching anything. He'd have to circle all the way around it to cast a containment spell on it. Charm at the ready, he sprang for it.

The winged snake guessed his intentions and flew up to the ceiling, out of reach. It wasn't going to let the clumsy-footed ones catch it. So he had seen it making its mischief. Well, that was no more than they all deserved, invading its land! The force they had cast about this place, earth and sky, was painful, and they tried to keep it away from the tasty fire-water in the barrels. How dare they? Bad enough that it could not escape from the small square of land. It had tried hundreds of times to make its way out, but it had to watch, helplessly, as beings without power went back and forth unhindered through the glowing barrier, while it, a spirit of the earth, was sealed in like the sweet fruit in glass it had destroyed several days before.

The golden-haired one was determined. The winged snake watched through glass-bright eyes as he approached, weaving back and forth to confuse it as to the direction from which it would lunge. As if the earth-spirit had not seen every dance made by the flesh ones for centuries! Out of anger it was making plenty of mistakes in its strategy. The winged snake was angry, too, but it had been biding its time, hoping for revenge against its captors. It would not err.

Tantalizingly, it lowered itself a foot or two closer to the floor. The golden-haired one leaped forward, arms out. The snake flicked its wings and was out of reach in a twinkling. It almost laughed. As the being charged by, it slapped him hard with its tail, knocking him sprawling.

The little male was tougher than he appeared. In a trice he was on his feet, hands working in the air. Too late, the snake saw the weaving and retreated. A few feet behind, it ran into the makings of a thin barrier hanging in the air. He was trying to capture it! Unspeakable! It dodged backward, around the glowing strands of power. Its tail caught on another strand, left there by the being before he made his first lunge.

The snake's thin temper frayed. It was a spirit of the earth, eternal. What did this blunt faced, clumsy-limbed flesh-being think he was doing? It would teach him what its actions meant!

Holl threw up his hands to ward off the fire-creature as it shot towards his face. Holl felt fire singe his skin. Too late, he began weaving a charm to protect himself. The snake being battered at him, bruising and burning at the same time. Holl saw a malicious light in the eyes he had not noticed before. He backed into a barrel, which rocked on its cradle, and settled back again with a tremendous *boom*!

Footsteps stirred overhead at the noise.

"What is going on down there?" Curran called out irritably.

"Don't come down!" Holl shouted back. "It's..." His warning was cut off as the snake-thing coiled itself around him, attempting to squeeze. Holl pushed at it, gasping for air. His hands passed partway through it. It was substantial only to itself, but not to him. What kind of being *was* this?

He chanted the charm of protection against fire as fast as he could get the words out. Now the pressure was hot, but not searing. Heedless of his own pain, he wove a net of power, hoping to get it into a cage so they could get rid of it without letting it hurt anyone else. The snake-thing thrashed, knocking Holl's arms upward. It shot a muscular coil around his leg, tripping him to the ground. Holl's head hit the cellar floor and he saw stars. When his vision cleared, he saw a hot, red mouth lowering toward his face, long fangs dripping fire. He grabbed for its throat with both hands, holding the head away from him.

By now half a dozen males piled down the stairs. Instinctively, when they saw Holl's assailant, they threw charms of protection and repulsion. The snake-thing, Holl still gripped its coils, was propelled partway across the floor.

But it was not to be captured. As Enoch and Bracey jumped down to grab it, it unwound itself from Holl's body, and slithered like mercury down the drainpipe. Aylmer, Dennet and two of the others sent nets of power down after it, but they retreated, shaking their heads.

"It moved too fast," Aylmer said.

Enoch helped Holl to his feet. "Look at you," he said gruffly. Holl's clothes were singed, and he had bruises on his face and arms. He yanked up the hem of Holl's shirt. "My sister's not going to be pleased with you. What did you mean, starting a fight with it alone?"

"Couldn't be sure it *was* an 'it'," Holl said. "I had to find out. I reacted too fast."

"Not fast enough."

"Stubborn to the very end," Aylmer said, shaking his head. "We knew weeks ago it was a being."

Enoch glared at the bearded male. "Then why did you not make this attempt yourself in force, and save him from a beating?"

Aylmer shook his head, but he took Holl's other arm. "Some folk need to learn lessons on their own."

The snake-being was gone but traces of malign power still informed the room, making it feel tainted. Curran raised a commanding hand and gathered the malice in a ball, which he threw to the ground and stamped underfoot to dispel.

"Now we know the horror is a livin' cretur," Curran stated, as soon as a village council could be called. "To be sure, it comes and goes as it pleases."

"It was affected by the containment charm I tried to use on it," Holl said, wearily. He sat on the Progressives' side of the room with his shirt off. Maura and Candlepat treated his scorches and bruises with salve. Only one scrape on his wrist and another at the base of his throat were bad enough to bandage. Even so, he felt as if he'd rolled around in a tumble dryer with a wheelbarrow load of rocks. "It could feel the wall, and avoided it where it could. We can capture it."

"How?" Rose asked. "It appears insubstantial."

"It's substantial enough," Enoch said. "Look at Holl."

"We can contain it," the Master said, "but we cannot control it. Did it communicate with you in any way?"

"No," Holl said, then corrected himself. "I am wrong. It *felt* at me. It felt angry. And when it was angry, I was, too."

The Master raised his thick eyebrows. "So. This may be the cause of all our black moods."

"That's a mercy," Dennet said. "Now we're aware of that, we can counter it. No need to let it play with our emotions whenever it pleases."

"But what to do about it?" Shelogh asked, standing up. "Now we know it's a live thing, however ye define life. How can we make it go away?"

"Strengthen the fence," a couple of the Conservatives insisted.

"It's on this side of it," Maura pointed out, reasonably. She gave Holl a gentle pat on the shoulder. He pulled his shirt back into place. His back and arms ached. "How is it we didn't know where it lies, if it leaves so large a footprint in our souls?"

"Did anyone ever sit down and try to trace it, as Holl did?" Marm asked. It was a surprisingly wise question for a simple soul. The others wondered why they hadn't suggested it first.

"We weren't looking for it," one of the Conservatives said, with a sour glare at the Progressives.

"Well, if it's a magical being, as we saw, it ought to have been hard to miss," Tay said, with a nod of support for Marm. "Doing damage we've been blaming one another for." Marm looked surprised, then pleased. He relaxed on his spot on the bench and gave the younger male a good slap on the back. It was an ill wind that blew no one any good, Holl thought. It was worth a sound thrashing to him to see the two of them friends again.

"Clearly it's been here for some time," Holl said, rising. "It appears to like the cellar. We need to block the drainpipe and prepare for a fight."

"We'll have to move all the breakables and foodstuffs," Rose said. "Including the beer."

"No!" Marm protested. "It'll ruin it!"

"Would you rather an evil intruder rendered it undrinkable?" Rose asked, frowning.

"Moving it does just that," Marm protested. "Master!"

The Headman shook his head. "Uf all things in this household, it appears to haf left the contents of the barrels alone."

He held up a hand to forestall Marm's protest it. "Apart from draining them, that is. Can ve not now agree that it vas this being who has been stealing mead, and not vun of us?"

It was Marm's turn for an apology, and he didn't stint. "I am sorry for any false accusations," he said. "I care for my art. It's the heat of the moment that made me forget I do not do this for myself alone."

"Handsomely said," the Master acknowledged. The others murmured assent. Even the normally sour Curran seemed appeased. "Now: action. Vhat must ve do?"

"That would depend on what it is," said Holl. "I've never seen anything like it in my life."

"Nor I," said the Archivist, "but I will research it more closely. Will everyone give me their best images of it, on the computer, if you can render it there?"

"And if it does not ruin the computer again in the meanwhile," Tay said.

"Ah!" Bracey said, raising a knowing finger. "Do you think this is a new kind of demon? A computer virus? We've heard enough about them in the newspapers, not to mention in the on-line digests."

"No, you fool," Enoch said, peevishly. "What would it be doing in a barrel of mead?"

"Well, where do they go, and where do they come from?"

"I don't know," Holl said. "We must think. This is destroying our peace."

"In the meantime," Aylmer said firmly, "we must put the guards put up still more strongly."

"You can't do that," Holl said. "They're almost powerful enough to kill now. Sooner or later some innocent is going to fall victim to the protections, and we'll be guilty of its death. Have you not noticed that birds rarely sing in the mornings any longer? At least not close by. No crickets. No rabbits. All living things with any wits about them avoid this place. We might as well be back in the library."

"And that's where I wish we were," Keva said, going nose-to-nose with her younger brother. "At least there we had no mysterious enemies attacking us."

"We were starving, too," Enoch said. "If not for the inter-vention of the kindly ones such as Ludmilla and Lee and espe-cially Keith Doyle, we'd be worse off. There's no reason to flee. Something must be done, but it's clear that increasing the protections we have won't work."

"What about," Marm asked, carefully sorting out his words, "something specifically meant to flush out electrical beings? It's done all the time on the computer, isn't it?"

"You can't put a virus checker against malign beings in the air," Enoch said, impatiently, with a curt gesture.

"The least we can do is warn those we send messages to," Holl said. "It sounds as though Keith Doyle's computer has sustained some damage from each of our sendings."

"You may not tell him," the Master said at once.

"Why not? We're going to warn the Niall. It's not fair to let the Big One think his machine is at fault every time it loses its programming, when, in a way, it's our doing. And what if it does something to him while he's here? It can't poison him, since he only drinks from the cup we gave him, but it could harm him in other ways."

"No," the Master cut off his protest. "Not yet." Holl was unhappy. He sensed a new edge in the air, as his folk prepared themselves to undergo a siege against their intruder. "I understahnd that you feel responsibility for our friend. Try to behave normally. To do otherwise is to alert the Big Folk that there vas something wrong, and that, in spite of our troubles, is something ve are not yet prepared to do."

"Then what in heaven's name should we do?" Holl asked, springing up from his place. "The Big Folk will still come and go. If we close off all doors and let no one know, we will be shut in alone with this thing. It may kill one of us next. How long are we to pretend to the outside world that nothing is wrong?"

The Headman spread out his broad hands. "Until ve can conceal it no longer. This is our problem."

"Our shame, you mean," Enoch said. "If you will not think of Keith Doyle, what about the other students? They have not his experience with the unseen facets of life. You owe them a debt of care. What if our unknown monster attacks one of them?"

"This is not a new problem," his father said, raising his eyebrows. "It has been going on for some time. It has not attacked anyone whom it did not perceive as hafing attacked it first. It regards Holl's action as an attack."

"So we don't listen for it any longer, pretend it's not creeping around here?" Holl asked. "If mere perception is enough to set it off, then it's dangerous indeed. We'll have to take our chances in order to study it, whatever it might cost one or more of us. I'd be willing to take the risk. Who else will help me?"

His suggestion caused an outburst. "No one!" a Conservative snapped. "You're not Headman yet. It's for the Master to gi'e an order like that 'un."

Holl flinched at the accusation that he was overstepping his position. "I meant only that we need to be brave enough to do the research which will bring us answers. We don't know what it wants."

"It wants our land," Curran said. "It wants us out of here. We'd best be prepared to give it that, in the name of peace."

Catra hung her head. Holl glimpsed tears glittering in the corner of her eye, but she nodded stoically. She, like he, loved their new home. "I will start reading the classified advertisements."

"We can't run off and pretend this never happened," Enoch growled, not accepting the attitude of surrender the other villagers were assuming. "What if we have awoken something that craves vengeance? What if it follows us? What if this is a monster of our own making?"

That was too horrible for most of them to contemplate.

"Then we'd best figure out what it wants," Holl said, resolutely, "and try to solve the problem, or we might end up taking it with us when we go."

Chapter 17

"Sit down, Dorothy," Doug invited her, patting the swivel chair beside him. "Come on. There's still half an hour to go."

"I can't," Dorothy said, pacing in a corner of the boardroom. Not that there was much room to pace, Keith thought, watching her lipstick-colored back shifting up and back like a matador's cape. Everybody who could fit into the room was there, watching the big television screen. It was D-Day, or rather, O-Day, the last Thursday in October, the week before Halloween—the day the advertisements for Origami would hit the streets for the first time. Bill Mann and his executive staff were in the boardroom of PDQ with the executives and the creative staff. They were waiting for 3:05 PM to click over on the digital clock on the wall, when Janine and Rollin's commercial would air for the first time, introducing the Origami to the world. Keith himself was so excited he couldn't sit still. He'd been swiveling back and forth in his chair, to the obvious annoyance of Jason Allen at the head of the table. He stopped, not wanting to annoy the executive further, but found himself fidgeting endlessly with a coffee cup. He thought briefly about learning to knit. It'd be an allowable outlet for the nervous energy in his hands, and he'd have eight or ten sweaters by the end of the week. Success or failure now rested squarely on the backs of those who were in the room. If they did their job, there'd be millions in sales, and more ad revenue. If they didn't—well, Keith knew he'd be first out the door, perhaps with Dorothy not far behind him.

"Demographics said give the businessmen a toy after the markets closed," Paul said. He'd said it a dozen times in the last ten minutes. He stood with his arms crossed close to his chest, pulling pensively at his lower lip with thumb and forefinger. "You don't want to promote something expensive after Triple Witching in case the markets have dropped. They'll still be optimistic now."

"I've got forty store buyers ready to call me the minute they sell their first unit," one of the salesmen said. "We've got shelf-talkers, POP displays and posters everywhere."

"What about the Internet banners?" Jen Schick asked.

Paul nodded at the clock. "We're going to give TV first crack at live media. At 3:06 the banners and ads hit the Net. One of my interns is monitoring chat sites. Our PR firm representative assured me the releases are going out to every techno site he can reach."

Bill Mann spread his hands on the table. "Then this is it," he said. Jen had fingers crossed on both hands. Theo Lehmann sat drumming his fingertips, body tense, his eyes fixed on the screen.

"Newspapers and magazines started this morning," Doug Constance said. "The ads will run in all editions tomorrow and all weekend. The ball's rolling."

"And my ad, I mean, our ad?" Keith asked, anxiously.

"And Toto, too, my dear," Doug said, in a sugary voice. He passed a file to Keith that contained tearsheets of foreign translations. "'One of Everything' will be annoying everyone from billboards in a dozen cities by next week. Take a ride out on west Ohio Street. It's going up there right now."

"Yahoo!" Keith shouted, springing up out of his seat. It was real! His party was going to happen!

"Shh!" Dorothy ordered. "Here it comes!"

The camera faded to black on the CNN announcer. Psychadelic colors burst upon the eyeballs, accompanied by the bouncy sixties song. The Origami started its little dance, twisting and flying around the screen. It looked irresistible, perfect, fun. Keith wanted to grab it right through the screen and play with it. Everyone in the room burst into wild cheers, with Rollin shouting, trying to get them to be quiet so they could hear his dialogue. It was impossible. Dorothy seized Keith and whirled him in a circle.

"We did it!" she cried.

The Origami folded in the actor's breast pocket. The minute-long spot ended with only the last four words of the script audible, "...motion machine from Gadfly."

Bill Mann's dark eyes were shining. "We're in business."

"It's a success," Doug said.

"Champagne!" Dorothy announced, standing at the sideboard. She handed the first bottle to Doug. "Go on, you do the honors."

The cork hit the ceiling. Over glasses of the effervescent wine everyone continued to hash and rehash the appearance of the commercial, and speculate on how it was going over. Within minutes the telephones began ringing. Queries started to hit the chat rooms at once.

"Mostly 'what is this thing?'" said one of Paul's interns, coming in with a sheaf of printouts. "They're intrigued. Half of them say they've got to have one."

"We've tickled the technos," Rollin said, throwing himself into a chair with his hands behind his head. "We have arrived. I love the Silicon Age."

"It's wonderful," Jen Schick said, over and over again, staring at the big television display, which was now occupied by a woman in a suit reading the news. "I saw the commercial going together. We even screened it, but it didn't feel real until this moment. How often will it air now?"

Doug handed her a folder. "Here's this week's schedule. I'll keep you up to date. If you need any more information at any time, call, but we'll continue to be in touch."

"Nice work, everyone," Jason Allen said, rising from his chair.

"Thanks, Jason!"

"You've got good people," Bill Mann said, rising to shake hands.

Allen's eyes scanned the creative team, landing last on Keith. Keith gave him a hopeful smile, and was rewarded with a grudging expression of approval. His stint in purgatory was over.

"Best in the business, Bill. See you later." The executive retreated, followed by the account people, all suddenly busy with cell phones or notebooks. The celebration was over. Time to get back to work and sell more ads. No one had the luxury to sit back and rest on the laurels of one commercial, however successful.

And successful it was. The ad for Origami had everybody talking. On his way home from work conversation in the bus was all about the terrific new toy they'd seen advertised. One highly envious young urban professional said that his partner had one, had run out for it right after the first ad. Everybody wanted details. Keith felt special being involved in the campaign. He badly wanted to tell them he'd seen it months before any of them had, but in a way he felt that would retroactively violate his non-disclosure agreement. Besides, the other riders would probably beat him to death with their briefcases. Anyone who had a PDA or a pocket computer seemed to look at their old device with jaundiced, unsatisfied eyes.

But the event that made Keith happiest of all was early the following week, when the bus pulled to a halt at his stop. There, on the side of a genuine city of Chicago vehicle, as large as a sofa, was the Origami. And there, in the middle of the screen, was his invitation to all the little people all over the world, asking them to come to his party. Keith was so overwhelmed that when the woman behind him nudged him to remind him to get on the bus, he spun around, seized her hand and kissed it. Before she could recover from her astonishment, he grabbed the metal handbar on the bus door, swung himself to the top of his steps and flourished his bus pass.

"To PDQ, Jeeves, and don't spare the horses," he said, grandly. He bowed the woman past him and sauntered down the aisle to the nearest empty seat. Now, if all those Little Folk out there who saw the invitation would just respond to it, Keith would be the happiest man in the world.

Within that same week, he began to see Origamis popping up everywhere. On the bus. Where he went to lunch. In the library. On the street, where excited buyers, fresh from the telephone/wireless activation process, dialed the person nearest and dearest to them to say, "Guess what I'm talking to you on!"

"The buzz is phenomenal," Dorothy said, greeting Keith as he came into the office. "We are getting press everywhere. Nothing like it has been seen since the cell phone." She shook a handful of papers at Keith. "Jen Schick is already getting queries about tying in the programming to i-business in the US. It's all over Europe and Japan. She wants us to be ready with ads saying that the Origami supports i-data."

"Any time," Keith said, cheerfully. "I'm ready to change the world."

"Well, we already know you're its number one fan," Dorothy said. It was a running joke around PDQ how besotted Keith was with it. He had only two photographs on his windowside table: Diane and the Origami.

"I wish I had one," he said. "It's tough saving for an engagement ring and a pocket computer at the same time."

Dorothy looked at him with disbelief in her eyes. "What, on what we're already paying you?"

Keith grimaced. "I've still got tuition expenses. Everything went up when I transferred to the condensed Saturday courses. I didn't know they cost more than the regular program. And it looks like I might need some serious engine work on the Mustang. The wear and tear from my weekly commute isn't helping. And rent and food, of course."

"Hadn't you better think about retiring that horse?" Dorothy asked, putting her hands on her hips. "It's ancient, and it's got to be a gas guzzler."

"It's a good car!" Keith said. "And it gets pretty good mileage. Really." It did, but the economy was not due to the design built by the Ford Motor Company. Not prone to metal-burn like the Little Folks, Keith had been magically tinkering with his beloved old car until it earned respectable mileage. He was a little concerned about what would happen when it went in for its yearly emission-control testing. He had no idea if anything unusual would show up in his exhaust fumes. How he'd explain it to the testers he didn't know.

"Well, you ought to be able to afford to replace it in a year or so," Dorothy said, sitting down at her desk. "Your work on the campaign has been good. Everyone upstairs is happy. If you can keep it up this could secure things for you. On a permanent basis, such as that is in this business."

"That would be great!" Keith said, scooting his chair up beside her. "So, what's next?"

"We build on success. Why don't you get to work on those i-business tie-ins? That's where you're walking down the street and the screen of your phone or PDA, or in this case your Origami, lights up with an e-coupon for doughnuts for the shop you're walking past. You go in and give them the pin number on the coupon. You get pastry at a discount, the shop gets business, and everybody's happy. Go down to Research and get information on how they're doing it—the greatest usage is in Japan, but Europe is coming up fast—and start thinking about how it fits in with the Origami and the US."

"Roger, captain!…Oops," Keith said, looking at his watch. "I can't right now."

"Why not?" Dorothy asked.

"I'm sorry. I forgot Dola is coming in today. I've got to get her from the train station."

Dorothy thought for a moment, then her brows went up. "The Fairy Footwear girl? Your cousin?"

"Uh, yeah," Keith said. "Time for the Christmas ad campaign. I'm her legal guardian on the set. Besides," he added, with a grin, "she wants me to take her shopping."

"Uncle Keith generous to his niece?"

"To a fault," Keith said, "as the Californians said about the San Andreas. So, is it okay if I…?"

Dorothy waved him out the door. "Later, champ. Bring her by to say hello. I know some *really* expensive stores I think you should take her to."

"Ouch, my aching wallet. Thanks, Fearless Leader."

The production house handling television spots for America's Shoe was within walking distance of PDQ, but too long a hike from the train station, especially for one of the Little Folk.

Keith took the Mustang to the Amtrak station just in time to meet Dola on the platform. There was just a split second of concern as Keith wondered if he would recognize her in the crowd, then realized he was silly to worry. The girl he thought at first was a five-year-old coming towards him on the platform, wearing pink coveralls and a flowered shirt and a floppy hat pulled down over her ears, started waving when she saw him. Unlike some of the other Little Folk, Dola was not in the least disoriented by being in a crowd of Big People.

"Hi," Keith said, coming to meet her and pick up her suitcase. "Ready to become more famous?"

"It is a job," she said, with a grownup air that made Keith laugh.

"You're doing it really well. You're getting fan mail, you know. The company thinks you should be answering it."

"I know," Dola said, "but must I? They don't know anything about me other than what I look like. I get such funny questions, such as what do I like to eat and what music I listen to. I am afraid they may become more personal, and we don't want that."

Keith didn't have to ask who 'we' were. He shook his head. "I can ask the rep handling America's Shoe to get someone to answer the letters for you. If you want, you can give her some information so she doesn't have to make it all up."

"I think I would like that, Keith Doyle," Dola said solemnly. Keith chuckled. She was just like a miniature grownup sometimes. The elves matured slower than humans physically, but they had an old, wise view of the world from childhood.

"Let's see what we can do." He bowed her into the Mustang as if she was visiting royalty, and pulled out of the underground parking lot. "Great weather we're having for November," he said, knowing he was talking too fast. "No snow yet. I can't take you back tonight, but you can stay in the apartment tonight. You can have my room. I'll sleep on the couch. Is that okay with you? We'll drive down after work tomorrow."

Dola cocked her head. "You are going to ask me about how things are going at the farm," she said, following his train of thought far too well. "Please don't ask me again, Keith Doyle. I'm not supposed to talk about home. Please."

Keith tried not to look disappointed. She had followed his train of thought far too well. "I won't ask, if you promise me that there's nothing I can do to help." She hesitated, and he jumped on it. "There is something wrong. Is someone sick?"

"Well...no..." but she sounded uncertain.

"Is it me?" Keith pressed. "Something I've done?"

Dola reached over to the steering wheel and laid her hand on his, another surprisingly grownup gesture. "You must never think that. Never. It is not you. You are our friend. Will you trust me to say that, and ask no more?"

"Well...all right. Sure I will."

"Thank you, Keith Doyle," Dola said. She sat back against the ancient upholstery and relaxed for the first time since she'd gotten into the car.

Keith chewed on what little she'd given him all the way to the studio. All right; if no one was ill, and it wasn't something he'd done, what was bothering the elves? Keith thought about the phone call Dennet had fielded, about the problem with the cable installer they wouldn't let him straighten out. The chatter in the kitchen suggested they were being hounded by other people. Debt collectors? Maybe they didn't want him to get involved because they were in over their heads. Could they be in debt? They weren't accustomed to having a lot of money, and there were so many expenses involved in having a new home, it was easy to fall behind. They'd been dealing on eBay, for example—could they have lost money, too? He'd better get to work selling for them again. Make contact with those galleries, as Holl wanted him to do. He could even give up his commissions. His heart sank when he thought of his own mounting expenses, but there were 80 of them and only one of him. He could get by on less. An idea struck him: they'd mentioned selling to galleries. He'd ask around how you got started.

On the set, the chatter wasn't focused on America's Shoe's new line as much as on the new gizmo in town. The director and product producer kidded Keith about not letting them in on the ground floor of the Origami craze.

"C'mon," said the director, whose name was Gary Von Ard. "You knew all along! I could've told my broker and been rich this week."

"I wish I had had a broker to call," Keith said, ruefully. "But as far as I know Gadfly's not being publicly traded yet. This is their first big product."

"It's a doozer," the producer, Gail Cohen, said. "I know Lana Tarleton who did the ad. She's been grinning at the rest of us over lunch. It's like a poker game, guess who has the neatest assignment we can't talk about. She wins. I think eight of us owe her drinks."

"So you're taking it out on me?" Keith asked, flinging up his hands in mock fear.

"Why not? You're handy. If you can't rag on the one you want, rag the one you're with."

"To make up for it," Gary said, "you can recommend me to direct the next batch of commercials for Origami. I've got some terrific ideas."

"Sure," Keith said. "I'll mention it to Dorothy."

He had nothing to do while waiting for Dola to run through her paces but watch her in action. She had the acting thing knocked. The director loved her because she was poised and professional, but still behaved like an energetic little kid once the camera was rolling. The only reason he was there at all was because Dola was under legal age. SAG and the child labor people were always pulling surprise visits to the studio, making sure they weren't exploiting child actors. Keith shifted in the chair behind Camera Two. Underaged or not, Dola could take care of herself.

With time to himself, his thoughts drifted back to his poster. Who knew what magical being was looking at it right now? He hoped that Catra had gotten it right in describing how to get in touch with him. He didn't know how he'd explain it to the neighbors. Maybe he'd tell them the building was haunted. He grinned. Funny how people were more willing to believe in ghosts than elves.

Chapter 18

"I tell you that it is more than an 'impression,' Beach," Maria said impatiently. "I have received word of a burst of great magic. It is in the south, south from here."

Beach was getting bored with her. Technology had proved more reliable for leads to their goal than her psychic mumbo-jumbo. At this stage he was keeping her and Stefan around for amusement as much as anything, but the novelty was wearing thin.

Ming had not come up with any fresh hits from their predator program, and he was becoming impatient. If he had not been so certain that the language was tied to arcane knowledge and devices that defied physics, he would have been away from that tedious city and elsewhere in the time it took to buy a ticket.

"Where, specifically, did your 'word' come from?" he asked, handing her a map of the state. "Can you pinpoint it within a few miles?"

She drew her pendulum from her handbag. Stefan leaped forward to bring her a chair. She closed her eyes and let the gold weight swing. Beach had only one eye on her. The other he kept on the computer screen, in case word came from Ming. Maria's act would never make it on the stage. She didn't sigh or fall into a trance. She just closed her eyes and allowed her hand to move of its own volition. If he hadn't been such a cynic her lack of showmanship would have inclined him to believe in her and her spirits wholeheartedly. But, real or not, her spirits weren't talking to her that day.

"I cannot," Maria admitted, after several swings and twirls. She let her hands drop to her lap, like a ballerina describing a dying bird. "Perhaps a week ago, when I told you it occurred. It is almost as if the magic hides itself. I can only tell you when it allows itself to be seen."

"Very convenient," Beach said.

He leaned back in his chair and stared at the ceiling, thinking hard. Sooner or later he was going to figure out a way to make the magic show itself. It would be the best tool he could ever wield, but he wasn't going to wait a lifetime for it. There had to be something he could do to tweak his odds. A little arm-twisting, perhaps, if he could figure out whose arm to twist.

Keith slogged into the farmhouse kitchen after Dola. Marcy came to meet him as he dumped the bags and his backpack next to the counter.

"You look awful," she said.

Keith saw the worry in her eyes, and straightened up. "It's nothing," he said, clutching his heart and coughing melodramatically. "The walk across the desert was a piece of cake. It was the climb up the cliff that did me in. Seriously, it's just been a long week. Did you see the ads?"

"I can't miss them," she said, wryly. "They're all over Midwestern. I drove Delana in to the Ag Department on campus for a seedling sale. You should have seen her jump when she noticed the writing on the billboard next to the hotel, right out there in front of everyone. She had to read it a couple of times before she calmed down. Everyone's been talking about it." Marcy glanced around her before she continued in a lower voice. "Not all of them are happy."

"That's a shame," Keith said, ruefully. "But there's no other good way to get the word out. I could wear a sandwich board, but it would *really* limit the guest list to how far I can get on foot between now and April. Right now," he added, yawning, "that'd be about thirty feet."

"Well, come and sit down," Calla said, bustling up and taking charge of him in her motherly way. "Borget, go and tell Holl that Keith Doyle has arrived."

"Don't bother him," Keith said, sitting down at the table. One of the cooks brought him tea in his special mug. "Thanks. This commuting is turning out to be harder on me than I thought."

"That's only natural," Calla said, sitting down with a cup of tea for herself. "A body can only do so much."

"I feel like I've hardly done a thing," Keith said, spreading his hands before wrapping them around the warm cup. "Most of the week I sit in the office writing copy. They've got me doing ads for a new function the Origami has that they want to push. That's fun. On my lunch breaks I study. That's interesting. At night I just go home and collapse. I haven't even been hitting the Nerd Bar with Dunn and his programmer buddies. Oh, but today I did a lot of walking around. My mom came into Chicago to take Dola shopping. I checked out a bunch of galleries that might be interested in looking at your high-end stuff." He fished in his inside jacket pocket for the list. "Here's all the contact names. All the ones with stars next to the name are currently carrying sculpture. Like yours but not as good. In my humble opinion."

"But this is a tremendous job," Calla protested, scanning the sheet of paper. "You are far too kind. It's more than you should be doing for us."

"Never enough," Keith said, gallantly. She looked worried. Their money troubles must run deeper than he thought. "Has...er, has Diane called?"

"No," Marcy said. "Why?"

Keith looked sheepish. "She's mad at me. She's been complaining that I can't tell her anything about my work, but she figured out from the poster of the Origami that I must have told you about it in advance. I tried to explain that I needed the text for the invitation. That wouldn't have been covered by the nondisclosure agreement, but I guess the niceties just don't translate well."

"Give in," Holl said, coming to join them. "You lose the argument."

"I have," Keith sighed. "I rolled over and showed my throat, although total and abject surrender loses something over the phone."

"Tell her what you can," Calla said. "She'll understand the omissions if you don't hold back where you don't need to."

"I should have," Keith admitted. "I really clammed up after that man came up to me in the park with the copy of the ad. Probably too much. Now it feels like I'm banging my head against a stone wall. Speaking of which, am I imagining it, or is the barrier spell stronger?"

Holl didn't answer for a moment. He swung his leg over the bench and sat down, carefully, almost gingerly. Keith jumped up with an exclamation of concern. Holl held up a hand to forestall him.

"I'm all right. I'm just tired. Pay no attention. What's this I hear about galleries?"

Keith was eager to show him the list. "I have to make an appointment to meet with the buyers. If you can give me some photographs, or one of the pieces to bring with me...?"

"It would be a pleasure," Holl said at once. "We would be very glad to have them do our selling for us." He caught Keith's dismayed expression. "Oh, it's not against you, Keith Doyle. It's become a wearisome task to keep track of the auctions on line. We missed a good sale because the line...went down. It would be worth it to have the selling overseen by a person. We will research this list of yours and settle on which ones are our best prospects."

"Right you are, sir!" Keith said, tossing him a salute with all the energy he could muster. "By the way," he added tentatively, "let me know if anyone would like to make some extra money. PDQ is auditioning kids to play Santa's elves in holiday spots filming now."

"Hmph," Holl snorted as his mother's smooth face dimpled with laughter. "And will I never be able to convince you that we're not interested in perpetuating a sterotype? It's bad enough that I know four months in advance you're going to ask us if we want to be leprechauns for the St. Patrick Day sales."

"Okay, so it's typecasting," Keith said cheerfully. "I'd do it, but I'm too tall."

"And why should you not? Are you not the one who's always telling us about the magic of television?"

"Why use me when they could have the real thing?"

"Is it worth it," Holl asked, "knowing that we must disguise the reality for the sake of not provoking a riot?"

"You know," Keith said thoughtfully, "it'd be a whole lot easier if we didn't have to."

"Tell me more, Mr. Doyle," Professor Larsen said, leaning forward with interest. "What's an example of the small niche handcrafts manufactory you speak of? You sound as though it's a business you have had personal experience with. *Considerable* personal experience."

"Oh, it's more theoretical than anything else," Keith said, wishing he'd had a tape recorder running while he made his presentation about the operational structure of a small industry. Since it was always on his mind, he'd described Hollow Tree Industries as best he could, naming no names, giving no clue as to location. From the amused and keen looks on the faces of his fellow students he must have waxed very lyrical. "I've just been, er, thinking about it for a long time."

"Really? Then, please, tell us more about your *theory*," Professor Larsen said, tenting his long fingers on his lectern. "What kind of woodworking factory has no concerns with pollution control? I've looked over the balance sheet you provided. It shows material statistics, detailed down to the types of wood and sizes of nails. It details safety measures including the minimum thickness of goggles to be worn whenever power tools are used, but I do not see any provision for worker's compensation, not even a claim for bruised shins."

"Well, there haven't been any…yet," Keith said.

"But according to you, this company has been operating for several years. In all that time, you want us to believe that they haven't had a single accident?"

"No, sir," Keith answered truthfully. The elves were incredibly careful, and used magical safeguards as well as physical ones, but he couldn't say that.

"That'd be a miracle, wouldn't you say? The workers must be of supernatural skill, turning out a myriad of toys and gifts without ever getting so much as a splinter."

"Oh, they are, sir," Keith said, as inspiration lit up his eyes. "You see, when you're talking about an *international* reputation, the workers take particular pride in their safety record. Their target market would get upset if there was a suggestion that the goods came to them at the expense of someone else's well-being. The training program lasts several years, and the employees are always getting additional education. The turnover is very small. They've never had a strike."

"*International* reputation?" a male student asked curiously.

"Sure. And as for distribution…their entire output is shipped only once a year. Admittedly it sounds very limited, but they do cover every single country on Earth. The CEO is also the Chief Operating Officer. He handles product distribution personally."

Keith's classmate shook her head. "One of those small businessmen who can't delegate, huh?"

"Well, there are some things that you can't really delegate," Keith said. "I mean, where are you going to replace a guy that can make toys, handle public relations, oversee the workforce, *and* drive the reindeer?"

The class burst into laughter. Professor Larsen raised his eyebrows.

"We're talking about Santa's workshop?" he asked, dryly.

"Why not?" Keith asked.

"That's a captive workforce," an African-American woman said sternly.

"No, it's not," said a Hispanic woman in a tan shirt-dress, getting into the swing of things. "They don't have to work for Santa. They'd like it."

"They'd have to *want* to work for Santa," Keith said, warming to his topic. "I mean, think of the Arctic climate. Nonstop snow all year, and part of the year the sun doesn't rise at all." The class burst out laughing.

"Where else could elves work?" asked a man.

"Hollywood?" suggested Keith glibly. "Think of all the movies starting from *The Wizard of Oz* that used little people."

"Hey, woodworkers with talent can get a job anywhere in the world," another called, grinning. "Santa ought to be glad they stay with him."

"People, people!" Professor Larsen shouted, over the hub-bub throughout the room. "Let's get back to Mr. Doyle's de-fense of his thesis. It's a fascinating fiction, but it's not really *viable*, is it?"

But it was hopeless. Everyone was talking and laughing about the idea of Santa Claus as a small business owner.

"If you're talking about clear leadership, customer interac-tion, and a good product, that's an ideal model for..." Keith's female defender exclaimed, only to be interrupted by a man with a deep voice.

"You have a spreadsheet here showing manufacturing costs against income!"

"Well, Santa must pay something for materials," Keith said, happily, tapping a pen on his palm. "He'd never cheat."

"What about the income? He doesn't charge for those gifts. Where's the money come from?"

Keith thought furiously for a moment, looking at the ex-pectant faces of the class. Maybe trying to equate the elves' business with Santa's workshop hadn't been such a good idea. "Corporate sponsorship!" he exclaimed, then shouted over the resulting laughter. "You don't think it's a coincidence that mil-lions of kids get Sony Playstations or Cabbage Patch Kids all in the same year, do you?"

"Since we're not talking about a cash economy, where's the opportunity for profit sharing?" an older male student asked. "There's no decent possibility of personal enrichment."

"What about all the milk and cookies?" asked the woman in the tan suit.

"No profit-sharing per se," Keith offered, "but you'd have to guess he couldn't consume all that by himself. The elves'd clean up on goodies."

"At least this is entertaining, Mr. Doyle," Professor Larsen said. "All right, I'll let it pass." He put Keith's paper back into the folder and slid it into his portfolio. He glanced at the clock. "All right, folks. Next week, we're going to cover just-in-time versus traditional warehousing. Reading in Molino, pages 45-70, and Deming, chapter 6. I'd like to see a brief paper showing me your understanding of the assignment. You can write it as it applies to the businesses we studied this week—except for you, Mr. Doyle. I really don't want to see a paper on Santa flying toys all over the world via reindeer power."

"No, sir," Keith said, as the class broke up.

"You are crazy, man," said the young man behind him, clapping him on the shoulder before climbing the stairs up to the ground level entrance.

Keith strutted out of the building, to find Diane waiting for him at the curb in her little car.

"So how was class?" she asked, as he tossed his backpack into the rear seat and climbed into the front beside her.

"Oh, you know," he said casually, "same old thing. It's just like being an undergraduate."

Diane let out a shriek and held down the DELETE key. "This is garbage!" she exclaimed.

"No problem," Keith said soothingly, leaning over to read what was left of her philosophy homework on the screen. "Let's try again. 'Nietzsche's views on the state of existence could be equated with the story of Creation, passing from the state of chaos into one of order.' That's pretty good."

"Yes, but everyone's going to say the same thing," she said. "I know I should say something about the mechanism of society, or compare him to his peers. I hate this."

"The Master is teaching philosophy this semester."

"Yes! Socrates, Plato and Aristotle. We did them already. He's lingering on the Great Classic thinkers, and my general study course for non-majors is already on the 19th century."

Keith glanced out of the window. Their precious Sunday together was ticking away.

Since she had made up with him, he'd been careful to focus on her needs when they were together. It didn't help that she was struggling in her classes. In order to graduate in June, she had taken the maximum number of course hours. Having to work her half-time job on top of that schedule, she was falling behind in the elves' class. Keith felt partly responsible. Changing his schedule had put stress on her as well as on him. His conscience was as uncomfortable as his back. The couch he was sitting on was the one he slept on when he visited her. Its most notable feature was the number and variety of lumps in the aged cushions, which left a topographical impression on his vertebrae. He thought of it as penance for enjoying himself when she was having such a hard time.

"I don't know," he said, after they'd erased paragraph after paragraph of her essay on her computer and were staring at a nearly blank screen. "It's philosophy. Will your professor even be able to tell if you just put down any kind of stuff and tell them that's your interpretation of Nietzsche?"

Wordlessly, Diane threw herself back in her chair, which rolled all the way to the wall of her small apartment, which consisted of a room and a half with bathroom in a converted attic. He eyed her sympathetically. "We can work on it later. Are you ready for the Master?" he asked.

"No," she said, mournfully. "How about you?"

Keith held up his pocket recorder. "Almost ready," he said. "Just a few more thoughts to insert. I'll print it out when we're finished with yours."

"Forget it," she said. "I'll never get it done in time. My brain's run out of battery power. I'll have to tell him I can't handle the load. I'll drop out if he wants me to."

"No! Don't do that. I'll take the blame," Keith offered. "I'll explain that you've been coming out with me to visit clients and wasting all your homework time. It's my fault we're having to concentrate being together into your only free half day."

Diane shook her head. "He won't buy it. If you can keep up, I should be able to do it. I just can't."

"Tell him," Keith pleaded. "Talk about it. We'll work something out."

Chapter 19

To their surprise, the Master was very understanding.

"I haf been vaiting for this, Mees Londen," he said, his chin tipped so he could peer up at her through the gold-rimmed glasses perched on the bridge of his nose. "I am merely surprised that only *you* claim fatigue. Mit the schedule that this vun is keeping, he ought to be exhausted as vell." He swept a hand toward Keith.

"Not me," Keith said, cheerfully, handing over his essay with a flourish. He'd finished it hastily that morning and printed it out on Diane's computer. "Hit me with your best shot. I'll take it."

In spite of his bravado, he felt a little light-headed. He put it down to the protection spell around the farm.

His teacher raised his wiry red brows high on his forehead. "Ve vill see. In the meanvhile, Mees Londen, I am not unreasonable. Let us change your responsibilities. Attend class, listen, participate, and I vill not ask for written work from you until the end of this term, and then, vun paper only. Is that acceptable?"

Diane's eyes shone. "Thanks, sir. I really didn't want to quit. It's just that something had to give."

The Master chuckled.

"Your villingness to continue despite your situvation inclines me to be generous in return. You are velcome. Now, please sit down. The others haf been vaiting for you. Now, Meester Doyle, as you are so ready to offer your interpretations, in the writings of Hegel, ve find a correlation betveen..."

By the time class was over, Keith felt as though his brain had been shampooed, set with steel curlers and blow-dried on high. He'd come out of the session in reasonably good shape, but not without a good mental workout. The Master, never loath to take an opportunity to burst a self-important bubble, called on Keith as often as possible, and insisted that he defend his answers. Holl and the others enjoyed watching the grilling. It gave them a chance to take it easy. Tay in particular thought it was fun.

"Thanks for the show," he said, slapping Keith on the back in the vicinity of his kidneys. "I didn't have much time to study, but you drew all the lightning today."

"Glad to be of service," Keith said with a playful grimace. The white-haired elf went away, sharing the joke with Candlepat. Seeing the smallest children playing at the far end of the big room watching him, Keith rose from the bench and gave them his most melodramatic stagger, as if he was so weak he'd collapse within steps. Diane applauded.

"Fantastic," she said. "Can I tell the paramedics that you died of Nietzsche?"

"Bravo." Marcy joined in, rising from her seat among them with Asrai clinging to her. Enoch was working with a fine rasp on a small piece of sculpture a few paces away. Dola sat among the toddlers and babies, helping them string big wooden beads on a lanyard. "For both the performance and keeping up with the Master."

"Piece of cake," Keith announced blithely. "I've got crumbs all over my hands. I thought he would never finish teasing me about the wrong homonyms in my essay. That'll teach me not to proofread something I dictated. Hey, any news from home?"

"My father called," Marcy said.

"And...? How did he sound?"

Marcy made a face. "Like he's...thinking. He said he hasn't talked to Mom, yet. I can't stand it much longer. I have to know that it's all right with them!"

"Is there anything I can do to help? Do you want me to go and talk to him again?"

"No. I don't think so." Marcy straightened her shoulders. "If they can't handle the reality, then...too bad. I'm getting married anyway."

"Bravo back at you," Keith said. "I mean, brava! And hurrah! But I thought he handled the concept pretty well when I hit him with the pictures."

"Daddy never makes up his mind in a hurry. It makes him a good attorney, but it was awful when he took me to buy a used car when I was 17. *This* time, I don't care if it takes him forever, but he has to see things my way for a change."

"It's a lot to absorb, his daughter marrying outside his species, so to speak," Keith said.

"Are you seeing things our way at last, Keith Doyle?" Holl asked, wryly, following them from the corner set aside as the classroom.

"Well…only for the sake of argument," Keith said. "I don't want Mr. Collier to get spooked off by too much all at once. I still think we're related. But, hey, I don't have to prove it. Marcy will. I took biology class. If she can…" He stopped talking as the dark-haired girl blushed scarlet to her hairline. "Oops, sorry. Letting my mind run away with me."

"You've done a lot for Marcy and me, Keith Doyle," Enoch said. His face twisted into an expression that, if Keith didn't know him so well, would make him think the dark-haired elf was feeling shy. "When the time comes you'll aid me at the ceremony, eh?"

"Best man?" Keith asked, astonished. "Isn't that Holl's place?"

"It is. No, you'll be part of the challenge. Do you mind?" Keith reddened. Having him take that role in their marriage rite was appropriate, since at one time he'd tried hard to date Marcy himself, giving up his pursuit in favor of Enoch's obvious devotion, and the more obvious return of that affection by Marcy. "That is, if we ever manage to have the ceremony."

"It's not an if, it's a when," Keith said firmly. "I'd be honored."

"Well. Good, then." Enoch sat down and went back to his sculpture, a modern impression of an owl in flight.

He *was* abashed to have asked. Keith felt like ribbing him a little, but looking at Marcy's pleading eyes, couldn't bring himself to put in the needle.

Holl listened, wondering if indeed Marcy thought at present it was the very best thing to tie herself down to beings who had such a curse on them as the Folk did, virtually haunted by a being they could not control, and that could pop up at any time. He wondered if he should offer some oblique kind of warning, in spite of the Master's caveat. Keith was so happy, Holl hated to be the wet blanket.

"Hey, how about a magic lesson?" Keith looked at his watch. "I've got a little time before I have to take off."

"Sure," Diane said, encouragingly. "I watched him stick his head into the lion's mouth. Now I want card tricks."

"No time," Enoch said, suddenly curt, bending his head over his work.

"I've been practicing," Keith wheedled. "I can make a fountain of fire. It's really cool. Only, I have to do it outside. I think I've licked the *oomph* problem. I've discovered these rivers of energy in the earth that I can tap into sometimes. The problem is I don't know where they are until I start trying to magic something. I'm still working on control."

"I have to see this myself," Diane said, one eyebrow hitched skeptically high. "You didn't tell me you could make fire."

"Yeah!" Keith said happily. "I've been practicing in the break room at PDQ. Luckily there aren't any of those energy sources close by, or I'd set the place ablaze. The smokers on staff think I've got an invisible lighter. You want to see?" He shot back his cuffs and held out his hands.

"No!" said Enoch, looking alarmed. "Don't do it here. Go away and practice some more. I'll tell you when I'm free to grade your parlor tricks."

Keith sat down next to him and leaned toward him with an expression of huge-eyed wistfulness. "Aw, come on, Enoch. This isn't the same guy who just asked me to stand up at his wedding, is it? All I want to do is prove I've actually absorbed what you've been teaching me."

Holl gave his brother-in-law a hard look. Enoch sighed and put down his file. "All right, then. I'll tell you why you can't. We've been having county inspectors and other Big Folk bumbling around near the property a good deal lately. I don't want you calling attention to us, especially with something like a flaming geyser."

"That's awful!" Diane exclaimed. "You must feel like you're under siege!"

"More than you realize," Holl said.

Keith's expression turned sympathetic. "I'm sorry. I didn't know."

"Well, now you do," Enoch said. "Practice on your own away from here, to spare us."

"Sure. Whatever you say. If there's anything I can do to keep from causing you trouble, you know I'll do it." He hit himself in the forehead. "I almost forgot! You know, Dola is supposed to do another commercial at the end of the week. If you put her on the train on Thursday, I can bring her home Saturday. Is that all right?" Dola sat up eagerly.

"No," Holl said at once. "Not this time. She won't be able to make it."

"What?" Keith asked, surprised into a doubletake. "The Fairy Footwear people will be expecting her."

"Well, they'll have to go on expecting her," Holl said. "She's not available."

Evidently, no one had told Dola about the change in plans. Her lips pressed together into a tight white line. Her eyes grew wide and bright. Silently, she rose to her feet and left the room with her head held high. She must have been on the verge of tears, but no one was going to see her cry.

Keith was shocked. He met Marcy's eyes. She shook her head an almost imperceptible amount. She knew nothing of this.

"Is she being punished for something?" Keith asked, lowering his voice, though he knew all the elves would still be able to hear him.

"No."

Keith frowned. Curtness was a very unHoll-like response. "Is it those county inspectors you want to avoid? I could drive her up today. Nobody will care about a car with a man and a little girl in it. Marcy could get her from town when she gets back on Tuesday." Holl's young-looking face set into a mulish There was more to this than county inspectors. Diane and Marcy retreated, clinging to one another. Keith sidled up beside Holl and leaned over, pitching his voice just above a whisper. "Holl, we need to talk."

Holl didn't lower his voice. "There's nothing to talk about. You've said many times that they expect temperament from actors, and that she's unusual because she doesn't show any. Tell them she showed temperament and wouldn't come. No other explanation is necessary."

Keith was puzzled and troubled. "C'mon, Holl, I thought we were friends. Talk to me. Is this connected to what's been bugging you since August?"

"And we are friends," Holl said, with a softening of his expression. "Enough, I hope, for me to tell you this is something I cannot talk about. And do not give me that cat-at-the-mousehole expression. You'll get no more details from me. I mean what I say. Go home now. You're tired, and we're tired. There's nothing we need to discuss now."

"You'll confess," Keith said darkly, sweeping his bookbag to his shoulder with a flourish. "They all confess in the end."

"There, do you see?" Enoch shouted to the whole of the workshop when the Big Folk had left. They'd all been listening anyhow. "We're running out of excuses! Holl must hold off the forces of the outside singlehanded, while none of you offer to assist getting rid of the problem at its heart!"

Shelogh put down the lantern she was polishing on the table with a *snap!* "We have discussed it every day, young pup! What will you have us do?"

"Discussion is nothing," Holl said, "if it doesn't result in action. The creature zooms in and out as it pleases. Anything we do to enhance, alter or improve attracts its attention. I had my heart in my mouth throughout the entire weekend thinking that it would turn up and attack Keith Doyle or one of the other Big Folk."

"They'll be protected as long as they do no magic," Catra said. "Living more simply is good for us. 'Simplify, simplify,' said their Thoreau."

"It's unnatural for us," Holl said. "We're used to using our talents whenever we please. And what of the goods we produce? I believe we're cheating if we don't send out lanterns that light, or baking molds that protect against burning. Otherwise, what is the difference between our work and that of a human-run factory? But we're afraid to use our natural talents. I've seen it—I've done it! It's absurd. There we sit on the porch, waiting for the UPS driver, casting the very last enhancement as he's coming up the drive, hoping he doesn't see us as we sneak away, and hoping the being doesn't attack him on the way out!"

"If talent's the chief thing that attracts it, we shouldn't use it," Bracey said reasonably.

"We're living enough like Big Folk as it is," Curran snapped. "Slam the door on them all."

Tay appeared in the big doorway. He caught Holl's eye and beckoned to him. Holl left the others to argue and followed his nephew.

In the very center of the farm property, the land sloped gently upward to form a low hill. In the precise center of its peak, nearly hidden by tattered cornstalks and drifts of snow, was a forlorn little figure in jeans and long-sleeved overshirt. Dola's cheeks and ear-tips were pink. When she saw her father and her granduncle coming up the rise, she turned her face away from them. Tay stopped, holding up his hands helplessly. Holl patted him on the shoulder and went to sit down beside the girl.

He gathered her close to his side with one arm, willing warmth into her. She was shivering but trying hard not to show it.

"What are you doing out here, little one?" he asked, gently. Dola shook her head. "Is this about not being able to go to Chicago?"

"Not just that." The girl raised her eyes. They were full of unshed tears, and the end of her nose was pink. "I do not like having to stay here all the time. It hurts. I feel what it is like when I am outside our land. It's comfortable. I can have peace. I hate it in here. I feel as though I'm going to die, all the time. Sometimes I wish it *would* happen so that I would be free of the endless *humming*." She threw out her arms.

"Oh, no, my dear," Holl said. "Never feel that way. Life is too precious." Tears began to roll down her cheeks. He dabbed at them with the edge of his sleeve, while feeling in his pocket for a handkerchief. Holl realized she hadn't chosen her haven at random. Dola had withdrawn as far from the boundary spell as possible. He, too, felt the tooth-gritting buzz that underlay all the other pulses of life on the farm. He had gotten to the point where he could ignore it, but it was always there at the edge of his consciousness. For the first time he realized how it irked him, digging at his normally even nature and affecting his judgement. It was affecting everyone's quality of life.

"Can't we go back to the way things were before?" Dola asked wistfully, leaning her head against his shoulder. "I thought the fence was meant to deflect the outside, not shut it off completely."

"You're right, child," Holl said. "And it would be well if we told them so."

"Now?"

"Now." He stood up and took her hand.

"Take down the boundary spell?" Curran asked, outraged. "We can nae take it down!" Intimidated by the old one's fury, Dola held fast to Holl's arm. He gave her hand a squeeze for confidence.

"We're doing this all wrong," Holl said. "We have shut this thing in with us. It's angry because it's trapped. Let's set it free."

"It is a radical idea," the Master said, coming to stand beside his heir-designate. He had been summoned from the house by Catra during the last argument. "I propose ve call a formal meetink to decide the matter. Here and now. Archivist?"

Catra reached for her pad and pencil, never far from her side, and sat down on the nearest bench. The rest of the Folk gathered around them, arranging themselves on one side or the other, Conservative and Progressive. Catra nodded to them. The red-haired Headman turned to the rest of the anxious-eyed village.

"Very gut. I declare this meetink to be open. I recognize Holl." He sat down on the old one's bench as grandly as if it was his armchair in the living room.

Holl had to admire the Master's tactics. Such a move forestalled the inevitable arguments, subsuming them under Robert's Rules of Order. Everyone must now listen, if impatiently, to what he had to say. He knew he was laying down his reputation for this proposal. He chose his words with care. Dola glanced at him, asking with her eyes if she ought to sit down. He shook his head, indicating that she should stay. She stood tall as a princess beside him, gazing proudly at her family and friends. It was the first time she'd been included in a village meeting, a function always reserved for adults.

"We've been living under siege for months now. You all know it. I did not realize until Dola showed me how unbearable it's become, living inside a spell that harms us while it seems to do nothing whatsoever to our tormentor. Turning up the power does not work. Perhaps turning it down will bring peace."

"No!" The outcry from the Conservatives was automatic. "Destroy the thing," Aylmer said. "Then ve vill talk about opening the fence."

"It's entitled to its life, as we are," Holl said. "Let's let it escape."

"We can't let Big Folk bumble onto the land," Candlepat pointed out.

"All right, let us not take down the spell entirely," Holl offered. "Let's put holes in it so our unwitting guest can come and go—go, we hope—in places where Big Folk cannot accidentally wander through; say, at the wide part of the stream, and over the compost heap, and go back to behaving as usual."

"You're asking them for an act of faith," Enoch said, rising after being recognized by the chair. "They won't act until someone else steps forward. You've got my vote. I say we do it."

"Seconded," Tay said automatically.

"But we may attract more things that we do not wish to know about us," Calla, Holl's mother, pointed out gently.

"We'll be careful not to use too much of our skills," Holl said. "We have not really become used to living in the open again—I never lived outside the walls of the library. The rest of you must remember what it was like and teach us. To survive we must keep our heads down and do what we may, safely and prudently. Catra quoted Thoreau earlier. Let us moderate our actions. Humans have laws to guard against public nuisance because they are aware that they are capable of creating one. It would seem our actions have more consequences than we knew. We are self-governing. Simplify, and we will not draw unwanted eyes."

"In favor of tryink this new approach?" the Master said. All the Progressives' hands went up and, to Holl's surprise, a number of sheepish-looking Conservatives. "Opposed?" Curran's hand shot into the air, followed by only a few of his fellows. "Very vell, it is carried. Ve vill lower the protections, opening them entirely in places to be selected mit care. Ve vill review its effects in vun veek. Any other business? No? Adjourned." The Master rose from Curran's bench and strode magnificently to the door.

"Done and done," Enoch said, with a wry grin. "He gets things done most efficiently, doesn't he? Keith Doyle will notice the difference. He's not stupid."

"No, he's not," Holl said. "I hope he will remain patient until he can be told."

The top of the dining room table was invisible under the heaps of papers, ledgers and textbooks. Keith felt underneath the nearest stack of notes, hoping he could find his pencil without looking away from the line of tiny numbers on the spreadsheet he was filling in. Staring at something made it hard to keep his gaze on it. The document seemed to bloom with light, twitch, then blur. Unable to stop himself, Keith blinked, and lost his place. Damn! He groaned and rubbed his eyes. Since he was now free to look, he could search for the pencil. Calculating the costs of running a franchise restaurant versus an independently-owned unit in the same chain was a job for expert accountants or actuaries, not a tired grad student who could just about balance his own checkbook. Keith had just discovered that his pencil had been in his breast pocket all along when a key rattled in the lock. He glanced at the beer-sign clock on the wall. Eleven forty-five! He'd better get to bed pretty soon.

"That must be the star coming back from rehearsal," said Dunn, without looking up. He had been working on his laptop on a board balanced between the arms of their one good arm-chair, in front of the television. He kicked down the volume on MTV. "Yo, Pat."

"Hello, dear, I'm home," Pat said, slinging his shoulder bag on the couch. "Did you two miss me?"

"Always. Did you bring me anything?" Keith said, glancing from one column to the next and making a note so he would remember his thoughts about franchise viability the next evening.

"Sure! This…piece of paper," Pat said, stooping to pick up something from the floor. "Is this anyone's? No, forget it; it's blank."

Keith glanced up idly at the yellowed square in Pat's hand as his roommate headed for the wastebasket. Something glinted on its surface. Keith leaped out of his seat and grabbed it away from him.

"What's with you?" Pat demanded. "Manners, boy. It's scrap paper."

"I don't think so," said Keith, holding the fragment gingerly. "It's not paper. It's parchment.". As he'd been taught, first by Holl and later by Enoch, he sent an inquiring thread of sense into it. To his delight he could sense a tiny measure of magic in the paper. The feel of the power was unfamiliar: deli-cate and wispy; not at all sturdy and matter-of-fact like the elves, or cool and airy like the air sprites, or rough like the bad-tempered *bodach* of Lewis and Harris. This had been made or at least enchanted by a type of being he had never met before. Enormously excited, he brought it over to the lamp to look at it more closely. Pat followed him.

"What is it?" he asked.

"Not sure," Keith said, looking closely.

As he tilted it under the light he saw a pattern of faint, transparent tracery on the surface. "Does anyone have a magnifying glass?"

"There's one on my Swiss Army knife," Dunn said. He got up, carefully setting the board and computer down on the couch. From his pocket he brought out a thick, red-cased knife. Keith unfolded the little lens and peered at the paper.

The silver threads seemed to spell out tiny words. Keith sat down at the table to transcribe them onto a sheet of notebook paper.

"Not does your correspondent use invisible ink, he also speaks fluent gibberish," Pat said. But Keith recognized a few of the words. He didn't know what they meant, but they echoed the text of the invitation on the billboard ad.

"You almost tossed out my very first RSVP," Keith said with satisfaction.

"You're kidding," Pat said. "Who from?"

"More like *what* from?" Dunn asked.

"Finding out's going to be half the fun," Keith said. He took a blank sheet and carefully copied out the pattern of silver lines. He compared the transcription to the bit of parchment, which he stowed carefully in a new file folder marked 'Attending.' "I've got to send this to the farm," he said, waving his piece of paper. "Dunn, can I use your scanner?"

Keith took the disk with the file back to his own room. He sent the tracing as an attachment to an e-mail to Holl for translation, then went back to read his other messages.

The Little Folk must have been on line already that night, because before he signed off there were excited e-mails from both the Illinois Little Folk and the Irish Little Folk. The message was a variation on their own language, Catra wrote, dating back over a thousand years. They'd no idea who or what it was from.

The Old Ones were even more taken aback. The Niall swore he would check every record they had dating back to the Flood to see if they could figure out with whom they had contact so long ago.

"It's an exciting thing, so it is," the Niall's message con-
cluded. "You are doing a great thing, young one. We are all
sorry it is not possible to get any of us over to you in time for
this knees-up, and surely we wish that it was. Could you draw
pictures or take videos so we can see who these mysterious
correspondents were?"

"Of course I will," Keith sent back. "I'll have to photograph it just to reassure myself it happened."

"Are we invited to this thing?" Pat asked, after Keith read
the replies out to his roommates. "Or am I just going to die of
curiosity waiting to hear what it was like?"

"You have to come," Keith said, eagerly, his eyes shining. "Both of you. All the elf-friends ought to be there. I
don't want to be the only Big Person besides Marcy who re-
members this in years to come. This will be a historic occasion." He struck a statue-like pose with one finger pointed
toward heaven.

"You mean a *mythologic* occasion," Dunn said, wryly. "But
you couldn't keep me away with barbed wire."

"Excellent," Keith said, pleased, grabbing a pencil to make
a note. "That's *three* RSVPs. It is going to be one great party."

"If anyone else replies," Pat said, ever the devil's advocate.

"Come on," Keith said. "I know these can't be the only
other beings out there. I just hope some more understand the
invitation."

He wasn't disappointed. The spider-writing was only the first
of a flood of replies. Some of the responses Keith received
were in picture-writing. He particularly enjoyed the ideogram
that showed a pretty good caricature of him and a wooden
keg. Keith hoped the guest, whatever it was, understood the
whole message, and wouldn't show up in May at his apartment looking for a drink.

A few replied only by repeating the image from the ad,
some in loving and exact detail that included the ad copy in
the corner. Others sent written notes in alphabets that neither he nor any of the Folk had ever seen before. The linguists at the farm were going crazy with delight trying to

translate them. Most were on some kind of paper or parchment, one or two on scraps of leather, and tended to be small
in size, except for one.

Late one November evening, Dunn was interrupted by the
sound of hammering at his bedroom window. He rubbed the
condensation off the glass to see a pair of blackbirds, flying
with their wings close together. As he watched, they threw
themselves at the pane, tapping frantically until he let them in.

The birds skimmed in and hovered over his desk. Narrowly missing a stack of CD-ROMs they let go of leather
strings they clutched in their claws, and dropped a stone the
size of a plate. It landed with a loud BANG! that shook the
desk. The birds fluttered out into the night. Dunn stared at the
stone. Impressed into it was a single, enormous thumb-print.

"Doyle!" Dunn yelled. "It's for you!"

Chapter 20

"Beach!" Maria shouted, pounding on her employer's hotel room door. Stefan stood beside her, his eyes shining with excitement. "Beach, open!"

The door opened a crack, and the tall man peered out over the security bar. The two Eastern Europeans stood on the threshold in a state of high excitement. "What do you want?"

"Beach, you must look!" She held up a brown paper bag.

Beach groaned. Every day for the last several weeks, despite the worsening weather, the pair had gone out shopping. They seemed determined to cover every single store in the Chicago area, one block at a time. Most of their purchases were horrible, tasteless and cheap. Bags packed their room, adjacent to his, and every bag was labeled with a name in their own language. 'Uncle Illian,' or 'Cousin Katya,' and so on. They must have larger families than the Osmonds. "What is it now?" he asked nastily. "Something for Granddad Janos?"

"No," Stefan said, avidly. "We found one of something."

"*That's* descriptive," Beach said, but the others paid no attention to the acid comment. They pushed past him into the room. Maria swept the desk clear and put her bag on top of it.

"Hold on, what the hell are you doing?" he snapped, grabbing at the swirl of papers. Ming had sent him a cluster of graphics of the magical language. He had been sorting through them, looking for common elements with previously known documents. "This is important work I'm doing here!"

"Ignore those," Maria said grandly. "Those are dead. *This* is alive."

She unfastened the top of the paper sack as though it was made of silk and drew from it a parcel wrapped in tissue paper. Beach eyed it with curiosity as she removed layer after layer, finally revealing... a lantern. It was about six inches square with twisted pillars, pierced screens on three sides, a peaked roof topped by a ring, and a candle inside. The whole thing, including the candle, was carved out of wood. Only the wick was soft cotton.

On the tip of Beach's tongue was the word, "so?", but it died as he recognized the object. He reached for his computer mouse and started clicking through the images of artifacts until he found the one he wanted.

"Yes!" he breathed.

No doubt about it, the lantern on his desk matched at least one object in the possession of Maria's government. He saw plenty of differences in ornamentation and fashion, but that could be the whim of an individual creator. According to the documentation, the old one had been discovered in 1632. This one was new.

"Does it work?" Beach asked.

With a triumphant smile, Maria picked it up and blew on the wick. It ignited.

"As you see," she said. "It burns without consuming itself."

Beach sat down slowly, his eyes never leaving the dancing flame. "Well, I'll be boiled in oil."

He stared at the lantern for a long time. At last, he had evidence that there was some connection to the magic right here in Chicago. It had been five years since he had seen the artifacts held in that secret vault. He had begun to lose faith in his dream. Here it was, restored. He played with the lantern, igniting and extinguishing it. It never failed to react to his breath. Beach laughed. Maria and Stefan looked pleased with themselves.

"Good job," he said, chucking Stefan on the arm with the side of his fist. Something scratched away at his memory, begging to be let in. He pointed at the lantern. "I've seen one of these."

"Yes, right here," Stefan said, looking puzzled.

"No," said Beach, thoughtfully. "I have a strong impression that I have seen another just like this one recently. Very recently." Automatically, his hand reached out for the stack of surveillance photographs from the Doyle apartment. Reluctantly he tore his gaze from the object on the table to flip through it.

The image was so small he almost missed it on the second pass through. In a snapshot of the young man's living room, in the midst of a collection of junk on a wooden mantelpiece over a nonfunctioning fireplace stood another lantern.

"The boy?" Stefan asked, his eyebrows drawn together in a puzzled frown. "But he is too young to be trusted with the great secrets of power."

"If that's true, why are most hackers under twenty?" Beach challenged him. "No, it's plausible he has some connection to the source. I've run into nothing but dead ends trying to make a connection either through Perkins Delaney Queen or Gadfly Electronics. *He's* the one who had the lingo on his home computer. This Doyle has to be deeply involved. He must be the conduit, if not the source itself." Beach tapped his chin with a forefinger. "Very, very interesting. He acts like such a total wally you'd never suspect him."

"We will go over his apartment again?" Stefan asked.

"No," Beach said, narrowing his eyes dangerously. "This time we have to question him directly."

Keith hunched over the wheel of his car, steering with one hand and holding his pocket tape recorder in the other. It was just his luck that the first heavy snow of the season was falling on a Friday evening as he was trying to get down to the farm.

"PDQ note," he said. "Personal assistant with personality. Personalize your Origami…no, too repetitive. How about, never forget a coupon again. I-discounts always in your pocket, courtesy of Origami. This'll be for the home shoppers, not business buyers."

His windshield wipers began to click and scrape, drawing lines on the window instead of wiping clear. Keith wasn't worried about ice accumulating on the blades. They had fouled half a dozen times already, but a new little gimmick he'd taught himself was working out pretty well. He put down his pocket recorder, held his outspread right hand to the cold glass and concentrated on his newfound skill. He had to drive peering between his fingers, but it was worth it. Within five miles the rubber blade had melted clear. *So there, Enoch*, he thought, triumphantly. *One fire spell to order.* He put his fingers down against the hot-air vent to thaw them. Maybe when the weather started to warm up he'd work on a spell for cooling, and save wear and tear on the air-conditioner in the aging car.

He picked up his recorder and tried to get his mind back on the mysteries of international franchising. He hated to admit it, but the Master had been right when he said Keith might be wearing out under such a heavy schedule. He was. The last couple of Mondays it had been a real challenge to get out of bed to go to his job. If working for PDQ wasn't so stimulating he'd drop the whole thing and go back to a regular schedule and living off campus. He wouldn't have to eat crow. Things changed in the business world so ofter the school had several grad students going up and back every term. The professors wouldn't mind if he changed back, providing he could make it past the semester break. Just then that respite felt a million miles away. He hoped his good karma with the powers-that-be at PDQ would hold out until he received his MBA. He hated to give up the job completely, for several reasons. Thanks to the generous salary trickles of money flowed slowly but steadily into his three saving funds: house, ring and Doris. He was getting valuable work experience. And it was fun. He ought to ask Dorothy what PDQ would think of letting him have a shorter work-week. Some of the really senior creative directors seemed to come in only a couple of times a month, but stars like that were given a lot of leeway. Keith shook his head. He was the most junior person on staff. He'd be pushing it to ask for special favors less than three months in.

He had left the expanse of well-lit interstate freeway miles behind him for the empty, four-lane road that led due south toward Midwestern. The shorn cropfields on both sides of the tarmac looked like a shaggy beige carpet under five or six inches of snow. His headlights, on for safety though it was still daylight, lit up the rooster-tail flurries swirling across his lane. If it got thick enough he wouldn't be able to see the lines. There was nowhere to pull off for miles yet. The soft shoulder sloped sharply down into drainage ditches on both sides of the road. He hoped the promised storm rolling in from Iowa would hold off for another hour and a half, until he reached the farm. At least the temperature was cold enough for dry snow rather than sloppily wet. Though the road wasn't slick, a crunchy, half-inch film of snow had already accumulated, enough to fill tire treads and make the going treacherous.

How lonely it was out here. He couldn't see another car ahead or behind him. Chicago was wall-to-wall with people, but downstate Illinois, flat as God's ironing board, was a patchwork of farmland speckled with small towns and cities. Normally Keith enjoyed the endless sky stretching to the horizon. At that moment his world had shrunk to the area his headlights could illumine under lead-gray clouds and worsening snow. It would have been a relief to find a pair of red taillights to follow towards town.

A tiny speck of bright white appeared in his rearview mirror and grew steadily larger. One more car on the road. Keith smiled at the reflection. He always wondered who was in other cars and where they were going. Dola chided him for wanting to care about the business of every person in the world. *But why not?* he thought with a wry grin. It was a dirty job, but someone had to do it.

Seventy miles more. He'd be grateful when winter break came and he could stay in Chicago for a few weeks straight. He'd miss Diane and Holl and the others, but they could come up to visit him for a change. Some day, when he was finished altogether with school he'd have to make up his mind where to live. He had almost $5,000 in the house fund already. By spring there ought to be enough for that down-payment on at least a modest starter home. Would he and Diane stay near the university, or in Chicago? He'd hate to be too far away from the elves, but it was tough to make a living in advertising in a small city. The major business was in the big cities. But where did she want to live? He wanted her to be happy.

The bright light in his mirror divided into two and continued growing. The other car was coming up pretty fast. Guy must be in a hurry to get where he was going. Keith dropped the recorder and put both hands on the wheel in case he had to maneuver. He pulled into the right lane to give the other room.

The car pulled level with him. Out of the corner of his eye Keith got a glimpse of metallic paint, white or silver, and the silhouettes of at least two men in the car. The passenger, a pale face with dark hair and eyebrows blurry behind the foggy glass, turned to look at him. Keith tipped him a grin and put his attention back to driving. It was kind of nice to have company.

The other car weaved back and forth in its lane, then started over the dashed white line into Keith's.

"Hey!" he cried, as it came within inches of his fender. "Watch it!" He stomped on the brake, dropping back a length or two. The other car immediately slowed to match his pace, and loomed toward him again, this time clipping the left edge of his bumper. It swerved back, then hit him again with a BANG! The driver must be drunk. Not wanting a worse collision, Keith put his foot down hard on the accelerator. The powerful Mustang engine growled to life, and he shot ahead. His cell phone was beside him on the seat. He ought to call in a drunk driver, but he didn't want to take either hand off the wheel. The snow was getting thicker.

The white car fell lengths behind him, but started to pull forward, homing in dangerously on Keith's bumper. What was wrong with those people? Did they *want* to cause an accident? Keith urged the Mustang onward.

There must have been one mighty engine under the other car's hood. No matter how Keith tried to maneuver, no matter how fast he drove, the white car kept beside him, and it was gaining ground. Keith slowed. If he could drop back quickly enough, he could pull a bootlegger's turn across the sunken meridian, and head north toward the nearest town. This was a dangerous driver. He ought to be yanked off the road before he killed someone.

To throw the other off guard, Keith increased his speed past 90 and hung on to the wheel for dear life. With any luck a state police car would spot them as they roared past. Keith might end up with a ticket, but so would the other guy. Glancing in his mirrors to make sure no other vehicle would be endangered by a sudden change of direction, Keith hit the brakes hard, then spun the wheel in a circle. The back end broke loose and fishtailed for a moment, then the car bounded over the uneven grass barrier in the center of the road to the northbound lane. Keith stepped on the gas.

Within moments the other driver turned his vehicle to follow. Keith saw the headlights bob as the white car crossed after him. It was chasing him! Keith peered ahead through the dancing dots of white. How far ahead was that last turnoff?

The other gained on him. Keith held grimly to the wheel. The white car swerved into the other lane, rocketed forward until it was halfway ahead of him, then edged over, forcing him closer to the edge of the road. In a moment they'd both go into the ditch. He tried slowing or speeding, but the stranger had his measure now, and matched him move for move. Keith felt gravel under his right tires as he felt the white car nudge him in the front left fender. He hit the brakes hard and threw down a mental anchor, using the thickest thread of magical sense he could muster, to keep his car from spinning out. He bumped over the loose rocks on the shoulder. A cold stone was in his belly as he heard the drive train drag through the gravel.

The white car didn't have brakes as good as his, mechanical or magical. Its tires, clogged with snow, skidded on the smooth road. As Keith watched in horror it went off the road and crashed into the ditch, finishing tilted over at a 45° angle against a fence. Keith heard the impact as he overshot the site. He hauled his wheel over to the right, rolled to a stop on the shoulder, then threw his car into reverse. He turned to look behind him, steering with one hand, the other outstretched along the top of the car seat. He hoped no one was hurt.

As he got closer, he could see figures staggering up onto the roadside. He thought he saw at least four of them. He could just about fit them into his car while they waited for the tow truck. He'd better call in the accident, then give Hollow Tree a ring just to let them know he was going to be late. But first to find out if anyone had been injured.

Putting his phone in his pocket, Keith pulled on his gloves and got out.

"Are you folks all right?" he called, heading toward them.

Lit by the red glow from his taillights, three of them stood hunched against the cold in short leather jackets and jeans. The tallest man, pale-skinned and pale-eyed, dressed in an expensive overcoat, turned toward him.

"Come here," he said, in a nasal, flat voice that sounded Australian or something.

In one horrible moment Keith recognized him. It was the guy from Buckingham Fountain who'd had the advance copy of the ad. Automatically, Keith started to back away. The tall man stuck his left hand into the front of his coat and brought it out again. Even in the gloom Keith realized he was holding a gun. "Come eeyeh! Naow!"

"Now, wait a minute," Keith said, alarmed. "I don't want any trouble. I haven't got anything you want. The ad's out. Everyone knows about it."

"To hell with the ad!" the man yelled. "Where did you find the lingo in the middle?"

The lingo...? The elves' language? "No place," Keith said, defiantly stopping where he was. The tall man's three companions swarmed around him, roughly taking hold of his arms and shoulders. "I made it up."

"Liar," Beach said, narrowing his eyes at the boy with a leering grin. "You feel you have something to defend. Now we're getting somewhere. Maria!"

A slender, black-haired woman appeared from near the car, swathed to the chin in furs. She had dark, intense eyes that even in the gloom bored into Keith's like diamond drills. Oh, no. He'd watched enough spy movies to know that he ought to be afraid when they brought out the spooky lady. They were going to make her bend his mind until he told them all about the elves and their language. Well, they didn't know everything about *him*.

"Maria," said the tall man, "has he got any of the glamour on him?"

The woman moved closer. Her eyes seemed to glow. "Yes," she said. "A power, growing...growing...growing..."

The men holding him obviously weren't too crazy about the spooky lady, or her pronouncements either. Keith could feel their grip loosen involuntarily. Good.

With a wiliness borne of years wrestling with a stronger and larger younger brother, Keith ducked down and slipped out of their grasp. At the same time, he used Holl's favorite trick on them, one the Big student had wheedled his friend into teaching him. He jumped away. They flailed for him, and ended up windmilling their arms, unable to follow because their feet were stuck to the ground. Keith stood just out of reach, panting from the exertion, as they swore at him. Three at once was a lot to deal with, and not a single river of power anywhere to draw upon. He had to do it again, though, because the tall man himself was coming at him now, gun pointed at Keith's head.

"Come back here, young man," he commanded. "We haven't finished our conversation yet."

"Beach, we are stuck!" the dark-eyebrowed man cried.

Keith wasn't waiting to see what else this Beach had in mind. Summoning up every erg of energy from the depths of his soul, he threw another sticky-spell at the man's feet and ran for his car. He jumped into the waiting Mustang and gunned it out onto the snowy road.

He didn't dare turn around and head south again, not here. The charm couldn't last long on his limited ability, and they'd be after him pretty soon. That is, if their car was drivable. With a sigh Keith reached for his cell phone. No matter if they were trying to pry secrets out of him, they were still people. He couldn't let them freeze on the Illinois tundra in the middle of the night. He called in the accident to the state police, pulled off on the first secondary road, and began to wind his way slowly toward Hollow Tree Farm.

"No, we did not foresee the incident," Holl said, offering Keith hot cider in his unicorn mug at one thirty in the morning. Keith's frenzied pounding on the door had awakened most of the household. Everyone had gone back to bed but Holl, Keva and Dola, who was sitting next to her granduncle with wide eyes. "But you are right: it is a good thing that Dola was not with you."

"We'd just be coming back from her commercial shoot," Keith said, taking a long, deep sip. Ah. The icicles in his bloodstream began to thaw. He slumped with his elbows on the table. Exhaustion weighed down every limb. The drive along unfamiliar, narrow lanes steadily clogging with snow had shredded his nerves. "If we'd been talking I might not have paid attention to those people until they'd run me into a fence. It's bad enough they banged up my bumper. That's going to have to be pounded out. So, it's better you didn't come, sweetheart." He reached over and tugged a lock of her blond hair.

Dola was not mollified. She tossed her head, tilting one pointed ear toward her uncle. "I might have been able to help you, Keith Doyle. You say you nearly ran out of strength."

"Just about," Keith admitted. Circles were etched in the pale skin under his eyes, which were muddy green with exhaustion. "I was woozy for the next twenty miles, and driving through a blizzard, that's not too smart."

"You did amazingly well, for a Big Person," Holl said seriously. "Holding down four grown men, one with cold steel in his fist, is a worthy accomplishment."

"Shucks, it was nothing," Keith said, pleased at the compliment. "So when this man, Beach, came up to me in the park it wasn't about the ad itself. I shouldn't have had to worry about PDQ or my job. That's a relief. But this is worse!" he exclaimed, sitting up suddenly. "This guy could be after *you!*"

Holl nodded. "But they cannot find us. Our land is surrounded by many protections, not the least of which is the 'electric fence' you like to complain about. But there will be those who will say you've given us undesirable exposure to the public, by publishing your invitation."

"I know," Keith said, his shoulders sagging. "I'm sorry. It just seemed like the easiest thing to do. But it's working! I've gotten about twelve responses so far. From what, I have no idea, but I've got the RSVPs. The Niall sounded really happy about it. I thought you guys liked it, too."

"We do." Holl smiled. "Pay the growlers no mind. They also believe we will bring down all of modern civilization on our heads by putting out a mailbox on the main road. But I'm curious: how did those Big Folk come to associate our written language with…what did the man call it, the glamour?"

"An old word for magic," Keith acknowledged. "He didn't say, and I wasn't going to stick around to find out. But this Beach isn't going to leave me alone. Following me over a hundred miles from Chicago to ask me a question means he's serious. What can I do?"

Holl tilted his own head to regard his friend. His carroty coloring was distinctive enough, but his native enthusiasm drew the eye regardless. "You *are* difficult to lose in a crowd. Ah, well, you were asking Enoch for a lesson. He won't mind if I take this task on myself."

In spite of his exhaustion, Keith perked up. "What is it?"

"Our means for avoiding sight. It's a skill of misdirection more than invisibility, so don't get your hopes up, you overexcited infant." Holl grinned at him. Working at the sink, Keva let out a sharp exclamation. She came over to stick a dripping forefinger in her younger brother's face.

"Don't you dare teach him about the pulses of the earth," she said in their own language. "It's not appropriate for a Big Person to know!"

"He may need to know it one day," Holl argued. "I thought you trusted him."

Keva smacked a tray down on the table and dried it with rough strokes of a towel. "To a point! He's still a Big Person!"

"He kept our secret despite the risk to his own safety," Holl said. "We owe him what protection we can give him."

"I don't like it. I wouldn't do it." She spun on her heel and went back to her dishes.

Holl scowled at his sister, then turned to Keith, who had been watching them curiously. He probably guessed that he was being discussed, but was too well-mannered to say so. "In any case you're in no shape to absorb the information now, Keith Doyle," he said in English. "Go to sleep. You've got your classes to attend in the morning."

Keith groaned and looked at the clock. Only six hours until he had to be awake again. "I'll call and tell them I died," he said.

"Not yet," Holl assured him, taking the mug out of his hands. "Come on. Do you need help getting down to the barn?"

Keith made a face. "I'm not dead yet. Wait until morning."

Beach sat in the cab of the wrecker, waiting for the two men in boiler suits to winch his car out of the ditch. Though they weren't pleased to have to come out to the middle of nowhere in the middle of the night, they showed the concern of decent people for the four passengers who needed help. They had been sent by the highway patrol, they told him, who were informed by an anonymous phone call. Someone had seen them go off the road. The boy, Beach thought. His mind went back over the events of three hours before, replaying them again and again. He still could not believe what seemed to have occurred. The four of them had been glued to the ground while their quarry ran away.

"What did he *do*?" he asked Maria for the fiftieth or sixtieth time.

The psychic was huddled against the door, staring out into the snowy night. "I do not know. Suddenly there was a feeling. My spirits tell me the earth is his friend...but I know no more than that."

Beach frowned. He wanted to know more, and right that very minute, preferably with illustrations and footnotes. "But what is it? A hereditary skill? Or did he learn it somewhere? How? And from who?"

Chapter 21

"Not like that," Holl said, sternly, early the next morning. "I can still see you. You want to lead my eye away from you." Keith, flattened against the wall of the farmhouse living room, thought harder about not being there. He edged slightly to the right, and was pleased to see Holl's gaze stay fixed on the same spot.

"Now I can see you," Enoch said. Keith shifted back the other way, and Holl looked him straight in the eye.

"This doesn't work so well on more than one person," Keith complained. Holl reached up and tapped him on the chest.

"You're concentrating on the wrong thing. Don't think of *you*. Make something else the focus of all attention. Use your strength to make an object so attractive that no one will be able to resist looking at it. It can be anything. The lamp. A scrap of paper. A vase of flowers. A pigeon."

Keith grinned. "I can see having these guys run after a flying pigeon. They'll wake up wondering why they're miles across the city."

"It's momentary," Enoch said, sternly. "That's why it can be such a strong effect."

"I get it," Keith said. Marm came through at that moment, carrying a ball of twine and a pair of scissors. Evoking all the energy he could, Keith applied the attraction to the plump brewer. Involuntarily the other two elves' heads turned toward their fellow as he stumped toward the basement steps.

"What are you two looking at?" Marm asked, puzzled. Keith took the opportunity to scoot across the room and seat himself on a footstool near the fireplace. When Holl and Enoch came around to face him again Holl was smiling and Enoch had his brows raised.

"Well," said Enoch at last. "No one should be surprised any longer by your proficiency."

"Not bad for a shirt-tail relative, huh?" Keith asked, grin-ning so wide he could have swallowed his ears.

The two elves looked at one another. "If there was ever a Big Person I'd consider being related to..." Holl began.

"Don't push too much," Enoch said, interrupting his brother-in-law but looking at Keith.

"Oh, well," Keith said cheerfully. "A guy's got to try."

"You need more practice," Enoch said. "One more time."

"Have a heart!" Keith said, trying to look pathetic. "I'm starved. I can smell breakfast from here."

Holl looked at him slyly. "If you can sneak out into the kitchen without us seeing you, you can eat."

"Ah, yur a turrible, turrible hard taskmaster. Both of you."

Tiron stuck his head into the room.

"The orders are ready," he said, with a wink at Keith. "Is the delivery van ready to roll?"

"Saved by the bell," Keith said, wiping his forehead with an exaggerated gesture of relief. "How are the samples coming?"

"Ready for you when you go home," the Irish elf declared positively. "And you'll never see finer."

"I bet," Keith said, looking at his watch. Everyone seemed cheerful that morning. It was such a pleasant change from the last several weeks. Keith felt good, too. Despite his long drive the night before and the worries that followed he felt refreshed. "Oh, boy. I'd better get going. I'll be late for class. I'll get them later, Tiron. Thanks again for taking the time to show me, guys. I was just too excited to wait for Sunday."

"It's a small thing," Enoch said, as Keith went out the door. The two males heard a squawk of protest from one of the morning's cooks as the Big student filched three muffins out of a basket about to be set on the table.

"Vhy do you denigrate his accomplishment?" the Master asked from his big chair near the window.

"Well, he never saw you, did he?" Enoch countered. "You've been here throughout, and he didn't sense you once."

"But that vas not the subject of this lesson, vas it?" his father asked, mildly. "He understoot the teaching very vell, and made use of it most creatively." The Master smiled. "He took advahntage of the arrival of Marm to show you vhat he had learned. I gif him high marks for that. But to be able to mislead your eyes at all—who vould haf expected that vun of the Big Folk could efer haf done it? He has advanced farther than efen I vould haf thought possible mitout training, or the assistance of a device. He is extraordinary among his kind."

Enoch shook his head. "That's exactly why I didn't want to make a fuss. If that notion was anywhere in the back of his mind, he might freeze at a time when he needs to use the skill. I want him to think anyone who studies hard enough can do it."

"Ah. Misdirection." The Master's eyes twinkled. "I hope that your purpose does not backfire and leaf him helpless vhen he most needs the skills."

Holl laughed. "Keith Doyle? He's as resourceful as a backwoodsman. If one thing doesn't work, he'll try another. When have you ever known him to give up?"

The Master looked grave. "Nefer. But he has chosen much too heavy a schedule this year. I vorry that he is growing too tired to make intelligent choices."

"Ah," said Holl. "Now, that I can do nothing about."

"Well, well, strangers," Ms. Voordman said, looking up as the bell hanging over the front door of Voordman's Country Crafts jingled. Keith edged his other foot in the glass door and nudged it open far enough to carry in the huge box in his arms. Diane was close behind him with a small carton. The proprietress, a slim, well-groomed, dark-haired woman somewhere in her forties, gave Diane a peck on the cheek. "Welcome! Is this my holiday order?"

"Yup," Keith said. "Everything. Plus, we'd like you to look at a couple of things."

"I'm sure I'll love them," Ms. Voordman said. "Come on back. I have fresh coffee. Hot," she added, glancing out the door at the falling snow. "This is getting ugly. I will either have a lot of business this evening, or none at all."

"I'd love some coffee," Diane said, gratefully. "It feels like we've been driving forever, but it's only been about an hour." She held up the box. "Do you want me to stock these?" Diane had worked for Ms. Voordman during her freshman and sopho-more years and knew the business well.

The shop owner shook her head. "If you'll just help me unwrap them that would be fine. I'll take care of the busy-work after you go. How often do I have a chance to chat with you?"

Diane looked pleased. "Thanks."

"I have to get the other two boxes out of the trunk," Keith said, pulling the door open. "Be right back. Don't wait for me."

Few cars passed the small parking lot in the gathering gloom. Keith looked at the sky, hoping it would clear up before Monday. He didn't relish another drive like the one the night before.

He hauled the second box out of the trunk and piled the third box on top of it. In order to cary both through the door-way he had to bend his knees slightly, but he made it. The doorbell jangled behind him. Ms. Voordman peered around the tower of cardboard.

"Very nice," she said, approvingly. She pointed at the floor next to the cash register. "Just set them down here."

Keith rubbed feeling back into his hands and stamped snow off his shoes. "Where's Diane?" he asked.

"In the back." The shop owner paused, her normally sharp brown eyes studying him with worry. "Keith, we've known one another a few years. As a friend, I'd like to say something. You can tell me it's none of my business."

"Sure," Keith said, concerned at the serious expression on the older woman's face.

After a quick glance over her shoulder to make sure they weren't being overheard Ms. Voordman lowered her voice. "I think of Diane as my own daughter. I know how she feels about you."

"Well, I feel the same way," Keith said. "I mean, I love her."

"Good. You should show it a little better than you have been. She's feeling neglected. You ought to spend some more time with her."

"I know," Keith said, with a sigh. He kicked the lower carton with the side of his foot. "I'm so busy this year. I wish I had more time."

"Make some," Ms. Voordman advised him, in the direct way she had. He raised his eyebrows.

"I must be in real trouble," Keith said playfully.

"Don't joke, young man. She's worth taking care for."

"I know," Keith said, his narrow face serious. "I love her so much, I couldn't imagine the rest of my life without her."

"Don't tell me, tell her!" Ms. Voordman smiled at Diane, who came out of the back room with two cups of coffee in her hand. She gave one of them to Keith. "Now, please let me see the specials you brought me."

Keith took Ms. Voordman's advice to heart.

After the bad start the weekend turned out to be wonderful. The weather improved so that the setting sun threw red and orange rays over a glistening, white landscape that raised Keith's spirits and filled him with enthusiastic plans. A new restaurant specializing in Indian cuisine had opened up near the university. Keith took Diane there that evening. Though unfamiliar, the food was good enough to earn Diane's critical approval. They lingered over rich, gooey desserts and sweet, milky tea, enjoying the exotic music that went so well with the food. Keith made sure that she enjoyed herself, taking care to defer to her, and let her do most of the talking. He felt rewarded by the pleasure shining from her eyes. Mentally, he thanked the shop owner for giving him a nudge to remember what was most important in his life. He didn't mention the near-collision or the encounter with the man from Chicago, judging that the news would only frighten her and ruin a happy time. Nothing had happened, anyhow.

When he returned to the farm Sunday morning it was with fresh orders in hand. One was from Ms. Voordman. She'd been very impressed by the original sculptures, and put in an order for three small pieces valued between $100 and $300 to put in the glass case she reserved for special items. A couple more of their old clients asked for one each, but even a single art piece made the little cash register in Keith's mind go *ka-ching*!

"They'll really be thrilled about this," Keith kept telling Diane. At the back of his mind he mulled over the shop owner's words about his girlfriend, watching her face out of the corner of his eye as he drove. She seemed perfectly contented to share in the Little People's good fortune. He began to think ahead of things he could do to please her. She liked yellow flowers. Maybe he could have a surprise bouquet sent to the food service facility where she worked, to arrive in the middle of the week.

More good news awaited them at the farm. Marcy must have heard the Mustang crunching up the drive, because she and Enoch were waiting for them at the kitchen door. Her milk-white face was flushed with pink. Enoch, as usual, looked dour but grimly pleased.

"My folks called," she said, her eyes dancing with excitement. "They want to meet Enoch."

"That's great!" Keith exclaimed.

"How wonderful!" Diane said, hugging Marcy. "I'm so happy for you."

Marcy returned the embrace, and turned to give Keith a shy hug. He put an arm around her awkwardly, aware of Enoch's gimlet eye on him.

"Thanks," Marcy said. "Dad said it was after you came to see him the second time that he really started thinking. He's all set to approve, I can tell. They're coming down here this week. We want to get married around Christmas. Will you come?

"You bet," Keith said.

"Try and stop us," Diane said, positively. "This is *terrific* news."

"We've got so many plans to make," Marcy said, as though she still couldn't believe her own words. "They're going to come to dinner—should they meet everyone at once? Would that be too much?"

The Master gathered them up for class, causing the question to be tabled in favor of the musings of Aristotle.

By the time they finished with the session in the quiet corner of the barn, the sky was clear and blue with a few wisps of cirrus cloud pointing in the direction of the departed storm. Keith pulled his hat down over his ears, but the wind didn't seem as cold as it had before.

"Look at that," Tiron cackled. He, Enoch and Holl were helping Keith carry armloads of swaddled sculpture up the slope to his car. Marcy and Diane trailed behind, picking their way carefully. "The gods are so eager to see the back of you that they've cleared the weather to speed your departure."

"Yeah, thanks," Keith said, concentrating on not slipping.

"You're permitted to let any of the galleries keep these works to sell," Catra said, trotting beside him in the snow. She offered a sheaf of papers in a manila folder. "Here is one invoice for each piece so that they all do not have to go to one place." Her face and ears were pink from the wind, but she was so absorbed in her task that she didn't realize she had come out without a coat. "I am keeping a central list, but here is a copy for you. Tell us who takes what. And we will accept commissions."

"Gotcha," Keith said, sticking out two fingers to take the folder.

"I've got it," Diane said, accepting it for him. She pulled the hood of her parka tighter around her face. "Go inside! I'm freezing just looking at you."

Keith stowed the packages in his trunk with a blanket tucked around them so they wouldn't roll around. He slammed the trunk lid. "There! Ready to take to the snooty side of town."

"Our thanks, Keith Doyle," Catra said. "I would like to hear all details of your discussions with the buyers, and any comments they have."

"I'll even tape record them, if you want."

"That won't be necessary," Enoch said, sourly.

Diane huddled into her coat and moved her feet. "It's too cold. I'm going to go. Call me?" she asked Keith.

"Of course," he said, gathering her into his arms. "Soon as I get home. Love you."

"Love you, too," Diane said. She glanced over his shoulder at Marcy, standing a little way off with Enoch, and felt a touch of envy for their happiness. "Promise me something?"

"Sure," Keith said at once. He raised his right hand. "I solemnly swear I will buy a black Armani shirt when I get home and wear it to the galleries." He leaned down into the circle of her down jacket's hood to kiss her.

"Good," Diane said. She paused a moment, thinking she might say something more, and decided not to. "Bye." She went to her car and got in.

Keith noticed the troubled expression on her face, and thought of running after her. Was she still worried about her schoolwork? He thought they'd made real headway on Saturday. He shook his head. She'd be all right. He'd write her a long, loving letter as soon as he got back to Chicago. But why wait? He could dictate it on the way. He patted the little tape recorder in his coat pocket.

"Do you need to rush off?" Holl asked him. "Would you like a warming cup before you go?"

"That'd be great," Keith said, forgetting what he was thinking about. He wanted to take advantage of the relaxed feel of the farm. He couldn't put his finger on what was different, but the elves seemed happier and less pressured. Maybe whatever had been bothering them had gone away. "Now that it's clear it ought to be a pretty easy ride home. I can stick around for a little while."

"Let's not go in," Holl said. "I'll bring some hot cider out here. I hate to shut out such a glorious sky. You wouldn't be too cold, would you?"

"No. I'm fine." Keith brushed off a stair tread at the bottom of the kitchen steps and sat down on it. His jacket was too short to shield his bottom from the cold board. He got up and used a little of his new heat charm to warm it to a comfortable level. When he looked up, Holl had returned and was watching him.

"Did Enoch teach you to do that?" Holl asked.

"Nope," Keith said. "I figured it out all on my own. I know he didn't want me doing anything big, but something this small shouldn't attract anybody's attention, would it?"

"I hope not," Holl said. He handed Keith his unicorn mug and sat down beside him. He wondered if Dola had talked. But she'd been adamant in her protestations that she had not, and that Keith had not pressed her once she had asked him not to. So were they broadcasting their fears to him in a way that he'd understand? Holl had always scoffed at Keith's protestations that the Big and Little Folk were related, especially with regard to him, but he had a sensitivity rarely seen in those of his kind. What had he picked up, anything about the monster troubling them? There hadn't been any fresh incidents in the last forty-eight hours, but the boy was sensitive. It was on the tip of his tongue to ask, but he pushed the question back into his mouth. The Master would have a few words to say to him if he broke confidence now.

"Ah, luxury," Keith said, stretching his legs out in front of him. He took a deep drink of the fragrant spiced cider. It warmed him all the way down inside, but not as much as having his best friend beside him, behaving normally again. Holl filled his pipe and lit it, sending a jet of smoke toward the distant horizon. It was cold, but one of those crisp, still, cool evenings full of peace.

"It's going to be a handsome sunset," Holl said. "I love being able to sit out here, feeling infinity before me, as though I could reach out and touch the edges of forever. Soon the sky will be full of stars. I look up, and I still marvel that it's not a ceiling, with a sunset we made ourselves out of light-strips. I love this place."

"I do, too," Keith said, feeling solemn. "Every time I come here I still get a thrill out of it. Every time I go I hate to leave. Sometimes when I'm watching the house disappear behind the trees I wonder if it'll be the last time I ever see it, forever. I hope that will never happen, so I try to enjoy it while I can."

"This is a philosophical side of you I've never seen," Holl said, surprised.

"Maybe it's maturity," Keith said, turning to him with a twinkle in his eye. "Don't tell anyone. I've got a rep to protect."

"They'll never hear it from me," Holl assured him. "Ah, but you're right. So much of life is fleeting. That which we have known and loved...could vanish in the next moment. For this reason we have to be prepared, to move on, to sever ties, to start over again."

It was so melancholy a sentiment that Keith was alarmed. "I hope you don't ever send me away."

Holl shook his head. "One day you may absent yourself of your own purpose."

"Never," Keith vowed. "Not if there's anything I can do to prevent it."

Chapter 22

Keith looked down at the lapel of his new shirt. He was used to wearing colored shirts, but the black under the jacket of the dark suit took a little getting used to. The price for good designer clothes had been a revelation, even though he thought he was prepared. The cost of the outfit had put a deep hole in the house-buying fund, but Diane had been so pleased when he called to say he'd bought it he decided it was worth the money. He wasn't sure he liked so many dark colors together. The outfit was too chic to be funereal. Instead he felt like a Mafia don or a game show host. He straightened his pewter-gray tie, feeling like he was wearing a grownup Halloween costume, all the more stark against the pure white walls of Galleria Tony. The outfit did the trick, however, as it had at the last five places he'd visited. The young woman with black, moussed hair and a fringed shawl behind the high counter focused on him right away. She glided out from behind the desk and came to a graceful halt beside him.

"May I help you?" she asked.

Keith introduced himself. "I represent Hollow Tree Studios," he said, offering one of the new business cards the elves had run up on their computer. "Your buyer, Mr. Albert, reviewed our portfolio and wanted to see some of the artwork." He indicated the rolling luggage cart beside him. Three of the best pieces were in a box on its platform. The paperwork and the portfolio were in his briefcase, which he had polished for the occasion but was beginning to acquire salt splashes from being pulled along the sidewalk in the slush. He'd had to make the journey from his office by bus. His car was in the shop having the bumper repaired, something that was cutting into his house-down-payment account, the only surplus savings he felt he could sacrifice. Dipping into it depressed him because it meant he was moving away from instead of towards his goal. "I've got an appointment. Is he here?"

He didn't feel optimistic. In spite of the fact that he had arranged to meet with the buyers from seven galleries that day, two hadn't been around, and one had been busy with another meeting and dismissed Keith without speaking to him.

"Ah, yes," she said, sounding like an extra in a vintage British movie. "He is here. Please wait." She sashayed away behind a white partition wall and returned shortly with a man dressed exactly like Keith, except that his tie was electric blue. It was a good omen. Keith began to feel hopeful. The man's brown hair and short, clipped beard had been spiked with mousse. Keith wondered if he ought to use some on his hair. He might fit in better.

"Well?" Thom Albert asked, raising his eyebrows at the bundles on Keith's luggage cart. "Don't stand there, darling, open them up!"

Like anyone else who saw the elves' work, Mr. Albert couldn't wait to get his hands on them, and didn't want to let go of them once he'd touched them. Keith watched him carefully as he moved the pieces around the broad table in the back room of the shop, holding them to catch the light, studying their construction, touching the smooth curves of wood. Still, this was the point at which the last two had decided not to buy anything. Keith had a better feeling about this man. He was not disappointed.

"This is mine," the buyer gloated, his long, pale hands battening onto the figure of a fan-tailed koi rendered in warm, golden cherrywood. He petted it gently, running his fingers around the elaborately carved dorsal fin and tail. "Magnificent for feng shui. I know just where I'm going to put it, on the north side of my condo. I'll take the others for the gallery, the bull and the abstract—what did you say the artist called it?"

Keith peered at the master list Catra had given him. "Winter Sunset." This was a piece of ragged oak burl shaped into the form of a wild, old tree whose upper branches surrounded a small, open circle. Placed against the white wall, the tree seemed to capture a pale, watery sun.

"Now, the bad news," Albert said, reaching for the invoices Keith handed him and examining the numbers. "Darling, you really need to charge more for these. Unscrupulous art dealers will pay what you're asking and quadruple the price. I might do it, too, but I'll tell you about it first."

"Maybe next time," Keith said, guardedly enthusiastic. "Think of it as an introductory special. The artists want to establish a relationship with a gallery."

"Well, you're mine," Albert said, firmly, setting the papers down and putting his hand on them. "Don't go anywhere else. I want to see everything you've got. The pieces you showed me in the portfolio—how many of those are still available?"

Keith opened the book and gave it to him. "Anything without a red dot on it."

"These photos are terrible," Albert complained, thumbing through the pages. "They look as though they've been taken with one of those cheap electronic cameras. They don't do the work justice. You should take them to a professional. They're worth it. Is Hollow Tree connected to an art school?"

"Independent crafters," Keith said. "They have an apprenticeship program, but they're really fussy."

Thom Albert laughed. "Well, so am I. I would be very pleased to display their work. I am sure we can do them justice. Let me show you the space I have in mind."

"This is great, Mr. Albert," Keith began.

"Thom, please."

"Thom. I'm Keith. The...people I represent are going to be really happy."

"Wait until we see dollar signs," the buyer assured him, "and then we'll all be happy."

After talking over how many pieces would fit in the space, appropriate lighting and financial terms, only the last of which was ground Keith was certain of, he folded up his luggage cart and put his overcoat back on.

Through the narrow window in the door, he could see that it had grown dark already. He was too tired to strut, but he couldn't help having a little jauntiness in his step. He'd succeeded in finding the elves a really good spot for their high-class work.

Funny, he thought, as he descended the short flight of steps to the street, that he hadn't seen any sign at the farm of where money would be needed. Everything seemed to be okay. Had one of them taken up online gambling? Or were they being blackmailed by someone? Who?

"There!" a woman's voice cried, pointing through the open door.

Keith glanced down. Light coming from behind him caught the features of the woman coming toward him. It was the scary lady! He flattened himself against the railing. He hadn't expected to see them back in the city so quickly.

I'm not here, he thought desperately. *I'm somewhere else. I'm not me. I'm not here!* Then Holl's lesson came back to him. Make something else more attractive to the eye. He focused on the gallery desk he could just see inside. He put the whammy on it and stood very still.

"This way," Maria said, gesturing to the two behind her. "I feel something here."

Obediently, Stefan followed her. Beach was less avid. He didn't appreciate being pulled out into the cold winter weather again, not that soon after they had spent a night on a remote Illinois highway, nor hauled along through the slush behind Maria and her spirits.. But he had to admit he did want to see that desk. Something brushed his arm as he mounted the steps, as if a person had gone by. He glanced around, but no one was near him. He shook his head.

"Hurry!" Maria cried. She burst through the door, her elegantly long nose almost twitching like a bloodhound's. She made straight for the counter. "What is here? I must see behind it."

Beach stared at the desk, too, unable to take his eyes off it. He had no idea what was so attractive about it. A trick of the light?

"There's nothing back here," the girl said, opening large eyes fringed with mascara in alarm at the blackhaired madwoman grabbing things out from under the desk and throwing them. "Thom!"

"Excuse me, may I help you?" A bearded man in Armani black came bustling out from the back room. "Please," he said, putting a hand on Maria's arm. "Don't do that." She threw him off, circling around the white-paneled counter to look. The girl tried to head her off, too. Stefan, always protective of his charge, interposed his stocky body to allow Maria to conduct her search.

"I will call the police," the bearded man cautioned them.

"I'm sorry, this is the inmates' day out from the asylum," Beach said. "They get a little excitable."

"Well, they shouldn't be here!"

"They respond well to art," Beach explained. "It's part of their therapy."

"It is gone!" Maria said. "I feel it back there, now." She headed for a partition wall at the rear of the room.

"Please!" the man said, getting ahead of her and blocking the doorway with both arms. "This is a private room."

"But I must go in!" Maria wailed. "The spirits guide me there."

Beach turned to the man. "Do you have anything back there like little carved lanterns or boxes with gauze panels on one side?"

Offended, the man straightened himself up. "God, no. This is a reputable gallery. We carry one-of-a-kind objets d'art. You want a knickknack shop."

Beach glanced over the man's shoulder at the room. He glimpsed a coffee machine, a couple of chairs, a file cabinet, steel shelves and a large worktable with a mismatched trio of sculptures clustered to one side. Nothing seemed out of the ordinary. He took Maria firmly by the arm and steered her toward the door. "Sorry to have troubled you. Come on, sweetheart. Stefan!"

"But something is there, Beach," Maria insisted as he hustled her down the stairs.

Beach looked over his shoulder. The man and the girl were behind them, making sure they went away. "We'll investigate it after hours, but not now. Didn't you hear him? He was about to call the police! You can't go diving into everything that attracts your attention."

"But that is why you bring me here," Maria said, hurt.

"The one thing I want you to find right now is Keith Doyle," Beach said. "Find him, and we'll find our answer."

"Very well," Maria said, sulkily. "I will ask the spirits."

"That's the spirit," Beach said. He put up a hand to hail a cab.

Dorothy opened the door of the PDQ boardroom just in time to hear Keith exclaim in an enthusiastic voice, "So the account rep says, 'Well, if you don't mind, then it doesn't Mather.'"

Jennifer Schick and the PDQ staff groaned and broke into laughter. Mann wore a puzzled expression until his marketing director explained to him who Ogilvy and Mather were.

"Your guy here is an absolute database of bad jokes," Mann said, as Dorothy slid into her seat at the end of the long oval table

"He sure is," Dorothy agreed, longsufferingly.

"You bet," Keith said, sitting down. "Wind me up and I go on for hours."

"Is that a threat?" Mann asked, easing back in the springy armchair.

"Try me," Keith said, with a look of playful insanity.

"No threat," Dorothy said hastily, watching her clients with a trepidatious eye. "We're not threatening anyone."

"That's just a joke," Mann said, turning to her. "Don't worry. I don't mean anything by it. He's been a good host while we're waiting for you."

"Everyone have enough coffee?" Dorothy asked, nervously. "Try the pastries. They're from that good place up the street."

"We're fine," Theo said, stretching out his long legs. "No problems." He felt in his pocket and came up with his packet of cigarettes. Though there were NO SMOKING signs displayed throughout the room, none of the PDQ staffers said anything. Keith even ignited his invisible lighter and held the live flame out for him to use. Theo leaned forward to touch his cigarette to the light, but Jennifer Schick caught the furtive glances of the others and elbowed him in the ribs. Theo sat up, a hurt expression on his face. She pointed to the signs, and understanding dawned. "Sorry."

"You are welcome do whatever you want," Dorothy said. "You're our guests."

Theo shook his head. "We play by house rules. But, thanks."

"*So*," Doug said. "You're the talk of the 'Net. How are you feeling?"

Mann nodded, indicating his friends. "Pretty amazing. Sales have just zoomed out of sight. We don't come from big money. We're just a bunch of friends from North Carolina, been together since college, working on one idea or another. This is the one that stuck, and now, well, suddenly it's all real. We're a major company. It's awesome."

"Since October, other businesses are setting up shop near us," Theo said. "We're thinking of calling our zone Silicon Ridge, to distinguish it from Silicon Valley or Silicon Prairie."

"Sounds intense," said Doug. "Well, you don't need us to tell you how good the response has been to the campaign."

"It's fantastic," Jen Schick said. "My researchers have been tracking sales in the major markets and in a hundred minor ones. I can't believe the numbers. You folks have done an incredible job."

"So, are you happy?" Dorothy asked.

"Oh, yeah," Bill Mann said.

"Good," said Doug, "because it's time to talk about what comes next."

"Next?" Mann asked. "We don't have a new unit coming out for a long time yet. Even the upgrade's a year off."

"That's especially why we need to plug the original one again. While the Christmas market is still going on is the time to think about winter and spring rollouts. Rita?"

"Lights, please." Keith, seated nearest the door, sprang to turn off the switch. Rita Dulwich, from the research department, put a graphic up on the multimedia wall screen. "Here's our suggestions that would be good followups, good value for money, to the campaign that's already running." One after another, the print ads appeared. Boxes sprang off from the central one, each containing a mockup of another advertisement.

Janine, Rollin, Keith and Dorothy had been working nonstop for weeks to come up with enough ideas to choose from. "Print ads, including catalogs for the new year, will offer a further, more subtle push for the Origami, to add another level to the high-visibility ads we're already pumping out there." A television screen appeared in the center, displaying the "Bend Me, Shape Me" commercial. "We'd like to produce at least two more series of spots to supplement our original television ad."

"Why?" Jen asked. "I like that one."

"Well," Rita said, "people have already seen it. Some of them will already be sick of seeing it." When the marketing director looked stricken, Paul hastened to explain.

"This is not a slam against the product. We do broadcast the first ad quite a few times over a very short term, to introduce the product and get it before the most eyes possible. A small percentage of the market saturates out on first viewing. It doesn't mean these customers are writing off the unit. The ones who already bought an Origami are going to be humming along with the ad. It's the slow shoppers, the ones who take their time to make up their mind that we want to capture. We want to give them a new way of looking at something they're already considering. And for the people we didn't catch the first time around, a new approach will wake them up. The buzz is good. We're getting terrific feedback. Our people," he turned a hand toward Keith and Rollin, "are already working on some good ideas."

"Well, all right," said Mann, a little uncertainly.

"Trust us," Doug said, offering his most winning smile.

"I dunno," Bill Mann said, his small mouth curling up at the corners. "When someone tells me that, I always count my change."

A surreptitious, after-hours visit to Galleria Tony turned up nothing that appeared to connect with Keith Doyle. VW and Beach's other operatives took apart the white desk, searching for whatever had attracted Maria's attention. Beach watched them, tapping his lip. He was puzzled, and he didn't like to be puzzled.

Like everyone else in the world, Galleria Tony kept their books on computer. In another shocking example of American arrogance with regard to security, the hard drive had no password. Anyone who could get by the primitive burglar alarm setup protecting the premises could have whatever they wanted and be away long before the staff returned in the morning. Beach ordered VW to copy the gallery's database to disk for Ming. If there was a connection she would pick it up.

As to what had set Maria off earlier that evening, Beach could only postulate a random emanation from the world of the unseen. These were old buildings, former warehouses turned into lofts and trendy shops. They'd have to check to see if anyone had ever reported the gallery haunted. In the meantime, Keith Doyle was their main target. Find him, Beach was certain, and he'd find what he was searching for.

Vasques disconnected his pirate drive, and nodded at Beach.

"Very well, gentlemen," Beach said. "Let's blow this pop-art stand."

Chapter 23

"I don't know if you're ready for television ads, Keith," Doug Constance said, shuffling the pile of roughs that Keith had set on his desk. "You're doing very well with the print ads. I like what you and Dorothy have been turning in. I think you should keep going. You can study what Janine and Rollin are doing, and we'll consider media scripts later on. I know you're gung-ho, but we have to be careful. The Origami's big money for the agency. Really big money. We're going great with Gadfly. I know you'll understand when I say it's nothing personal, but we don't want to queer this second line of ads. Maybe later."

"Come on, Doug," Keith pleaded. "Let me try. I've got a terrific idea. It'll look great." An inspiration struck him, and he grinned at the executive engagingly. "Look, if I bring you a rough, will you consider it?"

"A rough? Not a storyboard."

"No," Keith said, positively. "I'll bring you a real-time run to look at. Will you leave the assignment open until you see it?"

Doug looked at Dorothy, standing by the door. She raised her hands to her shoulders and shrugged.

"All right," Doug said, reluctantly. "I'll hold back for a couple of days. Is that enough?"

"Should be plenty," Keith said, backing out of the office. Dorothy followed, shaking her head. "Thanks!"

"What have you got in mind?" she wanted to know, as the two of them took a taxi northwards. "By the way, where are we going?"

"My apartment. Now that the Origami isn't a secret any more, can I bring someone in to help?"

"Will he want a consulting fee?"

"I don't know," Keith said. "I'll have to lay the whole thing out for him and see."

"All right," Dorothy said. "What about non-disclosure?"

Keith tapped the portfolio on his lap. "I've got the form right here. He knows all about them. He's a programmer."

Dunn was waiting for them in the Crash Site. He looked businesslike, his short hair freshly styled and wearing a pressed cream shirt, brown khakis with a crease down the front, and deceptively expensive shoes. Keith introduced him to Dorothy. Dunn shook his head as though doing a doubletake and took in the whole woman from head to foot. Keith grinned. She was a picture that day in a moss-green pullover and plaid skirt that hugged her curves. Dunn even admired the matching plaid shoes. "Mmm-mm-mm mm-*mmh*!"

Dorothy was flattered. She looked him up and down, a cool, amused expression on her face. "Easy, tiger, I'm taken."

Dunn raised his eyebrows. "Too *bad*. Well, if we can't run off and get married, what can I do for you?"

"Coffee might be nice. You programmers do drink it?"

"We live on it," Dunn said. "Come on back."

With two more chairs squeezed into Dunn's bedroom office things were tight, but it meant everyone could see the sheet of paper Keith pulled out of his notebook.

"I've got an idea for a commercial for the Origami. I need you to help out on the animation."

Dunn's eyebrows went up. "Sure."

"Great!" Keith exclaimed, talking with his hands. "Here's the idea. There's this architect on a flight. Everyone around him is bored. They're watching a boring movie, being served boring food, flying over boring landscape —we can have everything sort of grayish. He's working on technical drawings with a stylus on his pocket computer. He's the only one who isn't bored, of course, because he has the great new product, the Origami. His drawings are great. The line drawings get filled in with color, become real buildings, on streets with real landscaping. There's a kid kicking the seat behind him. He glances back, thinking he's going to be ticked off, but he decides he feels sorry for the kid. So he sketches out a stick figure on the screen, and makes it dance or something. He tilts his seat back and holds the screen so the kid can see it. The kid starts to get interested..."

"I get you," Dunn said, getting interested himself. "So he starts to make a cartoon for the kid right there in the plane."

"Yeah!" Keith said. Dorothy watched the two, nodding to herself. "So, then he sends the figure on a new little adventure, sketching in stick houses—the houses he was working on—and animals. He can draw because he's an architect, of course. People begin to lean over and watch. The man fills the images with color. He uses the infrared link—we'll animate the red line, because I know infrared is invisible—to pipe his little story to the movie screen, taking over from the constipated movie. His video is primitive but more alive and animated than the film. He adds music. People start to relax. The kid adds his own ideas, which the guy can sketch in or grab from clipart and his own video collection, you know, having the stick figure dance past home movies of the guy and his cats. Color spreads out from the screen, affecting the whole plane, even the world around it. By the time they land, the kid and the man are friends, and nobody on the jet is bored any more."

"That's great, Keith," Dorothy said. "How hard will that be to do?"

"So easy even he could do it," Dunn said, flicking a hand toward his roommate. "You use a commercial animation program, something you'd load to it from your desktop or using a CD-ROM. Dunno if they've got any of those programs on mini-CD yet."

"You can use the infrared link or even modem it over to an Origami," Keith said. "I thought you could use AnimaToaster 3. It's compatible with the system."

"No, man. This is the program you want." Dunn clicked an icon on his computer. "If the Origami can use AnimaToaster it can run ToonUp. It's faster and uses less memory. Here, watch."

Following Keith's idea, Dunn brought up the blue-line of a city plan. With a flurry of clicks on the mouse, he filled it in with color.

"That looks like fun!" Dorothy said. "Let me try!"

"My pleasure," Dunn said, standing up to make way for her at the keyboard.

"He must really like you," Keith said, playfully. "He won't let me touch his setup."

"And on the first date, too," Dorothy said, looking at Dunn through her eyelashes. In just a few minutes they had an animated stick-figure walking jerkily along the blueprint. "I'm hooked. Say, I've got a suggestion to make your storyline even better. What if somewhere along the way, along with colorizing the city, he puts in the actual image of the little boy, so he's the one having the adventure?"

"Yeah!" Keith said, raising his eyebrows. "That would be better."

Dorothy looked around. "I don't suppose you have any video of a child around here we can use to try it out?"

"I'll go check the video collection," Keith said.

He returned in a few moments with his magic lantern. He carefully avoided Dunn's eyes as he set it down. Dorothy eyed the carved wooden box with its gauze screen.

"What's this?"

"It's, uh, like those greeting cards that store a message on a chip," Keith explained. "This stores a couple of minutes of video." He set it screen to lens with Dunn's peripheral camera and invoked the charm to play. A small boy in a blue-striped tee-shirt with light brown skin and a mass of dark, frizzy hair sat looking at them. He had one and a half front teeth and a dimple in his right cheek.

"What a cute little darling!" Dorothy said. "Who is he?"

"It's me from third grade," Dunn admitted, giving Keith a dirty look. "You had to do it, didn't you?"

"Well, I don't have any of *my* school pictures here," Keith pointed out reasonably.

"Well, you were adorable," Dorothy said, soothingly. "Let's use it."

In no time they had incorporated the footage of Dunn's school picture, so he appeared to tame tigers, fly from building to building, wade in a fountain and slide down the stone bannister in front of a library. Dorothy sat back in delight and grinned at Keith. "You're practically out of the picture on this one, hot shot," she said. "It doesn't need any dialogue. We can use this one worldwide as is."

"Yeah, but it was *my* idea!" Keith complained.

"There's no 'I' in 'Team,' and no 'my' in 'advertisement,'" Dorothy said dispassionately, and turned to Dunn. "And this'll cost what to do?

"You're looking at it," Dunn explained. "Substitute film of actors and you can actually use this animation. Or I can do custom. My brother's company," he produced a business card for Uhuru Enterprises, "charges very reasonable rates. By the way, if you're giving these Origami things away, I'm in line right behind Red here."

Dorothy raised her eyebrows at Dunn's cheekiness. "Yeah, you and the rest of us. I'll see what I can do about getting you paid. You've got something here, Keith. Let's take it to the man and see what he says."

Doug didn't need a lot of convincing. He called in Paul and half a dozen others into the boardroom to watch the rough Dunn had made and burned onto a CD-ROM. Even Rollin had to admit it was a good storyboard. "You've got to cross-culturalize the actors," he pointed out. "Get all the combinations in there. Maybe a black architect and a white boy, a white man and an Asian girl, a Hispanic woman and a white girl. Got to cover all the bases."

"Sure," Doug said. "It'd be easy. God, I love this new technology. I cannot believe how fast you cranked this out."

"It's one of these days," Paul said, slapping Keith on the back, "when I'm proud to be in advertising. Let me call up Bill Mann and see what he says."

"How could he say anything but 'go'?" asked Dorothy.

That was exactly what he'd said. Within fifteen minutes of e-mailing them the MPEG of the rough animation, PDQ had the go-ahead to take it to production. Dunn showed them how to capture frames from the file to use as a storyboard for the director.

"Man, I like this," Paul said, happily, leaning against the wall. He offered a toast to Keith, Dorothy and Dunn with his coffee cup. "We'll never have to call a messenger service again. Start calling kids' agents. Hey, we ought to get the Fairy Shoes girl in there as one of the kids. Think she'd be interested?"

Keith grinned. "She'd love it. She's the techno-whiz in her family."

"Dorothy will be the producer for PDQ at the post-production house," Doug explained, "but both of you can oversee the filming. Jen Schick said she wants to be there, too."

"Fine by me," Dorothy said. "I'll schedule it."

But a new commercial for Dola wasn't the big news at Hollow Tree Farm. When Keith called that evening to see if the elf girl was interested, she told him to hold on the line.

The next voice that reached his ear was so excited he hardly recognized it as Marcy's.

"Keith? My folks love Enoch. We're getting married!"

Chapter 24

Snow falling in the field outside the big picture window in the living room of the old farmhouse only added to the beauty of the scene inside. The Little People had nailed up pine boughs and clusters of holly leaves and berries, making the whole room smell fresh and new. Luscious aromas of baking bread and bubbling gravy floated out of the kitchen, adding to the bouquet. Orchadia, mother of the groom, had a large crew of volunteers marshalled to take care of every task that arose. The event would be organized, if she had to worry herself to a nubbin before it began. The Master, and anyone who had the sense to stay out of her way, were helping Enoch and Marcy get dressed, in rooms as widely separated as possible. The Colliers, mother, father and younger brother, had been seated in a corner of the living room to be entertained by Dola and Borget.

Keith, who usually prided himself on being equal to every occasion, was himself having an uncharacteristic attack of nerves. Diane had had to remove him to the cellar to get him out of the way of everyone trying to get the room set up for the big moment.

"What if I blow my lines?" Keith asked, pacing up and back in between the wine barrels. "What if I say something stupid?"

"No one will mind," Diane said, placidly, seizing him and pushing him up against a wall so she could straighten his tie. "Don't fidget! This isn't a movie. These are our friends. They asked you to participate because you're a part of their lives. I mean, I could get really bent because Enoch's having you play the part of the old boyfriend, but do you hear me complaining?"

Keith looked at her as if he was seeing her for the first time and grabbed her hands. "*Do* you mind? Because if you do, I'll go up there and tell them I can't do it."

"No way," Diane said, crinkling her eyes. "You just want to get out of having to do it. You'll be fine."

"Thanks," Keith said, breaking loose to pace again. He stopped to straighten his tie and comb his hair into smooth waves. After one experiment with the mousse he decided he was happier with his own style. The stiff, rubbery feel of dry hair gel made his scalp twitch. He glanced down at Diane. "By the way, you look absolutely gorgeous."

Diane smiled shyly, turning so he could admire the cream velvet dress she was wearing. "Thank you. I bought it especially for you."

Keith, overcome, felt his throat go dry. "Diane, I..." At the serious tone of his voice she stopped twirling to face him. He took her hands again. "Listen, I wasn't..."

"Come on, you two," Holl called down the stairs. "We're starting!"

To outsiders the Little Folks' celebration of the joining of lifemates didn't look much like a modern wedding. The pair entered separately, to be met by friends, family, even old rivals, to challenge them and ask them if they were certain they were making the right decision. The Little Folk considered matches to be forever, and with their lifespans, forever was a very long time.

Though he was in the thick of the action he found himself watching Marcy's parents. Mr. Collier, dapper in a black suit just one step down from a tuxedo, kept his face expressionless. His eyes were always on the move, settling on one of the elves or another. Keith thought he was still having trouble reconciling their childlike faces with the fact they were adults. Candlepat in particular added to the confusion. The size of a ten-year-old, the blond elf girl had a curvaceous shape that her lipstick pink dress hugged tightly. Mr. Collier glanced at her frequently, then looked away, his pale cheeks flushed. Keith could also tell by the mischievous light in Candlepat's eyes that she was enjoying his discomfiture.

Mrs. Collier, whom Keith had only met once or twice a few years before, was emotionally in pieces. Fashionably thin, with small delicate hands clutching a handkerchief, her soft brown hair gathered in a loose knot at the back of her head, she looked too young to have a grown daughter. Marm stood next to her, thoughtfully holding a tissue box up to her whenever the tissue she had became too sodden. Her light blue eyes were rimmed with red. Marcy also had a younger brother, who looked a great deal like his mother. Curly-haired Josh was watching the whole proceedings with huge, gleaming eyes, torn between disbelief and excitement. If Keith had had to put a caption over his head, it would have read, "Oh, wow!"

Diane had been worried about Josh. When he'd arrived she dragged Keith aside. "I don't want to ask Marcy this, but can we trust him not to tell anyone what he's seeing?"

"It'll be okay," Keith had assured her. "If he got in here, someone will have put the whammy on him so he can't tell anyone, or just one other person. And that person can only tell one person." Diane looked dubious, but the elves had been getting by with that system for years.

He had other things to be worried about. Enoch arrived, wearing a silky tunic of ruddy bronze embroidered about the hem, neck and sleeves. He always bore an aura of dignity, but today he was majestic, passed the challenges set him by his mother and Holl, answering their questions about his intentions with quiet pride. Last came Catra, looking proud and lovely in a high-necked dress. Her hair was swept up to frame the tall points of her ears.

"You and I are of an age," she said. "We are both intelligent and hardworking. We would make a good pair. We are also," she said, with a surprising sly gleam in her eyes, "sufficiently strongwilled to withstand one another. Consider before you step outside your own circle for a bride. There is joy now, but what of the future?"

"I have thought," Enoch said, and though it was part of the tradition, he frowned, lowering his brows at being questioned. "And I have considered. I am fond of you, but there is not that spark that lights a fire within me. I would not take this step, if not to join Marcy. I am fortunate that she came into my life. What of appearances? If the souls meld, why should the lives not join? She is the only one that I love."

Catra bowed her head. Keith was deeply touched. Enoch didn't speak easily of his feelings. He stepped back a pace as Enoch passed, afraid to brush against him and break the mood. Diane and Mrs. Collier were sobbing audibly. The black-haired elf stepped proudly into the center of the room, turned to face the opposite door, and waited.

Rustles and whispering heralded Marcy's appearance. Her sable-brown hair was spread out on the shoulders of her dress, white velvet for a winter bride. The roses embroidered on its rich surface stood out, almost like real flowers. Their color matched the pink glow in her usually pale cheeks. A cloud of white and red flowers was in her hands, and on her head a wreath of magical white bellflowers, without which no joining of lifemates was complete. She looked ethereally beautiful. Pat, who had taken over from Keith the duty of movie-cameraman for the occasion, let out an audible whistle.

Shyly, she came into the room. The elves made an aisle for her as they might for a visiting queen.

Keith was so entranced by the moment that it took a poke in the back from Marm to remind him what he was supposed to be doing. He jumped forward, blocking her way.

"Don't do it," he said. The moment of placid grace was broken by the sound of his voice. He was sorry, and Marcy looked a little shocked. "You know I was crazy about you. We could still be a couple. You don't have to live on a farm in the boondocks. What do you think?"

It wasn't as eloquent as he would have liked. He blushed, the ruddiness drowning out the freckles on his cheeks. Marcy reached up to touch the side of his face.

"You're my best friend, Keith," she said, softly but clearly. "You showed me the truth about myself. You gave me the confidence to admit what I'd been feeling for months. I'll always love you for that, but my heart belongs to Enoch. I can't imagine turning back now." Her hand dropped to his, squeezed it, and let go. Keith stood aside. No one could have stayed in her way after a speech like that. At the center of the room, she came to stand beside Enoch. The usually dour elf looked so happy that Keith felt tears start in his eyes.

Before the community, their friends and relatives the couple declared their love for one another. There was nothing child-like about Enoch as he stated his vows. The Elf Master, as the Headman of the village, and Mr. Collier, looking nervous, came forward to join their hands together. It was so nice, so natural, so about time that Keith was nodding at the rightness of the whole event.

"Before our friends," Enoch said, "I swear that I will be a good husband to you, support you, and provide for you. Not only a lover I'd be, but a friend and partner in all things. No other will ever supplant you in my heart. I promise to enjoy and suffer life alongside you all the days of our lives. I will protect you from your fears and nurture your dreams."

Marcy's voice was almost inaudible as she replied. Her cheeks were scarlet. "I knew from the time I met you that I love you. I come to you with joy."

He kissed her gently. The Elf Master beamed at them.

"As you haf claimed one another, none of us shall stand between you or compel you apart. I offer my congratulations and good wishes." Marcy embraced him, then her father, as everyone broke into cheers and applause.

"A toast to the couple!" Holl cried.

"A toast!" Marm echoed, springing up to stand beside the punch bowl and a tun of his best wine. He put Keith's mug in his hand.

"To Enoch and Marcy!" Keith announced.

"To Enoch and Marcy!" everyone echoed, and drained their glasses.

"Another toast!" shouted Tay. "Long life and happiness!"

"It is over so quickly," said Ludmilla Hempert, seated in front of the wide fireplace among her beloved 'little ones.' One toast had led to another and another. Drinking progressed naturally to eating. The guests sat wherever there was a flat place, partaking of the feast. The cooks and bakers brought out platters, baskets and bowls of delicious food, offering re-fills to the diners who overflowed all the 'public' areas of the big, old house.

"They're good cooks all the time," Diane said, grabbing another biscuit from a passing basket, "but they've just excelled beyond anything I could have imagined. This is ambrosia!" She and Keith were perched on the windowsill. It was cold, but they had it to themselves. Nearby, Mr. and Mrs. Collier shared a bench with their son. Already the dutiful son-in-law, Enoch had brought them a small table for their plates and glasses. The Elf Master and his wife were next to them at another small table. The newlyweds had a place all their own in a nook next to the big fireplace, hung with garlands and glorious, out-of-season flowers that Keith was sure had been brought to bloom by one of the plantwise elves.

"Keith," Mrs. Collier said softly, leaning toward him and putting a hand on his, much as her daughter had done, "I heard what you said. I'm so sorry. I didn't know how deeply you felt for Marcy."

"I...don't," Keith said, hastily. "It's part of the ceremony, Mrs. C. Both of them have to meet the challenges. It's traditional. She's my friend, nothing more, I promise. Enoch roped me in as one of the 'disappointed suitors' because I used to have a crush on her. She ended up with the right man, I swear."

"Really?" she asked, her smooth forehead wrinkling.

"Really," Keith assured her. He took Diane's hand. "I found the right woman for me a long time ago."

"How lovely!" Mrs. Collier beamed. "So, when are the two of you getting married?"

Diane and Keith exchanged glances, hers expectant, his uncomfortable. "Well, you know," Keith said, at last. He didn't want to give away details of his savings plan, and he knew the Folk were listening. "We want to be ready. Both of us are still in school."

"Of course," Marcy's mother said, nodding knowingly. "You're right. It's so expensive these days to set up a household."

"By the way, is this...wedding...legal?" Mr. Collier asked, uncomfortably.

"It can be legally registered," the Master assured his new in-laws affably. "Though my son has no official birth records, the correct officials can be persuaded that they haf seen the right documentation. If this is important to you."

Mr. Collier seemed uncomfortable at the open manipulation of legal matters, but he tried to recover the mood. "Oh, well," he said jovially. "How else do you explain leprechauns in the family?"

Enoch glowered at the description, and a wave of muttering swept through the room. "Never mind," Tay whispered to him as he refilled his glass at the long buffet table. "You won't have to see the in-laws very often." Marcy, close enough to hear, blushed.

"How did your final exams go?" Holl asked Keith, a little louder than necessary.

Keith answered at once. "The most you can say about them was that I survived. I think I did okay, but I'll wait for my report card."

Mr. Collier looked embarrassed. He seemed to understand that he had committed a social gaffe. "Say, honey," he called to Marcy at her little table in the inglenook, "you were going to give me the e-mail address down here."

Marcy looked thankful to change the subject. "Yes! Of course!"

"Good. Give me a moment." Mr. Collier reached into the inner pocket of his suit coat and came out with an Origami. He touched the ON button, and the little screen hummed to life.

"Hey," Dunn said, elbowing Keith. "Isn't that one of your things?"

"Why, so it is," Catra said, from her perch on the arm of Ronard's chair. "Keith Doyle has been telling us much about them for some time now."

"Yours?" Mr. Collier asked, interested. Keith explained that he was working for the advertising company hired by Gadfly to promote the Origami. "They're pretty terrific. Do you have one, too?"

"No, sir," Keith said, fervently. "I wish! I'm saving up for one. They're pretty expensive."

"I'll say! I bought this one bundled with business software. It set me back $2,500. It's the greatest thing I ever had, though."

Mr. Collier started playing with the unit's panels, flipping up the screen to show the telephone face below. The graphics on the screen reversed at once so the lettering would be the same side up as the numbers on the keys. "It's a workable office machine, but it's like a toy, too."

"I know," Keith said, fixing fond eyes on the blue-green device. "I am just crazy about it. I can't believe how good the graphics are. The buttons are just far enough for good game play. And you can have three or four applications running at the same time. If you've got Doris, you don't need most of the stuff in your office!"

"Doris?" Mr. Collier asked, blankly.

"He's got a pet name for it," Pat explained, his long face twisted in mournful amusement like a Lewisian marsh wiggle. "He's in love with the darned thing. There's a framed picture of it on his desk. Uh, right next to one of you," he hurried to explain, as Diane tapped her toe meaningfully on the floor.

"Bad timing, Shakespeare," Dunn scolded him.

"Oops, sorry," Pat said, ducking his head.

"Doris is my only rival," Diane said, plaintively to the room at large.

"Not a serious one," Keith said. He tried to recover the situation without explaining his secret plan. He realized the only way to save the situation was to jump in with both feet. He looked at Diane with sincere hazel eyes. "I mean, I would never think of asking *her* to look for engagement rings with me." He took Diane's hand with a meaningful expression. The Folk let out little exclamations of surprise and pleasure.

Diane brightened right away. "Oh! When?" she asked. "I don't have to work tomorrow."

"No, not tomorrow," Keith said, hastily. His heart sank when she looked hurt all over again.

"So you're not serious," she said, with a wry twist of her mouth. "It was just a ploy to get out of trouble over Doris."

"Yes. I mean, no! I *am* serious. About us, I mean. Maybe I'm being too cautious, because we haven't graduated yet. Let's go look at rings. Really."

Diane's eyebrows went up. "So why *not* tomorrow?"

Keith spread out his hands. "Because I've looked at both jewelry stores in town. I want something nicer for you. There's a lot more to choose from up in Chicago. You promised to go home for Christmas, and so have I. Why don't you come up the week after New Year's? We're both still off classes then. We'll make a special occasion of it. I might even spring for play tickets. What do you think?"

"What do I think?" Diane asked, kissing Keith as the elves beamed their approval. "It's a date!"

Chapter 25

"Still nothing on Doyle?" Beach demanded. VW shook their heads, looking ashamed of themselves, like a couple of schoolboys caught not having done their homework. "You've been trying to find him for almost two months! How the hell does he do it? He's eating and sleeping, right?"

"Yeah," Vasques said, sulRily. "We've been in his apartment a dozen times. His bed's slept in. His clothes are in the laundry basket. There's stuff with his name on it, but we have never found him there, no matter what time of day we go in."

"Has he changed to the night shift? Is he sleeping days?"

"We thought of that," Wyzinski said. "I got a jumpsuit and a toolbox, went in as an electrician sent by the building management to look at the wiring. The black kid was there, but no Doyle. We keep going back to PDQ, using every excuse in the book. Everybody's just seen him a minute ago, but no one ever knows where he is. He's ducking us like a pro."

Beach stroked his chin. "I didn't believe he could be a government agent, but I'm changing my mind. This could be bigger than we thought. Keep your eyes open. I must talk to him. I can't wait forever."

Leaning into the wind blowing bitterly off the lakefront, Keith trudged beside Pat across the street and onto the edge of the Navy Pier complex. January was making its presence felt with near-record snow. For the first time in weeks the temperature had risen above freezing, but that meant only there were puddles of slush under curbs, waiting to shoot up the pants legs of the unwary. Pat's jeans were tucked into theatrical-looking boots that went along with his mood and his current job. Both of them had woolly hats pulled down over their ears.

"I'm going to have 'hat hair,' and the makeup crew is going to make fun of me all through rehearsal again," Pat complained.

"I thought Uriah Heep was supposed to have hair that stood up," Keith shouted over the wind.

"He is, but mine won't stay that way without a ton of hairspray!" Pat called back. "They'll have to blow dry it, and I'll look like a lacquered hedgehog."

"The show must go on," Keith said, encouragingly. "It's a great role. You're the villain."

"Please! We villains prefer the term 'antagonist.'"

"You mean you don't believe in a specific God?"

"Thanks," Pat said, crisply, yanking open the door of the Children's Museum. The two men scooted inside out of the cold. "That's so old it went out with vaudeville. Say, speaking of doubles acts, how's the old married couple getting along?"

"They're still in their own little world," Keith said with an avuncular smile. "Neither one seems to hear anything anyone says. It's getting really old as far as Holl's concerned. He ought to know better, but he doesn't remember what it was like when he was walking into walls whenever Maura said his name."

Pat made a face. "Yeah, you're a fine one to talk. How many people here think Keith is going to walk into walls for six months when he and Diane finally get hitched?" Pat hoisted a long arm into the air. "Brr. That gust just went right up my armpit. How come it's this cold inside?"

"That's Mother Nature getting even with you for being unsympathetic. Enoch and Marcy had to hang on longer than Holl did before they got married. They're so happy. The others ought to give them a break."

Pat took off his hat and ruffled his hair. The lank, black strands tumbled like a limp haystack. "I am sure they are, my dear boy. But when you're not in love everyone who is just seems so sappy. How many people don't think they're going to wait a whole year before trying to hatch a baby?" Both he and Keith raised their hands. "Unanimous. Nice to *see* you, there, by the way. I appreciate you keeping that spell off, or whatever it is. Not that I object strenuously. If I have to have one thing blocked from my sight, it would be your silly mug."

"Thanks heaps," Keith said, sourly.

Ever since the snowy night he'd nearly been run off the road, Keith had been using the anti-attention charm Holl and Enoch had taught him almost all the time. Pat and Dunn hated it because they found it uncomfortable to carry on a conversation with someone whom they couldn't look at directly. Moreover, the parameters of the spell meant that they ended up staring at whatever Keith had made the focus of the spell at the moment, such as the television or a wall fixture. Dunn finally started asking him to lay the glamour specifically on what he wanted to look at at that moment, such as his dinner plate or manuals he was reading.

It was worse at PDQ. Having the spell going all day meant that people were always looking for him and never finding him. The only places he felt safe leaving it off were in the security of Dorothy's small office or the men's room. He had to go without it during sessions in the boardroom, but the rest of the time he was basically invisible. It meant limiting his involvement in the filming of the new commercial. The script had been changed by Rollin when Keith couldn't be found. Keith still been able to offer a change that he thought was pretty effective: adding images of Origami's features to the adventure the child had on the little screen. But Keith could tell his invisibility was wearing on the tempers of even his champions like Dorothy and Paul. He couldn't help it. Staying out of sight was not for his sake, but for the sake of more than eighty others.

Since he had the opportunity, Pat studied him.

"You look tired. Are you that worried about these people?"

"They're a real threat to the elves," Keith said seriously. "I've got to keep out of sight until they get bored and go away. The trouble is, I'm just running out of gas. It's nice to have a few weeks off from school. I thought I could handle it all, but between the commute, my classwork, my job and...you know..."

"The bibbity-bobbity-boo," Pat interjected lightly.

"...I barely have time to breathe." Keith frowned as they trudged up the concrete stairs that led to the theater. He pulled open the glass door without seeing it. "I keep wondering if I shouldn't have postponed business school when PDQ hired me. I thought I could do it all with no problem, but my class assignments are getting more complicated, taking up hours I don't have because I'm working full time. It's blowing up the rest of my life."

"Nearly threw the whole Diane thing in the dumpster last week," Pat said, with sage sympathy.

"Yeah," Keith said. "I'll make it up to her. I was going to wait until I could just buy the ring and give it to her right there. I mean, I've studied the literature. I do not have anywhere near the two months' salary saved up yet."

"Two months' worth?" Pat exclaimed in horror.

"That's what they say, but I haven't been working a whole year yet, and who knows if I can stay on this gravy train? I hope she doesn't mind picking one out and waiting for me to make time payments."

"Don't worry. She'll forget all about the disappointment of not being engaged to you when she sees me utter the famous phrases of the odious Uriah Heep. 'Too 'umble,'" Pat said, his lanky body collapsing into a comma over his clasped hands washing themselves.

"It's type-casting," Keith said, grinning. "It's you to the letter."

Pat gave him a superior smile. "Thank you. I thought it was a brilliant portrayal, some of the elements of which I drew from my very rich life. I'd be living in very much more 'umble surroundings, if it wasn't for you and Dunn taking me off the streets. You guys keep a much better grade of food in the fridge than my other acquaintances of the theat-ah."

Keith tugged at his carroty forelock, peeking out from under the edge of his gray wool cap. "Our pleasure. We've got to support the arts, you know."

"You're getting your money's worth. This is a very true-to-life *David Copperfield*. I think the CSR is pretty brave for trying to make money off Dickens."

"Brr. This is a Dickensian season, for sure. Whenever I had to read *Oliver Twist* in school I always pictured England being cold and bleak."

"He ought to have lived in Chicago," Pat said. "That'd teach him what winter is *really* about. But it's worse out here on the pier. Well, here's where I get off. You mere mortals will have to wait until the opening to see our brilliant performance."

"Oh, yeah!" Keith said, remembering. He reached into his pocket. "I got paid today. Here's the money for the tickets."

"Thank you," Pat said, plucking the white envelope out of his fingers. "I'll make sure you get good seats."

"Thanks," Keith said. "That'll help."

"Hold still!" a woman's voice pleaded over the sound of wailing that echoed off the walls. Pat's dark eyebrow arched.

"Somebody needs to go home for a nap."

"No," Keith said, spotting the source of the sound. "She's hurt."

A little girl no more than four years old with black pigtails sat on the hard tile floor, sobbing, as a room mother tried to spread a bandage over a scrape on the child's shin. The girl wasn't cooperating, kicking her leg out of the harried woman's reach. Keith dropped to his knees beside them.

"Hey, don't cry," he told the girl. "It's not so bad. Hey, look! See the clown?"

The girl's lip stopped quivering long enough for her to ask, "What clown?"

Keith took his handkerchief out of his pocket. He put his two hands together and spread them out with the white cloth in between. On its surface he allowed the image of a jolly, brightly colored clown to appear. Its white face had a bright red nose and mouth and eyes with exaggerated blue lashes around it that matched its bright blue hair. Its baggy costume was covered with spots in all the colors of the rainbow.

"Look out!" Keith said, in mock alarm. "Its spots are going to fall off! Catch them!" He made the dots rain off the clown's coverall. The little girl put out her hands, but the blobs of color dissolved into air. She giggled, her bruise forgotten. "Whoops!"

"Are you a magician?" the woman asked, fascinated. She finished the bandaging job as quickly as she could while the child searched her lap and the floor for the missing spots.

"Wizard in training," Keith said.

"Like Harry Potter?" the little girl asked, brightly.

"Not exactly. No owl," Keith explained. He tapped a finger on the end of the girl's nose. "See if you can catch the spots next time." He rose and stuffed the handkerchief back in his pocket.

"Thank you," the woman called, as the two men turned away and climbed the stairs.

Keith caught Pat looking at him with a peculiar expression on his face. "You know, that is very impressive," his friend said hoarsely. Keith realized that neither of his roommates saw him do magic very often.

He waved a dismissive hand. "It's nothing. Enoch would be all over me for using a background. He thinks all illusions ought to be free-standing."

Pat cleared his throat. "Nothing but special effects, eh?"

"Sort of. I've got to get back to work. See you later."

"Thanks for the escort and the floor show," Pat said. He waved to the uniformed black man standing by the glass doors. Recognizing him as one of the cast members, the guard stepped aside to let him in.

Pat flipped his hand in salute as he disappeared through the auditorium doors. Keith pulled his scarf tighter and hitched his collar up around it. He retraced the route he and Pat had just taken in. To his surprise, there were shops and pushcarts all along the pier. He could have been shopping for little trinkets to give Diane! Oh, well. He could do it on the way out.

There was just too much on his mind. When classes began again he'd have Entrepreneurship and Business Accounting, two heavy courses. The Master had stated that from Classical philosophers they were moving on to ancient poetry. With Keith's luck he meant to have them learn it from the original Greek, Latin and Chinese. He worried that the course load was becoming so heavy he'd have to give up commuting to Chicago or consider transferring to a distance-learning program. Neither would work, he thought, browsing to the next cart, which carried small wooden goods, among them a few baby teething toys made by the elves (Tiron's and Candlepat's, by the maker's marks on the bottom). It was the Midwestern connection he didn't want to lose. If only Holl could teach him teleportation, and take the commuting time off the table. He grinned, wondering how the cost for power expenditure for a transporter would look on a spreadsheet. No, better not to annoy Dr. Li right off the bat at the start of term.

Okay, forget school, Keith thought, stopping to turn over earrings on a pushcart display, and let the new Origami ads percolate at the back of his mind for a while. New file folder: Make Diane Happy week. Dunn's brother had recommended a good Italian restaurant for a fancy meal, maybe to celebrate finding that perfect ring. Keith had also been scoping out nice places on the Mag Mile. Diane wouldn't be able to resist the after-Christmas sales. Banners and signs were everywhere trumpeting deep discounts on leftover merchandise. Keith had examined them all with a newly-educated eye, seeing if he could guess which stores were offering real deals. It didn't really matter. He'd end up going into whichever ones Diane wanted. He might not be in the walking-into-walls stage, but his ladylove could ask for what she wanted. If it was in Keith's power to grant, it was hers. In the meantime, a pair of blue-green crystal earrings that just matched her eyes would serve as an suitable offering.

Speaking of walking into walls, the crowd was surprisingly thick for a weekday afternoon. Hordes of grade-school kids crowded the front hall of the Pier, most likely waiting to go upstairs into the Children's Museum. Keith was jostled by bored children rocketing around the enclosed space, their voices echoing off the high ceiling. Teachers and room parents, in desperate pursuit of their wandering flock, shoved through the crowd.

A man pushed close to Keith. He tried to make room, guessing that the other wanted to get past to the bookstore, but the man hung close until they were past the door. Wondering if he was about to have his pocket picked, Keith tried to dodge away toward the Information desk in the center of the atrium. A grip like a steel manacle closed around his upper arm.

"You're tough to locate, pal," a harsh voice said in his ear. Keith tried to tilt his head to see his captor's face, but his scarf and hat prevented him from turning that far. The man jabbed him in the ribs again, this time with a blunt cylinder. "Don't try to yell. I've got a silencer. They'll never know why you dropped. Move. Out the door."

Keith's heart pounded. He'd forgotten to put his invisibility spell back on! If he could just slip away in the crowd he could put it on again, but the man had a solid grip on him. He had to get away. The Information desk was within reach of his fingertips. If he could get loose he could vault the edge and explain to the security guards when he wasn't in danger of being shot. He didn't want anyone else hurt, either. The pier was so crowded, with all those children. He couldn't disable the gun, but he could stop the thug from going anywhere. He worked his arm around until it was pointing toward the floor, and fired off a quick charm.

The guy jerked to a halt as his feet stuck fast in place, but he didn't let go. Keith felt cold metal jab him in the back of the neck, just under the edge of his scarf.

"Undo it or I'll kill you right here," the man growled in his ear. "You're not going to pull that on me again."

So it was one of the guys Beach had with him downstate, Keith realized. Reluctantly he closed his fist, releasing the glue-spell. The grip on his arm propelled him forward again.

Keith sensed the presence of another, larger man coming up alongside his captor. He heard the sound of electronic beeps, the new man dialing a cell phone. His voice was deeper than the first. "Yeah. Got him. Pull up."

"How'd you find me?" Keith asked, resisting an impulse to hold his hands in the air.

"Shut up."

They emerged into the cold January day and stood in huddled in a knot on the curb. Keith felt his mind spinning as he tried to calculate how he could get away from the pair of thugs without getting shot. His nerves were so strung out he almost burst into laughter when the car that zipped in to the curb in front of them was a black Volkswagen Beetle with dark-tinted windows. It hardly looked like a gangster's ride.

"Get in," said the first man. He pulled open the door and pointed with his elbow, a gesture that allowed him to keep the gun in his hand concealed. He yanked open the door, pulled the seat forward, and shoved Keith at the back seat.

"Come on, guys," Keith said, looking up at his captors. He tried valiantly to keep his feet on terra firma. The moment he got into the car he was lost. "You must have the wrong guy. You want Harry Potter, right? He lives in England. I can't give you his address, but..."

A hand holding a white cloth emerged from the front seat and smothered the rest of his sentence. Something wet and medicinal-smelling smeared his face. Keith opened his mouth to complain about the odor, but he had trouble forming words. The world blurred into a mosaic of dark and light. Something hard hit him in the cheek and barked against his knees.

He heard a thread of music. It was his cell phone ringing. Answering it seemed like the most important thing in the world, but he couldn't work up the strength to take the kingfisher-colored phone out of his inside coat pocket. So nice of the second big man to do it for him.

"Take a message, huh?" Keith muttered through his gag, as his leaden eyelids drooped closed.

"Sorry," Wysinski said, holding down the POWER button until the phone turned off. Vasques grabbed the unconscious Keith by the belt and shoved him into the back seat. "I don't do secretarial work."

Paul Meier put the receiver back in its cradle.

"No answer," he said. "He told me he was going to lunch with a buddy who's in a play on Navy Pier. Probably you can't get a decent connection inside the building."

"I don't like it," Dorothy said, tapping her long, coral fingernails on the tabletop. "The client likes his style. I hate to go on with the meeting without him. This meeting's to clear an ad budget for five different trade shows all spring and summer. I left it in his hands. He knows these i-business ads backwards and forwards. I'm not sure which is which. Maybe we ought to cancel."

Paul shook his head. "You've got the keylines. The preliminaries were already approved. Pitch 'em for all you're worth. I'll help out. We've got the final of the new commercial to show. That always cheers 'em up. Don't worry. Keith'll probably waltz in here fifteen minutes late with a weird excuse, a box of doughnuts and a bad joke."

Chapter 26

Wasn't that his belt buckle? Keith wondered, staring at the mysterious, square silver object in front of his eyes. Why did his head hurt so much? And who was groaning like that? The sound made it hard for him to think. He tried to rub his temples to drive away the pain, but his hands were stuck. Trying to tug them loose, he discovered they were tied behind his back. And his feet were attached to the legs of the chair he was sitting in. He was freezing. Where were his coat and hat?

"Awake at last?" Beach's supercilious voice asked from somewhere behind him. A hand grabbed the back of his neck and dragged his head up, away from the familiar buckle to a face he'd seen a couple of times before: the scary lady, crouching before him. She was dressed in a cheap-looking fur-trimmed coat with a hood that framed her narrow face, and fur-trimmed gloves. No, one glove. The bare fist grasped a gold chain. Keith peered at the object dangling at the chain's end. It looked like a golden plumber's weight.

"He is aware," she said, staring at Keith avidly. He couldn't put his finger on her accent. She sounded like Dracula's younger sister. With those burning eyes, she could have *been* Dracula's younger sister. He turned away from her gaze, trying to figure out where he was. He was not going to give Beach and his minions the satisfaction of the usual question.

The concrete ceiling of the chilly room was low, with water stains visible in the corners. One bulb, protected by a wire cage, burned in the center of the ceiling. The sealed concrete floor was divided by a long metal grate a foot wide that ran the length of the room. The room smelled strongly of chemicals. Cleaning supplies, a metal pail on wheels and a cluster of brooms were propped against the walls. A few feet away was an ancient and filthy industrial sink with a rag slung over the

lip. Some kind of janitor's closet? Maybe, but it was a strange
janitor's station with the noise of car engines so close. But the
ratiocination helped him to gather his wits. He saw the shadowy forms of two men in the corners in front of him, flanking
the only door he could see in the cinderblock walls. Besides
Beach, he could hear someone breathing behind him.

"Now," Beach said, pulling a chair up in front of Keith
and swinging it around so he could sit with his arms propped
on the back, "let's talk."

"Can't," Keith said, promptly, though his lips were stiff
with cold. "I'm late for work."

Beach pursed his lips wryly. The boy had seen too many
spy pictures. He thought that by acting manly and holding out
he would keep his secrets. Beach shook his head.

"I'm only civilized up to a point, Keith," he said. "I thought
you were a nitwit when I first met you, but there's deeper
thoughts going on in that noggin of yours." He thumped Keith
on the top of the head with his knuckles. "It looked like a
fluke—what could a lad like you know about the higher powers? And then we found this in your stuff." He nodded, and
the dark-eyebrowed man stepped forward with a bag. From it
he drew Keith's magic lantern.

"Hey, that's private property," Keith protested.

"So we stole it," Beach said, with a nasty grin. "This, too."
The man with black eyebrows produced the candle lantern
and lit it. "Goes on with a breath. Goes out with a breath. Do
you have anything to tell me about how it works?"

"What about it?" Keith asked, nonchalantly. "'S a space-
age chemical that's carbon-dioxide activated."

"Yeah, I might have fallen for that explanation if it wasn't
that I've seen the very same design before. Stefan?"

Stefan had one more item in his bag, another lantern.
He turned it in his hands as if it was a priceless gem. In
spite of himself Keith leaned in close to see it. The ornamental carving, fluted pillars and a complicated band of
beading top and bottom, didn't match any of the elves'
styles, and there was no maker's mark on the bottom.
"Where did you get that?"

"Not space-age technology, lad," Beach said, pityingly. "It's hundreds of years old. Found in backwoods Romania. But it still works." To prove it, he breathed on the wick. It burst into flame. "Now, would you mind just telling me how you come by a lamp that's the absolute replica of one that dates from the Renaissance?"

"I bought it," Keith said.

Beach hauled back his fist and drove it into Keith's cheekbone. Keith gasped. His chair rocked onto two legs, and settled down again, while his head rang from the blow. "Wrong answer. Let's try a different one. What's this thing do?" He held up the magic lantern.

"It's a toy," Keith said. "A replica of the old movie projectors from the turn of the century. It doesn't do anything."

The scary lady made a noise. Beach glanced at her with raised eyebrows and turned back to Keith. "Maria thinks you're lying. What's it do?"

"It shows a picture," Keith said with the greatest reluctance. "Anyone can use it. Just hold it flat on your hand and look at the screen."

Beach followed his instructions. The image of Dunn as a second-grader appeared on the light gauze. Maria let out a fascinated coo.

"How's it work?" the Australian demanded, nearly shoving the box in his face.

"I don't know how it works," Keith said. It was nearly the truth: he didn't know *how* it worked, just that it did. Beach drew back his hand again. Keith recoiled to the extremes of his bonds.

"You do know *something*," Beach said. "You made us stick to the ground like glue. You did it again at the pier. What was that?"

"Would you believe hypnotism?" Keith suggested, not very hopefully. "The power of positive thinking. I didn't want you to move, and you couldn't."

Beach shook his head, narrowing his gaze on Keith. "It doesn't make any sense, lad, and I'll tell you why: I don't believe in coincidence. I should have twigged it when you ran away from the advert I showed you. You knew what that writing was. No, don't try to tell a lie," he said, as Keith choked out a protest. "I can't find anybody else who even reacts to it except to say that it's pretty. You bugged out like a rabbit with a firecracker under your scut. I've been chasing that lingo for years, now." He poked Keith in the chest with a forefinger. "I know it's got something to do with magic. *Real* magic. You've proved, twice now, and maybe more, that you're tied in in some way. And you've got the goods, the candle and this magic lantern. You can't tell me that it's just chance that put all three of those elements together. Now," he said, dangerously, leaning close and lowering his voice, "I'll be reasonable if you will be. Who taught you to do that?"

"I just picked it up," Keith said. "You can get books on anything these days. I practice."

"Oh? What were the names of the books?"

Keith shrugged, as far as his pinioned arms would let him. "I don't know. Something I got out of the library." Well, *that* was true, but it didn't satisfy his tormentor. Beach grabbed hold of Keith's left ear and twisted it. Keith yelped.

"You think someone would write this stuff down? You think I'm stupid? Hasn't it occurred to you what might happen to you if you don't cooperate?"

Keith ground his back teeth together as images of trap doors into the Chicago River and machine-gun massacres in garages popped up in his mind. "I can guess."

"Yeah," Beach said, with amusement, as if he could see for himself what Keith was thinking. "You're the one who's seen too many pictures. Fine. Let your imagination go wild. I know everything about you. I know where you live. I've read your mail and listened to your phone conversations. I know if you tell a lie. I'm a businessman. I can make it worth your while to help me. I want the power. Take me to wherever you learned what you know. Is whoever taught you still alive?" The cool eyes watched Keith, who was determined to give away no information. "We've been watching you, you know. We've tapped your phones, read your e-mail, gone through your stuff.

You've got no secrets from us. Yes," he said, watching as the boy tried to remember every single contact he'd had for the last several months, "if you've got something it'd be better to tell us when it's easy to do it." He got up. The chair legs emitted a horrible groan as they scooted across the floor. Keith winced. "I'll give you a while to think about cooperating."

"This kid's got rocks in his head," Wyszinski complained. "It's two in the morning. We've been asking him the same questions for hours. He's not going to give it up."

"No, he's a wily one," Beach insisted. "He can't hold out forever. Pretty soon he's going to want to eat and use the toilet. He'll want to sleep. We won't let him. We'll see how long his resolve is good for once he starts feeling miserable. He's a *nice guy*. He wants people to like him. He's had a soft life. That kind's got no stamina. Knock him around a little more, reason with him prettily in between, and he'll be begging to tell us what he knows."

"How do you know he's not going to magic himself out of here," Vasques asked sourly.

"Wouldn't he have done it?" Beach argued. "He may know a few fancy tricks, but there's got to be plenty more powerful spells out there. Look at him. He's a boy. Who'd trust him with the whole grimoire, eh? We want more than spells; we want tools. The lantern and the other artifacts are toys. You can be sure there are weapons."

A low tapping on the door interrupted them. Wyszinski stood to the side and opened the door a crack. "Yeah, Miller?"

"Clean-up staff's coming," the operative whispered. "We're going to have to get out."

Wyszinski relayed the information to his employer, who frowned. "I thought you said we could have this room for a few days."

The burlier half of VW shrugged. "He said he couldn't promise. At least he's giving us a warning. We don't want the cops."

Beach drummed his fingertips on his thigh. "We'll have to take the boy back to the hotel. We don't want to attract attention. Get Miller to distract them. We need five minutes." Wyszinski nodded and sidled back to the door.

At the other end of the gloomy room, Keith lolled in the chair, trying to ease the cramp between his shoulder blades. He watched the bad guys huddle and whisper, his heart sinking. Whatever Beach and his friends were up to, he knew he wouldn't like it. He wished he could hear what they were saying.

His head hurt. Beach had been relentless, coming at him time and again, in different ways, but always with the same questions. He sounded pleasantly reasonable: all Keith had to do was tell him where he learned to do magic, and who was making what he called 'the artifacts,' and he could go home. When Keith refused to answer they roughed him up, hitting him or twisting his fingers or ears. The air was freezing, but they'd taken away his coat and hat. They ate carryout Chinese food in front of him, not giving him so much as a noodle. He didn't like it, but he could take it. For now.

Worry ate away at his insides, gnawing at his empty stomach. If he didn't give them information willingly, sooner or later they were going to try drugs or serious torture, and he'd be spilling everything he knew about the Little Folk. Suddenly his bright idea of having the elves sell handcrafts to support themselves was backfiring all over the place. Why did it never occur to him that somebody might figure out the toys and things were magical? Why didn't he think that somebody might want to learn how to do it for themselves, the way he had? Keith didn't think this Beach character wanted to learn charms and enhancements for the purpose of recharging his car battery. No, he was all set to abuse it in some bid for world power, or something else underhanded and international-spyish. Thank heaven Keith hadn't gone all the way with his plans for a Hollow Tree website. Beach would have been able to find not only the lantern, but every other gizmo the elves made.

Keith steeled himself. He had to keep silent, no matter what they did to him. If they tried to force him to talk...Keith gulped. The elves trusted him. He might have to make the

ultimate sacrifice to keep them from harm. Tied up like this
there was only one weapon at his disposal, his home-made fire
charm. He dreaded how his parents would feel claiming a
charred body at the morgue, but at least he could take the bad
guys with him. The elves would be able to live without fear.
He only wished he could tell them why. And Diane. Oh, God,
he was never going to see her again!

His ears perked up as he caught the edge of a whisper.
Keith thought Beach say something about going home, but
sudden voices passing by outside the door drowned out the
rest of the sentence. People! He hadn't heard other people in
hours. No one was near enough to cover his mouth this time!
He took a deep breath to yell for help.

"Psst! Red-crested land man!"

The air rushed out of Keith like a balloon deflating. The
voice sounded as though it was coming from inside the room.

"Psst!"

Very slowly, he turned his head to see who was speaking.
Over his shoulder he saw a human figure at the rear of the
room. He jumped, then realized it was only a set of coveralls
on a hook. No one was there. Had the knockout drops the
black-eyebrowed man given him affected his brain?

A rustle from the other end of the room distracted him.
Keith hunkered down in the chair as Beach approached him
again. The tall man pulled a gun out of his pocket and shoved
the barrel against Keith's chest.

"We're going to move now. Since you know the drill from
all your movie-watching, I don't have to tell you that it would
be a bad idea to try and give us the slip." He nodded to one of
the men, who bent to untie Keith's legs.

Tingles shot into his feet as blood returned. It took a few
tries before Keith could stand up on them. Stefan set his coat
over his shoulders and the hat on his head. Keith huddled into
the coat, grateful for the warmth, but it felt too light. He jogged
the garment on his shoulders. No jingle.

"Are you looking for these?" Beach asked, holding up his
telephone and keys. He kicked aside a section of the floor
grate and dropped them. Keith heard them clatter against

concrete. He tried to dive for them, but the gun barrel prevented him. "Whoops! Clumsy me. Now, move it."

Keith blinked at the acid-bright lights. His eyes focused in the new light to see row upon row of fat concrete pillars painted red and tarmac striped with yellow lines and blotched with oval stains. They were in a parking garage, echoingly empty because of the lateness of the hour. Two more men in blue and green down bomber jackets moved in close to the group and nodded. In the harsh fluorescent light all their faces were drawn and worn. They looked as tired as Keith felt. Beach nudged Keith in the shoulder blade, and they edged away from the black-painted metal door.

They trudged along the cold pavement, stepping over the occasional floor grille. Now he knew they were drainage channels to funnel away rainwater and melted snow that came into the building on car tires. The garage was divided into sections containing five or six rows each. Keith kept his eyes open for a place to hide, should he be able to get away from Beach and the gun.

"I hear my spirits," Maria said suddenly. "There is power here."

"I've heard this place is haunted," said the man in the green bomber jacket, kicking the wall painted with the words "Row N" as they went by, "like the garage where they had the St. Valentine's Day massacre."

"Shut up," Beach said, biting off the words with his teeth. They walked past rows P through W. "This building can't be more than thirty years old. It hasn't had time to accumulate ghosts."

"I know," said the blue bomber jacket, a man in his early forties with an acne-pitted complexion and curly, greasy hair, "but we're going after pixie dust stuff. We might trip over something that wouldn't bother anyone else."

"Such as?" Beach asked, in a tone that did not invite a reply.

Blue bomber didn't reply. With a look of deep horror on his face, he pointed toward the far wall. Keith followed the line of the finger and stared. The figure of a woman floated weightlessly toward them. Translucent, sea-green garments fluttered around a slender-boned body, and waves of long, russet-brown hair flowed over her shoulders, framing long, slim neck and a narrow, huge-eyed face the deathly color of sea-foam. Her pale, narrow feet were bare as they seemed to float slightly above the soiled pavement. She raised a long-fingered hand and pointed unsmilingly at the advancing group. Keith had never seen anything so beautiful in his life. A ripple of delight ran through his body.

Beach's men reacted rather more negatively. Maria dropped to her knees, clutching her pendulum. Three of the men froze. Stefan let out a howl of fear and raced away.

"Come back here!" his employer howled, then exclaimed, "What in 'ell?"

The gun barrel dropped away from Keith's shoulder. He glanced back. Beach had fallen to the ground, his foot caught in an open grate. He lay on his back, waving the gun in the air. Keith wasn't about to waste the opportunity. He ducked behind the nearest pillar.

Ping! A bullet hit the wall not far from his head. Keith dropped into a crouch, but started running for the next pillar anyhow. His coat billowed out behind him like a cape.

"Psst! Red-poll! Here!"

A pale hand beckoned from beyond the last wall. Beach was scrambling to his feet now. With his heart pounding in his throat, Keith ran toward the hand. He ducked around the corner as another bullet sang by.

The hand grabbed his arm and pulled him against the inside surface of the wall. The owner of the hand, a black-haired male with the same greenish-pale skin as the female spectre, held his fingertip to his lips.

"This way! There is no time!" The male pointed to an open grate in the floor. "Down there."

Keith threw a glance over his shoulder. The others had snapped out of their trance and were shouting. Without hesitation, he jumped through the opening. He landed in a shallow concrete trough about half his height and rolled out of the way. He landed on his side, struggling to get upright without the help of his hands. The space he was in was just the width of his shoulders. The male came behind him, hefting the grate quietly into place just half a second before footsteps thundered overhead. His eyes seemed to glow in the dimness as he repeated the gesture of touching his forefinger to his lips.

"Where did they go?" Beach shouted.

"He's disappeared!" one of the men yelled.

"How? He can't turn invisible! He's wearing handcuffs! He must be behind one of these pillars. There's only a few staircases and the vehicle exit. Don't let him escape!"

"Who…?" Keith began, as his rescuer moved closer to him. He expected the figure to shimmer right through his body and disappear. Instead, the male flipped aside the folds of Keith's coat to look at his hands and made a tut-tut noise. "You're *solid*," Keith said.

"Shh!" his rescuer hissed, planting a long, cool and slightly clammy hand over Keith's mouth. "Wait. The guards are coming." The two of them crouched as low in the pipe as they could as the sound of an engine rumbled toward them. Through the grate Keith spotted a revolving blue light. A shadow stopped directly over them, belching diesel smoke. Keith shoved his mouth and nose down against the fabric of his collar to filter out the irritating fumes.

An irate voice shouted, "What are you people doing down here?"

"Sorry, officer!" called Beach's voice, smooth in the face of authority. "We couldn't remember where we parked."

"Hop in," said the security guard. "I'll help you find it."

"That's not necessary…"

"Hop *in*."

The van sagged noisily as Beach, his four henchmen and the spooky lady climbed in. Not until it chugged away, letting light in through the grate, did Keith dare to raise his face. The newcomer studied him, and Keith returned the honest scrutiny. His rescuer was tall, his long legs folded up in the narrow space, but very slender. A fillet of worked gold sat on his thick, dark hair, and jewels decorated the tight gold bands around his wrists. His skin was moonlight pale with an undertone of green that showed in the hollows of his sharp cheekbones and pointed chin. His eyes were a dark, mysterious green that made Keith think of deep sea and deep forests. On either side of his beautiful face were tall, pointed ears even more elegant than the elves', and he never imagined such a thing was possible.

"I cannot undo your bonds," the being said. "We must wait for my lady."

"I can't thank you enough for rescuing me. My name is Keith Doyle."

The male smiled, no, *grinned*. It changed his face from austere to approachable. "That's a name that'd be familiar in either place we've lived."

A gentle rasping sound and a rattle surprised Keith so much he jumped, knocking his head on the grate above him.

"Your pardon," a soft voice said. Unable to turn around, he glanced back. The female had come up behind them. She set down a cardboard box full of loose metal. "I will try to find a key to undo these bonds. You would not be surprised how many keys people lose in the water. Garbage forever raining down on our home...." She clicked her tongue.

"What...who are you?" Keith asked, finding his voice at last.

"We are the *sidhe*," the female said, trying one small key after another in the cuff lock.

"Really? Cool! I'm giving a party in May at the home of some friends of mine. They're...Little People. They come from Ireland, too."

"Sh! We know. You are just as you're described on the advertisement," the male said. "We saw you today on Navy Pier, but you were walking in a dream. Then those men took you. We were going to speak to you. We plan to attend."

"Oh? Oh!" Keith said, his fear abated by enthusiasm. "That's *great*. My friends will be *thrilled*. I mean, I'm thrilled, too. So you could read the invitation? Does that mean you come from the same lineage as them? You're related? They kind of look like you, with the ears, but they're shorter than me, about two-thirds of my height." He tried to give a more coherent explanation, but the male continued to look puzzled.

Keith heard a *snick!* and his right hand began to tingle. "There, that worked!" the female said. A second click, and the nerves in his left hand screamed as blood raced back into the tissues. Keith brought his tortured extremities around in front of him under the shelter of the coat and began to rub life into them.

"Wow, that's better," Keith said. "Wait, I know how I can show you my friends." As soon as his fingers could grip, he reached for his wallet.

In the flap underneath a photo of Diane he kept pictures of his family. Among them he knew there was a shot of Holl and himself from his overseas vacation in Ireland. With a crow of triumph he picked it out and gave it to the male. Holl and he were standing in the middle of the Callanish stone circle. Keith worried for a moment that Beach had seen the photo when he'd gone through his pockets, but Holl's ears were hidden by the baseball cap he always wore when he was out in public. Anybody could see the difference in their height, but someone who didn't know better would think the blond kid was human.

The male smiled and handed the picture to the female, who studied it and gave it back to Keith. "We are not the same. We are of the First People. We learned their tongue when we knew your friends of old, they or their ancestors. They are the Second People."

"Like me?"

"Your race came third."

"Oh," Keith said sadly. "No relation at all, huh?"

"We are all related," the woman said, more kindly than the male. "Some closer than others. My name is Liri. He is Rily."

"I'm honored," Keith said.

"And I believe these are yours," Liri said. On one long palm she held his small telephone and his ring of keys.

"Thanks," Keith said, relieved, as he tucked his property into his side pocket. He was startled to see that her fingers had shallow webs between the third phlanges.

"I really appreciate your helping out a...Third Person."

"You're a friend to us, or at least not an enemy," Rily said, drawing his fine brows down toward his thin nose. "The subtlety is important."

"I know. I follow Chicago politics. But I hope you'll come to think of me as a friend."

Liri touched Keith gently on the shoulder. "You were pinioned a long time. Can you crawl? Security is on patrol. I do not think you wish to be found."

"You're right about that," Keith said. He followed his new friends on hands and knees through a maze of troughs until they came to a metal grate. Rily grasped it with one hand and set it aside to let the others through. Keith poked at it curiously as he passed it. The grille had to weigh fifty or sixty pounds, but the sidhe had picked it up with one hand. He was impressed.

The pipe was enclosed on the top outside the garage walls, cutting off the light. His invisible whiskers detected a wall a few inches from the side of his head. He put one hand on the rough concrete surface to guide him. Soon the conduit expanded to a height in which the three of them could walk upright. Rily helped Keith stand. Keith stretched his cramped muscles, letting his hands brush against the rough ceiling. His back eased, and he sighed with pleasure. They walked for a long distance in the darkness, until a small, distant light came into view. Soon he could see what they were headed toward: another grille. The slope of the tunnel dipped sharply. Keith found himself trudging through two or three inches of hardening slush. Rily opened the grating far enough for them to slip through. Keith noticed that their lovely clothes were entirely unmarked by either the water or the long crawl through the drainage pipe. Both of them might just have come from chairing a formal dress meeting of the Seelie Court. That was some useful magic. He probably looked like he had just come out of a brawl.

"The drain flows out from here into the lake," Liri said. "We know every waterway in the city."

"You do? Where do you live?" Keith asked. He was hungry, cold, achy and still on edge from his ordeal, but curiosity about these wonderful beings was making him twitch to the end of his whiskers. "Have you been here long?"

"Long enough," Rily said, curtly.

Liri had more patience than her lord. "Our home is under the water," she said, with an impish smile that made her face look even more fey and wild. "I cannot tell you exactly where... but you can see the Drake Hotel from the surface."

"Along the Inner Drive?" Keith asked. He looked up as his voice caused an echo in the pipe. "Sorry. I knew there had to be other, uh, folk somewhere. I never dreamed that you were so close."

"Then I believe you will continue to be surprised," Rily said, with a hint of amusement. "There are more. Some are our friends, and some are not our enemies...but there are others." Keith opened his mouth to ask who, but the severe look on the sidhe's face kept him from voicing the question. The three of them emerged under a piling at the edge of the lake. A long pier ran to their left. Lights glimmered in the distance, but the spot in which they stood was draped in shadow. "We must go. We cannot stay long away from the water, but we saw you in danger. Your offering to entertain us was a kindness seldom extended by your kind to ours. We look forward to allowing you to become a friend."

"But I want to know more," Keith pleaded. "Please! When did you come to Chicago? How did you get here?"

"We can speak at more at the party," Liri said. "Goodbye for now, young friend. You are safe. You can find your way now, but we must leave you here."

"Here?" Keith said. "But the water's frozen."

"No matter," Rily said. As gracefully as a salmon, he leaped toward the water. The jewels on his forehead and wrists caught the distant light like sudden comets. His back arched, and the ice seemed to part before his outstretched hands. He slipped beneath it, becoming a pale streak beneath dark gray glass. His bare toes, pointed like the best Olympic divers, were the last things to disappear. Liri smiled gently at Keith's astonished face before she followed her lord. Keith just caught a glimpse of green as they slid away. Not a single ripple or crack in the ice betrayed their passage. It was as if they had never been there at all.

Wow, he thought, shaking his head. *Right here in the city*. Wait until he told Holl. And Diane. And everybody.

But once he started walking back toward the city, alone again in the cold, empty night, his mood began to sink with the temperature.

It was four o'clock in the morning. In just four more hours he'd have to go back to work. Keith stumbled up the access steps of the pier to street level and found himself at the far eastern end of Randolph Street near the Yacht Club. He began to trudge west, feeling the cold wind batter him from every direction at once. Despite his gloves, his hands were as cold and numb as his feet. It seemed like a month ago, not a day, that he was supposed to anchor the discussion with the Gadfly team about ads aimed at the B2B market, business-to-business, for the upcoming run of trade shows. Dorothy was probably very upset with him. He had *never* missed an important meeting. He owed her an apology, to be delivered from his knees with a box of chocolate-covered caramels as an offering. She wouldn't be interested in an explanation, and she wouldn't believe it anyhow. *Jason* was probably chewing the curtains with fury, and no bribe would placate him. Keith was pretty sure that in the back of the boss's mind the notion was still there that somehow Keith was responsible for the leak of the ad sheet several months back. But he had to go back and resume his normal life.

But how could he? he thought despairingly, listening to his footsteps echoing on the icy pavement. He'd only gotten away from Beach because the sidhe were there to help him. Next time he'd be on his own. Beach would be looking for him, harder than before. It was his fault they'd found him. He had been careless. That could never happen again. Next time they'd be looking for tricks. They would make it impossible to get away, by whatever means necessary. Keith shuddered. Beach was right: his imagination was their greatest weapon against him.

Anger at his own stupidity making his gestures fierce and sharp, he restored the eye-avoidance charm on himself. He stalked along Washington Street, changing the focus of the spell every few feet to an inanimate object or a shop window. *No one* would ever catch him off guard again. No matter how much it annoyed his friends or his co-workers, they'd have to put up with it. *He* wouldn't be the one who caused the elves a moment of trouble, not when they'd been having such problems themselves. *He* wouldn't be the liability that cost them their long-sought freedom.

Chicago before dawn was populated by people on their own missions. A thin stream of cars and trucks hurtled by him, the drivers clutching the wheels with purpose. A man wrapped in an old brown sleeping bag sat in a sheltered doorway rocking and talking to himself. He didn't look up as Keith passed, just kept on repeating in his rough, tuneless voice the same line of a song. Keith felt lost. This wasn't his time of day, his place.

The hollow feeling of despair reminded him that he was literally empty inside. Somewhere in the vicinity there had to be an all-night diner. At the next intersection a passing taxi drew with it the fast-cooling aroma of hot coffee. Keith turned in the direction from which the taxi had come.

Wandering down the street, he looked into shop windows. Advertising was his business, at least until PDQ canned him, but he couldn't bring himself to be interested in the point-of-purchase displays or the merchandise they showcased. Makeup, boots, stereo equipment, books, candy—they all ran together in a blur, until a white chevron caught his eye.

It was a seagull in flight on a poster in the window display of a card shop. The words, in white over the photographic background said, "If you love something very much, let it go…" Keith was prepared to forget about the old cliché until he was reminded suddenly of the conversation he and Holl had had not that long ago. "You might absent yourself on purpose," Holl had said, as though he had foreseen this very moment.

How could he have known? Keith turned away from the display window, stricken. He balled his hands up, shaking them furiously at the air. How could he let the Little Folk go? They meant so much to him. They were his best friends, his second family. He *loved* them.

But that was the point, he realized, after stalking block after block of empty stores and offices. If they needed him to let go, how could he deny them that? He would never want to be the cause of harm to them. Beach was a danger to them. Keith was only the means to that end, he realized that now. He wasn't the source of magical toys or weapons-grade spells; *they* were. He had to keep Beach from finding the Little People. The Australian would probably have a hard time enslaving them, but once he knew they existed they would have no peace.

All right, he thought, if he wasn't just paying lip service to his ideals, if he *really* meant he would never cause the elves harm, then he would do it. He would do anything, if it would prevent anybody from reaching them and disturbing the peace and safety that they had worked so hard to attain. Even though it could mean he would never see them again.

Keith felt a pang of misery. It seemed like his whole world had been swept away. Even if he got it back again it would never be the same.

Beach would *never* find him.

Chapter 27

"No, don't take that. Please."

The short Hispanic waitress in the blue uniform and stained white apron looked down at the pair of pale hands clutching the coffee cup she had just tried to pick up.

"Sorry, I didn't see you," she said, instead taking the empty platter that was pushed to the edge of the table. "You need a refill?"

"Please."

She poured out the contents of the glass pot in her left hand, upending it for the last drops. Keith pulled the cup closer to him, inhaling the sour, bitter aroma. He'd wolfed down a giant-sized truck-driver breakfast so fast he didn't remember what it tasted like. There'd been pale yellow blobs and dark crumbs on the plate. So he had eaten eggs and toast. *Part of this complete breakfast*, said the advertising genius in his subconscious.

Once he had food in his belly he had nothing to do but think. He couldn't go back to work. That was the first place Beach would look for him. He was afraid to go back to the apartment. They'd been in and out of it. Beach knew about all of his possessions. Keith worried what had been on his hard drive. Was the spy-guy responsible for all the troubles he'd been having with his e-mail account?

Most of all he was afraid to go back to the farm. The last thing he wanted to do was draw attention to the elves. If Beach trailed him there...

He had to talk to Holl. He fumbled for his cell phone and began to dial. Fear overwhelmed him, making his hands shake. Hastily, he hit the END and CLEAR buttons, wiping the number off the screen. What if Beach was serious about having listened to Keith's phone calls? Did he have bugs on this phone?

He smacked it on the table and stared at it as if it was a poison snake that hadn't made up its mind whether to bite him or not.

An unshaven, tipsy-looking man in the booth facing Keith's had watched his performance with the phone. "Wha's the matter with you, pal? Girlfriend throw you outta the apartment?"

"No," Keith said, staring glumly at the paper placemat. "I was kidnapped and beaten up by international spies."

The man regarded him with owlish sympathy. "Don't y' jush hate when that happens?"

"Emil, don't talk to yourself," the waitress said, coming back with a full pot of coffee. She filled the drunk's cup and shoved it into his hands. "You come in here so drunk and you expect me to sober you up before work. I'm not your mama. Drink this. I'll be back to give you a refill."

"I'm not talkin' to myshelf," Emil argued, pointing at the booth across from him. "This guy here...where'd he go?"

The jingling of the bell on the door was his only reply. The waitress sighed. She picked up the check and the twenty-dollar-bill sitting on the table in the abandoned booth. At least the other man had paid before he went. Funny that she couldn't remember what he looked like.

Dunn was doing a crossword puzzle and eating a bowl of cereal when he suddenly found his attention fixed on an individual spoonful of Cheerios.

"Keith," he said positively. He tried to turn his head, but his eyes were riveted on those floating O's. "Where have you been, man? We've been worried to death. Your boss called when you didn't show up. They sounded pissed."

"I was kidnapped," Keith said.

"What?" Dunn demanded, standing up. "Daggit, Keith, take the whammy off me!"

"Not here." Keith looked around. "The apartment might be bugged."

Dunn thought for a minute. "The laundry room. I've got an excuse to go, and if I talk to myself, no one cares."

While his roommate filled a washer with khaki pants and chambray shirts, Keith told him all about the situation. "And he said he could monitor my phone calls and my e-mail."

"He could at that," Dunn said. "If this is the guy who's using something like Carnivore he can find information about you that's translated into electronic bits in any online database, including any time you use your credit card. All it takes is time. Sometimes a lot of time. So how'd you get home?"

"My bus pass is anonymous; I paid cash for it. I stood in the middle of the thickest crowd of passengers I could find, and took the first bus heading north. I couldn't go to work looking like this anyhow."

"And how is 'anyhow'?"

Keith lowered the spell. He let Dunn get one brief look at him before refocusing. His clothes were soggy, stained and torn, and the bruises on his eye and unshaven cheek were already turning purple. Dunn was shocked.

"You can't let 'em get anywhere near the little guys," he said to the detergent dispenser. "What can I do to help?"

"I need you to call Diane," Keith said, sinking down on an upturned laundry basket. "I'm afraid to get on the phone. If Beach's tappers hear my voice they'll know where I am. She's supposed to come up here this weekend to shop for engagement rings. Call her off. Tell her not to come up. I know she'll think I'm trying to get out of committing, but I don't want her involved in this."

"Too late for that," Dunn said, shoving his quarters into the machine and pushing the slide home. The roar of the washer nearly drowned out his next words. "She's here."

"*What?*"

"She's asleep in your room." Dunn turned around to look at Keith, but his eyes were still fixed on the coin slide. "She wanted to surprise you. I guess she has."

"You have to let me see you sooner or later," Diane said, sitting cross-legged on the couch in a pair of pink-flowered pajamas like a grade-schooler at a slumber party. Dunn slumped in his favorite armchair. Both of them had their gaze fixed on a folder that lay on the coffee table. The radio was playing six-ties favorites at conversation level.

"Not here," Keith whispered. He was perched on the arm of the couch between them like the Ghost of Bar-room Brawls Past. "They've got to have someone observing the building. They'll go back to all the places they know I go. I'm taking a risk even talking. There could be a bug."

"Doubt it," Dunn said, "but I've got a friend in law en-forcement who can come and find out."

"Well, how's this spell work anyway? Do people who are across the street suddenly get interested in a dropped cigarette butt they can't actually see when they look toward you?"

"Uh, not really," Keith said. "At a distance their eyes just slide off me. It's not until they get really close that they look at what I want them to."

"Okay," Diane said, reasonably. "Even if they're watching they don't know you're here, because their eyes keep sliding off you. Is there a big closet with a light?"

"Red here is living in it," Dunn said. "There's a pantry cupboard, where we keep the broom and cleaning supplies. Pretty tight quarters, though."

"That will do," Diane said. She got to her feet and beck-oned to the air. "Come on. I came all this way to see you. I can take it."

Keith stood in the utility closet straddling the vacuum cleaner with his hands behind his back like a shamed little boy. Diane, one foot on an upturned pail, wiped his face with a wet kitchen towel. He tried to keep from wincing. "It doesn't hurt so much any more."

"Shut up," Diane said fiercely, though her hands were gentle. In the light of the single bulb Keith watched a tear roll down her cheek. "Why didn't you tell me there was someone stalk-ing you? They tried to run you off the *road*? Is this tied up with what's going on at the farm?"

"No. I mean, not really, but it could be. I didn't want you involved," Keith said. He put the misdirection spell back on himself and opened the closet door. "It could be dangerous."

"Well, I *am* involved," Diane told the thermostat. "I love you. If something happened to you I'd be furious. When you didn't come back last evening I thought Dunn had called to warn you I was here. I didn't believe him when he said he didn't know where you were." Diane looked upset, but with herself, not at him. "If I hadn't been so suspicious, we could have been out looking for you."

Keith felt a chill go right through his bones. He grasped her hand and kissed it. She jumped, not knowing he was going to do it. "It's a good thing you didn't. These people mean business. Dunn, did you call the police last night?"

"No, man. Considering the people that we know. I mean, what would I tell them? You were stolen by the fairies?"

Keith gave a bitter laugh as he emerged, blinking, into the light. "Not this time. The fairies rescued me."

"Good morning. May I help you?" asked the young woman in the elegant black coat-dress behind the counter.

"Yes," Diane said, feeling dowdy by comparison in jeans and her Irish sweater. She wished she'd worn something nicer, but her dress blouse wasn't warm, and it was snowing hard outside. Besides, she thought, steeling herself, she was a customer. "We...I'd like to look at engagement rings."

The woman smiled, totally unaware of Diane's insecurities. "Of course. Right back here."

"I don't like this," Keith whispered, following Diane along the narrow aisle on the left side of the store to the case where the saleswoman beckoned. He glanced at the black-flocked walls and the mirrors lining them. He was sure most of them had security cameras concealed behind them. His spell could fool human beings, not video tape. "We're only a block from my office. If Beach came by..."

"He can't see you," Diane murmured. "We can't only look in the big department stores. Shopping ought to cheer you up. Besides, you promised. Now, shut up."

"Do you want to look at wedding sets?" the saleswoman asked.

"No," Keith whispered.

"No?" Diane asked. "Why not?" She smiled at the saleswoman, who had been giving her puzzled looks. She would question Keith later, when she could see him face to face. "Just engagement rings, for now."

"Of course. Do you want a solitaire, a solitaire with baguettes, or something more modern?"

"I don't know," Diane said, her eyes dazzled by the blaze of blue-white in the case. She loved to look at jewelry, but mostly as a window-shopper. It felt different to be choosing a piece that she'd be able to keep. That made it more fun, but exciting, too. These weren't just pretty stones in pretty settings—they were engagement rings. At *last*. Four years of dating, talking, planning and endless dodging the subject were over. The man she loved was making a commitment to their future. She looked at the ring finger on her left hand and tried to picture a diamond there.

Suddenly, she felt shy. She curled her hand up and took it off the counter, out of the way of any rings that might jump up and climb on her finger. This was a big step for her, too. Was she ready? She had thought she was. When Marcy and Enoch had gotten married she had been so happy for them, but jealous, too. Why them and not her? She wasn't kidding herself that theirs was an easy relationship. The reaction of Marcy's parents alone would have been enough to break up a stable love match. But her turn for happiness and stability was coming. This ring would be its symbol. The skin of her palms tightened with nerves. She put her hand up under the light.

"All right," she said.

The woman pulled a tray of rings out of the case.

"Do we have a price range we're trying to keep within?"

"I'm not sure," Diane said. Keith was silent. He was probably as nervous as she was. She leaned backward, feeling his warmth, tickled by his breath in her ear. The saleswoman had no idea why she smiled.

"Well, why don't we pick out a few things you like, and and you can find out what your fiance says."

Diane nodded.

"Here's a pretty one. The center stone is a round brilliant, about two-thirds of a carat, and an excellent cut. The color is good. It's G. Do you know about the GIA scale?" The saleswoman went on talking, offering information on the quality of each diamond as she put one ring after another on Diane's hand. "Well," she said at last. "I've been showing you my favorites. Which ones do you like?"

"I...I don't know," Diane said. Some of them were wonderful, but the prices shocked her. Three thousand dollars for the square diamond set compass-style in the broad band? Four for the smaller diamond in the platinum setting? Did it really matter to her whether the stone was colorless or flawless? Maybe, she thought, cocking her head to look at a trio of round diamonds channel-set in a band. If the ring was meant to be a symbol it ought to be as close to perfect as possible. But was that realistic? One thing she had never been able to get Keith to discuss was how much he could spend on a ring. She didn't want him to beggar himself, but there was that little voice deep inside her that wanted to impress her sisters and her friends, to let them know she was marrying a man with potential. But she wanted to be practical, too. It was stupid to spend the price of a year's tuition on a bauble that didn't do anything, but still, these were so beautiful some primal urge was interfering with her common sense.

At least Keith wasn't interfering with her looking at whatever she wanted. Whenever the saleswoman brought out a new case of rings she was able to browse freely. She looked at colored stones as well as diamonds. One of them was really beautiful, an eye-clear, champagne-colored oval topaz tilted on its side and slashed along its left edge with three horizontal grooves, set on an exaggeratedly wide band. In the end she pushed that case away. "I'd rather stay with the diamonds. I guess I'm more old-fashioned than I thought."

The saleswoman smiled. "Well, someday you might like that one as a cocktail ring. Keep it in mind."

"Do you like any of these?" she asked, when the saleswoman turned away for a moment to lock up the semi-precious stones.

The three remaining cases had lots of good choices, but no particular one leaped up and shouted at her.

She felt a compulsion to turn her head toward the case to the left. Part of her wanted to fight the urge, to look any-where else. She knew it was Keith's best way of communi-cating with her, but she hated being controlled like that. The force relaxed when she let her gaze settle on the third row. A modest round stone with rich, rainbow fire glistened up at her. From her brief lesson in quality, she knew that it was a fairly good diamond. She liked the setting, a pair of flared lips of bright gold that looked like a thumb and forefinger holding the stone delicately between them. She tried it on, turning her hand this way and that to catch the light. "Mm-hm. That's pretty." She put it back in the box.

Her eye was drawn farther to the right and one row down, to a single princess-cut stone. She studied it for a moment. The setting was beautiful but Diane didn't care for the way the light bounced off the center of the stone in flat glints. "No, I don't think so. I like round or oval stones."

Her invisible tourguide steered her eyes left and down again, skipping over winking points of light until it brought her to the bottom corner of the center case. Set into the blue-black velvet was a round solitaire with small, triangular baguettes on either side of the gold setting, wide edge facing the center stone. The band itself was pinched on either side of the diamond, emphasizing it and making it look larger. Diane tried on the ring. She was captivated by the gleam of the stone and the way the band resembled a ribbon tied in a bow around a gift. "That's beautiful. Oh, no. It's over five thousand dollars. That's too much."

She heard a gentle sigh from behind her. "You think so, too? Oh, well. I like the first one a lot. Should we get it?"

She gazed at the expensive ring for a moment, then her sight was dragged to the handle of the front door.

"Let go," she hissed. Her gaze freed itself, and she turned to see the saleswoman staring at her as if she was crazy. "Will you excuse me for a moment?"

With as much dignity as she could muster, Diane marched out the front of the store into the snow, and turned into the nearest doorway. "What's wrong?"

She caught a momentary glimpse of Keith's face before her attention focused on the darkened metal plaque studded with doorbells for the businesses up the stairs of the building behind the security door.

"I can't buy the ring now," Keith said, plaintively.

"Why not?" Diane asked, pretending to read the names as a police officer walked by. "If you can't afford it all at once, I'm sure they'll let you buy it on time. I thought you would. You can put the down payment on your credit card."

"I can't use my credit card. Beach and his people said they're tracing me wherever I go. They have access to all my computer files. Dunn thinks with the kind of program they're running they could even find me if I use my ATM card."

"You've known this for weeks!" Diane's eyes blazed bright green with outrage. "So you asked me to come all the way to Chicago to look for rings but you didn't intend to buy one? This whole afternoon was just to mollify me? I feel like I'm marrying into the witness protection program!"

"I did intend to buy a ring!" Keith tried to take her hand, but she jerked it away from him. "I want to. I would do it this minute, but I'm afraid they'll catch me again. I don't think I could stand up to their questioning, not so soon. I haven't had any sleep." He sat down on the doorstep. "I'm sorry. I'm not explaining myself very well. I can't endanger our friends. And they are *our* friends, not just mine."

Diane spat the words out bitterly. "Sometimes I wonder if you care more about them than you do about me."

"It's different," Keith said, putting his head in his hands. "I'm the one who's responsible for helping them go public in the first place. They need my protection. No, not exactly. They need my discretion."

"Well, they need mine, too!" Diane said, trying to turn her head away from the doorplate. Keith realized her dilemma, and let her focus on a spot at the edge of the street. "*I* know where they are. No, I'm not going to lead some power-mad nutcase to them, but come on, Keith! They've gotten along for thousands of years without you, and they will go on after we're all long gone."

"Will they?" Keith asked, a little sadly. "Look, I swear I was going to buy you a ring. If it hadn't been for last night, I would have. You know you mean everything in the world to me. I have to think. I've been knocked off balance. I don't know where to go. I don't feel safe anywhere. I'm just so tired."

Diane sank down next to the sound of his voice. She could almost see him out of the corner of her eye. When he reached out to put a hand on her knee, she didn't pull away. "I'm sorry, too," she said. "You sound exhausted."

The invisible hand squeezed hers. "Can we start your visit all over again?"

"Sure," Diane said. "Let's pretend I got here Saturday morning, the way I was planning to originally."

"But, that's tomorrow."

"Right," she said, briskly, rising to her feet. "You're going right home and going to bed. I was freaked out about you telling me you'd been kidnapped and everything. I wanted things to be okay and back to the way they were before, even though they're not. You go to sleep. I brought my new textbooks with me. I can get a head start on the semester while you sleep."

"You are the best," Keith said. His voice rose until it was close to her ear. "I wish I could buy you a million diamond rings."

"I'll settle for one," Diane said. "And don't worry about the elves. When I go back I'll tell them the whole story in person. That way no one can phone-tap you. They'll decide if you're too much of a danger to them. But I doubt it. You're the best friend they've ever had."

Chapter 28

At the sound of the door shutting behind her, Dorothy sat bolt upright in her seat, but she didn't turn around.

"Whatever your excuse, I don't want to hear it," she said.

"Okay," Keith said. "Do I still work here?"

"Maybe." Very slowly, Dorothy rotated her chair, then bolted out of her seat when she saw him. Her angry expression changed into one of concern. "Oh, my God, Keith, what happened to you?"

He winced as she probed the bruise on his cheekbone. "Four guys, all bigger than me. Believe it or not, they didn't want my wallet."

"Were you in the hospital? Did you go to a police station? Your roommate didn't know where you were."

"I was wandering around for a while, but I'm okay now. Can I stay? I'm ready to go back to work."

"Maybe," Dorothy said again. "Jason wants to see you. But I think he'll go easy when he sees that eye."

As Keith could have predicted, Jason Allen gave him a dressing up one side and down the other, bringing up the issue of trust, responsibility and reliability but he stopped short of firing him. Keith ate crow willingly, without salt or ketchup, hoping for another chance. If this was the soft treatment, he'd wear a suit of armor if he had the rough treatment coming.

"The only reason I'm keeping you," Allen explained, after an extended tirade that Keith accepted without rancor, "is that the client really likes you. They're coming in for another briefing today. You've got six hours to come up with some more copy to replace what they rejected on Thursday. Got that? Get out of here."

"Yes, Jason. Thank you," Keith said, backing out the door as quickly as he could.

"Remember, you're still an independent contractor. You could be out of here any time."

"I know, Jason. Thanks."

Misdirection spell firmly in place, Keith scooted back to Dorothy's office. He spent the next several hours hunched over his desk scribbling all over ad roughs.

In spite of Dorothy's nervousness about having had to lead the discussion over Keith's i-business ads, the meeting must have gone pretty well. Keith found initials denoting approval in the corner of more of the proposed ads than he'd thought. The twenty remaining still needed to be winnowed down to four, one for each major trade show, but all of them needed to be given the quality treatment. Keith found it easier than he'd thought to buckle down and concentrate on rewriting copy. A feather of creativity began to tickle the back of his mind. Surprised that such a thing was possible after all he'd been through so recently, Keith made notes, chortling to himself while he wrote. Busy with layouts in the keyline department, Dorothy left him alone.

Around lunchtime, he heard a rap on the door.

"Hey, there," Paul Meier called. "May I come in?"

With a cautious glance at the window behind him, Keith let the charm drop and opened the door.

His mentor's compassionate brown eyes looked him up and down. "Dorothy was right. You look like you were run over by a train."

"I wish it had been that easy," Keith said.

"So you knew the guys?" Paul asked, concerned.

"Yeah. At least, I've seen them around." It was on the tip of his tongue to say that their leader was the man who'd shown him the leaked ad, but Keith held that back. Such an admission would spawn too many questions, and open up speculation again about whether Keith had betrayed the agency months ago. Since it had turned out the ad was only a means to an end, as it had been for him, he wanted the matter left alone. And he didn't want to touch on the subject of the elves.

"Well, a clear ID ought to help the cops find them. Is the girlfriend going to join us for lunch?"

Keith shook his head sheepishly. "She went back this morning."

"Oh?" Paul asked, his saturnine face sympathetic. "I thought she was supposed to be here all week. Things didn't work out?"

"I…" Keith took in a deep breath and let it out before he spoke. "Let's just say the weekend was a strain. We're still together. I think. I hope." His heart gave a painful squeeze. He didn't know whether that was entirely true. "It was pretty hard on her that I got mugged. I hate to admit it, but I'm glad to be back at work."

"Well, you probably need a little time alone after a trauma. Want me to bring you back a sandwich?"

"That'd be great," Keith said, taking a ten out of his wallet. Paul held up a hand.

"Today's on me. I'm just glad you're back here in one piece." Giving Keith a friendly chuck in the arm, Paul headed for the elevators. Keith reinitiated the charm and went back to his table.

Paul was right: a little time by himself would do him good.

He felt guilty how relieved he was to return to the office. He had escorted Diane to the six A.M. bus back to Midwestern. They had said a very formal goodbye to one another. He'd given her a peck on the cheek before she boarded the bus. She hadn't returned it. Keith was pretty sure they hadn't broken up, but being around one another was just not working. Keith knew it was his fault. He had disappointed her about once too often. He had some major trust-rebuilding to do with her, too.

When they had returned to the apartment from the jewelery store on Friday, Diane insisted on fixing Keith a second big breakfast. He laid out his sleeping bag under his desk, the only place in the apartment out of the usual foot traffic, and slept for nineteen hours.

He awoke at eight o'clock Saturday morning to the aroma of cooking. Diane had taken care of meals, enlisting Dunn and Pat to help her shop so Keith didn't have to leave the apartment.

Watching her stand in the kitchen, slender in tee-shirt, jeans and fluffy pink slipper socks, her long blond hair floating around her shoulders, with a recipe card in one hand and an eggshell in the other, he had a sense of future nostalgia, but the present reality couldn't live up to his hopes. Diane greeted him briskly, not warmly, acting more like a caretaker than a girlfriend or fiancee. The latter sure didn't seem possible any time soon. He felt like a ghost in his own home, having the others walk past him without seeing him. They even began to talk to one another as if he wasn't there.

He was ashamed of himself for not being able to follow through on his promise. His roommates were no help. Pat pointed out, more accurately than tactfully, that Keith had agreed only to *shop* for rings, not to buy one. Keith backed away from that argument, knowing that sticking by the letter of the law was only going to get him deeper in trouble. Diane had observed, acidly, that that was why Pat wasn't in a permanent relationship. The comparison led Keith to hope that she hadn't dismissed completely the idea of them as a couple, but he didn't get any reassurance from her. He was on probation, and he knew it.

The evening that Keith had set up to be so special was a failure. They'd gone to the play and out to dinner, but he had had to keep his guard up the entire time they were in public. Diane understood why he had to do it, but she hated being with someone she couldn't look at. He couldn't blame her.

Sunday had been worse because they had made no advance plans. Unable to decide on an outing that required the minimum possible public exposure, they decided to stay inside and just chat. That, too, was chalked up in the disaster column. It was difficult for Keith to find a topic that wasn't full of land mines. School: Diane was pretty certain she'd gotten a low grade in a key subject and might need to retake it during the spring semester. Work: Keith didn't dare talk about the Origami, which left him little scope except to tell her the latest news about the people in the office, and that was of little interest to someone who had never met them. Marcy and Enoch: too close a subject to their own situation. Keith got enthusiastic about showing off his folder of responses to the party invitation, but not even telling about meeting the sidhe in the storm drains was enough to cheer her up. The story only reminded Diane that Keith was in trouble because of the Little Folk. She assured him that it wasn't his fault, but he knew she still felt let down. They spent the day being painfully polite to one another, but the truth was that their nerves were jangling. Only the undeclared truce they were observing kept them from releasing the tension in an extended argument. He'd accepted without quibbling when she said she was leaving the next morning.

He couldn't feel any worse if he tried. It made him weary looking into an infinite future of having to stay invisible. It could be years before Beach gave up looking for him. Diane would never consent to marry him if he insisted on staying out of the wedding pictures. He loved her so much that it half-killed him to hurt her feelings, but he hadn't yet figured out another way to cope.

He kept thinking they should have found a way to get past the badness. Were they just too young to be considering making a lifetime commitment?

It also half-killed him to be thinking about limiting contact with the elves. There was no way he would lead Beach to them. Beach was based somewhere in Chicago. Keith wondered if he should call the local Hollow Tree clients and asked them not to cooperate if someone asked about him. No, he thought, crumpling up a sheet of paper and tossing it into Dorothy's wastebasket, fifteen feet away, that would only draw attention. Maybe he could say that someone was trying to steal Hollow Tree's designs, and ask them not to give out any information. But that sounded fishy, too. He didn't know what to do.

With a sigh, he went back to work. Two hours to go before the client arrived. Advertising only sounded like it came out of Never-Never Land. In reality, it was always Right Now Land.

"Hey, sharp tie," Jen Schick said, smiling as Keith sidled into the boardroom behind Dorothy.

"Thanks," he said, flipping the bright orange, blue and green-swirled strip of silk in his fingers. He took a place at the table opposite the window. If he hunkered down a little, he was shielded from view by Bill Mann and Rollin Chisholm. An intern came by with his decaf quadruple-sweet mocha latte. "I took it from a clown."

"Really?"

"Yeah. He thought it was too gaudy. Might ruin his reputation as a serious artist."

"What's with that eye?" Theo asked.

"The clown. He got mad because I wouldn't take the rest of his outfit."

Mann chuckled. "Sorry to miss you last week."

Keith glanced at Dorothy, Jason and Paul. "Sorry about that," he began.

"No problem," Paul said, cutting him off. "Right, folks? Dorothy gave you all the briefing. And Keith's been going over all the changes you requested."

At Dorothy's nod, Keith passed out copies of the rewritten ads. The client read them over, nodding here and there. Mann made two more changes. "The facts have altered since last week," he said, glancing at Keith's worried face. "How you phrased it was fine. We've finally established the phone link for software upgrades. Might as well say so. We've got an upgrade coming out this week."

"That's very cool," Jason said. "I'll try it later. My wife bought me one for Christmas, you know." From the inside pocket of his immaculate jacket, he brought out the smoky-blue colored unit. "It's so slim it doesn't ruin the line of my suit."

Jen Schick smiled. "That is one of the things we've been hearing across the board. It's nice to see it in use."

"Everywhere," Doug assured them.

"I've watched guys with Origamis on the bus," Keith said.

"That's great," Mann said, opening his hands in appeal. "But how many women?"

"Uh...none so far."

The Gadflies looked at one another. "Gadget-envy just doesn't hit women the same way," Jen admitted. "That's one of the things we wanted to talk to you about."

"That's what the second line of commercials is for," Dorothy said. "You've approved the initial one, male architect and boy. We're ready to start on others, woman and boy, woman and girl and so on, and, as Rollin suggested," she nodded at the other art director, "mixing the ethnicities so no one gets left out."

"That'll get the fast-track businesswoman," Bill Mann said. "But an Origami could really change anyone's life. Guys will pick up an Origami. Women just aren't."

Rita from Research cleared her throat a trifle sheepishly. "Our numbers show that presenting female role-models in the ads could produce increase in female buying anywhere from five to fifteen percent."

"Better," Jen said, making a note.

Keith cleared his throat. "When you're ready to commission a third line of commercials," he said, "I had an idea today. It's kind of goofy." Rollin made a noise.

"That's your middle name," Doug said, clearly taken aback. He looked at Dorothy, who held up her hands. The Gadflies noticed the byplay, and Mann looked concerned.

Keith hurried to explain. "It's just something that struck me funny when I was rewriting the copy. What if you showed a soccer mom standing at the kitchen counter? She's throwing things into a bowl and mixing. It's really noisy. The camera comes in close enough to see that she's adding things like a telephone, a notepad, a modem, a still camera, even hoisting a television up and dropping it in, but you can't see in the bowl."

"Good thing," Doug said.

"Then a time-skip when she pulls a pan out of the oven and the kids cheer. She's made an Origami. The kids cheer. I thought it could have a closing tag like, "To heck with cookies," or "Something the whole family will like." Then you could show her taking pictures of the kids at a game. It kind of takes the mystique out of the Origami, maybe, but it's hard to push something everyone uses while being esoteric."

"I like it," Jen said, with a grin.

"Me, too," Bill Mann said.

"The wording's pretty rough," Jason said, one golden eyebrow rising high on his forehead.

Keith felt his face reddening. "I just thought of it today. I wasn't going to mention it, but they brought up the female demographic. It just came out."

"It does address the need," Paul said.

"We can fix it up," Rollin said hastily. Janine nodded.

"Good," Jason said. He waggled a finger at Keith. "Give Rollin your notes. Janine, work on some preliminary scripts. We'll have them for you to look at next week."

"Hold your horses," Mann said, raising his hands. "Don't spend our money too fast. We're still going with the architect spots, right?"

"Of course," Dorothy said, vainly trying to take the meeting back to its original purpose. "On Monday. We're including the Fairy Footwear girl. She's got a terrifically animated face, very gamine."

"She's a little older than most of the children," Rita Dulwich said, "but the research shows that we lose a lot of girls in her age group because they don't have models showing interaction with technology. She's familiar to the viewing audience. Girls will connect her with fashion, and to be honest but not very PC, they do respond to fashion cues at her age."

Keith felt a shock. He'd almost forgotten Dola had been cast. "Uh, I don't know if she'll be able to do it."

"Why not?" Dorothy asked, frowning at Keith.

"Well, she's got school, you know. Second semester is just beginning. I...uh, hate to bring her to Chicago and have her miss out on so much school."

"You said her parents had no problem," Doug said, his forehead drawing down. "Is she copping out?"

"Now, now," Paul said, holding out his hands for peace. "Keith, why don't you call your...?"

"Cousin," Keith supplied hastily.

"...Cousin, and we'll settle this right now." He pushed the phone toward Keith.

Keith picked up the receiver. A loud dial tone sounded through the room. Immediately, he hit the button that disabled the speakerphone. Jason looked disapproving. Keith put on a sheepish face. "C'mon, Jason, these are my relatives. They still act as if I'm five years old. Do I have to let everybody hear the stuff they might say?"

"Of course not," Paul said, taking the initiative, nodding at the executive "We'll let you save your pride."

"All right," Jason said, mollified.

"Too bad," Dorothy said, a wry expression on her face. "I'd like to hear some stories about you as a kid.

Keith dialed. He had never felt so nervous in his life. Even though it was only an electronic connection, he didn't like mixing his everyday life with the elves'. The phone rang only twice before it was answered.

"Who is it?" Keva's shrill voice came loud and clear through the receiver. Everyone in the room grinned.

"It's me, er, Aunt...Keva, Keith." His face felt hot. This was not going to be as private as he'd hoped.

"What do you want? Everyone's down in the barn!"

"Well, can I talk to Tay? Or Holl? It's about Dola, er, coming up next week?"

There was a long wait. He heard the receiver being picked up. The next voice on the line was one he wasn't expecting: the Master.

"Meester Doyle?"

"Uh, hi, uh, uncle."

"Ah. Ve are being overheard?"

"Not exactly."

"Your end, then." To his relief the Headman spoke in his usual low, calm voice. The others seated around him lost interest because they could no longer hear what was being said, and started chatting among themselves.

"Yeah. I, um, called about Dola *not coming* up here next week."

"Not coming? Vhy should she not? You had our word.

Vhy vould you assume she vould not be available? Has something occurred?"

Keith struggled for words, not wanting to say too much. "Uh, well, it's been pretty busy...in school."

"Ah, yes. Ve know of your exploits. Mees Londen came to us this ahfternoon and told us all. It has been qvite a difficult time for you, but undertakings have been made, and must be kept."

"Well, I wouldn't want to cause any problems...with her classwork."

"You will cause none," the Master said firmly. "And you must not seek to diminish contact mit us because of your experiences. It vill do us no harm."

"Are you sure?" Keith asked, conscious that his voice was threatening to break.

"I am sure. Come back to us," the Master said. "Your stoicisim is admirable, but your absence vill leaf a most unpleasant gap in our lifes."

"But..."

"But," the Master put all of his authority into that single syllable and stopped Keith's protests cold. "You vill make it here safely. Thereafter ve haf our own means of preventing prying eyes. Your classes begin again on Saturday. Therefore it vill be confenient for you to convey Dola back mit you on Monday. She is looking forvard to the experience. Ve look forward to seeing you on Friday efening. Goodbye." The connection clicked off. Keith stared at the phone for a moment, overwhelmed by the trust the Little Folk were putting in him. He wasn't sure he was worthy of it.

"Well?" Jason asked.

Fighting with his own uncertainties, Keith looked up at the waiting roomful of people. "She's in."

"Good," Paul said, rubbing his hands together. "Now, let's get back to business."

Chapter 29

The road to Friday took forever. After the meeting Dorothy dragged Keith back to their office and chewed him out thoroughly for bring up an idea that hadn't gone through channels first. He felt he'd been punished enough not only by having it taken away from him, but by seeing Rollin and Janine gloating about it.

The new vigilance Keith had to employ wherever he went was tiring him. Long before he got home every night he was worn out from the mechanics of keeping the charm going and looking over his shoulder to make sure no one was taking notice of him in spite of it. For the elves' sake he needed to keep his wits about him. He didn't go out anywhere unless he had to. He felt lonely and isolated, all the more because Diane never answered his phone calls. She had even set her e-mail account to bounce his messages back to him. Dunn suggested that he go to an Internet café and use a house computer to try again, but Keith didn't like the idea of tricking Diane. He'd see her when he went down to Midwestern and have the discussion both of them had avoided so soon after his assault. It wasn't going to be easy, but he wanted things to go back to normal between them.

Dunn had helped him get his car without attracting extra attention. Keith climbed into the back seat while his roommate drove to the grocery store. Dunn waited for a few minutes to make sure no one had followed him into the parking lot, then went inside, leaving the keys in the ignition. Keith rolled over the front seat and started the engine, feeling like a thief stealing his own car. Thanks to the spell dozens of people probably got the impression that there was no one in the driver's seat. He took a circuitous route out of town. By the time he was headed southward, he was certain there was no one behind him.

He never risked the interstate highway, instead taking the side roads through endless little towns he hadn't known existed. It took a couple extra hours to drive all the way to the farm.

The twinkling lanterns on the side of the house glittered with the same promise as Peter Pan's second star to the right. He devoured the sight like a starving man. It had been a terrible week, thinking that he would never come back to the farm house. Inside, like the most precious and anticipated birthday present, were all of his friends, safe and happy.

Keith pulled the car in and rolled to a halt, more tired than he wanted to admit. He was thanking his lucky stars that it was the first week of term and he didn't have any work to turn in. It wasn't until at last he walked in the kitchen door and saw the Master standing there with his hands on his hips to realize guiltily that he *did* have more homework that he should have done, and that not a single word of it was written.

"Well, Meester Doyle?" the Master said, peering at him over the top of his glasses.

"Well, sir?" Keith asked, nervously, as a thousand excuses jumbled themselves in his mind.

The red mustache parted in a wide smile. "Velcome back."

"Thank you, sir," Keith said. His muscles sagged with relief.

His other friends hurried forward to take his bag. Borget grabbed a cloak off the peg and raced out the door behind him. Dennet and Aylmer brought Keith to the dinner table where Keva plied him with food and fresh bread. Marm's round face shone as he poured a mug of cider.

"Tapped just today," he informed Keith.

"It's great," Keith said, too overwhelmed to say more. Dola huddled in on the bench beside him as he ate and drank. "Thank you. Thank you all."

"A sacrifice deserves recognition," the Master said. "Mees Londen told us eferything."

The door opened. Borget, his cheeks pink with effort and the cold, stepped aside to let Holl enter. Holl came over to grasp Keith's hand.

"I was putting Asrai to bed. We didn't know when you'd arrive." The blond elf's voice was hoarse. Keith swallowed, feeling a lump in his own throat.

"You were sure I would come? I'm still not certain I should be here."

Holl gripped his hand tightly before letting it go. "Where else should you be? Wherever we are is a home to you, now and forever."

Gifts on top of gifts. Keith bent his head over his plate, taking in the good feelings along with the good food. He didn't trust his voice for a while. The others must have known how he felt, for they filled the air with stories while he ate.

"I made a butterfly," Dola said, producing a folded triangle of colored paper. "It even flies. See?" She let it go, and it began to flutter over the table.

"Take it away, girl," her great-grandmother snapped, snatching it out of the air. "The man's trying to eat."

"It's okay," Keith assured them. "It's beautiful."

"The cow calved two days ago."

"Tim's Craft Hut bought tventy lanterns."

"Asrai's cutting a new tooth."

"Candlepat has a new dress. The Conservatives are scandalized."

"Vhy vear a garment vun can see through?"

Keith just let the news wash over him. More serious matters could come in a while. For the moment, he just wanted to enjoy being with his friends again.

"Turn *up* the electric fence?" Holl asked, astonished, when Keith brought up the subject Sunday morning. "When you were complaining endlessly and forever that you wanted it turned down? Whatever for?"

"I told you those creeps are snooping around," Keith said. "It's you they want, not me. I don't want them even getting a glance at you."

"We have protection," Holl assured him. "And you have your defense."

"And I use it, even if it knocks me out by the end of the day. I'm afraid even to sleep without it on. I've learned to fine-tune it so it only affects people in the immediate area. But focus like that is extra-tiring. Beach found me because he was looking for me. He knows where I work, where I go. Are you sure you want me to take Dola to Chicago under those circumstances? With me half-invisible all the time? If the SAG representative thinks a minor is on the set alone he might call Child Welfare."

Holl waved away the concern. "You won't let that happen. You'll cope. We have faith in your endless creativity. Keep your ears open, as you have, and act as wisdom dictates."

"Wisdom, huh?" Keith grumbled good-naturedly, following Holl down the hill to the barn for class.

"Or imitation thereof," Holl said, grinning back at him over his shoulder. "We trust you."

Keith glanced around uncomfortably. He was the only one who didn't have a paper on his desk. Holl sat at his ease, sanding the arms of a wooden doll for his daughter, giving Keith an occasional glance. None of the others looked his way, especially Diane, who arrived late and, despite Keith's frantic semaphoring to her to sit by him, placed herself as far away from him as possible.

The Master wrote a word in Greek on his easel blackboard and tapped it with his fingertip. "*Agape*. Eferyvun has reviewed the poetry ve discussed from last veek?" All of the students, Little Folk and Big Folk nodded, except Keith's. Here it came. "Fery good. Meester Doyle?"

Keith rose to his feet to explain why he didn't have his paper, a subject he had been avoiding all weekend. But the Master forestalled him.

"Meester Doyle has been vorking on a long-term project in comparative sociology in vhich he is making contact mit other non-human beings. Perhaps he vould care to bring us up to date on that?"

Keith felt his mouth drop open. The others turned to him with fascinated faces. Keith met Diane's eyes. She gave him an encouraging nod. Did he even spot a hint of softening in her expression? She might have been mad at him, but she was still on his side.

"Um, yeah," he began awkwardly, but warmed at once to his subject. "Well, for years I've been thinking about throwing a party. It's planned for the beginning of May. You're all invited. I have to tell you about a couple of the guests I just met a week ago. Their names are Rily and Liri. They're sidhe...."

Vasques threw himself into the desk chair in Beach's hotel room. "Nothing," he said, disgustedly. "We searched that entire garage a hundred times. We didn't find a trace of Doyle or a clue as to how he got out of there. We even got the city workers in on it."

"How'd you do that?" Beach asked, curiously.

"Told 'em we'd lost a bag of diamonds," Wyszinski said, with an evil grin. "They opened every door and turned over every floor plate in the place."

"Devious," Beach said, pacing to the window. "Like that boy. Damn him, he's gone to ground again. He has to be using some kind of spell or device to keep out of sight."

"Well, we can't find someone who's magically invisible," Vasques said. He looked at his partner and tapped his temple, schooling his face into innocence just as their employer turned around again. "Miller and O'Dell kept a lookout on the apartment. A girl slept in his room all weekend. No sign of Doyle, though. He must not have gone back there. What do you want us to do now?"

"We'll have to hunt him down from the other end," Beach said, after giving his operatives a hard look. "The artifact in his apartment came from somewhere, as did the one that Maria and Stefan bought. Did he find a hidden hoard, or is he making them?"

"These are new," Stefan said. He sat in a corner between the others and Maria. Oblivious to the rest of the world, the psychic was communing with her pendulum. Stefan's job was to protect her from interruption when the spirits spoke. She wouldn't have heard a gun go off next to her head. "That was what made us excited."

"So the chances are that he made it. How? Is the the heir to a long history of spell-crafting?"

"There wasn't any sign of woodworking tools in the apartment," Vasques pointed out.

"What if he just makes them as a hobby?" Wyszinski asked. "One or two at a time?"

"We'll have to discover that," Beach said. "But if he is, he must be working somewhere. That one was for sale. There are probably more. I must know the source. A factory—no, there's the cold-iron issue with machinery."

"The boy did not burn when we put the handcuffs on him," Stefan pointed out.

Beach looked amused. "He's not a fairy, Stefan. But *magic* is affected by it. Therefore it's not a large operation. A workshop of some kind."

"Chicago is full of artisan workshops," Vasques pointed out. "It could take years to locate the right one."

"Ah, but we have three things in our favor: you, my investigating friends, Ming, and Maria, who located our quarry the moment he put a magical foot wrong. Keep your eyes open, darling." The psychic nodded at his words without looking up. "Ming will search the web for public records of any facility rented in his name. The rest of you, legwork. I want observation on his usual haunts, but I want you to hunt down anywhere else that he has sold more of these artifacts. Get on the phone. Make friends. Sooner or later he's bound to return to one of those places, and then..." Beach narrowed his pale eyes, "we will have him."

Chapter 30

"This is beautiful stuff, Tiron," Keith said, admiring the sculptures as the elves wrapped them in newspaper and packed
them in cartons for delivery to Galleria Tony. Far from wanting to withdraw from the marketplace, they were looking forward to expanding. Keith considered it, but decided that it
would be okay to bring more merchandise to the Galleria
because Beach had already been there. He wouldn't back-
track to places where he hadn't found anything. Besides,
Thom Albert had called him three times a week since January asking for more.

Keith kept glancing toward the door with an ever-diminishing sense of hope. It was Valentine's Day. He wanted to
take Diane out for dinner, but he hadn't heard from her yet.
He'd had left numerous messages, hoping he wasn't sounding
as desperate as he felt. Since their disastrous weekend at the
beginning of January she'd been screening her calls through
her answering machine, nor was she responding to e-mails.
She came to the Elf Master's class, but she arrived only minutes before it began, and always left before Keith could catch
her alone. She was going out of her way to avoid him. He
missed her tremendously. He had tried showing up unan-
nounced at her apartment, but she had not opened the door.
He'd sent little presents with love notes attached. She'd call or
e-mail to thank him, but that was about it. Their conversations were short, always ending with Diane saying she had to
go study. Before he'd left Chicago he had had flowers delivered to her with a note asking her out to dinner. He had even
worn his new Armani suit to please her.

He hadn't had as much time as he would have like to
devote to making up or anything but work and homework.
Professor Larsen was riding the Entrepreneurship class hard,

demanding that they revise the assigned business plan over and over until any of them could be an instant success in the real-life marketplace, just add money. And luck. Keith had kept in mind from first semester the basic premise of a business like Hollow Tree– anything to take some of the foot-slogging research out of the way—but he was designing it as though it was meant to employ Big Folk and pay actual expenses. There was an incredible amount of planning and calculation to come up with a property that could survive its first two years without going bankrupt. Thank goodness Dr. Li's afternoon class in Business Accounting dovetailed into the morning course— no accident on the part of the program's designers, of course.

Keith stroked the cherrywood carving of a doe and was surprised to feel a smooth force under his fingertips. "Why do these have magic in them? Do they move, like some of the kids' toys?"

Tiron grinned. "And wouldn't that make the Big Ones drop their jaws? Nothing so dramatic. I've given them a bit of enhancement to keep them from ever deteriorating. I don't mind it if the wood takes on the luster of age, but I'd take it amiss if I should outlive my work."

Keith clicked his tongue as he set the carving down on a pile of newsprint. "I wish I could do anything half as well as you carve."

"Ah, well," the Irish elf said, coloring faintly with pleasure, "I just see what's in the wood, and I bring it out with me knife. You've got your own talents, you do."

"Not like this," Keith said, folding paper around the doe. He regretted hiding its beauty away, but even a mild protection spell might not keep it from getting banged up in the trunk of his Mustang. He looked forward to the expression on the face of the gallery owner when he unwrapped it and all of the other treasures the elves had made. Holl brought over a dolphin made of a fine-grained, pale, yellow-green wood. It leaped, effortlessly, from a heavy base that allowed it to arch outward without support underneath. "Holl, that is terrific."

"Catering to the masses, are we?" Tiron asked, in his leisurely fashion. He leaned back with a lazy, insouciant grin. "All the rage with the nature-lovin' Big Folk, dolphins are. And baby seals—have you done a baby seal as well?"

"The wood suggested the shape," Holl said, not rising to the bait.

"Did it? Did it look like a dollar sign, then? See the way the grain fights against the line," Tiron said, pointing to the dolphin's side. Frowning at his cavalier tone, Keith leaned close.

"I can't see anything wrong with it. It looks great to me."

"Oh, well, you're not an expert. He's forcing his design," Tiron said, taking his knife out of his sheath and using it as a pointer. "This grain suggests a more undulating design. You could have done a squid or a mermaid out of the same piece, with a natural flow. This is poor workmanship."

"It's nothing of the kind!" Enoch burst out. He had listened as long as he could to the criticism. How Tiron dared pick on Holl, knowing the burdens he was carrying!

The Conservatives continued to harp upon how naked they felt without the boundary charm, and how lowering it hadn't solved the problem with their unwanted visitor. In addition, they were on the lookout for Keith's attackers, another reason that they thought the charm should be renewed at full strength. Even they had to admit morale was better now that they were not so much under stress from the spell, but they were smug in the knowledge that Holl's grand plan had failed to do what he had claimed it would. Enoch didn't consider it a failure. Holl had been able to keep an uneasy truce going, believing that leaving the ways open was the only possible solution.

The fact was they no idea why the creature should still be hanging around since they opened the portal, but there it was. The initial peace of mind the Folk had enjoyed was fading fast. The creature was attracted to the energy that arose from both magic and strife. He could feel its influence behind the occasional battles that arose, suspecting that it had a role in creating them. It continued to behave like a poltergeist, knocking things over, interfering with the cellar and spoiling everyone's mood, but its visits were far less frequent. Of all this Enoch could say nothing so long as the Big One was listening, but Tiron ought to have known better. Why bring it up now?

He glanced around the workroom. Oh, ho, so it was a show. The pretty sisters were behind Tiron. His cockle-doodling was for their benefit, not to impress Keith Doyle. Enoch said flatly, "Holl's work is good work. If you can't give a compliment where it's earned, then keep your words to yourself."

"Well, you've hardly done better, have you?" Tiron asked, his plot discovered. He stood up, ready for a fight. "Ye've carved a piece of tree to look like—a tree!"

Enoch turned to regard his handiwork, the depiction of a gnarled old oak, its crown leaning protectively over a doe and its fawn nestled in the knobby roots. "And what's wrong with it?"

"Well, it's hardly imaginative, is it?"

That was so unjust that Enoch stared at him for a second. Keith sat there with his mouth open, not understanding the fires that were raging under the surface. Holl hastily put aside his own hurt feelings to restore calm.

"Let's keep peace in the house," he pleaded.

"Will you not defend yourself?" Enoch asked Holl, openly annoyed even though he knew the bogie must be enjoying his display of bad temper. "You've reason to be proud of your work. This popinjay thinks because he's traveled a thousand miles he can lecture us."

"Three thousand," Catra said, with a record-keeper's passion for accuracy.

"Don't you go defending him," Enoch snarled. "His rudeness is inexcusable."

"Don't you snap at me," Catra said, shocked. "I'm not a part of this."

"I don't wish to cause more upset," Holl said, carefully.

"Hey, what's going on here?" Keith Doyle asked, his kind face wearing a puzzled expression. "There's no reason to get bent out of shape. *All* these pieces are great. Thom's going to go nuts. People will be buying them as soon as I unwrap them."

"Keith Doyle is right," Ronard said. "Our skill's un-matched. That's the point."

"What do you know?" Tiron said, shoving his red face into the bigger and slower male's face. "The only thing you've hewed worth using is firewood."

"That's not fair," Ronard said, working his big jaw. Nor-mally a pleasant, good-natured soul, he was controlling him-self with difficulty.

"The tree should be saying that about your use of its wood!"

"And who do you think you are, babbling on about your over-ornamented baubles?"

"They're not over-ornamented," Catra said, with perhaps more care for accuracy than for her longtime boyfriend's feel-ings. "Tiron's style is very classical."

Grinning, Tiron thrust his chin at the bigger, slower male. "There, you see? She agrees with me."

"Catra!" Ronard said, his feelings hurt.

"I'm being no more than accurate," the Archivist said, sur-prised. Ronard looked dumbfounded.

"He insulted me! What accurate thing have you got to say about that?"

"Well, it wasn't nice of him, surely."

"What kind of a boiled-egg response is that? Can't you tell him off as smartly as you did me?"

"Why? What good would it do?"

"Don't you call my sister a boiled egg!" Candlepat snapped.

Ronard's nostrils flared out like a bull's. "Stay out of this!"

"Don't you shout at my sister," Catra flared.

"Well, the two of you don't seem to know who your friends are, do you?" Ronard replied, hotly.

"I think I do know," Catra exclaimed. She grabbed Tiron by the arm and marched away.

"Wait a moment," Tiron protested. "I wasn't..."

"Tiron! Don't go!" Candlepat cried, her lovely face run-ning with tears. "There's a curse on this house!" Keith felt in his pocket for a handkerchief.

"Here," he said, offering it to her. "It's just a spat. You'll all fix it up before dinner, right?"

"Ah, no, it'll never be the same again," Candlepat wailed, throwing herself into his arms.

"It'll be okay. You'll see." Keith said.

"Oh, Keith Doyle," Candlepat said. She nestled against him and put her head on his chest. Keith sat awkwardly with the attractive elf on his lap, wanting to pat her on the shoulder comfortingly but not knowing quite where to put his hands. She may have been the size of a child, but she had the body of a full-grown woman, and a very attractive one at that. He was also aware of the eyes of others on him. The room felt suddenly hot. Candlepat grabbed his face between her hands and brought it eye to eye with hers. "You're the only one who cares about me." She started to kiss him over and over.

"Candlepat, no, mmph!" In between passionate smooches, he protested and tried to pull away, but she paid no attention. He was terrified, intrigued, embarrassed, horrified and astonished all at once. It was a fantasy and a nightmare.

"A-hem!" Keith looked up at the sound of a throat being cleared.

Diane stood over them, her hands on her hips. The balance of the moment tilted abruptly and inexorably to nightmare.

"Uh," Keith said, weakly, "Happy Valentine's Day?"

Of all the wrong things to say in the universe, that was at the top of the list as the most incorrect choice of any he could possibly have made. For one second her face was blank with shock. In the next moment, anger flooded in, changing it into a reddening mask of rage.

"So this is what you mean when you say you miss me! I never want to see you again!" Head high, she spun on her heel and marched away. She paused on the threshold of the barn to add, "And you can forget about the cold cuts for your party!"

"Diane!" Keith shouted. He tried to detach himself, but Candlepat hung on like ivy clinging to a tree.

"Ah, no, now, don't run away again," she pleaded. "You're always trying to skip away from me."

"Look, Candlepat, I'm sorry," Keith said, trying to fathom the depth of the disaster that had just occurred. "Diane!"

Diane strode up the gravel path toward her car, slipping every other step on the ice. It wasn't bad enough that Keith was still lusting after "Doris;" now he was starting to get involved with elf women! Or maybe, she thought, choking back an angry sob, that had the problem from the beginning: why he wouldn't commit to her. Why stick with one woman when he had a farmful of willing females who owed him their lives? He hadn't even looked up at her when she'd arrived. And that Candlepat! Kissing him right in front of her! A fireball had erupted up out of one of the table saws at that moment, exactly defining how Diane felt. How dare she! How dare he!

She resented all of them, but Keith most of all. This elf business was his deal, not hers. Oh, she was grateful for the extra education, and God knew she'd never have made it all the way through college without the scholarship money that they gave her—money she fully intended to pay back one day—but other things had happened to her, things that would never have happened in a million years if not for them. She'd been kidnapped by a Secret Service agent in Ireland, spent days being frantic about Keith when he'd disappeared down a sinkhole in Scotland, and spent the most humiliating morning of her life shopping with the Invisible Man. For all she knew, she herself was being stalked by bogeymen. Well, never again.

She was so angry that she couldn't separate her car key. It fell out of her hand into the snow next to the path. She fished it up, bit her glove off and pried the freezing tongues of metal apart. She hurried toward her car, only wanting to go and hide somewhere. Humiliated in front of everyone, and by the person she thought she could trust most of all in the world.

She heard shouts over the wind whistling between the house and the trees.

"Wait, Diane!" "Wait, don't go!" "Diane!" She stiffened her back, thinking it was Keith, but the voices coming up behind her were female.

Diane ignored them. If Keith didn't have the sense to know when she was serious, she'd find someone else who would appreciate her. Her eyes were full of tears, freezing into slush in the cold. Her lashes clumped together, and she brushed at them with her glove. She bumped into something, someone, and blinked her eyes hard to clear them. A heart-shaped face with sympathetic blue eyes framed by a white parka hood peered up at her.

"Go away, Marcy. You're responsible for this."

"Me?" Marcy asked. "How?"

Diane thought of saying that she'd been the one who led Keith to the Little Folk in the first place, but the truth was that Keith had followed *her* to their hidden classroom. Marcy wasn't to blame just because she got married and Diane wasn't even engaged yet. It was all Keith, as usual. Maura and Dola hurried to take her hand and offer her a handkerchief before she was aware that she was crying.

"It's all his fault," Diane burst out. "He's got time for everybody but me."

"That's not true," Maura said, putting a motherly arm around her waist. "Everything he does is for you, in the end." Marcy patted her on the shoulder, offering silent support.

"He thinks about you all the time," Dola said. "He *talks* about you all the time, and he does talk." She was wrapped in a huge shawl, probably grabbed off a hook when she dashed out into the cold to comfort her. Diane had always thought of the little elf girl as a kind of rival. She knew it was silly. She and Maura were both so good-hearted, but they couldn't understand that their kindness made her feel worse. Diane tossed her head back, forced herself to stop crying. Her eyes still stung. The others watched her with sympathy.

"I have to get out of here for a while."

"I understand," said Marcy.

"Diane!" Keith called. With difficulty he shook loose from Candlepat's embrace. The elf maiden went flying. Keith babbled an apology and dashed out of the barn.

"Did you have to do that?" Holl asked Candlepat, who sat where she had landed on the floor, inspecting her nails. She didn't want to meet anyone's eyes.

"It was the only way I could think of to keep him from seeing the fire spirit," she said, her long eyelashes lowered. Her cheeks were rose pink with embarrassment. "My heavens, what he must think of me!"

"I'm sure it will be all right," Ronard said, offering a hand and helping her gallantly to her feet. "You showed amazing presence of mind so soon after an argument."

Candlepat gazed up at him with large blue eyes shining. "Did you really think so?" Ronard's breath caught, and he swallowed then nodded slowly. Holl grinned. Poor Ronard was out of his depth. The girl bounced back faster than a rubber ball.

Enoch frowned. "There wouldn't have been an argument if the four of you had behaved civilly."

"Ah, well," Candlepat said, putting her arm through Ronard's, "Tiron started it."

"*Do* you think Keith Doyle saw it?" Enoch asked. "There'll be questions."

"So long as he gets no answers," Curran said, with a sharp look at Holl from under his snowy eyebrows, "it will no' matter."

Chapter 31

Keith's thoughts pounded in his head in time with the slap of his windshield wipers. Of all the rotten luck, to have Diane walk in at just that moment! She was ticked at him already. Now she thought that he was cheating on her! As if he could have predicted what Candlepat would do. Everybody had seemed all right when he arrived at the farm. Now they were fighting. It was just like September. Why would Tiron attack Holl like that? Why wouldn't Holl speak up for himself? Why did Enoch have to do it?

But the first thing, the main thing, was to find Diane. With one hand gripping the wheel tightly, Keith dialed her number on his cell phone.

"Hi, this is 217-555-3663," Diane's voice said brightly. "No one's here, so leave a message."

"If you're there, please pick up, Diane! I can explain. Nothing happened! Candlepat got into an argument." Hastily, he clicked off. That wasn't the best way to start off an apology. He tried again.

"...Leave a message."

"Diane, I'm sorry you had to see that. She just wanted someone to be nice to her after Tiron and Catra..." He hung up again. He just wasn't doing this very well.

"...Leave a message."

The third time Keith just turned off the phone without saying anything. He needed to see her in person, to plead for understanding. Not that he deserved it, he thought, guiltily. One tiny little voice inside his head said that he had liked kissing Candlepat, but the rest of his inner voices broke out in a chorus that he hadn't sought out the contact, didn't want it in the first place, and Diane was his true love. He agreed with the overwhelming majority. Alas, none of them knew anything about time-travel. It was impossible to go back and undo the last ten minutes. He was stuck with the status quo.

The logical place to look first was her home. She was probably too angry to go back to the small confines of her apartment, but he went there anyhow. Not that she was likely to open the door to him, but he judged by the lack of tire marks in the new snow covering her reserved parking place that she had not been there. Keith went to her job next. The food service was always grateful for extra hands; she might have gone there to work off some of her fury. No such luck. None of her coworkers had seen her since Friday.

Out of a sense of desperation, Keith turned the Mustang toward Voordman's Country Crafts.

No white Saturn was in the parking lot, but the shop owner's baleful expression told him more than words could that Diane had been there. She was waiting on a customer when he arrived. The moment the teenage girl had left, Ms. Voordman swooped down on Keith and dragged him into the back room.

"What is the matter with you?" she asked, her dark eyes flashing. "Diane came to me as a friend who would listen to her. She was so angry she couldn't cry. She was almost ready to forgive you for backing out on your word in January, but you seem to have taken fear of commitment to a new depth. Don't you dare lead her on as though it's a done deal if it isn't."

"But it was! It is. Didn't she tell you..." Keith began, trying to figure out how to explain a kidnaping, the supernatural and an invisibility spell without using any of the buzzwords. Ms. Voordman waved away his explanation.

"She told me she found you with another girl. Are you trying to drive her away?"

"No! It wasn't like that, honest to God. The other girl was crying. She's a friend of ours." Keith felt terrible. "It's just a mistake."

"That's one way to put it," Ms. Voordman said. "I warned you this could happen."

"It wasn't my fault," Keith said. "I mean, not this time. She has to give me another chance. Where did she go?"

The shop owner shook her head. "Leave her alone. She needs to have some time by herself, to think through exactly what it is she wants. You're just too busy. Both of you. See if you can pick things up when you are prepared to devote your attention to her."

"I will. I swear."

Ms. Voordman gave him a stern look. "Let her have some space. You need to think things over yourself."

"I already know what I want. What I need. I just blew it. Thanks...for listening to her."

"Go on," the shop owner said, waving him out, but less harshly than before.

On the way back toward Midwestern he tried Diane's number again. The message had been changed.

"This is 217-555-3663. No one's here, so leave a message. Unless this is Keith. Just hang up and don't call back."

"Diane, I'm sorry," Keith said, as soon as the tone sounded. But it was followed by another noise, that of the receiver being picked up and slammed down with great force. He didn't try again.

"What do I do?" Keith asked Holl, at the conclusion of his story. He sat on a bench in the kitchen sagging over a mug of Marm's best brewing as though he was the only patron left in a bar. Holl regarded him with the air of a sympathetic tavern keeper. He knew the other kitchen helpers were listening, but were tactfully pretending that they weren't. Keva had saved a plate of stew from the supper pot and furnished half a dozen of her best rolls on the side. Keith ate them without tasting them. They might as well have been from the food service. "Ms. Voordman told me to leave her alone for a while, let her get over being mad."

"I'd say the woman has a great deal of sense," Holl said, "and a kind heart besides. Nothing you could say will change Diane's mind for a while. I'd volunteer to be your go-between, but I agree it will do no good. All you can do is to let her temper cool."

"That could take a while," Keith said glumly. He rubbed his eyes with the heels of his hands. "It's taken almost six weeks just to get her to agree to a date. Ms. Voordman said I'm too busy to have a relationship. Maybe she's right."

Holl's face lit up. "Now, *there's* that memory I've been try-ing to draw back! It was her name that has reminded me." He took a pale green slip of paper from his pocket and presented it to Keith. "Here you are. The last three months' commis-sion. A bit larger than the usual," he said, as Keith's eyebrows climbed to the skies, "adding Galleria Tony's portion added on top. You've done so much for us it's nice to be able to reward you, though truthfully you've rewarded yourself. It's your hard work."

"Oh!" Keith said, as he suddenly remembered that other people besides himself had problems. Guiltily, he glanced around at the others, who quickly turned away, not meeting his eyes. Things must be worse than he'd imagined. He pushed the check back at Holl. "Thanks, but I can't accept this."

"Why not?" Holl asked, bewildered.

"Well, don't you folks need it?"

Holl eyed him. "What makes you think that?"

"I think I finally figured it out," Keith said, gently. "It's been bugging you folks since before September. Why you were in such a hurry to move into the high-price shops. Why you started selling over the Internet but wouldn't let me build you a website. You guys must owe some serious money. That's why you've had the power so high on the fence. You've been having problems with Big People hanging around. What hap-pened, did you max out the credit cards? You can stop credi-tors from dunning you, you know. There are laws to protect people from harassment; I'm surprised Catra hasn't come across them...why are you laughing?"

"You incredible infant," Holl said, caught by surprise. "Did Dola tell you that?"

"Heck, no. I tried every way I could to weasel the truth out of Dola on the way up or back from Chicago. She held out better than a spy behind enemy lines. All she'd say is she feels like she's being watched. She's been good. I worked it out for myself. Everybody's been on edge for months. Someone's bugging you. Let me at' em. I can make them back off. One look at me and you'll never hear from them again."

Holl shook his head. "No. Big People are always a problem to us, but it's not that." He sighed. "We've our own worries, unrelated to our success as capitalists."

Keith pounced at once on the word. "What kind of worries? Come on, Holl. Something's been eating you for months. Tell me. Are people spying on you again? Pestering you?"

Holl opened his mouth. "I...no. You've caught me by surprise, but I am not supposed to talk about it."

"If it's been a problem since August—or before!—then you're not having much success solving the problem yourself. Tell Uncle Keith."

Holl hesitated again. "It's true we haven't been able to work it out for ourselves...but I cannot say anything. I've been forbidden."

"But I'm your best friend," Keith said persuasively.

Holl smiled at him, sadly. "And so you are. But you can't help with this."

"How about Twenty Questions? Sounds like...? If it's not money, and it's not interference from other people, what could be bothering all of you that much?"

Holl had to stop himself from blurting out the whole story. It would be so easy to share the burden, especially with this generous and willing Big Person, but he was all too aware that they were not alone in the room. "No."

Keith turned huge puppy eyes on him. "C'mon, Holl! Okay, don't tell me. Let me guess. You're the subjects of one of those new reality TV shows, and you can't decide who to vote out of the village. No? You've become addicted to cybersurfing and you can't keep up with the orders. No, wait a minute, I know that's not true because I delivered this week's myself. How about...?"

"Stop!" Holl said, wearily. "Enough guessing. ...We...don't have the privacy we thought we would have here. We have our freedom—you helped us buy it—but we can't enjoy it. For months now we have been unable to stretch our wings as we'd hoped. We'd wanted to research our talents further, but we can't do that either. You know before we left the library we dreamed of having a place of our own so we could give free rein to our skills, and perhaps invent more, but it's attracted...attention."

Holl heard a gasp from the others in the room and stopped short. The noise was inaudible to Keith Doyle.

"From who? You have to tell me the rest now!"

"No more," Holl said, wishing he could take back even those few words. He was mortified with himself. He would never be headman now. "You've caught me by surprise. I was not to tell you a thing about this. I've broken confidence."

Keith frowned, concern creasing his forehead. "But it's been bugging you for months!"

"That it has. It'd be good to get it out at last, but I can say nothing else."

"That's it? You can't use your talents? Why not? What's stopping you?"

"I..."

"You gave someone your word not to talk," Keith said shrewdly. "It has to be the Master. I'll go get him. If he absolves you of your promise, you can tell me." He stood up. Alarmed, Holl jumped up and put out a hand.

"Don't go. I made *everyone* a promise, not just him."

"Well, he's the one who counts, because he's the Headman. Right?"

"In a way."

"Good," Keith said, with a decided nod. "I'm going to go ask him now. It'll only take a minute. I'm sure he'll say yes."

Holl's heart pounded. "No! Keith Doyle, come back here. Don't plague him with your nonsense. He's teaching the youngsters now. You wouldn't want to interrupt class." Holl strode after Keith, but it was in vain. The juggernaut was loose; beware all who stand in his way!

The rest of the Folk stared at them as they left. Holl's ear tips were red with embarrassment. He'd failed. He'd failed the village, the Master, but most of all himself.

The barn was quiet on a Saturday evening. Work had ceased before supper, leaving the elves free to pursue hobbies, such as music, embroidery, making and mending clothes. With the noise of the power tools stilled, families could enjoy time together and have conversations with their kin. The strips of light on the ceiling that mimicked daylight were just beginning to take on the color of sunset. It didn't exactly match what was going on on a February day in Illinois, but Keith had never known any of the elves to suffer from Seasonal Affective Disorder.

The room was so quiet, in fact, that everyone heard his footsteps long before he entered. Every eye was on him as he slid open the door. Holl slipped in behind him. Keith offered a smile all the way around. Most of the Folk met his eyes then went back to what they were doing, but he could tell their handsomely pointed ears were tuned in on him like radar antennae.

The Master was watching him, too, but he didn't drop his gaze when Keith met it. Instead, he watched the Big student approach. His round face was expressionless.

Dola, the eldest in the children's class, looked at her favorite with curiosity in her large eyes, but said nothing. Keith quaked a little in his shoes for what he was about to throw at his formidable little teacher, but he'd been watching Holl suffer for months. Enough was enough. He cleared his throat.

"I'm very sorry to interrupt, sir," Keith said, formally, "but may I have a moment of your time?"

"So *how* is he supposed to get rid of this fire-snake thing?" Keith asked. They'd withdrawn into Keith's sleeping area in the corner of the big room for privacy, but with the elves' sensitive hearing he might as well have been on a stage with a public address system. He'd asked the Master to give Holl permission to tell him the whole story. It was granted freely, making Keith wonder why no one had simply asked before. "You've forbidden him to ask for help. How's he supposed to do something he doesn't know how to do?"

The Master was as imperturbable seated on the old brown couch as he might have been on a jeweled throne. He peered at Keith over the gold rims of his glasses. "He is supposed to improvise, to use tools at his hand."

Keith threw up his hands. "And if those aren't sufficient? When does the breaking point come? He's been trying to fix this situation for months, hasn't he? And no, I had no idea what was wrong. I just knew he was going through hell and he wouldn't tell me why. Nobody would."

"No vun vould. It is a test of his leadership skills, to solf a problem for the sake of the village."

"Look," Keith said, appealing to the Master, "It's no secret you're grooming him for your job, in a century or two. I don't pretend to be an expert, but I am studying management techniques. One of the things I did learn is that when you can't handle something on your own, a good manager takes the job to a subcontractor who can handle it. So far you've let him get banged around. Everybody's been living under a cloud because you can't get rid of this thing. You have to let him ask for help. I'd help. I'd do anything for him. I'd do anything for you. You know that."

The Master tapped his lower lip with a thoughtful forefinger. "I see. But you must also see vhat I do, that he has lessons to learn in leadership."

Keith frowned. Something in the Master's words rang a bell. Keith turned to Holl. "Now that the cat's out of the bag, can I give you a piece of advice in handling this situation? A quick lesson in good leadership and task management?"

"Certainly, Keith Doyle," Holl said.

"Delegate. Let me go down there."

Holl's eyes went round with alarm. "No! You're out of your head."

"Holl, I can do it," Keith said. "I'm good with supernatural beings. Look at the air sprites and the sidhe."

"What about the bodach?"

Keith tilted his head humorously. "Two out of three isn't bad. But how else can I keep my title as the world's only research mythologist if I don't try? What do you think, Master? Shouldn't he choose the best man for the job?"

"You think you are the vun who can help qvell this angry being?"

"Maybe. Maybe not," Keith admitted. "But what harm can it do? You've already spent months living with this thing. If I fail, you're still in the status quo. If I succeed, all to the good. No one else here seems to be able to break through. I do have experience talking to other species. Okay, so one of them kicked the stuffing out of me, but I survived. And look, better me than your handpicked successor. There's only one of him."

"And only one of you," the Master said, gently.

"I consider it a calculated risk," Keith said, with a shrug. "Why not? He could have asked me to do it from the beginning. I'd have said yes then, too."

"I could not allow it because ve knew you vould accept the task and the risk. It vas too easy. He had to come to the point vhere he vould succeed or fail. At that point he vould haf to make the decision himself. He broke confidence, vhen he knew that vould haf consequences, for the vell-being of us all."

Keith was outraged. "So by failing he passes?"

The Master shrugged. "It took him longer than I had assumed. He had to veigh blind obedience against the task at hand, and efen still he did not open up completely vhen it vas clear the situvation had gone far beyond his abilities. It is a lesson in leadership he vill only haf to learn vunce."

Holl shook his head. He was too tired to be angry.

Keith looked at Holl sympathetically. "I'm glad I'm not you. I've only got to keep my grades up and try to make up with my girlfriend, if I can."

"You are more important than that, Keith Doyle."

"Not at the moment," Keith said, trying to sound more offhand than he felt. He was nervous about confronting a being that had knocked the wind out of almost the entire village at once, but he was excited, too. "Well, boss? Do you want me to go into the basement and try and talk to that thing?"

Holl looked at the Master, conscious that what he said now would have repercussions for years to come. "I would be grateful if you would try."

"Then, I'll do it," Keith said, getting to his feet. "Keep the first aid kit handy." Holl rose, too. "Where are you going?"

"I'm coming with you."

"No," Keith said firmly. "You're not. You are not expendable. And I'd rather try this alone. If I screw up I don't want anyone else in the line of fire." Cocking an imaginary hat over his eyes, he stumped out of the barn.

"He's one of a kind," Holl said, shaking his head in pure admiration. "He's right, though: he has more experience than any of us in confronting an unknown menace. Why did you let this test go on so long?"

"You had to know the price of this gift," the Master said. "A few months' consideration vill haf done you no harm. And you might haf solved it yourself. It is not over yet. He may still fail."

"Then I'd better have the first aid kit ready," Holl said. "You underestimate me. I know the price of this gift." He hurried out of the barn. The Master watched him go, smiling a little in the depths of his red beard.

Chapter 32

"Hello?" he called, as he walked down the cellar steps. "Come out. I won't hurt you."

He heard a rustling, then realized it was footsteps coming from upstairs. Half a dozen people saw him go into the basement. Most likely a sizeable group was gathering, wondering if he was going to be walking back up there under his own power. Of course he was, Keith thought, firmly.

The small windows high in the wall between the lanterns were dark. Sunset was long past. Keith should have felt tired. Instead, he experienced a rush of energy brought on by the possibility of experiencing something new. Human nature was a funny thing, Keith thought. He was likely to get thoroughly roughed up, even killed, but his steps were light. Beach scared him, but he was genuinely looking forward to meeting Holl's poltergeist. Both parties were capable of beating the living stuffing out of a person, both obviously had their own agenda, both were unpredictable and dangerous, yet Keith preferred his chances with something out of the unseen world. He was sorry Candlepat had distracted him from seeing it. He knew she meant well. She had made herself scarce by the time Keith had gone to confront the Master.

Holl had last found the fire monster in a wine barrel. Keith lifted up the lids of a few, but saw nothing except liquor. It had also once emerged from the drainpipe. He looked. Nothing down there but an echo. Holl had told him all about the creature's visits, how it seemed to bore its way in to drink up Marm's beer and cause trouble. Keith felt his way along the walls, sensing the spell that protected the house. It was a version of the charm that ran all the way around the property: more thorough but less powerful, and smooth as plastic under his fingertips. Not completely; he sensed rather than felt jangling edges where the charm had been disrupted. An answering tingle ran down his spine. It had broken through again. Was it here now?

The sound of crackling answered him. He suddenly realized that he was casting a deep shadow that danced against a wall suddenly lit in orange. His spine still tingled, but it was growing very warm, too. Slowly, Keith turned around. Hovering in the air at eye level was a ball of fire about the size of a cat. It had small black eyes that glared unblinkingly at him.

"Hi. I'm a friend of the owners. Who are you?"

Wham! An invisible cannonball hit him in the stomach, propelling him the short distance to the wall. Another knot of force met him there, and sent him sprawling across the room.

"Hey, wait, I'm friendly!" Keith protested, picking himself up. The poltergeist, or whatever it was, had uncoiled like a snake and was swimming toward him in the air. He threw up his hands to protect himself. Quick as lightning, the streak of fire was behind him. Another kick sent him back the other way. He rolled to a halt against the wall under the stairs. Reaching up, he grabbed hold of the newel post and wrapped his arms around it. The next kick hurt, but he managed to hold on. "Stop! Why are you doing this? Look, my friends are nice people. You're scaring them. They haven't done anything wrong. All they want to do is live here. Look!"

He hooked one elbow in between the treads of the staircase. With one hand he started drawing illusions. Enoch might have taken off points for technique, but under the circumstances his images were pretty good. First he showed the village the way he remembered it first: everybody sitting down to dinner in the basement of the library. Family groups, happy, eating and talking and laughing, but somewhat subdued. Then, he created a really detailed image of the farmhouse sitting on its hilltop, surrounded by a glow. The elves, looking much happier, started farming and gardening and building little houses. The fire creature didn't let up. Once it discovered it couldn't throw him around any more, it started ramming him with its nose, burning his shirt and pants in patches the size of Keith's fist. As Keith set the figure of Dola dancing he'd originally thought up for the Fairy Footwear commercial over the miniature field he'd drawn, the fire monster came straight for his head. Keith ducked, covering his face with both arms, but he didn't let the image die.

"Wait, you've got to see more! This place is very important to them. They're really nice to be around." The one thing he vowed not to do was hit back. He had an idea that that was what got Holl and the others in trouble with the creature in the first place. No matter what it did to him, he'd respond with more information. It was his only chance to break through. If this didn't work, the elves would have to keep from doing magic here forever. Keith was determined to make peace. "See? The Master is my teacher. He's great. He's taught Big People as well as little people." He showed the Elf Master with the mixed class on Sundays, showing many of the students who had passed under his hands: Lee, Teri, Dunn, even Karl Mueller, who'd turned out to be a rat, and told the monster what they'd been able to accomplish because of their education. "Lee's a newspaper writer now. Teri designs clothes—oof!" Keith didn't dodge fast enough to miss the next pass. The snakelike tail whipped him in the cheek.

"Hey!" he exclaimed. "That hurt! You're not listening to me!"

Figuring to turn the tables, he went on the offensive. Wherever the little monster shot off to in the room, Keith had a picture waiting there for it: Enoch carving lantern screens, Dola babysitting for Asrai, Keva kneading bread. Each showed one or more of the elves engaged in a peaceful, productive occupations.

Two could evidently play at that game. Keith had to jerk his head back to avoid being smacked in the face by a wave of fire. It threatened to pin him against the wall. He wiggled out from behind it, only to be met by another wave. He ran across the cellar, meaning to take shelter among the barrels, and plunged directly through another that sprang up in the center of the room. It shed little heat. The creature meant to scare him, not hurt him.

"Oh, so you're not so bad after all," Keith said. "But I'm not budging."

He kept up the picture show, making visuals out of vivid memories. He had to grin at the recollection of Enoch trying to parallel park his car, his head barely showing over the edge of the steering wheel, concentration written all over his dour face. A powerful blow in the chest knocked him over backward. He found himself on the floor, looking up into the bright black eyes.

"Hi," Keith said. "Forget it. I'm not going anywhere. You might kill me, but you won't outwait me." He squeezed his eyes shut as the flames came closer and closer to his face.

"Not the ssssame," came a sibilant voice from inside the flames.

Keith's eyes flew open. It could talk! "As who? Not the same as who?"

Instead of answering, part of the creature seemed to dissolve into a haze as the rest of it gathered in a loop. Within the confines of the circle, a picture formed in flame. Keith recognized the elves, faces drawn in hair-thin lines of fire. "They fight and flee. You ssssstay. Ssssuperior."

"Me? Superior? Compared with them?" Keith asked, getting used to the hissing voice. "No way. I'm just more stubborn."

"Ssss."

"My name is Keith Doyle. What do they call you?"

The flame gathered itself into the long, narrow shape again, but this time there were rings at the end of its tail, which it shook with a menacing clatter.

"Nadouessioux," it hissed.

"Nadoss...nadussess...can I just call you Rattlesnake Person?"

"Sssssnake Boy," said the fire-snake in pictures of his snake self and a fiery human shape. "I have been called that before. The onessss who lived here before worsssshiped me. Offered ssssops."

Keith nodded. "Snake Boy. This land belongs to my friends. I know they locked you on it by accident, but the fence has been open for weeks. Why are you bothering them? What's the

problem? Do you want them to leave you some kind of trib-
ute? Wine? What is it you want?"

The fire-etched picture changed to a complicated web of
lines. Keith peered at it for a while, then decided it was a map
of some kind, with flowing roads traversing high and low
ground, running around and through waterways and canyons.
He got the impression by the depth of the lines that the roads
were very, very old. "Sorry, I've never been there. Where is
that? It doesn't look like any terrain I've ever seen."

"You *are* there," the fire-snake hissed. "It issss here. Below
you all around."

"Below? You mean underground?" Keith asked. When the
creature didn't seem to understand he showed his own image
sinking into the floor. The creature dove into the ground, then
erupted, its tail switching wildly.

"You did not go!"

"I can't," Keith said, bracing himself for another attack. "I
can just make pictures."

But instead of being outraged, the snake-thing was amused.
"You fooled me. You are the trickssssster. Your head issss the
right color."

"The trickster?" Keith plucked at his hair. "I know Loki in
the Norse mythology is supposed to have had red hair. Is it a
universal tradition for the color to go with the job?" But his
image-making skills didn't extend to abstract concepts. "Can I
see that map again?" The nadouessioux gathered into its coil,
displaying the complex pattern again. "So where are we?" A
tiny square appeared at the junction of three of the roadways.
The energy forming the lines seemed to stop at the square,
striking off sparks when they hit it. "Ah! I get it. They opened
up the protection charm, but not where you need it? If they
open the way, will you knock off trashing the house? Wait,"
Keith said, as the fire-snake lashed its tail impatiently. He made
a picture of Holl opening a door at each end of the cellar.
"What if they do that?"

"Ssss," the nadouessioux said, with satisfaction. "And
musssst give me some of the sssssweet liquid." It showed him a
picture of a barrel suffused with a brilliant glow. Keith grinned.

"Marm's got a fan," he said. "I've got to ask them, but I bet you've got a deal. Holl!" he shouted.

Footsteps clattered down the stairs. Holl was at the head of a crowd of Little Folk, with the Master following calmly behind. They all stopped short when they saw the glowing beast coiled on the air next to Keith. He almost laughed. Their arms were full of medical supplies. They seemed astonished to see him unharmed. He stood there with all the dignity his burned clothes and bruised limbs would allow.

"Let me introduce you to Snake Boy."

"Pleased to make your acquaintance," Holl said warily.

"I'm here to broker a truce," Keith said. "It looks like a bunch of the local magical roads run right through your cellar. All Snake Boy wants is for you to stop creating a roadblock on the main superhighway."

The nadouessioux formed itself into a circle and showed them the map. The Master came forward to peer at it. Snake Boy's flames were almost the same color as his beard. "A most astonishingly detailed representation of energy flow," he said. "And ve are at this junction?"

"Yessss."

"Uf course ve vill make such a vay," the Master said. "Ve vere avare of the flow, but did not realize ve constricted it."

"Obssssstructed."

"Yes. It vill be remedied at vunce. Is there anything else?"

The nadouessioux snapped back into its snake shape at once. "Ssssweet liquid," it said.

The Master smiled. "As you vish."

Most of the Folk withdrew from the basement, leaving the Master to finish arranging the terms of the truce and Enoch to open a hole at each end of the shield charm. Olanda and the other cellarers were wringing their hands over loosening the protections for the stored food, but Enoch had pointed out that they were likely to keep more of it this way. The others gathered around Keith to fuss over him. Shelogh and Calla exclaimed over the charred patches in his clothes and the reddened skin below. Tay ran for the healing salve. Keith stood like a mannequin while they daubed and bandaged him.

"I can't mend those until you're out of them," Rose said, fingering the burned cloth. "Do you vish to stay in the house tonight?"

"No, thanks," Keith said. "All I want to do is sleep."

"Are you all right?" Holl asked Keith. "I feared the worst when you called out."

"I'm fine," Keith said. "That thing packs a solid wallop!"

"Indeed it does," Holl laughed.

"It didn't mean any harm," Keith explained to the Folk gathering in the kitchen. Calla cautioned him not to move while the salve soaked in. He sighed with relief as the burns stopped stinging. "I think you were both freaked out to find one another on what you both thought of as your turf. It's going to be okay now. I convinced it you're okay."

"And how did you do that?" Catra asked.

Keith grinned. "I did the dog-and-pony show. I threw pictures of it, images of all of you doing normal, peaceful, everyday things. Eventually, it stopped hitting me, and told me what it wants. I told you it pays to advertise."

Holl laughed. "I should have believed you."

"Wait until I get my MBA. Then I'll have credentials." Keith stretched, then looked at his watch. "Two a.m.! Holy underwear, Batman! If you guys don't mind I think I'd like to go to sleep now."

"Do you want something to eat?" Dennet asked. "We're in your debt."

"Nope. Just sleep. Thanks."

"You've earned that and more, widdy," Holl said. "I'll walk with you."

Keith shrugged into his coat, feeling the aches in his back and arms. "I have got just one favor to ask."

"Name it," Holl said.

"Next time, if a problem comes up, would you just tell me?"

Holl reached up and slapped him on the back, catching him in the middle of the largest bruise. "I promise."

Chapter 33

"I tell you, Beach, we should be going south," Maria said, as Beach opened the door of Gifts 'n' Things, on the main shopping street of Lake Geneva, Wisconsin. Her dark Balkan looks seemed bleached out by the bright sunlight coming in off the ice-covered lake. "The power comes from there again, as it has not in many months. It grows ever stronger! The spirits call to me. I must go there."

"I'm happy to hear it," Beach said, waving her inside.

"There was a great *surge* of power. I have been telling you many days now. You do not listen," Maria said, sulkily. But as usual, she forgot about being upset as she sensed something in the store.

"I told you," Vasques said, pleased with himself, watching her scurry toward the display cases. He raised a finger to point. "The item is right over…"

"No," Beach said, pushing his hand down. "Let her find it. I want to know if it's real."

The two men watched as Maria went directly to the third case against the rear wall of the shop. She pressed her hands against the glass, as if communing with something inside. A pleasant-looking woman with round cheeks and light brown hair appeared out of a narrow doorway and bustled over to her.

"Hi, there. May I help you?"

Beach nodded to Vasques. "Keep them busy."

With one eye on the others, Beach slipped through the doorway and into the rear of the shop.

He was getting used to the jumbled mess of back rooms and storehouses that stood behind pristine gift shops. The tidier the showroom, the more of a wreck was likely to be found in the private area. This shop was one of the extremes. The owner had one file cabinet, but it was clearly overworked. File folders leaned out of every drawer and were heaped on every flat surface, including boxes of stock.

Beach flipped through the mass of papers on the desk. The owner did his or her accounting by receipt. Heaps of them were jumbled together in an incomprehensible mass. Beach listened with one ear to Vasques spinning the clerk a long story about a cousin's wedding while he dealt receipts off the pile in his hands as though dealing cards. Statuettes, figurines, Beanie Babies, Venetian masks… He had to hurry.

Suddenly, the word 'lantern' caught his eye. Hastily, Beach pocketed the invoice and rejoined the others in time to see Maria exclaiming over a magic lantern exactly like the one they had taken from Keith Doyle's apartment. Beach nodded to Vasques, who took Maria by the arm and escorted her firmly out into the street. Beach thanked the woman, then followed them, examining his prize as soon as he was out in the frigid sunshine. Wyszinski rolled the car up beside them within a few moments.

"Any luck?" Vasques asked.

"No Doyle," Beach said. "The same company name: Hollow Tree Industries. No address. No indication of how the lanterns were delivered. Typical," he spat. "Most of these places don't have a decent file system, ledgers or any kind of organization. I have no idea how they stay in business."

"So he is in business under this Hollow Tree umbrella?" Vasques asked.

"He has to be," Beach said, getting into the car. He drummed his fingers on the receipt. "Six delivered here, twenty or more that we can trace elsewhere. Probably hundreds more we've never seen. So there's no remaining doubt: they *are* mass produced. That means a large workshop of some kind, but not in the city, and some kind of delivery service. We need an address. They have a web site, but it's not active. That moron in there can't help; Doyle probably hand-delivers to her, and even if he doesn't she almost certainly thinks the shipments get there by magic."

He flipped open his cell phone and dialed Ming's number.

"It looks like a lock on Hollow Tree Industries, but still no return address," he said. "Can we trace one through the name?"

"Not easily," Ming replied. "If they pay cash for parcel post, there's no paper trail. Hacking the United States Postal Service for one package is like looking for a frog in a swamp. I could break the firewall, but is that the best use of my time? It would be easier if you can identify a delivery service where they have an account. And it would help if you can pin down a postal zone. Omnivore can do it, but it will take longer the bigger the area it has to search."

Beach snapped the telephone closed, feeling frustration overwhelming him. He pushed the sensation back, determined to let intelligence rule instead.

"I am missing something obvious," he said. "Think, everyone."

"We can go back and turn his place over again," VW suggested. Beach ignored them, cupping his hands over his eyes. He went over their first meeting. He sat down beside him in the park. The boy had been reading. When Beach asked him a question, he lifted an open, friendly face, then went back to his book.

His book!

"He was reading a *textbook*," Beach exclaimed suddenly, surprising Wyszinski, who nearly swerved off the road. "He's a college student."

"What kind of book was it?" Vasques asked.

Beach cudgeled his memory, trying to make the picture come into focus. At one point Doyle had closed the book on his finger. Business...business something. He just could not see the second word, but that was enough. "He's a business major."

"Too old for undergraduate," Vasques said, shaking his head. "We got his birthdate off the PDQ database, remember? He must be in graduate school, probably an MBA program."

"Excellent," Beach said. He dialed Ming's number and gave her the information. "Vacuum up all the data you can through Omnivore. VW, check all the business schools. All of us," he sighed heavily, "will continue to investigate craft outlets."

"Maria felt the source of the power is downstate," Stefan pointed out. "Also, that is where he was going when we followed him that time."

"True," Beach said. "We'll look there, but there are dozens of diploma factories throughout the Chicago area, too. He's holding down a full-time job. That can't leave much room for a full educational program as well. This could take another month or two of legwork, but we'll find his school. It's only logical to work outward from there to the power source, without having to canvass every small factory in a six-state radius."

"We're on it, boss," Wyszinski said.

"We'll get him," Vasques assured him.

The telephone rang.

Ming sounded triumphant. "Midwestern University. A Keith E. Doyle is registered in the MBA program there. Omnivore picked up right away. All those schools sell their student lists to marketers to make a few extra bucks."

Grinning, Beach passed along the information to his operatives. "I never thought I'd say this in my life, but God bless capitalism."

A severe-looking woman with dark hair looked up from the cash register when she heard the bell ring.

"Good afternoon," she said, her eyes flicking with a practiced air over Beach and Maria. There was a look of approval there for Beach's camel-hair coat and Maria's stylish black fur ensemble. "May I help you find anything?"

As tired as he was of gift and craft shops, Beach put on a big smile. When his operatives asked around the campus of Midwestern University, this was the store that everyone recommended for nice knicknacks and keepsakes. "Something special," he said heartily. "We'd like a little present for some friends we're staying with. Just a little gift for them to remember us by."

The woman smiled. "I am sure we can find something appropriate. How much were you thinking of spending?"

"Thirty...forty dollars?" Beach suggested. "More, if you've got a really special item." He put emphasis on the word 'special.'

"Ah," the woman said, nodding. "I think you might like something from this collection. Everything is hand made. They're very popular with my customers." She tilted a hand, indicating that he should follow him toward a shelf halfway back in the shop.

But he didn't need the woman's assistance. Maria was exclaiming with wonder. Almost as soon as they'd entered, she had made a beeline for the same display. "Look, Beach!" she said, excitedly, turning to show him a carved box she held cradled in her hands. The style of ornamentation matched other items in his possession, to a capital 'T'. "So many things, all of them...mmmph!"

Beach put a hand over the psychic's mouth and spoke to the shopkeeper. "Very lovely. As you can see, my companion here knows quality. I've hardly ever seen anything this nice. Is it locally made?"

The dark-haired woman started to reply, then her mouth snapped shut. She answered, very pleasantly, "I'm not sure. I buy them from a distributor."

"I see," Beach said. "Would it be an imposition to ask for the company's name? I'd be very interested to see if the artisans take private commissions."

The shop owner regarded them with open wariness now. "I'm afraid I never give out the names of my vendors."

"Ah," Beach said, nodding. He took the box out of Maria's hands and put it back on the shelf. "Thank you very much for your help. Come along, darling, we're done here."

The bell jingled behind them.

"Those were *more*," Maria said, as Beach dragged her toward the car.

"Yes, they were."

"New things, beautiful new things!"

He was losing patience with her. The farther south they had driven, the more frantic she had become. Her spirits were talking to her, compelling her to drive down country roads, steering them, in Beach's opinion, nowhere useful. Whenever they reached a dead end, as they invariably did, she would stretch out yearning hands over the endless snow-covered crop fields, reaching out for something none of them could see. He regretted, not for the first time, hiring a psychic.

"Yes, dear, many pretty things. Now, get in. I'm not standing out in the freezing wet any longer because you're in ecstasy. Early spring in central Illinois is like living in one of the frozen circles of Hell." Stefan and Miller jumped out to open the doors for them, looking curious. "Hollow Tree Industries sells to her," Beach told them. "A good long time, I'd say, by the way this woman reacted. She couldn't wait for us to go away. We can't be far away from his base of operations."

In the center of the back seat O'Dell was talking on the cell phone. He handed it to Beach. "Ming," he said. "She's hacked the UPS computer. We've got an address."

"Tourists again," Shelogh muttered, coming into the kitchen with a basket of crocuses. "So early, ye'd think they'll be in Flahrida."

"Never been there," Keva snapped. "And I'd never want to go. Full of snow-birds. Sounds unnatural."

"Snow-birds are Big Folk who go south for the winter, grandmother," Dola said, from the kitchen table, where she was doing her homework.

"Big Folk?" Holl asked, coming into the kitchen with a sack of flour from the store in the barn. Enoch, carrying a second one, came in behind him. "What Big Folk?"

"The ones who go south for the winter," Dola explained.

"No, don't listen to the girl," Keva said, impatiently. "The ones hangin' around the road."

Holl gave his sister an odd look. "What do they look like?"

"You haf seen them for yourself," Rose said, her mild eyes full of concern. "They vere there yesterday. They haf come back."

"The same ones?" Holl asked. "Enoch said that a clutch of Big Folk were trying to come up the driveway two days ago. A man in coveralls stopped the UPS driver on his way out. I thought they were land surveyors."

"They are back," Rose said, now worried. "Are ve beink spied upon?"

"I don't know," Holl said, pushing out of the door.

"Stay out of sight," Enoch ordered. He followed Holl.

Word spread throughout the village. In no time, everyone was clamoring to know more. When Holl and Enoch returned to the house, everyone was huddled in the living room, exchanging speculations that ran from harmless to wild. Holl went straight to the Master, who was in the midst of the crowd, calling for calm.

"It is as Shelogh said," Holl reported. "These must be the people who have been harassing Keith Doyle."

A few of the Folk began to wail in fear. The others were silent, but their faces were drawn tight.

"He's betrayed us," Curran howled. "He persuaded you to reduce the protection charm, and now he's sent other Big Folk to capture us!"

"Never," Enoch said. "You old fool, you don't know what you're talking about. Once we provided a front and back door for the fire-snake, such extensive wards were no longer necessary. We didn't have to expend the energy."

"He meant for us tae leave oursel's vulnerable!"

"That is a lie," Enoch snapped. "Keith Doyle has put himself at grave personal risk for our sakes."

"We'll have to call him," Holl said, cutting off all further argument.

"Is that your decision?" the Master asked. Holl looked at him levelly.

"You know it's the right thing."

The Master nodded. "I agree."

Keith turned the sketch of the Origami upside down, then onto its side. In another six weeks the promised scanning software would be available for purchase for the original buyers. It used the camera eye, set on fine-focus. Keith's palms still itched, wishing he had one of the devices of his own so he could play with it and get some ideas. A drawing just wasn't the same. A thread of thought concerning vacuuming up words was just beginning to form in his mind when a telephone rang. Absently, Keith kicked his chair backwards toward Dorothy's desk and reached for the handset. He heard a dial tone. The phone continued to sound. He realized that it wasn't ringing, it was playing a jig. His cell phone! Diane!

He scrambled to dig it out of the pocket of his coat, hanging on the back of the door.

"Don't hang up! Don't hang up! Hello?"

"Keith Doyle?"

"Holl, hi," Keith said, plopping down in his chair. He was a little disappointed, but still pleased to hear from his friend. "What's new? What do you think of a handheld device that can suck up words and store them in memory? Textbuster? No, wait, that sounds like someone going after dirty books. I just can't come up with a catchword I like…"

"Keith Doyle," Holl said insistently, "cease your prattling just for a moment and listen."

Keith was alarmed at the tone of panic in his voice. "What's the matter?"

"There are people outside the farm. They've been here three days already. We're staying out of sight, but the constant scrutiny is making us nervous. So far they have not managed to come onto the property, yet they will not go away."

Keith sat up straight. "How many people?"

"Six men and a woman. She has black hair and wears furs."

"Oh, my God, the scary lady. She can sense magic. She'll figure out what you are. Is there a big guy? Brown hair, laser beam blue eyes, fancy coat?"

"There's one like that," Holl said.

"He's their leader. Do not, repeat, do not let him get his hands on you. Don't even let them see you."

"We have stayed out of sight, but we cannot stop all comings and goings. Marcy went out for groceries. They tried to follow her when she returned. They could not go through the aversions, but they are not giving up. We raised the wards again, but such a thing takes time to come fully into effect. Everyone is frightened. They're afraid of being taken prisoner, like Dola was. Can these Big Folk break down the protection charm? Do they have the means?"

"I don't know." Keith got up and began to pace, one hand twisted in his hair, wishing that he could teleport down to the farm and see for himself. "Can't you make yourselves vanish, the way I've been doing?"

"Don't be silly. We need to see one another."

"This is terrible," Keith said. His mind raced. "You can't let them see you. The rest of us could protect you. You could teach us some kind of concealment charm. If we can make you seem to vanish, maybe they'll go away."

"Who is the rest of us?"

"Well, you know. The other Big students. I could teach Diane—no, not Diane," Keith corrected himself, since she hasn't spoken to him in a month, "—and some of the others how to do the 'Look the other way' charm, and maybe some of us could help with avoidance spells. We wouldn't even have to come onto the property. We could set up shop in the forest preserve next door."

Holl was silent for a long time. Keith checked to make sure they hadn't been cut off.

"Hello?" he said.

"Keith Doyle, I have to tell you something that Enoch should have months ago. There is no one else. You're the only Big Person we've ever found who can do what we do, cast the same charms we cast. Before you, no one had ever asked. Since you began to learn, we have looked hard at other Big students who come to us, but you have potential that no other has had."

"But that's not true," Keith said. "What about my brother? He could get the whole Fairy Godmothers Union involved, or the genies. They do magic."

"With a wand or a lamp," Holl corrected him. "And they have many restrictions upon their talent. It may not be the true wish of a child to save us, and where will you find enough lamps?"

Keith became very still as realization dawned upon him.

"Then it's just me," he said, simply. "All right. Holl, you've got to stop everyone from doing magic. Nothing. Don't plug leaks, don't enchant shortbread molds, don't swat flies. No anti-teething charms. Just turn up the electric fence, and sit tight."

"What are you going to do?" Holl asked.

"I'm going to get their attention," Keith said resolutely. He hung up on Holl's protest.

Beach paced up and down before the narrow driveway like a tiger in a cage. How frustrating to be so close to his goal, but not to be able to enter it!

A rustic sign next to the drive identified the property as Hollow Tree Farm. He was frustrated. All the threads he'd been following had come together at last, but they ended in one large knot. The database that Vasques had copied from the Chicago art gallery had an entry in its vendor file for Hollow Tree Studios, using the same UPS account as Hollow Tree Industries. If only he had known that Doyle was selling fine artwork as well as toys and trash, he could have ended this hunt a long time ago! In Galleria Tony Maria had gone after the scent like a bloodhound but because they hadn't known what they were looking at it they had not made the connection. He had wasted time, something he abhorred. He had a personal score to settle with Keith Doyle. The boy had lied to him about everything. Impressive, in a way. He wouldn't have thought a soft American suburbanite would have had the guts.

He had power, though. Try as they might, they could not go farther along the driveway than the first dip. One step more brought them smack into an invisible barrier as impenetrable as a brick wall. No, not a wall, but a compulsion to go away. *Very* impressive.

"The spirits are gone!" Maria complained, huddled in her fur hood. "All of the magic has gone away!"

"Ridiculous," Beach said. "How can it be there one moment and gone the next?"

"I do not know, but it is as if it was never here."

Stefan cleared his throat. "This is maybe why Maria cannot always feel this place," he said. "It is only magical perhaps when Doyle calls upon the power?"

"I don't know how it works! I can't find the young fool! Can you see Doyle anywhere?" Beach demanded, as Vasques came around the corner from the north. VW were using binoculars to scan the land. According to the plat of survey, the boy owned 20 acres. Most of it was farmland, but there were thin patches of woods, and a stream wove most of the way around the perimeter.

The swarthy operative shook his head. "Not so far. I saw that girl again. Not the same one who was in Chicago. Dark hair."

"I'll have Ming run the license plates from that land barge she drives. Wait, what's that?"

"I dunno. The girl?"

"No," Beach said. "Someone with light hair. Give me those binoculars. Hurry!"

He grabbed the glasses and peered through them. Before the person behind the window dropped out of sight he had a brief glimpse of large eyes, silver-white hair and tall, pointed ears. Beach goggled. "Did you see that?"

"Oh, my God," Vasques breathed. "It was, like, a pixie, only bigger. A whaddaycallem, a fairy?"

"So that's what Doyle is hiding!" Beach exclaimed, amazed and delighted. "What are they? And where is Doyle?"

Chapter 34

"I'll bring the boat back in about an hour," Keith called as he steered the light motor launch away from the rental slip at Navy Pier out onto Lake Michigan.

"No problem," the owner called, waving a hand at him. "Enjoy!"

Keith angled the boat south, aiming for the mouth of the Chicago River. The weather was mild for early spring, so he tossed his hat and scarf under the low seat. It'd be plenty warm soon.

For the sake of his friends he was determined to take on Beach and his minions. He had always feared the day would come when somebody tried to invade the Little Folks' space. Now the worst had happened: somebody had discovered where they were, somebody who knew what they were and what they could do. Keith had to draw them away from the farm. The scary lady could feel it when people were doing magic. That should have dawned on him when she found the 'glamour' on him, several months back. She was attracted to the emanations from the farm. Well, in just a few minutes he was going to make the biggest dent in the mental airwaves since Merlin moved Stonehenge. That should bring the creeps running north again faster than you could say "Abracadabra."

His control had improved enormously after living for months in the shelter of the misdirection charm, but his natural strength wasn't enough to do what he had in mind. He needed an external source of power. Thanks to Liri and Rily, he had found the biggest river of power in the state, and it happened to flow directly underneath the Chicago River itself. He couldn't draw on it unless he was right on top of it, but that was easily remedied, with an outlay of cash and a little fast talking. It was possible he'd get in a lot of trouble for doing what he was about to do, but the date was on his side.

The little green motor launch putt-putted into the canyon of buildings. Before Keith started looking for his power source, it found him. He knew what it felt like when Holl put out a thread of sense, like a tickle at the back of his mind. The well of magical energy underneath the river reached up to prod the tiny intruder coming into its midst. The sensation nearly knocked him out of the boat, like Moby-Dick capsizing Ahab's ship. Hastily, he pulled back all his feelers, and waited while the giant presence sniffed him all over, then subsided, evidently deciding there was no harm in him. He hoped it would feel that way when he was through.

"Hey," he asked it, "would you like to come to a party?"

Traffic on the river was light that day, for which he was grateful. He brought the launch to a halt well lakeward from the first bridge and shut off the engine. He didn't have to worry about concealing his presence, since he knew Beach's entire gang was at that moment besieging the farm.

Focusing hard, he began building the mental structure that underlay his fire charm. When he and Enoch had discussions about doing magic, the black-haired elf always told him to create a stable base in his mind so that the evocation of the charm itself was like setting light to the tinder under a bonfire. How apt a metaphor *that* was. Over time he'd internalized the process until it was second nature, just like the way his friends did it. His usual trick was to hold his hand as though there was a lighter in it, and let the flame hover above the circle described by his thumb and forefinger. This time, the difference in scale would be massive.

"Scary lady," Keith said, moving to stand in the very center of the boat, "this is for you."

He threw his arms wide and his mental ring wider, creating the world's largest thumb circle for a practical joke, and lit his imaginary fuse.

Whoosh! A blazing column of flame shot up from the depths of the river. Keith hit the deck, huddled in fetal position to shelter his face, but even close up the blaze wasn't that hot. The fire was well contained by all the preparation he'd done. Keith uncurled and sat enjoying his pillar of fire as it shot heavenward like a geyser, ten, twenty stories into the air. White-hot light lit up the river, reflecting off the water, the bridge and windows of the hotels and office buildings to either side. He could almost see the gleam on the underside of the fluffy white cloud way overhead. It was the most beautiful thing he'd ever seen, a dozen Fourth of July fireworks displays all rolled up into one big Roman candle. That ought to do it.

He heard a siren echoing down the river. A fancy speedboat with a revolving blue light on top arrowed toward him. Keith let the flames die down into the water, and sat waiting for the police boat. One of the two uniformed officers raised a loud-hailer.

"Sir, drop any weapons and put your hands in the air!"

Keith raised his arms up over his head. They pulled alongside.

"All right, buddy," said the first cop, a burly man in his fifties with graying black hair and a pockmarked complexion, "what's the big idea?"

"April Fool!" Keith called out.

"What?"

"It's April Fool's Day!"

"What's the joke?" the other policeman asked. He was a young African-American with a long jaw.

"Oh, *you* know," Keith said, with an innocent grin, "making a bonfire on the river. Like the East River in New York, the one that actually caught fire? Well, the Chicago River's not polluted like that one." He smiled at them, trying to make it sound obvious. "That's why it's a joke."

"Oh, yeah," the younger policeman nodded, looking as though he thought he understood. "It looked cool. I saw photographers running from the two newspaper buildings. You'll probably make the papers."

"Hope so!" Keith said, cheerfully.

"It's dangerous to play around with fire like that," the senior officer said.

"I was careful," Keith assured them.

"What kind of incendiary device did you use?"

"Nothing but the power of positive thinking. No explosives, no chemicals. I didn't even drop a gum wrapper. Look for yourself!"

The policemen did, scanning the surface of the river. Except for a few fish that probably wished they could blink, Keith hadn't left a permanent mark anywhere. He showed them his most harmless geek-face.

"Are you going to arrest me?"

"Well…" the older officer began, looking Keith over thoughtfully. "You can't really call it criminal damage to property. I mean, setting fire to the river? It was weird, but it doesn't seem to have endangered anyone else. I don't see any debris or chemical residue. It's not like you dumped dye in the fountain on St. Patrick's Day. Okay. You can go."

"Great!" Keith looked at his watch. "Well, I've got to get back to work. My lunch hour's almost over. And I'm expecting a very important phone call."

"Gedadda here," the older officer said, with a half-amused, half-annoyed wave. He nodded to his partner, who clambered back behind the wheel.

Keith didn't have long to wait for his call. The kingfisher-blue cell phone erupted, sounding almost frantic. He took it out of his pocket with delicate thumb and forefinger, and touched the SEND button.

"Hell-oooo-ooo?" he asked, musically.

"What did you do?"

"Got your attention, didn't it?" Keith asked, pleased. Beach sounded mad enough to chew solid metal.

"Where the hell are you?"

"In a motorboat. But that's not important right now," Keith said. "We need to meet."

"Where? Down here at your property?"

Keith blanched, hearing the farm refered to as his, but knew it would be better if he played along. The guy didn't deserve an explanation. "No. Somewhere neutral. Meet me…in front of Sue. The day after tomorrow. One o'clock."

"Sue? Sue *who?*"

But Keith didn't say anything else. Ignoring the shouting coming from the receiver, he just punched the END button and put the phone back in his pocket. Humming, he started up the motor and drove the boat back to Navy Pier.

"Sue?" Beach snapped, speeding back along the narrow rural road toward Chicago, heedless of the speed limit or the safety of the others in the car. "Who is Sue?"

Stefan, in the front passenger seat, cleared his throat sheepishly. "The tyrannosaur."

"The what?"

"Big skeleton, in the museum." He tilted his head toward Maria in the back, sandwiched between Vasques and Wyzsinski. "We went to see our first day in Chicago. Is very impressive."

"Hurry, Beach," Maria said, agitatedly. "The spirits call me. He is stronger than ever we dreamed."

"Yes," Beach said, leaning over the wheel. He ground his back teeth together, glaring at the lane ahead. "We underestimated him again. I've got to stop letting that silly face of his fool me."

A few minutes later Keith's phone rang again.

"They are leaving," Holl said. "The woman became very upset and made the men get into their cars."

"It worked like a charm, then. Sorry about the pun. On to phase two!"

"Be careful, Keith Doyle."

"Don't worry about me," Keith said, blithely. "I'm on a roll. Stay battened down."

Though the huge, classic hall was filled with people, Beach had no trouble spotting the bright hair of his adversary. The boy stood at his leisure, leaning against a rail just beneath the fearsome five-foot skull that Stefan whispered to him was Sue.

Beach nodded to his associates, who spread out throughout the crowd surrounding the dinosaur skeleton display. He pushed through until he was standing before Keith. The boy looked up at him with lazy interest, not seeming at all afraid of him. When had the balance of power slipped his way? Beach cudgeled himself mentally. When he'd come running at the boy's command, that was when. Well, it was going to change back, right quick.

"Hi," Keith said. "You're exactly on time. Can you believe it? This is supposed to be the most complete skeleton of a T. rex ever unearthed. Beautiful, isn't she?"

Beach almost spluttered with indignation as questions burst out of him. "What are you? Who are those people in your farmhouse? How are you doing what you're doing? Did you inherit the ability? And why are you making knickknacks when you could be making weapons?"

"Weapons?" Keith said, innocently, enjoying the beet-red color rising on the big man's face. He glanced around. Stefan and the others had to be pretty close. He needed to keep his escape route open. "That's for people with enemies, right? No one hates me. They think I'm a goof. You did for a long time, didn't you? But you don't now. Do you?"

He was taking his text right out of the comic books he used to read as a kid. It was amazing how easily the Evil Overlord trope clicked into place. Keith only hoped he was channeling Professor Moriarty instead of turning into someone like him.

"Yeah, I did," Beach said, pulling himself together with a visible effort. "I won't underestimate you any more. We've got your number now."

"Fine. Then we understand one another," Keith said, one eyebrow raised loftily. "I want you to leave…my property alone. And stop following me around. What'll it take?"

"I want your power," Beach said, loudly enough for Keith to want to shush him, but the deafening roar in the high museum hall kept anyone not standing immediately beside the two men from hearing him. Still, Beach noticed the concerned look on his face. "You're trying to keep your power a secret. Let me put it this way. If you choose not to cooperate, I will make my knowledge public. With one word," he held up a cell phone not unlike Keith's, "I will unleash an e-mail barrage which will make your cover company's annual output look like a mimeograph machine. Everything about you and your mysterious cohorts down south will be known around the world in minutes, and you won't be able to call it back."

Keith frowned dramatically. Pat had coached him all morning on how to look desperately reluctant. "How do I know you won't do it anyhow?"

"If you cooperate?" Beach shook his head. "There's no honor among thieves, Mr. Doyle, but I'm not a thief. I am a businessman, and this is a transaction."

"I see," Keith said, moving away from the rail. Two eight-year-olds had been digging into his sides trying to get behind him anyway. "What do you want?"

"Now we're getting to specifics," Beach said. He looked to his right and left. The dark-eyebrowed man and another huge thug appeared out of the crowd and flanked Keith.

"I'm not going anywhere," Keith said, with a glare at the two thugs which made them take a step backward.

"You bet you're not. I want to learn how to do what you do. You've managed to make yourself invisible for six months. Teach me that. You caused some kind of disturbance that Maria picked up on all the way downstate. Teach me that. You hold the secret to those little toys that can make fire or store images, all without technology. I want to be able to do those things. Once I can," Beach said, sweeping a hand sideways, "no worries. You'll never see me again."

"Or your minions?" Keith asked, raising an eyebrow. The huge thug on his right who seemed to take offense at the word 'minion.' He started to move towards Keith.

Beach swept up a hand, stopping the man in his tracks. "None of us will ever cross paths with you. We'll respect one another's territories. Fellow wizards. What do you say?"

Broodily, Keith put his chin on his knuckle and his elbow in his other palm. He took a dramatic moment to consider. "Very well," he said, mysteriously. "I have to prepare. You will hear from me. Now, leave me alone. I have work to do."

With that, he brought all his strength to bear, focusing the vision of three grown men on a nearly-invisible spot on the floor.

By the time they freed their gaze, he was gone.

"What do you plan to do?" Holl asked.

With the kingfisher phone held to his ear, Keith tripped lightly down the stairs of the Field Museum, knowing that he had at least a five minute head start on his adversaries. "I'll give them what they want, of course. It'll be great."

Holl sounded skeptical. "Great? Beach wants you to grant him something that comes from natural talent, instruction, hard work and years of practice."

"Right," Keith said, blithely. "So it must be easy to pass along, mustn't it? See you in a couple of days. I've got to get back to work."

"Hey, guys," Jason Allen said. The agency president had been summoned hastily from his corner office to the front desk. He shook hands with Bill Mann, Jennifer Schick and Theo Lehmann. "Nice to see you. We, er, weren't expecting you. Were we?" He glanced at Dorothy, who was regarding the Gadfly team with a perplexed smile. Behind the corporate officers were a couple of young men in khakis pushing a stack of plain brown cartons on two-wheeled carts that they wouldn't let anyone else handle.

"Nope," Mann said, smiling. "We're not scheduled to be here for another three weeks, but we just had to come by because we wanted to celebrate. We just received the order for the one-millionth Origami unit!" He held up bottles of champagne in both hands.

"Whee!" Dorothy cried. "That's fantastic, folks. Congratulations!"

"That is awesome," Doug Constance said, shaking their hands. "Come down to the conference room. We'll crack those bottles open there. Hey, Keith, run out and get us some munchies to go with the champagne, will you?"

"You bet," Keith said. "Fruit, cheese and crackers?"

"That's my boy."

Mann stopped him before he could run to the elevator.

"Don't go yet." He addressed the agency staff. "Jason, Doug, Peggy, you're all part of our success. We wanted to show our appreciation with a little gift for everyone on the team. Guys?"

Grinning, the Gadflies pried open the big cartons, and began to hand around giftwrapped boxes.

Keith thought he recognized the size and shape as one was handed to him.

"This isn't...?" he said, unable to believe his eyes. "I mean, it's not really...?"

"Yes, it is," Mann said, pleased with the dumbfounded expressions of the agency personnel's faces as they tore off the paper to reveal the very box they had helped to design less than a year before. "We want each of you to have an Origami on us. You've done us proud, folks, and we want to say thank you."

"This is one generous thank you," Doug Constance said, turning the box over and over. "Say, I'd forgotten how good looking this package is. We did do a hell of a good job on it!"

"Thank you all so much," Dorothy said, touched, folding the package against her chest. "I am really going to enjoy this."

"'My wife bought me one for Christmas," Jason Allen said, with a boyish grin, "Ever since she saw Keith's last ad she's been agitating for me to return the favor. Thanks, Bill."

"Look at Keith," Rollin said, holding his gift in both hands. "He's wanted that thing since you first handed him one. He's finally speechless!" Janine laughed. Keith shook his head.

"I can't believe it. Thanks a million. A trillion!"

"Our pleasure," Mann said. "Now, come on! Let's download some of this champagne!"

"Yay!" Jen Schick cried, holding a bottle on high.

Keith unwrapped his box and took the unit out of the protective polystyrene cradle. Even without batteries, even before it was programmed with his access numbers and MP3 files, it was already his Doris. He couldn't wait to get her on line, to start doing all the things that he'd been writing ads about for months now. They were going to take some beautiful notes together. He couldn't believe he had an Origami at last. Now he didn't have to wait to buy one. A thought suddenly struck him—a happy thought.

"Dorothy?" he asked. "Can I run out for a minute?"

She looked at him strangely. "What about the champagne?"

"I'll be back in no time," Keith promised. "Can I?"

"Okay. Don't forget about munchies."

"Sure thing!" Tucking Doris away in his pocket, he ducked into their office just long enough to grab his coat. Not bothering to wait for the elevator, he plunged down the fire-escape stairs to the ground level.

He all but flew into the local gourmet shop to leave the order. "And next time I can fax it to you on my way out of the office!" he told Sam, the owner, a mustachioed man in his fifties who knew all about the Origami and was delighted with Keith's good fortune.

"I can have this for you in fifteen minutes," Sam said, grinning at him. "Congrats, Keith."

"Congratulate me on my engagement," Keith shouted, swinging out of the door.

The elegant young woman in the jewelry shop looked more alarmed to have a grinning maniac come hurrying into the shop. He rushed to the case containing the engagement rings. He scanned the case, looking for the ring Diane had sighed over but that they didn't think they could afford, the big, round brilliant flanked by two little trapezoidal diamonds. Now that he had a surplus thousand-and-some dollars, he wanted to spend it all on Diane. The ring had looked so beautiful on her hand. He had to have it. If that didn't say undying love, then nothing would. The fact that she wasn't talking to him at the moment was merely a detail.

"Can I help you?" the young woman asked at last.

Keith straightened up, stuffing Doris into his back pocket. "Yes, you can," he said, pointing down through the glass, past the nose and fingerprints he had just left on its surface. "I want that ring."

Chapter 35

"Now, everybody knows what to do, right?" Keith asked the Folk gathered in the farmhouse kiitchen, while shrugging into a voluminous robe that Pat had brought from the wardrobe department at the Candlelight Theater. The costume was heavy purple velvet, painted with silver and gold astronomical symbols. Hokey, but you had to give the people what they wanted, as Pat explained. Marcy and Candlepat knelt at his feet, tacking up the hem with safety pins. "Where's Snake Boy?"

Holl gestured toward the cellar steps. "Asleep in an empty barrel. It wasn't happy when we shut off the exits through the cellar, but we left an image of you, and it quieted down. I believe it will always respond better to you than to us."

"He just has to get to know you," Keith said.

"You are enjoying this way too much," Pat said, tilting Keith's head up with one hand while he drew carmine liner on his lower lids and emphasis lines in the creases at the corners of his mouth. "There. You look sinister. The rest of it's all mental. Are you ready?"

"Yep. I just need to sing and dance, and let my fire-buddy do the rest."

Borget came hurtling into the room. He skidded to a halt on the polished boards of the floor as all the adults looked at him. "They're here," he panted. "Two cars full of Big Folk!"

Keith looked around at the roomful of anxious faces. "Everybody stay out of sight. If this goes wrong, I don't want anyone in the line of fire. He knows enough about magic to be packing cold iron. Maybe you should all take shelter in the cellar."

"No way," Pat said. "I'm not buddying up with that cross between a rattlesnake and a blast furnace."

Keith grinned. "He's really nice once you get to know him."

"Yeah, that's what I once thought about you."

"It's showtime," Dunn said. "Good…"

"Never say that," Pat interrupted, putting his hand over his roommate's mouth. "Break a leg."

Keith hoisted the long skirts of his robe with both hands. "I just might, in this thing. Here goes nothing. You guys stay low."

"No problemo," Dunn said. "Good… I mean, break a leg," he finished, with a glance at Pat.

Keith stumped up stairs, trying to remember the speech he had written. His mind was blank. He only hoped his mouth would remember in time.

Holl accompanied him to the door. "You're bearing the burdens for my folk again, Keith Doyle," he said. "It should be one of us confronting this menace, not you."

"How?" Keith asked. The blunt question betrayed more of his raw-rubbed nerves than his cheerful expression. "One good look at you, and Beach has just what he wants, for real. Let him have a genuine ersatz wizard to pick on. This'll be fun. Really."

"No one whistles in the dark like you," Holl said, sincerely. "We owe you more than I can tell you."

Keith was touched. "You've given me plenty, and I'm not talking about lanterns or magic lessons. You know that. Besides, this is at least half my fault. Let me fix it. If he mops up the floor with me you can jump in."

"I sincerely hope it won't come to that," Holl said.

"You and me both." Keith hitched up the front of his over-sized costume, and opened the door.

"Come out!" Beach shouted at the white farm house. Since the last time they'd been there, whatever had held them back from walking onto the property had gone away. The seven of them still could not approach the house. The invisible barrier had retracted inward until it surrounded the cluster of buildings. Maria was mewing to herself like a frantic kitten, running up and back with her pendulum. She was muttering something about the spirits being here, the spirits touching them all, the power everywhere. He knew that, curse it, or he wouldn't have been standing here in the first place! "Come on, Doyle! We've got an appointment! You called me! It's high noon! Come out!"

There was a creak of tortured hinges as the front door of the house swung open. A dark figure crested with flame shoved open the screen door and emerged, pausing with dramatic effect on the porch. Beach stared at the boy in astonishment. Doyle was clad in a ground-sweeping purple velvet cassock studded with enough rhinestone constellations to make Elvis Presley proud. He almost laughed, but something in the youngster's expression made the sound die in his throat.

"You are prompt," Keith said with grand hauteur, walking down the steps with the correct outward kick to get the fabric out of his way.

Beach had to back up hastily as Doyle strode directly through the wall he'd unable to penetrate, and stood almost nose to nose with him. It took him a moment to regain his composure.

"What is with the costume?" Beach asked.

Doyle lifted a golden-red eyebrow. He held up his arms so the huge sleeves fell back, revealing his bare wrists. "This old thing? You and the rest of civilization only see me in my mundane appearance most of the time. Here, I can throw off the trappings of the modern world and just be myself. Do you like it? I only wear it around the house."

"It looks like you've been robbing Dame Edna Everage's closet," Beach said, his voice expressionless. The boy looked disappointed. "But I'm not here to chit-chat. Let's do business. I have certain advantages; so do you. You have certain things you don't want revealed to the world at large. I believe that gives me the right to make the first demand."

"If you say so. Make it," Keith said, folding his arms. The five big men behind Beach spread out, prepared to close the distance and jump him, but a quelling glance from him made each of them back up a pace. That proved he had nothing to fear from them.

Beach beckoned to the scary lady. She approached, her black eyes huge, almost glowing. At her employer's nod she raised her pendulum and let it describe an arc over her other palm. Beach eyed Keith speculatively.

"First some questions. Maria will tell me if you speak the truth. Where do you get your power?"

The boy paused, looking him up and down, as if assessing whether or not he could understand the answer. "From a...distant relative."

Maria exclaimed to herself. "He speaks truth."

Beach almost crowed for joy. "I thought it was something that had to be passed down through the generations. Hereditary, then?"

"Yes. And no," Keith said. "In my case I had the talent, but I had help, er, learning what to do with it. Freezing people in place, and so on."

"Ri-iight," Beach said, breathing out slowly. "So it *can* be taught."

"Absolutely. And it can be augmented, almost to infinity!" Keith let his voice ring through the hollow. It impressed Beach's men, but not Beach himself.

"If you're capable of wielding infinite power, then why in heaven's name do you make nasty little toys and housewares?"

Keith imagined he could hear the elves sputtering in indignation as their work was impugned. Carefully, he kept his own ire capped.

"Tradition," he shrugged. "They've always been made. They're useful. I'm benevolent. Why shouldn't the rest of the world have the benefit of my...talent? For a price, that is. You notice my goods are for sale."

"You're out of your mind, do you know that?"

"I prefer to think of myself as pleasantly eccentric."

Beach regarded him with narrowed eyes. "I've discovered more of your secrets. You're not in this alone, are you? You've got a workforce making your little toys for you. Perhaps—*elves?*"

Keith's eyebrows shot up.

"Elves? Are *you* nuts?" he asked. "Where am I going to find elves?"

"I saw them," Beach said. "I saw them with my own eyes through that very window, and scurrying around the property. Are you going to deny you have a whole building full of little people carving wood for you?"

"You want to meet my workforce?" Keith asked, with bored insouciance. "Fine. Nothing up my sleeves!" He whipped out the Origami from a pocket hidden among the robe's folds. Beach looked skeptical at the high tech device in his hands. "We're very high tech nowadays, you know."

"Om whaddayacallem particularum om!" he shouted, while tapping in, "Holl, now!" on the tiny screen's virtual keyboard. He hit SEND. The electrical fence spell lowered slowly and majestically. None of the other Big Folk was directly aware of its passage except the scary lady, who got very excited. Her eyes tracked its descent to the ground. Keith was impressed. She had a remarkable natural talent. Too bad she was working for these losers.

"It goes!" Maria cried. "The spirits are here!"

"Come forth!" Keith cried out in a terrible voice, as Pat had coached him.

He stood facing Beach with his arms folded. He didn't look behind. He knew that from the house a stream of elves, only the ones without beards or gray hair, was approaching, solemn and silent. It was more fun seeing the reaction of the intruders. They were gawking, mouths open.

"What are they?" Beach asked avidly. "Elves, brownies, baby Vulcans, *what?*"

"Yeah, right," Keith said, grabbing Holl, who came up only a few feet away. He swept off Holl's favorite red baseball cap. "I told you not to wear that."

"Sorry, sir," Holl said, in a properly chastened voice. Underneath the cap his ears were rounded and small.

"They are… children," Maria said, in disbelief.

Beach shook himself almost visibly, as he broke out of the haze of expectation into the reality before him. "*Children?*"

"Duh," Keith said scornfully, as if this should have been obvious to them. "Who did you think? They've been working for me for ages. They're terrific on details. They work for very little. I've never had to give them a dime." All of this was exactly true, and calculated to inflame Beach to the very end of his patience.

"Child labor? You filthy bastard! You...you *capitalist!*"

Keith was stung by the insult, but remembered it was only make believe. He sneered at Beach.

"Yeah, I'm a capitalist and I'm proud of it. You've got to do anything necessary to make big money. You're right, I don't want the government to know about it—just as you don't want anyone to know what you're really doing in this country." Keith continued winging it, trying to remember anything he could from the threat sequences in old Mission: Impossible episodes. "There are plenty of sweatshops in this country. Mine's just a little nicer than most. I can do whatever I wish. No one can stop me."

"*Why?* Why do it when you have the power yourself?"

"You know power corrupts," Keith said. "And absolute power corrupts absolutely." He opened the circle of his hand and made fire spring up right in front of Enoch, who jumped backward five feet with a look on his face that boded no good for Keith later on.

"You disgust me," Beach spat. "It'll be a pleasure to rob you of your advantage."

"You think you can?" Keith asked, flicking another flame into existence in the palm of his hand. Beach clapped his own hand over it, extinguishing it. He shook a forefinger under Keith's nose.

"You'd better bet I do, sonny. We have a deal. If you don't turn over your power to me, right now, then I'll report what I know to the authorities. My men all have cell phones. You can't knock off all of us at once."

"I have no choice," Keith said heavily. "I want to keep my secret. And my wealth."

"You can have them as long as I get the power," Beach said, mentally rubbing his hands together.

"Swear it!" Keith demanded. "When you leave here, it's the last we will ever see of each other, forever."

"Done," Beach said. Keith put out a hand. Beach looked

reluctant to touch him, now aware that he was a corrupt child-exploiter, but he clasped the offered hand. Keith made a huge spark fly between their fingers. He could hear a few of the Folk behind him murmuring their approval.

"Very well, then! I command the genius of my power to appear before me in the shape of my familiar!"

A collective gasp rose from Beach and his minions as Snake Boy slithered out of the ground and lay coiled at Keith's feet, glowing like a blast furnace. It flicked its tongue at Beach, and shook the rattles on its tail. Beach's men seemed frozen in place by its beady black eyes.

Beach swallowed hard, determined not to seem cowed. "Well, give it to me," he demanded.

"Are you truly ready?" Keith asked.

"Yes, yes! Get on with it!"

"You'd better *be* ready," Keith warned him. "Taking power is simple. Holding onto it isn't so easy." He addressed the heavens, raising his Origami on high, and pointed at Beach. "I release my power, and hand it over to that man over there. Ready? Catch it! Hurry! The one who takes hold of it will control the magic!"

The glowing snake shot forward along the ground. Beach made a grab for it. He yelped as its burning sides scorched his finger. It twisted away from him. He dashed after it.

Keith's last statement had not been lost on Beach's employees. Power would belong to the one who could take it. Stefan, suddenly seeing an opportunity to become supreme boss for himself, made a dive for it. So did the rest of the henchmen. Snake Boy eluded them all and dove into the earth just as they converged on it.

"Where did it go?" Beach shouted, looking all around him.

"It is there!" Maria cried, pointing. A few feet away, Snake Boy surfaced for a moment, as though to say "nyah nyah nyah NYAH nyah!" and dove again out of sight.

"Is the magic gone from *here*?" Beach demanded. He pointed at Keith. "Is he stripped of power?"

"It is gone," Maria exclaimed. "All is open and ordinary. The fire that was here went that way!" She pointed to the northwest.

"Good." He strode up to Keith and socked him in the jaw. Taken by surprise, the young man tottered backward. His knees folded up and he hit the ground. Beach stood over him, glaring. "That's for leading me on a merry chase all these months." He gave him a kick in the side. "And that's for the kiddies. I hope the authorities lock you up for a century, you exploitative monster. It won't be me, I gave my word, but you're going to get yours in the end."

Beach hauled the protesting psychic to his car and shoved her in. Stefan ran after him, clambered into the rear seat. The car roared down the drive and up onto the road, rooster-tailing to the left. The second car zoomed away behind it

"They're gone!" Holl crowed.

Keith, his head ringing, tried to get up. Bodies surrounded him, hands reached to help him.

"I can do it," he said, feeling the ground rocking underneath his feet. "I'm mfffph!"

Lips covered his lips, kissing them soundly. Keith's arms flapped, finding their way around a familiar form that pressed against him. His vision cleared. Diane was there, smiling up at him.

"That was *wonderful*," she said. "I loved it, especially the look on his face when he called you a filthy capitalist. That was one of the most fantastic things I've ever seen. I especially liked it when he pasted you one. I've been wanting to do that myself."

Keith gaped at her, overwhelmed with joy. Then he kissed her, with all the passion of lonely months and unanswered calls. "I've *missed* you."

Diane hugged him, hard. "I missed you, too."

"I'm sorry."

She put a fingertip on his lips. "Let's not talk about this now." Keith nodded eagerly.

"They took off out of here in a hurry," Dunn said, frowning out at the road, "but what happens when they find out Keith sent them on a big-time wild-goose chase? They'll come back here with *bombs*."

"We put a forgetting on them the moment they arrived here," the Master assured him. "They vill not remember how to return to this place."

"Oh, so that's why you didn't mind showing your faces," Pat said, comprehension lighting his long face. "You've got to show me how you did the ears thing. I could use a technique like that for stage makeup."

Holl shook his head. "It's a Folk thing; you wouldn't be able to use it."

Pat snorted. "At least you didn't tell me I wouldn't understand."

Keith, one arm firmly around Diane, cupped a hand over his eyes to look into the distance. He thought he saw a faint dust cloud that was the two cars speeding off into the distance. "I sure hope Snake Boy can get back here in time for the party. I told him to lead them all the way to Hudson Bay."

"It's over at last," Holl said.

"Well, thank heaven," Enoch said. From the miniscule curves of humanlike pinnae, the elegant points of his ears sprang up. "I didn't want to spend a moment more as something I'm not."

Keith took off his robe and dropped it on his car hood. "Neither do I."

"An amazing performance, Meester Doyle," the Master said.

"Spellbinding, wasn't it?" Keith asked, pleased with himself.

"I was so proud of you," Diane said. "I couldn't stop biting my nails. All of those men had guns, but you held them off." Her eyes were shining. "You're a hero."

Keith bit his lip. The engagement ring was in his backpack, not twenty steps away in the kitchen. He wanted to go get it and give it to her.

He was saved by the appearance of Marm. The brewer held a pitcher of mead high above his head.

"A toast to the great and terrible wizard Keith Doyle!"

"No," Keith said, as glasses were passed from hand to hand. He gave Diane a regretful glance. It wasn't their moment. He wanted everything to be just right. The right time would come.

He was just happy she was by him again. "A toast to all of you!" He stood up, holding his unicorn mug aloft. "To the finest captive workforce a disgusting exploitative capitalist ever had!"

"Hear, hear!" Diane echoed, giggling, as she took a sip of mead.

The elves cheered.

Chapter 36

"Will ye no' put him somewhere?" Curran asked Holl sourly, grabbing his great-grandson as he came through the kitchen just after noon. "He's vibrating like yon tunin' fork, and gettin' in e'eryun's way."

May the first dawned brilliantly in a near cloudless sky over the Hollow Tree farmhouse. Long before the fingers of light began to stretch catlike over the land, Keith was out of bed, getting the site ready for the party. He'd mowed the lawn to smooth velvet the day before, and pulled up weeds anywhere he thought guests might sit. Around the grass still wet with dew he set dozens of flower arrangements growing in pots that had spent the night next to his bed in the barn in case it was too cold for them outside overnight. As for preparing the hot food, he filled with charcoal the two barrel-sized grills he'd wheedled the loan of from the local Lions club. Lighter fluid and cooking tools were laid out and rearranged a dozen times before he finally let that task rest. Cold food and drink would be arranged buffet style on four of the tables, two at the outer edge of the meadow near the grills and two close to the house. Several of the youngsters had promised Keith they would help keep the platters filled.

The Folk had offered him the use of all the refectory tables they used for daily meals, and built a dozen trestle-foot tables and two dozen benches to supplement those and the fifty lawn chairs Keith had rented for the occasion. He'd spent two hours dragging all the furniture around the field until the others woke up. The moment breakfast was finished he started urging everyone to help. They agreed willingly, but Keith was so nervous he gave the same jobs to several people, and issued conflicting orders to several others. The whole house, inside and out, was draped with garlands of flowers. Then greenery. Then flowers again. Then both. He changed his mind a dozen times over the decoration. The Folk put up with him for five hours, then found other tasks to busy themselves. There was really nothing more to do than wait.

"He's fussed over my rolls and loaves a hundred times already," Keva said with a peevish frown. She shoved her hands in the deep pocket of her spotless white apron. "I'm ready to lock him in the woodshed."

"It won't help," Dunn said. He and Pat had arrived around noon with a digital movie camera and a bag of spare batteries. "He'll just gnaw his way out through the floor."

"I'll take care of him," Holl assured them. "Calm down, widdy," he said, going over to grab Keith's arm. He pulled him to a chair and made him sit down. "There's no more to do. No one is expected until mid-afternoon. Everything is ready and more than ready. By the way, that's a fine shirt you have on. New is it?" He turned up the lapel to examine the light col-ored fabric.

"Light blue is the color of joy," Catra assured Keith. "And the polo-neck pattern is becoming to you."

"But what if they can't find their way here?" Keith asked, unwilling to be distracted. He felt as though he ought to be wringing his hands. "What if they miss the farm and end up in Springfield?"

"We've put up signs for those to see who can," Dennet said, touching his finger to the side of his nose. "Never fear. They'll be here in good time."

"Will they all come?" Keith looked forlorn. "I've wanted this party for so long. I'd hate to be wasting everyone's time for half a dozen pixies." Hastily he thrust out a hand. "Not that I won't be grateful to have pixies, I mean. I just hope more show up than that."

"Ye've half a hundred replies," Enoch said, trudging through toward the kitchen. "If any of the legends you've been filling yer head with for your whole life exist, they've got a firmer idea of courtesy than most of your relatives."

"That's true," Keith said, with raised eyebrows. "My aunt had to call most of the guest list when my cousin got married because no one responded." A new look of horror filled his face. "If they all come, we could run out of food! What if we don't have enough food?"

"We have enough food," Diane exclaimed. In honor of the good weather, she wore an aqua blouse and a swirling skirt of green and blue plaids that went well with Keith's shirt. "There's a hundred pounds of cold cuts on trays in the coolers, about twice that of sliced veggies and dip, chips, potato salad, cole slaw and three whole cheeses. At the risk of airing my education, that'll serve about three hundred people."

Keith jumped up, and swept Diane into his arms for a kiss. "You're wonderful."

Diane smiled, catlike with contentment. "Don't thank me now. You'll get the bill tomorrow."

Holl blessed Diane's common sense. They were well matched, he with his inexhaustible energy and good will, and she with her peaceful, centered mind and kindly heart. He wondered how long it would be before Keith stopped touching the small, square box drawing an outline on his hip pocket, and brought it into the open. The Folk were looking forward to the party, indeed, but they were hoping for further reasons to celebrate. Ah, it looked as though the moment was coming.

Keith dropped his eyes, a bit shyly, and took Diane's hand. His other hand went to the pocket. "Diane, I..." She looked up at him with an air of expectation.

Suddenly, Holl felt a rhythmic thrum through his feet that caused the floor to vibrate. He wondered if Marm or someone else was banging the cellar walls with a huge hammer. But it was no one in the house. Marcy, pretty as a spring flower in white blouse and lilac pants, emerged from the kitchen with an expression of astonishment on her face. Enoch, Keva, Marm, Dennet, Dola and all the others were behind her, wide-eyed. Silently, meaningfully, Enoch pointed back over his shoulder.

Loath to interrupt, Holl reached over and tapped Keith on the shoulder.

"Widdy, your guests are arriving. Do you not want to greet them?"

"Yeah!" Keith jumped as though he'd been stung by a bee, then stood, torn between his first love and his true love.

Diane looked amused and resigned. "Go on. You've been waiting for a year to see if anyone's going to show up. I want to see for myself what you've attracted."

"Well, come along, then," Holl said, his round face creased with amusement. Loud pounding resounded through the house. "There's one at the door. Why don't you answer it?"

The knocking came again. *Boom. Boom. Boom.* Keith bounded past Holl, grinning so wide he could have swallowed his ears. His first guest! He threw open the door and looked out. And up. And up. And up.

"H'o," said the enormous, black-bearded face on top of the huge body high atop the tree-trunk legs. "I'm Fet." He held out to the astonished human a sixpack of full-sized beer kegs. "Gift. W're do I put?" Keith gawked for a moment, then turned to Holl, his wits recovered in an instant.

"Don't you think it's inappropriate to call us Big Folk any more?"

"Ah, look at that," Marm said, taking charge of anyone who had anything having to do with his personal art form. He scooted out to meet Fet, like a puppy confronting a man. He eyed the kegs. "Well, then. Shall we take a wee taste and see if that's drinkable? And you must have some of my brewing, though if you take a fancy to it, there'll be none left for anyone else!"

"Good!" The giant's beard and mustache parted to show a generous, white-toothed, red-lipped grin. Before he followed Marm down the hillside he knelt to let a wriggling, writhing cluster of beings in his arms get to the ground.

Liri and Rily stood up and brushed off their glorious bejeweled clothes. Rily straightened the gold circlet on his forehead. The sidhe smiled, showing their sharp white teeth.

"We let the giant carry us here," Liri said, her pale skin greener than usual. "We should have taken the waterways."

"Greetings to you, Keith Doyle. These are others we know," Rily said, pointing behind him with a long, fragile-looking hand. Only Keith knew how very strong it was. "Min, Lar, Von, Sim."

Four black snakes clutching their tails in their mouths like hoops rolled toward Keith's feet and turned into people, four little men and women with bronze skins, black hair, and obsidian dark, shiny eyes that they blinked at Keith. "Lha Tan and Fha Whoh, visitors to these shores." A couple of tortoiselike creatures with scaly, gray-brown shells limned with slate blue stood on their hind legs and offered their host a beautiful basket woven of reeds filled with bright red eggs. "I do not know the names of these," Rily said, aiming a manicured thumb over his shoulder. "They do not speak much." Behind them were three tall, storklike beings that blinked shyly. The one closest to the door handed Keith a dripping brown paper bag.

"Hi," Keith said, utterly overwhelmed with joy, holding the bag against his chest until Diane pried it loose and handed it to one of the elves behind them. "Welcome. Thanks for coming."

Liri smiled. "It is rare that one of your kind wants to meet us, let alone seek us out a second or a third time. I admired your device of a sandwich board to attract our attention."

"It pays to advertise," Keith said cheerfully. "I hope you caught the big blast on April first." He heard a collective clearing of throats behind him. "I'm not the only one who's happy you're here. Let me present all of my good friends. This is Holl. And Diane. And Enoch and Marcy. And, of course, *this* is the Master."

Ever calm in the face of situations that threw lesser beings into fits, the red-bearded Headman stepped forward to bow to the regal sidhe and the others.

"My pleasure."

"And ours," Rily said, bowing back deeply. "We welcome this chance to meet our brothers and sisters of the earth."

"As do ve," the Master said. Behind his glasses, his blue eyes gleamed. "You are most velcome in our home."

Rily nodded. "We thank you. We knew of your folk of old, in a land far from here." He stopped and regarded the Master curiously. "Could it be that I have seen your face before?"

"Perhaps a relatif of mine," the Master said, just a little
too quickly. "Ve must speak more later."

"Yeah!" Keith said, as more of the Folk streamed up behind him, their eyes shining with excitement, waiting for their
turn to be introduced. "And this is Dennet and Calla, they're
Holl's folks…"

These early arrivals were only the first of many wonderful
beings to arrive, most of them bearing gifts of food or drink.
Fairies, real fairies like Sir Arthur Conan Doyle thought he
had pictures of, with floaty skirts and wands, turned up in a
flock like bright-colored tropical birds, twittering in high-
pitched voices. Keith took shot after shot with the elves' electronic camera, hoping they weren't moving too fast for his
lens. Wait until the Niall saw these!

There was a moment when the fairies, fluttering into the
garden in Keith's wake, saw the sidhe, and hesitated. Rily, who'd
been lounging at his ease in the shade of Olanda's prized cherry
tree, drew himself up and fastened large, angry, watery green
eyes on the little beings. Keith wondered if he was going to
have to jump in and break up a fight, but Liri intervened.

"There is peace in this place," Liri said, in a commanding
voice that cut through the hubbub. "Do not disgrace our host.
Someday we will settle our business, but not here and now." Reluctantly, Rily sat down again. The fairies withdrew across the
field and clustered around Marm, Fet and the drinks coolers. For
one moment Keith wanted to ask about their unsettled 'business,' but someone poked him in the back to ask him a question.

The stream of guests continued to arrive, amazing the Folk,
who had all but decided they were alone in the world. Most
familiar, to Keith, Holl and Tay at least, was the faint mental
image of a sunrise which told them that the air sprites, unable
to come down as far as the ground, were at least occupying air
space over the farm. Lee Eisley drove up in his new SUV, and
escorted Teri Knox and Ludmilla Hempert gallantly down the
slope. Teri squealed at the array of fantastic creatures hanging
around the garden. Old Ludmilla accepted it all without question, nodding and smiling gently at everyone she passed. Lee's
dark eyes showed white all around the irises.

"I dunno," he told Keith, when they exchanged handshakes and backslaps. "I'm too used to weirdo politicians and protesters now. I don't think I can handle anything this real."

"It'll all come back to you," Keith assured him. He handed Lee over to Candlepat and Tiron at the refreshment table, and went up to greet a few more of the Master's returning students.

A number of visitors were more animal, vegetable or mineral than humanoid. Keith was grateful for Liri's declaration of peace in the glade. Something minotaurish chatted placidly with something much smaller and rabbitoid. Something red about the size of a skunk with rows of sharp teeth lurked at the foot of the buffet table, waiting to devour delicacies that fell from the hands, claws, talons and paws of those others serving themselves. A tribe of ghostly, narrow wood spirits, claiming to be the last of their kind, shimmered into being among the trees in the garden and stood drinking in the atmosphere instead of enjoying the flowing beer and cider. Minute beings surrounded by colored haloes seemed to fade in and out here and there like blinking Christmas lights. No one could agree on what the creatures really looked like. Many of the more insubstantial guests simply appeared, rather than ringing the farmhouse bell. Keith wandered around in a happy daze, greeting newcomers and introducing them to one another.

"Don't pinch me," he told Diane, who was setting dishes of tuna salad on the ground for a group of gray-coated selkies who had gallumphed up from the river's edge in their seal form. "If this is a dream I want to enjoy it as long as possible."

"Oh, it's real, all right," she said, straightening up and wiping her hands on a paper towel. She kissed him. "You know what you've accomplished here, don't you?"

"I know," Keith said, his eyes very bright as he looked around the garden. It looked like the frontispiece illustration from a very comprehensive and imaginative medieval bestiary. Was that...a *unicorn* peeking out from behind the raspberry canes, or just a trick of the light? He rubbed his eyes, but the white-maned creature was gone. His voice dropped to an awestruck whisper. "It's incredible. I just wonder what I'm going to do for an encore."

"What?" Diane squawked, astonished. "You think you have to follow this up?"

"Build on success, that's what they keep telling me in advertising," Keith said, trying to sound nonchalant and giving it up without rancour when he failed to sound disinterested. He grinned. "I've got a reputation as a miracle-worker to build on. Speaking of which…?" He looked around hopefully.

"I haven't seen it yet," Diane said, shaking her head. "No one has."

"I hope it didn't get lost somewhere," Keith said wistfully.

But the nadouessioux had no intention of missing the party. Guests near the serving area began to jump around and exclaim. Keith himself felt heat radiating from a spot near the beer kegs. The giant Fet rose to his huge feet just as the ground erupted and a stream of golden fire poured upwards. The flame coiled itself in a loop and hung eight feet above the grass, blinking black eyes at the amazed guests and looking very satisfied with itself.

Keith rushed over to greet it. "I thought you wouldn't make it back in time," he said, triumphantly. "Where'd you leave Beach and company?"

"A favorite plasssse," the fire-snake hissed. A picture, flame-edged and almost painful to concentrate upon, appeared in the circle of the nadouessioux's body. It showed a dramatic landscape of high mountains and rocky outcroppings covered in snow, all drawn in fire, but in incredible detail.

"Where's that?" Diane asked, peering at it. Borget, on ground patrol duty to pick up dropped napkins and pieces of food the ground-browsing visitors didn't want, came over to peer at it. He was getting to be a whiz at geography.

"I think it must be the Yukon Territories," the blond boy said, airing his education proudly. "There are active volcanoes up there." The nadouessioux blinked as if in agreement.

"A long, dry journey," it said. "I wisssh for ssssome of the ssssweet liquid to sssslake me."

"Well," Marm said, heartily, grabbing up an empty tankard and placing it under the nearest spigot. "You have come to the right place for that!"

"Zo, Meester Doyle," the Master said, coming up to him with a plate in his hand that held ordinary sandwiches and clumps of more exotic-looking goodies. "I must congratulate you. Ofer the misgifings of many of our folk and against incalculable odds you haf accomplished that vhich ve vould nefer haf undertaken on our own. I must congratulate you on accomplishing your goal."

"I didn't do it just for me, sir," Keith said, earnestly. "Now that you're living out in the world, I thought it would be good for you to get acquainted with the neighbors."

"And I for vun am enjoying it greatly," the Master said, with a smile. "Catra and I are gathering data on all uf our visitors that I shall compile in a paper to add to our archives and send to my brother in Ireland."

"I'd look forward to reading that," Keith said avidly, then more hesitantly, "if I can, of course."

"Read it? You may write it if you vish."

"Uh, no," Keith said, backing away. "I really don't need another essay, sir. No offense, I mean."

"None taken," the Master said, genially. Diane laughed.

Keith heard the crunch of tires on gravel and escaped up the hill to see who was arriving. He recognized the bronze Cadillac as Marcy's parents' car.

Marcy had heard it, too. She scrambled to the top of the steps, and stood staring at the car.

"Oh, no, Keith," she said with a worried look on her face. "You didn't ask my folks! What are they going to think?"

"Sure I did," Keith said. "Come on, they can take it. Your dad's cool. As for your little brother…"

As for Josh Collier, he had already flung open the car door and was staring down into the garden with a blissful look on his face.

"Oh, wow!" he shouted. "Marcy, you live in *such* a cool place! Dad, I want to go to Midwestern next year!"

"Marcy," her mother said, getting out of the car, "who are all these people?"

Keith and Enoch both took Marcy's hands and led the protesting girl to greet her parents. Diane followed, grinning.

"Hi, Mr. Collier," Keith said, cheerfully.

"Hey, guy," Alan Collier said. "How's school going?"

"I'm going to pass, but I think I'll take the summer off. I've got things I ought to be taking care of, you know. How was your drive down?"

"Very long," Marcy's father said, rising from his car seat very slowly. His eyes were fixed on the scene in the garden.

"Would you like a beer, sir?"

"Huh? Oh, yeah, I'd love one."

"Great! A tall one or a short one?" Keith asked innocently.

"Oh, a tall one."

"Right down there," sir," Keith pointed. "That's the tallest one we have." Fet was sitting crosslegged on the ground listening as Marm talked, probably lecturing him about brewing. Mr. Collier goggled silently. His wife looked alarmed, swallowed, then drew herself up, proving that Marcy was not the only person in the family who could adapt to bizarre situations with grace.

"Well, dear," she said to her daughter, "you must introduce us to all your friends. Hello, Enoch, dear." She leaned down to kiss her son-in-law, who escorted her down the stairs.

"Keith!" Marcy hissed, her fingertips digging into Keith's arm. "Why'd you do that?"

"Do what?" Keith asked, turning guileless hazel eyes toward her. "It's just a little payback for them not taking you seriously last year. It won't happen again."

"That's for certain," Marcy said. She let go her tight grip and squeezed his upper arm affectionately. "You're a good friend."

"That's what it says on the label. C'mon, Mr. Collier," he said, taking the stunned lawyer by the elbow. "You met Marm back in December. Let me introduce you to a new friend of his who's into beer in a really big way."

He interrupted Marm and Fet's lively argument about fermentation and helped his newly arrived guest to a deep mug of Fet's personal brew.

"This is terrific," Allan Collier said. "Did I ever tell you that I took up beer-making in college?"

"No!" Marm said. "All right, I'll put it to you. This big oaf says ye need yeast in the proportion of 1:20 to the hops. Now, I say that's too much."

"Way too much," Marcy's father said, gravely. "Now, I prefer a mix of about 1 to 35 or 1 to 40."

"No, no," Fet boomed, thumping his fist on the ground for emphasis, rattling all the bowls on the serving table. "Too li'l!"

Keith left them to the technicalities.

Chapter 37

"Keith, you haven't eaten a thing," Diane said, appearing beside him. "It's after six already."

"I...is it?" Keith asked, rising from his crouch near the coolers. He looked at his watch in astonishment. "Wow. It seems like everybody just arrived a minute ago. I was just making sure the supplies were holding up."

"Well, I was worried how *you've* been holding up," Diane said firmly. "It's been hours since you sat down." She put a plate of grilled bratwurst and potato salad into his hands and clamped his fingers around it. "Sit down and eat this. I made it especially for you."

"Yes, fearless leader," Keith said. He glanced around. The back porch currently stood empty of guests. "How about there?"

"It's going wonderfully," Diane said, while Keith wolfed down the first sandwich. "I feel like I'm in a movie with fantastic special effects. Did you see the fairies making flowers grow instantly from seed? Olanda's trying to get them to show her how to force her roses into bloom. Can they do each other's kinds of magic?"

"I dunno," Keith said, washing down a tremendous mouthful with a gulp of soda. "I don't think *they* know. I've been talking with lots of them—most of them don't communicate. There aren't very many of them left in the world. I don't know if there ever were. That's something I would really love to find out. Maybe that's something I can do in the future. I'd never really worked out a practical application for mythology, but maybe that's it. I can make connections, help them to get along."

"Do you really want to be troubleshooter for all the world, Keith Doyle?" Holl asked, coming up with a sheet of paper clutched in his hand. "They'll come to you if you put up your shingle as a Big Person who will give aid and comfort to the Unseen."

"Well, I'd be happy to help the ones who really need it."

"And how will you tell which ones those are?"

Keith thought about that. "I guess I'll get fooled a lot," he admitted. "But I don't mind."

"Your innocence is your passport, as always," Holl said. "Catra's been looking for you, by the way."

Keith couldn't read the odd expression on his friend's face. "Is everything okay?"

"It'd be hard to make it better, but we've got your first mystery for you," Holl said. He gave Keith the document. It was in the elves' ancient language. "This came by the e-mail a little while ago. It offers thanks for the invitation, and regrets for not being able to attend the festivities."

Keith glanced at it. "From the Niall? But what's the mystery?"

"It's not from the Niall, or any of his people," Holl said, his face brimming with excitement. "The server codes say that it comes from somewhere else in Europe."

"Where?" Keith's ears perked up. He pushed the rest of his food aside. "Could there be other folk like you? Lost relatives?"

"Uh-oh," Fet said, rising suddenly, his head nearly brushing the crown of the trees. "Which way d'n stream?"

"May be more of us, Keith Doyle, but it's a challenge you'll have to leave for another day," Holl said, with a grin.

Keith hurried to point the giant in the right direction.

The sun began to set, and a luminous full moon ascended slowly from the eastern horizon. Keith sat on the back porch steps, his left arm around Diane, watching his long-held dream come true. He'd matched everyone of the guests with their RSVP, and was smug in the knowledge that all the folk who'd said they were coming were there and ready to party. Fairies danced on the lawn, their bodies gleaming with colored light: gold, pink, blue, red, green. The sidhe lolled at their ease in the bend of the river. Fet held up one of Marm's barrels with his bare hands so the little brewer could pour out the last few drops of the keg for the fire-snake, who was getting cheerfully drunk with the turtle-beings.

"This is," Keith declared, raising the pop bottle in his fist in a toast, "the greatest celebration of all time, anywhere."

"It's got to be," Diane agreed. "This is like the United Nations of mythical beings. Everyone's having fun, they like the food and especially Marm's beer, and no one's gotten sick yet. Marcy's folks are down there talking with a bunch of boggarts or something like they've known each other all their lives. The Master's happy. Holl's happy. And you are responsible."

"Oh, yeah," Keith said, his face aglow. Diane held his right hand tightly in her lap with both of her hands. He knew he had never been so happy in his life. "I feel like I'm in the middle of my favorite Creedence Clearwater song. 'Doo doo doo, lookin' out the elves' back door,'" he sang. Diane giggled a little at his efforts to make the overlong line scan.

"We don't have to have the tambourines and elephants, if it's all right with you," Diane countered, putting her head on his shoulder.

"Spoilsport," Keith complained, but he was grinning.

"Not a chance," Diane said, seriously, looking up at him. "If you want them, it's okay. I really don't mind living with you in the midst of the fair folk, as long as you don't forget I'm here."

Keith looked a little ashamed of himself. "I never mean to ignore you," he said, contritely. "I just..."

"...Get absorbed in what you're doing. I know. That's one of the things I like about you, the way you throw yourself into what you do. It's fun. Most of the time. And this was worth it."

Keith sighed and took a swig of soda. "It sure was," he sighed.

The early spring evening was cool. As the sky darkened overhead Dennet and a few of the elders laid a bonfire in a circle of stones at the center of the garden. Holl's father glanced up at Keith on the porch steps and winked at him from under his feathery brows. He cocked his finger at the pile of wood.

Keith grinned back, understanding the joke. No, he'd let them set the fire their way. He'd done enough for the day. Dennet took a tinderbox from his pocket and teased loose a small clump from the mass of fluff inside. Getting down on his knees, he set it underneath a pile of light brush and other flammable materials, then breathed on it. Some of the guests let out murmurs of admiration as the bonfire leaped to life, crackling and hissing. The sidhe stayed in their nice, wet stream, but other guests were glad to move close to the warmth of the fire.

As proudly as a prince, Enoch made way, leading Marcy into the circle of firelight. The dark-haired girl stopped on the edge, shyly reluctant to come in with the eyes of so many beings upon her, but he urged her forward until she joined him. Enoch settled her on a large stone in a good, warm spot and sat down at her feet. In his other hand he had a musical instrument that he'd probably made himself that looked to Keith like a cross between a lute and a guitar. Keith was surprised. He'd never suspected Enoch of being musically inclined. The black-haired elf tuned the strings as other elves came into the golden circle, carrying fiddles, pipes and flutes. Holl had a bodhran drum and a short, double-ended stick just barely wider than his knuckles. Maura, depositing Asrai in the care of her mother-in-law, joined her husband carrying a beautifully carved flute. Tiron had a little gilded harp. Even Marm left his post by the beer and brought out a small accordion. Tay put a fiddle on his shoulder, drew the bow across the strings in a flourish of notes, and they began to play.

Signalling the others to silence, Enoch played a solo ballad, looking up into Marcy's eyes. His music was for her and her alone. The passion that sparked between them was almost palpable.

"They're so good together," Diane sighed, squeezing Keith's hand. "It's been nearly six months, and they're still like newlyweds. It's like he's giving her another gift."

Rily evidently thought a more grand gesture was called for. He rose from his repose in the shallows, strode majestically into the circle and set his jeweled crown at Marcy's feet. Suddenly, other guests were following suit, showering the surprised girl with packages and trinkets.

"How sweet," Diane said, delighted. "I think they're giving her wedding presents."

Marcy gave her husband a kiss. He smiled, lightening his dark expression, and struck a merry chord on his guitar. The others joined in, playing a cheerful hornpipe.

As the music rose, the fairies swirled together in a cluster, rising high above the bonfire, and began to dance, weaving in and out, their wings underlit by the blaze fluttering doubletime to the beat. Other guests rose and joined in. Some of them, like the stork-creatures, took to the air, but the rest footed complicated patterns on the ground. Rily, treading a dignified measure with Liri and the turtle-people, spotted Keith sitting on the porch and beckoned to him. Keith started to refuse, but Diane got up and pulled him into the dancing circle. He thought he'd stumble, but the magic seemed to take hold of his feet.

As the fifth number began, Candlepat and Catra stood up and sang along. Voices that had been forced into silence in the library were free here, filling the air with wild power, beauty, longing and joy. At the second chorus the fairies joined in, providing a sky-high descant that almost shook loose Keith's fillings, but he was rapt with happiness.

Lights, strange scents, tiny breaths of wind passed by Keith, in and out of the great field. Tall, attenuated shapes formed in the cool moonlight. It seemed that all the guests had not arrived in daylight. Beside Keith, Holl's breath caught.

"Who are all those people?" Diane whispered.

"I don't know," Keith said. "But they must have seen the invitation."

He went out to greet them. Some of the new forms fled from the warmth of his body; some, Keith knew, because he was a Big Person. Others offered cool nods, but a few did stop to speak. Rily moved majestically toward the shy ones. Some of the newcomers bowed to him. To others he offered courtesies. He turned to beckon to Keith and the Master.

The dancers moved cautiously into the field. The newcomers joined with them in the spell of the music, long faces and legs and hands picking up gleaming rays of moonlight and firelight. Keith felt he was in a dreamland, and offered his memory bribes, threats, and any kind of persuasion he could think of to store everything about this night. When he couldn't dance another step, he and Diane went back to the stairs to watch and marvel.

As the moon began to set, some of the smaller lights departed, and larger, darker shapes took their place. Keith felt there was no harm in these, either. The field was under a spell of truce and peace. His Little Folk wandered among them, chatting with some, sitting quietly with others. Fet and Marm were asleep and snoring under the trees. Pat, Dunn and most of the other students were camped out by the food, talking with the turtle-folk. The fairies flitted here and there, dipping into conversations, but avoiding the sidhe, who danced and drank and chatted, all with the greatest air of dignity.

Holl joined Keith and Diane, flopping to the ground beside the wooden stairs.

"Ah! I'm worn out. Maura went to bed hours ago, but I couldn't miss a moment. You've done it again, Keith Doyle."

"I wish I had my camera," Keith said wistfully.

"Don't you start that again," Holl warned him. The last time we'd only a small island to cover to find you. We're sitting here in the middle of the great, broad North American continent. Don't court trouble." He returned to the band to spell Tay, who wanted to dance with Olanda. Other couples were twirling together in the firelight, Enoch and Marcy among them. Keith watched them, feeling like a successful matchmaker. Diane must have known what he was thinking.

She steeled herself visibly. "I know we'll talk about us one day. I know how busy you've been. I want to give you all the room you need."

"I don't want any room," Keith protested, grabbing her hand. "I've been...I've had this.... Oh, never mind. Here," he

said at last, taking the small ring box out of his pocket and
opened it before her eyes. The diamond caught light from the
fire and sent out rainbows.

Diane flushed pink, taking the small velvet box in her
hands as though it might pop like a soap bubble. "Oh, Keith,"
she breathed. Then one eyebrow went up, and she wore a
mischievous grin. "But what about Doris?"

He blushed, too. "I had a piece of incredible luck."
He told her about Gadfly's generosity and his savings plan,
all three parts of it, including his secret account for the
downpayment on a house with a yard and two bathrooms.
"It was supposed to be a surprise," he said, sheepishly.
"But I waited too long to tell you, and you got mad. I'm
sorry."

Diane looked surprised, then pleased and touched. "You
doll," she said, taking his face between her hands and kissing
him soundly. "You thought of everything. So you got an
Origami as a gift."

"Yup," he said. "That made it possible to run out and pay
off the ring in full. You always came first with me. I swear
Doris will never come between us."

"I see that now," Diane said, "Well, you know, when
something's meant to be, it's meant to be. Let me see her."

Keith handed over the Origami. He didn't have to explain
anything about it; he'd spent months babbling about it, telling
her more than she'd ever need to know. Diane looked it over
with growing interest.

"This is really special," she said. "I'm not a gadget person,
but wow. You're right. It's irresistible. Maybe I'll want one,
too." She handed it back.

"Sure," Keith said. "Whatever you want." The two of them
sat together, staring out at the ceidlh, still in full swing. Keith
was twitching with nerves. "Well?" he began, tentatively, "what
do you think?"

"Of what?" Diane asked innocently. "Oh, come on, you're
never short of words. Is that the best you can do? You, the
wonderchild of the advertising industry? Your job is to sell
people on things."

Keith opened his mouth. "I...you've been everything to me...you know how I feel... Um. We've been so together for years..." He stopped to grin sheepishly at himself. The more he tried to express himself eloquently, the more of a traffic jam the words formed in his mouth. Better not to say anything at all. With a smile, he turned on the Origami. Taking the stylus, he scribbled on the screen, and handed the little device to Diane. With lifted eyebrows, she read it.

"I love you more than anything in the world," said the message. "Will you marry me?"

Diane stared at it, then smiled up at him. The light of the dying bonfire set the emerald of her eyes ablaze.

"Of course I will," she said. Beaming, Keith took the ring out of the box and put it on Diane's finger. It looked just right there. Perfect, in fact. She smiled, her eyes crinkling at the corners in the way he loved so much. "At last." She brandished her fist at him, ring side out. "And don't think I'll ever give this back."

"I hope you never will." Feeling as though he was about to burst with happiness, Keith embraced her, touching his lips gently to hers. She snuggled into his arms, joining the kiss with all her heart. After an eternity they broke apart, looking at one another a little breathlessly.

Something *thlunked* to the ground at their feet. It was a small package wrapped in violet gauze.

Diane glanced down, surprised, as more parcels joined the first. "What on earth is that?" she asked.

Keith's face was as red as his hair. "Wedding presents," he said.

Author's Biography

Jody Lynn Nye lists her main career activity as "spoiling cats." She lives northwest of Chicago with two of the above and her husband, author, packager and game designer Bill Fawcett. Nye was born in Chicago, and except for brief forays to summer camp and college has always lived in the area. She was graduated from Maine Township High School East and Loyola University of Chicago, where she majored in Communications and English, and was an active member of the theater groups, the student radio stations, and the speech team (original comedy and oratorical declamation). She has three younger brothers: a pediatric neurologist, an electronics trouble-shooter, and a CPA. Her mother is a nurse and an artist, and her father owns his own accounting firm.

Before breaking away to write full time, Jody worked at a variety of jobs: file clerk, book-keeper at a small publishing house, freelance journalist and photographer, accounting assistant, and costume maker.

From 1981 to 1985, she was on the technical operations staff of a local Chicago television station, WFBN (WGBO), serving the last year as Technical Operations Manager. During her time at WFBN, she was part of the engineering team that built the station, acted as Technical Director during live sports broadcasts, and worked to produce in-house spots and public service announcements. She also wrote mystery game materials free-lance for Mayfair Games.

Since 1985 she has published 24 books and over 60 short stories. Among the novels Jody has written are her epic fantasy series, *The Dreamland*, beginning with *Waking In Dreamland*, four contemporary humorous fantasies, *Mythology 101, Mythology Abroad, Higher Mythology, The Magic Touch*, and two science fiction novels, *Taylor's Ark* and *Medicine Show*. Jody also wrote *The Dragonlover's Guide to Pern*, a non-fiction-style guide to the world of internationally best-selling author Anne McCaffrey's popular world. She has also collaborated with Anne McCaffrey on four science fiction novels, *The Death of Sleep, Crisis On Doona, Treaty At Doona* and *The Ship Who Won*. She also wrote a solo sequel to *The Ship Who Won* entitled *The Ship Errant*. Jody co-authored the *Visual Guide to Xanth* with best-selling fantasy author Piers Anthony, and edited an anthology of humorous stories about mothers in science fiction, fantasy, myth and legend, entitled *Don't Forget Your Spacesuit, Dear!*, "a science fiction book you can actually give to your mom."

Her newest book is a contemporary fantasy co-authored with Robert Lynn Asprin, *License Invoked*. In the works are two collaborations with Robert Asprin in his *Myth Adventures* series, and a third volume in her *Taylor's Ark* series, *The Lady and the Tiger*.

Over the last sixteen years, Jody has taught in numerous writing workshops and participated on hundreds of panels covering the subjects of writing and being published at science-fiction conventions. She has also spoken in schools and libraries around the north and northwest suburbs.

When not occupied in petting cats or writing fiction, Jody reads, travels, does calligraphy, bakes, or gardens.

Come check out our web site for details on these Meisha Merlin authors!

Kevin J. Anderson

Robert Asprin

Robin Wayne Bailey

Edo van Belkom

Janet Berliner

Storm Constantine

Diane Duane

Sylvia Engdahl

Jim Grimsley

George Guthridge

Keith Hartman

Beth Hilgartner

P. C. Hodgell

Tanya Huff

Janet Kagan

Caitlin R. Kiernan

Lee Killough

George R. R. Martin

Lee Martindale

Jack McDevitt

Sharon Lee/Steve Miller

James A. Moore

Adam Niswander

Andre Norton

Jody Lynn Nye

Selina Rosen

Kristine Kathryn Rusch

Pamela Sargent

Michael Scott

William Mark Simmons

S. P. Somtow

Allen Steele

Mark Tiedeman

Freda Warrington

http://www.MeishaMerlin.com